THE COURSE OF H

Ali had to get to Jim. He was engulfed in a war whose history was being altered by the minute, a war already over, but now reopened by the Iron Men to carry out their horrible plans. Ali had information Jim needed to turn those plans around. And it was important to get to the time machine quickly.

Once inside the machine, she heard the whine of the generator as the flow of subatomic particles was finally accelerating faster and faster, until time was no longer locked into historical events. In a moment her own brain waves would be attached to the stream, and her mind would travel until it finally came to rest inside the consciousness of a Vietcong woman. . . .

Time Warrior #2

Hour of the Scorpion

Matthew J. Costello

A ROC BOOK

ROC
Published by the Penguin Group
Penguin Books USA Inc., 375 Hudson Street,
New York, New York 10014, U.S.A.
Penguin Books Ltd, 27 Wrights Lane,
London W8 5TZ, England
Penguin Books Australia Ltd, Ringwood
Victoria, Australia
Penguin Books Canada Ltd, 10 Alcorn Avenue,
Toronto, Ontario, Canada M4V 3B2
Penguin Books (N.Z.) Ltd, 182-190 Wairau Road,
Auckland 10, New Zealand

Penguin Books Ltd, Registered Offices:
Harmondsworth, Middlesex, England

First published by Roc, an imprint of New American Library,
a division of Penguin Books USA Inc.

First Printing, December, 1991

10 9 8 7 6 5 4 3 2 1

Printed in the United States of America

Dedicated
to
Chris Clarke and Neal McShane

1

The noise swirled around Jim Tiber, loud, incessant. The chattering of GIs and tiny almond-eyed women. The big Seeburg jukebox was pumping out Mick's complaint that he "can't get no satisfaction."

A soldier, a lieutenant, sat on the stool next to him, talking to him, a tumbling mixture of southern, good-old-boy dialect laced with references to things that Jim didn't have a clue about.

Jim blinked, hoping that this particular dream—this potential nightmare—would fade.

What the hell am I doing here? he wondered.

But he knew where he was. That's what made it all the worse. He knew *exactly* where he was. Or—at least—where his mind was.

But how it got here? And why?

He had some unpleasant hypotheses about that.

So while this beefy guy next to him yammered on, talking about a "fuckin' S&D in Go Gong" and other things that Jim didn't have the ability—at present—to understand, Jim tried to put all the pieces together.

Starting with what happened.

And—not to coin a phrase—what's happening. . . .

This is what he understood.

He and Ali and Martin had broken into Columbia's Time Lab to see if—hot damn—the scientists had really stumbled upon a way to travel through time. Because—crazy idea—if they had, Jim would use it to get the evidence he needed for his rejected thesis on the Beatles. But as soon as they hooked Jim up and zapped him back to Hamburg circa 1962, to, yes, meet the Beatles, something very strange happened.

He was in a desert. With Rommel. The Desert Fox. No more Star Club in the Reeperbahn, no more Twist & Shout. And history had taken some unexpected turns. But he discovered that he wasn't alone. He met Port, who had been sent by the Time Lab. And Port told him that someone had to be killed—someone else from the future—if things were to be put right.

And somehow Jim did it.

And then he was packed off to Berlin, to fun and games in the wunderbar Third Reich. He was picked up by a zaftig secretary who turned out to know the location of all of his most secret erogenous zones.

It was Ali. In someone else's body, too. She had come back to warn him that the other time travelers, the bad guys, were still playing with history.

And I nearly screwed up then, didn't I? he thought. The other time travelers, the Iron Men, were ready to ferret away art worth billions . . . more than enough money to finance their plans to rearrange history in a major way. Who knew what crazy plans they had up their sleeves?

But what happened to Ali?

She tried to stop the Time Lab from pulling her back. Everyone else they tried to bring back turned out insane. Permanently. But she had given them another way to do it. With no guarantee that it would work. . . .

When he finally reached her and called the fraulein, Ali's host, Ali was gone.

Perhaps, he thought, made insane by the time transference.

No one from the Time Lab ever got back with all their marbles, she had said.

But the Iron Men, in Soviet Georgia, could go back and forth.

At least that's what McManus—head of the Lab—thought.

So Ali could be a basket case.

And somehow I was plucked from the wonderful world of Hitler's Reich and dumped in Vietnam.

America's Playground of the Sixties.

The saddest place in the world, I had once called it in a term paper.

The bottom of the universe. The place where the American Century ends.

And I'm here.

With one rather large question . . .

What in the world for. . . ?

"So the Top calls me in and says—now you just gotta imagine this with that West Point accent, Jacko—he says to me, 'Lieutenant Burnett, your losses are becoming unacceptable.' Shit, I nearly started laughing in the moron's face. You know, Jack, back in Atlanta I was taught to respect authority . . . but hell! A man's got limits."

This lieutenant, this great bull with a neck like steel cable, laughed. "And I say, if he's authority, then I'm the damn Wizard of Oz."

Jim nodded.

There will be time to continue my reverie later, he thought.

At least, he hoped there would be.

The man next to him turned as if sensing that something was awry. "What's wrong, McShane? Somebody piss in your beer?"

Okay, Jim thought. I'm Jack McShane.

Well, that's not bad for starters. I know my name. Jack McShane. And he read the man's name above his lapel. R. Burnett. Jim took a stab at it. Robert . . . Richard . . . Ronnie? From Atlanta?

It's gotta be Bob. Big Bob Burnett. . . .

"Er, Bob," Jim paused. No reaction, he noticed. Good guess. . . . "No, I just got a headache, all this damn noise, and—" Jim looked around. Mick's whining was done and a song that Jim never heard before was thumping out of the big jukebox. Something about incense and peppermint.

Who cares what game you choose?

Little to win, and nothing to lose.

Right, Jim thought. After all, this is the sixties. The rebirth of romantic nihilism.

He noticed eyes on him. Two women, their eyes glowing in the darkness, like magical cats, were studying him and Burnett. The slinky women wore skin-tight, iridescent, silky dresses that shimmered even in the blackness. They were cut way up to what Ali used to laugh and call "the nether regions."

He found himself staring back at them.

Then Jim felt himself being nudged in the ribs.

"Up for some action, Jack? Might be our last opportunity for awhile. Yessir. . . ." Burnett slapped his bottle down and turned to look over the lurking bar girls. Jim read the label on Burnett's bottle. Bahmi Ba. The amber color of this local beer looked a tad *too* amber.

"Do it again, Louie," Burnett bellowed to the bartender, a dwarf-scaled man who had a permanent smile and twinkle etched into his face. Jim watched the man laugh and take the empty away.

He'll probably wear that same smile the day the North Vietnamese storm the city in 1975, watching them run the bedraggled remnant of America's fifteen-year investment out of Vietnam on overloaded choppers.

He'll probably wear that smile right up to the second they shoot him as a collaborator.

"Yes, Lieutenant. . . ." The bartender took time pronouncing the word, obviously proud that he could say the words so clearly. "And you, Lieutenant McShane?" Again, the words rolled out slowly.

It took a second for Jim to realize that the man was talking to him. "Er, no . . . no, I'm just fine here." To prove a point, Jim took a slug of his beer.

The acidic brew felt good in his mouth. It was real, pushing away all the craziness.

"You're not yourself tonight, Jacko. Not at all. You usually match me one on one, brew for brew." Burnett turned, his bottle held in mid-shrug. "I hope you're not getting halfway jitters. You know what they say . . . you can be halfway home or—"

The two Vietnamese beauties slinked up to the bar, one on each side of them. The one next to Jim slid her stool real close, and he smelled her rich perfume, powerful, cloying.

"Or, pal, halfway into the grave."

Halfway . . . Jim thought. McShane must be halfway through his tour of duty. And Jim was getting the feeling that McShane's job wasn't just stocking the local PX. He looked at his hands. They were good, strong hands, laced with a fine network of cuts. His nails were bit down to the quick, and the skin was dry and rough. He squeezed one hand around the beer bottle.

Yes, battered, and cut, but a real strong hand.

He looked at Burnett. He didn't look like a desktop soldier, either.

Great, Jim thought. We're infantry, army infantry. Lieutenants.

And what was the average life span for an army lieutenant in Vietnam?

About five hours?

Something like that.

The VC just aimed at the nice shiny bars on the helmet. Ka-pow, and leadership was no longer a combat factor.

"Number One GI?" the woman next to him sung in a chirpy, birdlike voice. "Buy me some tea?"

As if to emphasize the point, the woman rubbed her leg against Jim's. He turned and looked into her face.

She was young, her face a bright wash of deep red lipstick and pinkish rouge.

"Er, I—"

He turned to see what Burnett had done. But the good old boy was already in close conference with his own bar floozie. Louie had slipped her a glass of clear amber liquid. In the dark cavern made by Burnett's body, Jim could see the other soldier's hands fumbling around, enjoying the feel of the young girl's body, the sheer silk of her dress.

Looks like fun, Jim thought. But I'd really like to find out more about my situation. God, what year is it?

He turned and looked at the girl. She smiled at him and repeated, "Number One GI . . ."

No sweetheart, no GI. I'm a Number One time traveler trying to operate with a minimum amount of information.

The girl reached out and gave his leg a tight squeeze.

Louie stood in front of him, his eyes still twinkling, grinning. Jim nodded to him and said, "Some tea, please. . . ."

Louie nodded.

"And another Bahmi Ba. . . ."

It was many beers later—after the bar had filled with GIs and the jukebox seemed to be on the second run-through of its late-sixties repertory—that Jim found himself being dragged upstairs by his giggling bar girl.

Burnett was ahead of him. He laughed and weaved a crooked line. And Jim discovered that his own steps were none too steady. He tripped on the stairs, his clunky boots catching the narrow steps. And then, at the top of the stairs, the girl pulled him into a tiny room.

It was somewhere above the bar. Though he wasn't really sure about that. He knew they had walked upstairs, and then down a hall filled with noises, squeals, a host of a strange and exciting sounds.

Burnett disappeared into another room, his girl tugging him along even as he kept swigging his beer.

So now, here I am, Jim thought. Alone with this not-exactly unattractive Vietnamese woman.

She didn't give him much time to ruminate about matters.

She unzipped her sheath dress and was out of it before he could gasp. Which was precisely what he did.

"No . . ." he said, not quite averting his eyes from critical points of her anatomy. She was moving fast. Some unspoken transaction must have been entered into and she was hurrying to speed it up. He stood up, repeating, "No!"

The gesture proved to be just the wrong one for what the bar girl had in mind. Her tiny, delicate hands—hands that aroused in Jim a feeling of protectiveness more than lust—were fluttering with his pants.

"No!" he yelled. In answer, he heard a drunken shout from outside. Some other rutting scene turning a bit unpleasant.

"You be Number One GI," she said. "Mai Tuan Ha make you feel good."

Jim took a step back, and another, a bit unsteady, four beers to the wind. "Yes. Sure," he said. "But I don't want—"

He was shaking his head, a message that she clearly read. Because now she stood up, and her face twisted. There was a burst of Vietnamese. Then some English. "You Number Ten GI . . . Number Tou-san GI."

I'm slipping down the Hit Parade, Jim noted. More Vietnamese followed, none of it intelligible to him except for one word, repeated over and over.

It sounded like "Pee."

Which, he assumed, had nothing to do with the bodily function connected to the expression. After another barrage or two, he finally flashed out what her problem was.

Her pay.

He quickly reached for his wallet. It was full of colorful money. He dug out a few bills and handed them too her. He saw the word piasters on them.

Pi.

Live and learn.

The Vietnamese girl stood still. A smile bloomed on her face.

She came close to him, still naked, still looking appealing. He patted her shoulder, and then with a deep breath backed away.

"It's okay," he said smiling at her. "Take the money. It's yours. You don't have to do anything . . ."

She was still smiling, but he wasn't too sure she got the drift of what he was saying. But he pointed to her dress, curled up on a wooden chair by the window.

"You can go," he said, gesturing to the door.

She slipped into her dress and Minnie Mouse heels with about the same speed she had slipped out of them. Then she went to the door, giggling, smiling, and blowing kisses at him.

She shut the door behind her.

Probably thinks I'm dysfunctional, he thought. Damn right, I'm dysfunctional. Who wouldn't be? Isn't this everyone's dream. I come from a generation that thanks their collegiate stars, that they missed the lottery—the 'Nam.

And here I am.

Jim sat down on the bed.

The bar sign flashed on and off outside the window, sending alternating blotches of pinkish red and sea green across the wood floor.

I'll have to wait, he thought. Just wait until Burnett comes for me. Then what? Find out the date . . . good idea, and maybe a better idea of what Jack McShane's job is.

Though he had an idea about that already.

Try to avoid as many screwups as possible.

And wait. Bits of McShane should drop into place, just like the other memories had appeared . . . the waiter in Hamburg, Wolfgang Prater, and Oberstleutnant Fritz Wagner in North Africa. Sooner or later, the host consciousness begins to seep through. . . .

Bits and pieces will come to the surface, slowly, to help me get through this—

He hoped.

There was yelling in the hall. Loud, angry, nasty sounds. A bottle smashed. Then the sound of someone being shoved against the wall. The dull thud of something—a head?—smacking against the wood. More yelling, and then a knock at Jim's door.

The door opened a foot or so and Burnett's bullish popped in.

"Hey, Jacko, pull up your drawers and let's get out of here."

"I'm all set," Jim said, standing up.

He felt Burnett studying him, watching him.

"You have a good time? She looked like a real party girl, that one."

"Great time. . . ."

Ask him the date, Jim thought. What's the damn date?

He followed Burnett, who turned to the right, away from the stairs leading back to the bar.

"Old Louie got a little pushy about his tip." Burnett laughed. "I suggested he fuckin' take it up with the legal boys at MAC-V."

"MAC-V?" Jim said.

Burnett turned, still walking, and shot him another which-planet-did-you-just-get-in-from stare. "Yeah, MAC-V . . . hey, are you feeling okay?"

It meant nothing. MAC-V. then, he knew it was an acronym. And then, almost at the same moment, he just knew what it meant. Military Assistance Command-Vietnam. Headquarters for the whole shooting match, over near the airport where he had landed with a lot of other naive lieutenants fresh out of ROTC.

ROTC? Yeah, that sounded right. Glad to know that he went to college.

Ton Sun Nhut airport. Gateway to the jungle paradise! "Sorry," he said to Burnett, as they clopped down dark, rickety stairs. The hallway was thick with a smell that Jim—thanks to his time in Hamburg—now recognized.

He sniffed at the heavy pot smoke.

Burnett cleared his throat.

"Damn," he said. "I can't stand the smell of that *shit.* You know, if I catch any of my men blowing weed—on or off duty—I put them on twelve-hour C&S duty for a week. I don't need any stoned grunts out on patrol."

Jim would have liked to ask what C&S was, but that could wait. Burnett might be a good old boy, but who knew how much weird behavior he'd tolerate. And as far as Jim knew, *everything* he was doing was weird.

So he just said, "Yeah," and followed Burnett out the door to the street.

It was night now. The sky was not quite black, still tinged with a purplish-blue to the east. Someone on a bicycle sporting a two-person carriage called out to them, but Burnett waved him away.

He shook his head. "One of those damned cyclos was playing real hardball with me for some American smokes," Burnett said.

Again, Jim nodded. "Uh-huh. Sure." Fortunately, Burnett didn't need much encouragement to finish his story.

"I said five thousand p. Take it or leave it. So he drives me down Cong Ly Avenue and then back up Tu Do Street, saying, 'Eee, that's too damn much.' I tell you, Jacko, the PX stuff just doesn't rate the prices it used to. Anyway—"

Burnett started walking towards the right, which was good since Jim didn't know where to go.

"Anyway, we're finally at the cathedral, and he says, okay, four thousand. His top price. I was so sick of being banged around in that little wagon that I gave him the damn cigarettes. Speaking of which, you got some smokes? I'm fresh out.''

Jim was about to say no. After all, he didn't smoke, But then he felt a squat box in his shirt pocket. He dug out the red and white box. He flipped it open and extended a cigarette to Burnett.

So I'm a Marlboro man, Jim thought.

And I probably should smoke them. As long as I'm here. Keep the questions down. . . .

(Who'd quit smoking in Vietnam? Why? For health reasons? Dubious. . . .)

''Thanks.'' Burnett stopped and lit the cigarette. His face was covered with golden light, and Jim noticed how dark the street was. Nobody was around. A curfew? he guessed.

''Say, get any word from home? I just got—''

Burnett was puffing on the cigarette. Its tip glowed brightly. He talked and sucked on it at the same time.

''—a letter from my dad. He tells me that those punk long hairs, those hippies, have—''

The wall of the building beside them puckered and sent a fine spray of rock flying at Jim.

First Jim just looked at it. Thinking, gee, how did that happen? A hole just opened and rock splintered.

But he remembered hearing a faint pinging sound and something like the dull snap of a firecracker.

''Jee-zus,'' Burnett said, pulling Jim down when he just stood there. ''Fuckin' sniper must have seen me light my smoke.''

It dawned on Jim that they had just been fired at.

They waited, crouching. Jim heard Burnett breathing, grunting, almost sniffing the air. He turned to Jim. ''Why the hell didn't you get down?''

''I thought—''

''Yeah,'' Burnett interrupted, nodding. ''You're probably right. They like to get off one shot and hightail it away.'' Burnett laughed. ''I get a little jittery in the city. Wouldn't mind going after the little VC bastard. . . .''

Burnett stood up. "It's too late to be walking around here," he said. "Let's get back to the Continental. It will be our last decent night's sleep for a long time, eh pal? A real long time . . ."

"Right," Jim said.

So where am I sleeping tomorrow? he wanted to ask.

But the answer to that one seemed all too obvious.

2

Alessandra Moreau looked down at her hands.

They weren't there.

Nor, for that matter, was any other part of her body visible. If she was seeing anything, that is . . . if the images that registered in her brain had anything at all to do with normal vision.

Which she seriously questioned.

A number of thoughts occurred to her. The first one out of the chute arrived with a weird lack of passion.

I'm dead.

Her last memory in the real world was scrambling to hide her note inside King Ludwig's castle in Neuchanstein before guards pulled her away. The note, of course, instructed the Time Lab *not* to yank her out of 1941.

Her idea of reversing the flow of tachyons sounded good when she proposed it. But life—even life in the Third Reich—was too sweet to risk serving as a guinea pig.

Besides, there was Jim. If Jim stayed, she was going to stay.

Then everything went blank, misty. Like a scene from that old Warren Beatty movie, *Heaven Can Wait*. A misty way station filled with blue smoke and pale lights in the distance.

I'm just floating here, she thought. And then the

terrible thought came. Something's happened. Oh, god, something's happened.

They didn't get the note—damn it! *They didn't get the note* . . . and they just yanked my mind forward in time, like ripping it out of my skull.

And then she knew . . .

I'm insane. This is madness.

This is what's *supposed* to happen. This whispery aura is just a schizophrenic fugue state. Great, I'm mad—trapped in my deranged mind, while my nicely toned body decays into a blubbery vegetative mess, kept alive by a host of life-support machines.

That had to be the truth.

Because—ha, ha—that was the only choice.

If they had pulled her out—and if she had survived with all her marbles—she should be back at the lab now instead of floating in this sick, gaseous vapor without any corpus delecti.

She looked around at her new world. My new home, she thought. I'm trapped here.

She saw bright flashes in the distance, fireworks seen through a gauzy mesh. There was no sound. It was horrible. No sounds ever again. And no feeling! Just those flashes of light. Perhaps, she thought, they were other disembodied souls, spirits winging themselves hither and yon on the astral plane.

(And—for a moment—that idea intrigued her. Maybe that's what the Time Transference process was all about, a kind of astral travel accessed through the stream of subatomic particles. An interesting thesis that could bear studying . . . later.)

If there was going to be a "later," a prospect that didn't seem too likely.

More flashes. They were the only thing to watch, and she wondered if she could move closer to them, in her madness, in her dead, spirit state, whatever was her problem.

Ali felt as if she could simply kick back and swim in that direction.

But she had no body, nothing to move, nothing to kick. She was stuck. So she just looked ahead, watching the flashing lights, noting the subtle shifts in color, waiting for something to happen.

But nothing did.

Time, amusingly enough, was probably unmeasurable here. For time to exist, her old quantum physics professor Dr. Clarence Hofstaeder used to chortle, there must be "events."

At which point, Hofstaeder would pick up a pencil and drop it. See, an *event:* a "before", the pencil held in my fingers, a "middle," the pencil plummeting to the ground, and an "after," the pencil crashing into the floor and finally coming to rest. And yes, Hofstaeder had said, the pencil has changed, not just in its location, but in its very nature. Electrons have been lost, kinetic energy generated, potential energy exploited.

Ali had raised her hand then.

She always raised her hand and asked questions. Most of her Columbia professors treated her very seriously. She was the best student doing postgrad work in experimental quantum physics, and everyone knew it. That was a source of no small pride to her.

Her question made Hofstaeder laugh.

Suppose there were no events? she had asked. Suppose we stayed perfectly still in this class, didn't move, didn't breathe. And suppose the same thing happened throughout the world? Then there would be no time, right?

Hofstaeder had raised his hand and tried to interrupt her question. Like a wily batter, he saw the screwball coming.

"Of course, if there are no events, there is no time. That's what time is. But listen, young lady, there are billions of events occurring every minute in this class, every nanosecond. Cells are moving, dividing. Neurons are firing, skin is aging. It is a relentless flow—and we are its prisoners."

Prisoners. Hofstaeder was referring to Columbia's Red Building's widely rumored experiments in time and motion, experiments that were reportedly related to some hope of accessing the great stream of time.

Hofstaeder didn't believe any of that nonsense.

But Ali did.

Prisoner, she thought. I'm a prisoner here maybe forever, whatever forever is. How long have I been here? A lifetime? A few seconds?

And will I ever get out?

(Not if this is my mind, she thought. You're home, sister, if you've just gone nuts.)

She saw more flashing. Or she *perceived* more flashing. She still had no empirical evidence that her light-gathering organs were working. But the flashing lights, the colors, the fireworks in the distance, seemed to be picking up an intensity, and, yes, a rhythm.

Something's happening.

Something good. Or maybe something bad.

Or maybe something neutral.

Hell, let it be good or bad, she thought, anything's better than this . . . nothingness.

And she got her wish.

"Pulse steady, Dr. McManus. Respiration approaching normal. Blood pressure still too high, but stabilizing."

She heard the words, and they sounded as if she was watching a movie. A soap opera in the afternoon.

Will my husband live, Dr. Goodwrench?

It's—it's hard to tell, Mrs. Bloomingdale. In any case, I am free for dinner should any—

"It's going down, Elliot. Blood pressure falling and—"

She knew then that they were talking about her. My

pulse, my blood pressure. And she knew whose voices she was hearing. Dr. McManus. Dr. Beck.

The Time Lab.

I'm in the Time Lab, she thought.

And I don't feel insane.

I feel perfectly normal.

She opened her eyes and found the matronly Dr. Beck leaning over her. Beck's ample bosom pressing against her.

"Elliot!" Beck screamed, noticing Ali's wide-open eyes.

Then McManus's pinched, gaunt, but very welcome face, was in front of her.

"Thank . . . god! Ali! You're—you're—"

Ali smiled. At least, she felt herself smiling. She had been getting used to not having a body. But she felt her facial muscles fall into a familiar groove.

"Hi—" she said. She noted that her voice sounded whispery, frail. But she heard it.

McManus's face smiled down at her. Then Lindstrom, the blustery historian came close. "Ali . . . welcome home. I must hear about everything that happened—"

McManus put up a hand and shushed the boisterous historian. "There'll be time for that, Lindstrom. But first—" McManus reached out and took Ali's hand. She felt him touch her hand! "First, let's make sure that Miss Moreau is one hundred percent recovered."

She saw Lindstrom smile at her. And he cleared his throat. "How about ninety percent? I'm still getting those damned reports . . ."

"Reports?" Ali said. She tried to struggle out of the contoured chair. But she felt something in her arm. She turned and saw the IV tubes and a plastic bottle suspended above her. The act of moving, of pushing back with her elbows seemed too difficult. She fell backwards.

"There, there," Dr. Beck said. "You rest a bit.

Everything,'' the doctor said looking at some meters and dials, ''looks very good.''

''Yes,'' McManus said. ''We want you to get all of your strength back. Just sit here and take it easy.''

The smiled looked uncomfortable, out of place on McManus's normally stern face. He was making an unusual effort to get her spirits up.

''Here,'' Beck said, bringing a sweaty cup with a special sipping lid up to her lips. She licked her lips and felt how dry they were. She sucked greedily at the cup. It was ice water, cold and wonderful in her mouth. She kept sucking even as Beck pulled the lip away.

''Wait a minute. Not too fast. Let that go down a bit.''

Ali nodded.

They were all there. McManus, Beck, Lindstrom. Gathered around her like the farmhands at the end of Dorothy's sojourn to Oz. And Dr. Jacob, the man who actually operated the tachyon generator, stood just behind them. He hadn't said hello or anything. But then he hadn't said anything from the moment she first met him.

He just muttered about his precious generator.

''Wh—what happened?'' she asked again.

She saw Lindstrom look at McManus, and then McManus looked back uncomfortably. They waited to see who was going to pick up the ball.

''What happened to Jim? Why isn't he here?'' She heard her voice rise. She pushed forward again, a bit stronger now.

''I'd better disconnect the IV,'' Dr. Beck said diplomatically.

Ali stayed on her elbows. ''I want to know what happened. . . .''

Her voice was strong, clear, and demanding. The old Ali, she recognized, the one who did what she wanted. The one who got her way, come hell or high water.

McManus cleared his throat.

And then he began his explanation. . . .

As was obvious to Ali, her idea had worked. Reversing the tachyon flow—such a simple idea now that they thought about it—made reversing the time transference a relatively easy and safe process.

Except, McManus explained, for one thing. It produced a series of stress reactions in the subject's body, from minor fibulations and erratic blood pressure, to the full-blown symptoms of a major stroke.

They saw that as soon as they started to bring Ali back.

"Then that's why I was in nowhere land for such a long time?"

McManus nodded. "That's the reason for the stress. The return is not immediate and the body is left unattended by a consciousness, if you will. At least, that's as much as we understand about the process now. Dr. Beck watched over you very carefully, but we quickly saw that this was not an easy thing to do."

Dr. Beck offered Ali some tea. It had a minty, cinnamon smell that was wonderful. "Thank you," she said, taking a sip of the nearly scalding liquid.

"If that sits well," Beck said, smiling, "we'll try some food in a bit."

Ali smiled, and took another sip.

McManus sat there, waiting for her next question.

Ali felt her face fall, afraid of this question, afraid of the answer.

"What about Jim?"

She said it aloud.

McManus rubbed his cheek.

"He's alive," McManus said.

Ali took a breath.

"And, what's more, he did what he had to. Whatever the Iron Men were up to with the stolen art was derailed, if you will. We saw the signs here almost immediately."

Ali looked up at the historian, Lindstrom. She expected him to be smiling, to be happy that they had won. But instead Lindstrom was backing away, looking around. . . .

There's something going on here, she thought. Something they're not telling me.

"Then—then you'll bring him back?"

McManus stood up, now distancing himself from Ali.

"You remember what I said, Ali? Reversing the transference produces extreme physical stress. It's very dangerous. And—we know from our readings—that Jim was wounded."

Ali sat up, tried to slide off the special chair.

"No!" Beck tried to soothe her. "Sit back and rest, Alessandra. You'll—"

"Wounded?"

McManus nodded. Lindstrom was near his table, flipping through his yellow pads. She heard him hit a key on the computer.

"Nothing serious, as far as we could tell. If the life readings we get here are accurate, Jim—or rather his host body—is fine. Mending nicely. But—" McManus turned and looked right at Ali. "There was no way we could bring him back here. He was already in stress from his wounds. It was too risky, too—"

"Oh, come on, McManus!" Lindstrom bellowed from his table, his face flushed and red. "Tell her the rest of it, damn it! Tell her the whole thing!"

"The whole thing?" Ali said. "What whole thing?"

McManus rubbed his cheek again, his response to an uncomfortable position. But Ali didn't care. She wanted to know what he was hiding from her.

"Tell me!" she said, her feet slipping to the floor—which seemed to wobble like day-old jello. She steadied herself with a hand on the chair.

"Well, what I said is true. I mean, he couldn't handle a return to his body here. At least, I couldn't be sure he could handle it. And—"

Lindstrom bulled his way past McManus and stood facing Ali.

"And they moved!" Lindstrom bellowed. "The Iron Men lost in 1941, so they packed up shop and moved somewhere else."

Wh—what?" Ali stuttered.

"Yes," McManus said tiredly. She noticed how drawn he looked. How many days had he been here. A few days? A few weeks? And how much sleep had McManus gotten? Or any of them? "They moved. . . ." McManus said.

"I don't understand. . . ."

Lindstrom continued. "Just as soon as you and Jim stopped them, we started getting crazy readings from outside."

"Small stuff, really," McManus said. "Little changes, discrepancies that might have passed unnoticed if we didn't have our computer isolated from the outside data bank. But it kept track of the changes, all the small discrepancies and—"

Lindstrom shook his head, still baffled by the idea. "They were tiny, *insignificant* changes. Nothing to worry about at first, I thought they were just fallout from what you did in 1941. But then they just kept coming. . . ."

"Quite right," McManus said. "And the small changes started to link together, until there was a *pattern.* The computer finally alerted us that the Iron Men were active again."

"In 1941? Is that what you mean? Is that why you left Jim there?"

"Please, Alessandra," Dr. Beck said, trying to push her back onto her chair. "Try not to get excited."

But Ali kept watching McManus and Lindstrom look at each other.

"No, not—"

The lab door flew open. It was the security guard, Toland.

"Er, sorry, Dr. McManus. But they're back. And they insist on seeing you."

Ali saw McManus's eyes widen. She moved to Lindstrom. He looked scared too.

"Damn," McManus said. "Alright. tell them we'll be right up. And whatever you do, don't let them come down here."

"Yes, doctor." Toland said and he hurried quickly away.

"What's going on?"

McManus walked close to Ali and put his two hands on her shoulders. "We couldn't bring Jim here. But we needed him somewhere else. It was a decision that had to be made quickly. We're still not sure what's going on."

"McManus, we'd better go up," Lindstrom said. "Those goons won't wait for long. . . ."

"Yes, in a minute . . ."

"Goons? Who's up there?" Ali asked. "What do they want?"

"We finally got a fix on the focal point of the changes. They are being more careful now, doing lots of groundwork. And what we're seeing is only a foreshadowing, a mere glimpse of something very big that will change the world forever . . . if it's not stopped."

"That's for sure," Lindstrom snorted.

"Where's Jim?" Ali asked, her voice brittle, flat.

McManus took a breath. "He's in Saigon. January 23, 1968."

Ali stared at him, not believing McManus's words. "You sent him to Vietnam?"

Lindstrom cleared his throat. "Er, McManus . . . It's now actually the morning of the twenty-fourth back there. . . ."

McManus let Ali glare at him. And then said, "Yes, and we had better go up and meet our visitors. . . ."

3

The sound of voices, loud, laughing, harsh in what felt like a painfully early morning, snapped Jim awake. He took a few seconds to get his bearings—a common struggle for him lately. Yes sir, he thought, no telling who I'll turn up being, or where . . . or when.

Isn't life grand?

The loud voices passed by the door.

He heard someone in the bathroom humming loudly.

"Aren't you out of the sack yet, McShane?"

Jim looked around at the simple hotel room, and he remembered walking into the building, the hotel, last night and onto its Victorian patio. He walked up the stairs on a threadbare carpet to a room that he shared with the bumptious lieutenant from the south.

"Getting there . . ." he mumbled.

Burnett came out of the bathroom, his face still half-lathered from a shave, a cigarette stuck squat in the middle of the foamy side of his mouth.

"Last call for breakfast is in five minutes, Jacko. I let you saw wood as long as I could."

"Right." Jim said, smiling halfheartedly.

"Besides," Burnett said, talking as he went back to the mirror and his whiskers, "the bus to the base is moving out of here in thirty minutes."

Does that mean we're leaving here? That this simple hotel and the other exotic sights and sounds of Saigon are about to become a thing of the past?

The torture of not knowing was just too much.

"Why the hell are we going back to the base?" Jim asked. He heard a squish and gurgle of water. Then Burnett came out rubbing at his face with a white towel as if he was a madman.

He was smiling. But he also gave Jim an odd look.

"What the hell are you talking about, boy? Didn't you get enough R&R for your free weekend? It's back north tonight, mama." Burnett put on his shirt. "Back to the jungle, Tarzan. So put all other thoughts out of your mind. Shit!" he said, looking down at his watch. "Look at the damn time!"

Burnett hurried past Jim and picked up a small duffle bag. "I'll meet you down stairs, Jacko. My stomach's getting mighty anxious."

Jim nodded.

"Get a move on . . ." Burnett said, dashing out the door.

Jim looked around the room. A pale, milky light seeped through the sere curtains. He saw McShane's uniform—*his* uniform—scattered on the floor. A Timex wristwatch sat on the battered end table next to a bamboo lamp whose shade was all a kilter. The watch was next to a half-full bottle of Bahmi Ba beer, with a cigarette floating vertically at the top.

Good thing I didn't drink it, Jim thought.

He put on the watch.

He had a feeling that time was going to be important.

Apparently, breakfast was over. The dining room was shut tight.

"Here, buddy," Burnett said, coming over to him, still chewing on something. "I saved you some chow."

He handed Jim a sticky bun with a red center that looked like a bull's-eye. It wasn't from any food group that Jim would normally eat. But his stomach, rumbling at full throttle, overrode any qualms he had about the sticky-sweet breakfast roll.

"Thanks," he said, taking the bun and chewing into it like a caveman let loose in a *patisserie.*

It was disgustingly cloying. But it had a doughy substance to it that Jim knew would keep the worst ravages of hunger away for a bit.

He was standing in the hotel lobby, surrounded by other soldiers, mostly army, but a few marines who clustered together looking a whole lot leaner and nastier than the army people. He was biting into the roll, devouring it, when he saw a stack of newspapers by the corner. A small man sat beside the pile with a plate in front of him.

The date, he thought. The paper will have the date!

He walked over to the man, and studied what coins sat in his plate. Jim dropped a few down. The man smiled a toothless grin, nodding and saying words Jim didn't understand.

He picked up the paper.

Stars and Stripes.

I was expecting The international edition of the *Herald Tribune?* he thought.

He didn't look at the date.

He read the headline.

PUEBLO COMMANDER AND CREW TAKEN PRISONER.

The *Pueblo* . . . Jim remembered the story from his studies, if only because it was symptomatic of America hitting the darkest part of its post-Fifties world. Here was this great power, the world's protector of freedom, and the tiny Communist country North Korea had the *cojones* to seize an American intelligence ship—and its eighty-two surviving crew members—and keep them prisoners for eleven months.

The commander—the name escaped Jim, and he skimmed the article. He found it. Commander Lloyd M. Bucher was left to hang in North Korea after having released statements that embarrassed the United States.

He needn't have worried, though. Worse was to come, much worse, until Americans were treated to the Marx Brothers' spectacle of the Fall of Saigon, the cartoonlike evacuation of the city that demonstrated that the country of John Wayne could hightail it with the best of them.

1968. It was a wonderful year.

No, it wasn't. 1968, along with its pal, 1969, were the twin stars of the grand Guignol decade. There'd be another dead Kennedy, yessir, as Bobby bought it in a hotel.

So much for security.

And Martin Luther King became a living target, ending a dream that, with benign neglect, would turn into a nightmare, culminating in the Housing Riots of '98.

And what else? Jim thought, his mind racing, trying to remember the key events of the year.

Because he knew, oh yeah, he *knew* he was here because something damned important was going on.

The Iron Men were here. And the Time Lab had sent him to the rescue.

And this time, he worried, maybe I'm on my own.

Because if Ali made it back, they surely wouldn't risk her again. And if she didn't—

"Time for your last smoke, Jack," Burnett said, coming up to him, startling him.

Jim nodded. He looked down at the date. January 24th. 1968. Burnett looked over his shoulder.

"Oh, you're reading about that shit? That's old news, buddy. I was talking to someone who works in MAC-V intelligence. He says they're planning some kind of action against North Korea. Hell, we'll fix their wagon just like we're taking care of Charlie here."

"Right . . ." Jim said.

January 1968, he kept thinking. What else happened in January 1968? The Beatles started to come apart, that he knew. After the not-so-*Magical Mystery Tour*—which hit the stores in the states only weeks earlier, there'd be the *White Album*. Helter Skelter, hello Yoko, and goodbye Fab Four.

But why am I here?

He thought of a book, required reading, by Norman Mailer.

Why Are We In Vietnam?

He looked around the hotel lobby.

Outside the great doors of the Continental Hotel he saw a dark-green bus pull up. A school bus gone khaki.

"There it is, Jack. C'mon, your squad must miss you. . . ."

Burnett walked back to his duffle bag. The old man behind Jim was scooping up his few coins, counting them. The lobby started emptying.

The old man muttered to himself.

Jim kept looking around.

He noticed decorations in the lobby. Twisting, foil streamers. They caught the morning light. And cardboard words in Vietnamese hung near the ceiling. They looked like Christmas decorations. Sure, he thought. There are a lot of Catholics here. A lot. Could be. That's what they are. Sure—

No. It's January 24th.

Christmas was a month ago.

More like—yeah—more like New Year's decorations.

The lobby was nearly empty. He reached down, and dully picked up his bag. He started moving to the bus, turning to look at the decorations, and the old man, now counting his papers. A middle-aged Vietnamese woman came out of a back room to stand at the hotel desk, her face sullen, serious, watching the soldiers leave her hotel.

He was nearly at the door, nearly at the bus.

And then he knew what the decorations were for.

Vietnamese New Year's.

He pushed open the door and walked out into the cool morning air. He smelled the foul exhaust of the bus.

The Vietnamese New Year.

Tet.

There wasn't a more crucial date in the last half of the American Century than the bloody days of what came to be known as the Great Tet Offensive.

Now I know why I'm here . . . he thought, moving out of the hotel to the bus.

The ride made him feel as if he was back on one of those rumbling school buses, the way they used to bounce and jiggle on even level road surfaces. All day long you'd sit in a class, immobile, and watch the clock crawl. Then you'd pile into an overcrowded bus with stir-crazy kids who screamed, exulting in their freedom, while the mad bus driver tried to shake the little bastards until they couldn't see straight.

Or so it seemed.

This bus was just like that. Except for two differences. It was green. Everywhere, a drab olive color.

And nobody was screaming. These were big kids now, hulking kids with beards and big black boots that weighed a good ten pounds. There was no screaming.

In fact, there was hardly any talking. There was just the belching groan of the engine. The soldiers—most of them—just looked out the window, watching Saigon slip away.

Most sat quietly.

But not Burnett. He sat still for just a few minutes, then he gave Jim a good-natured jab to his kidneys.

"So," he said. "What the hell's the matter with you? You sick or something? Drink too many beers? I hate to say this, Jacko, but your personality seems to be suffering. . . ."

Jim shrugged. And just what is my personality? he wondered. He guessed—from Burnett's friendship—that it was something that tended toward something more personable and carefree.

"Yeah," Jim said. "I feel sort of, you know, bilious."

The word stumped Burnett, but then his mouth made a great "O" of understanding. And he laughed, "Hey, don't shoot anything my way. Call the stewardess for an air bag, if you don't mind.'' Burnett kept laughing at his own wit. Then—in mid-guffaw—he stopped. He turned suddenly serious in that way some guys had of suddenly becoming Mr. Concern.

''You still worried about home? Your mom and dad . . . ?''

Jim's eyes widened. Home. Now, what the hell is this all about? Did Burnett mean going home, getting my ass out in one piece? What was he talking about?

''Don't worry. It will all work out.'' Burnett acted uncomfortable and he turned to look out the window. ''If that's what's bothering you, I wouldn't even worry about it. . . .''

Well, I certainly won't, thought Jim. Especially since I don't even know—

But then—like a breeze blowing off a lake on a hot summer's day—he saw them. A man and a woman. Mom and Dad McShane. But old, too old, as if they had children late in life. The woman—he could picture in his mind. Sitting in a kitchen chair, playing with a paper napkin, weaving it through her fingers as it became more and more frayed. And then, a man. Sitting in a dark living room, a bottle of beer beside a great maroon easy chair. His balding head resting against an antimacassar that—once white—had turned a golden yellow with age and grease.

There was someone else. Young.

My younger brother, Jim knew.

No, he mentally corrected himself in the interest of not letting this schizophrenic state get *completely* out of control—Jack McShane's younger brother. Will. The perpetual younger brother. We always fight, Jim thought. About everything, all the time.

Jim pictured him, with shoulder-length straight hair. And bell-bottom blue jeans. A fringed vest.

Hippie Americanus.

But Jim saw his face. It was amazing how these bits of memory broke to the surface. He was young. Fifteen, sixteen or so. And he was yelling. At the old man, at the woman. Filling the small—

(Apartment. That's all it was. Two small bedrooms, a gloomy living room, a kitchen, and—)

It faded.

And he felt the presence of someone else's life being lifted from him.

"Don't worry, Jack." Burnett said, still looking out the window. "That stuff will all take care of itself. You'll see. It will all be fine."

The bus turned off the big avenue, crowded with people, then onto another avenue. He read the sign. Hong Tap Tu Street. The big buildings and hotels gave way to smaller streets, narrow shops and flimsy shanties. He saw fewer GIs, more Vietnamese everywhere, hurrying around, crossing the street, slowing the progress of the bus.

Then the bus stopped completely.

Jim heard the driver honking his horn.

"What the fu—" Burnett started to say.

Jim stood up to see what was the problem.

There was a crowd of people in the street, most of them in black. Some men were holding something up near the back of the crowd.

"Another damn funeral . . ." Burnett muttered. "Seems like they've been having a goddam funeral festival all week. Out in the jungle they leave their buddies lying around to stink up the place. But here, it's a big parade. I tell you . . . we're going to have to win this damn thing despite ARVN's help. They're just looking for—"

The funeral procession cleared a path for the bus, and it jerked forward, cutting off Burnett's keen political analysis.

The bus turned right, and then Jim saw that the city was disappearing. He saw they were heading east, and he didn't know what lay east, whether that was a good direction to be going, or a bad one.

All he knew was that the city was behind him. And

ahead a long road ran up to the green hills to the northeast.

And, ironically, it all looked quite beautiful. . . .

General William Childs Westmoreland smiled and indicated that everyone should take his seat in the comfortable conference room in the main building of Military Assistance Command-Vietnam.

There were a lot of comfortable things here. MAC-V was located near Tan Son Nhut Airport, in Saigon. And he had no doubt that the command center suffered from a rear-guard mentality. It was hard to see the jungles and the rice paddles through the haze and neon of Saigon. . . .

President Thieu wasn't here for this briefing and it was just as well. More and more, his number two, General Nguyen Cao Ky, was the one making the important decisions. The alliance of the soft-spoken Thieu and the flashy Ky, with his jaunty grin and colorful silk flashy scarves, was an uneasy one. But it was vital that it work. This was not the time for any instability.

And there were other pressures on Westmoreland besides keeping things rolling on the military front, fighting the great war of attrition.

President Lyndon Baines Johnson was losing his nerve.

"General," LBJ had said during Westmoreland's last junket to DC, staring at him as if he was a hound dog about to be sent to the doghouse, "I don't want a Dien Bien Phu."

But that, Westmoreland told him in Washington, was impossible. Out of the question. The war is being won, in the field, and in the hearts and minds of the loyal South Vietnamese people.

Westmoreland believed that.

Especially now.

Ky took a seat, still chatting with the American ambassador, Ellsworth Bunker. He was recommending a new restaurant.

"The steak Diane is really wonderful," Ky said.

Westmoreland looked at Bunker and sighed. Ky

turned, still smiling, his cerise scarf looking like Christmas tree tinsel.

"I think I'd like to begin," the general said.

His chief adjutant for intelligence, a corporal named Wally Kline, handed him a manilla envelope.

"The information in here has been checked by a number of our usual intelligence sources. And—except for a few small details—it's all been verified." Westmoreland slid typed copies—both stamped *For Your Eyes Only*—to Bunker and Ky. "As I told you at our last briefing, a major offensive is set to be launched to coincide with the TET cease-fire."

Ky shook his head, and made an angry sneer with his lips. "Those bastards—"

"We now have more precise information. Sometime during the thirty-six hour period of the cease-fire, a major influx of NVA Regulars will attack key positions both in the north and south." Westmoreland handed them each maps showing the points of attack.

"Khe Sanh . . . Tay Ninh . . . Hue . . . ?" Bunker said. "I don't understand. Why Khe Sanh? And Hue has been left as an open city since the beginning of the war. I don't get it. . . ."

"It's not an open city anymore," Westmoreland said.

"No actions near Saigon," Ky said, sounding relieved. "Sure," he said, taking care to pronounce his words. "That would be crazy." He grinned and made a small laugh.

"Nonetheless," Westmoreland said, "we will have the 199th here, as well as a few divisions from II corps. But the city will remain primarily an ARVN responsibility, with help from the usual military police."

"Of course," Said Ky.

"Do you think," Bunker asked "that we need to take any special precautions at the embassy?"

Westmoreland shook his head. The ambassador was new, still unsettled by the popping sounds of ground fire that drifted on the wind from the surrounding countryside. But the new American Embassy had a massive wall and crack guards.

Besides, why would the VC want the building—even assuming they could get to it?

"No, I think you're fine. And—as I've said—we don't expect anything to happen here. . . ." he smiled. "Except, of course, some festive fireworks."

But Ky's face looked troubled.

"I'll need those sheets back, gentlemen. . . ." Westmoreland said.

Ky nodded, and then turned to the general. "But where did you get all this information, General? It's very . . . detailed. It's their entire battle plan."

Westmoreland smiled. He didn't want Ky—nor anyone in the South Vietnamese government—knowing his source. Not yet. It was rife with leaks, VC regulars, and people who'd sell their grandmother for a pack of American cigarettes.

Or so Westmoreland thought.

"An excellent source," Westmoreland said, gathering up the sheets, and putting them away. "Which, I'm afraid, I must, for now, keep confidential." His grin broadened. Have to keep our allies happy, he thought. "Until we've completely checked his credentials and can be sure that he isn't in any danger himself."

Ky nodded. And Westmoreland knew that the Vietnamese VP would try to discover the source behind Westmoreland's back.

Let him, the Commander of the US Forces in Vietnam thought. Let him. . . .

As he used to say back in Spartanburg, South Carolina. Rots of ruck.

"Gentlemen," Ky said, smiling again as he stood up. "May I suggest a place for lunch?"

And—damn protocol—Westmoreland knew he was trapped, at least for another hour or so. . . .

4

McManus and Lindstrom started to leave the Time Lab.

"We'll be right back," McManus said. "We have to stop these people from bothering us."

Dr. Beck had her hand on Ali's wrist, taking her pulse, but Ali pulled away and followed McManus.

"McManus, the girl shouldn't come with us," Lindstrom said.

McManus sighed. "Please, Ali, we'll be right back, if you'll just . . ."

Ali shook her head. The floor still wobbled as if it was floating somewhere in the mid-Atlantic. She took a deep breath and tried to steady herself.

"No. Now that I'm back I want to know what's going on. I want to *help* Jim."

"Elliot," Dr. Beck said gently from behind her, "I don't think—"

"Please, Alessandra," McManus said, "you don't understand what's—"

"I'm coming, Doctor. I want to see what's happened to the world I helped save."

Lindstrom grumbled, wiped his brow and shook his head. "We'd better *go!*" Lindstrom said, turning to McManus, sounding completely exasperated.

They left the lab and Ali followed them.

"You really should be resting." McManus said,

pushing the elevator button. "And you're not going to understand what has happened. . . ."

"I'm not even sure that *I* do. . . ." Lindstrom muttered.

"Try me," Ali said, her wooziness almost more than she could handle. She put a hand against the elevator door for support. "I'm a fast learner. . . ."

She saw McManus shoot her a knowing glance, knowing what she was going through.

They could have stopped me, she thought. If they really didn't want me to come, they could have kept me in the lab. . . .

The elevator door opened and they trooped in.

"Lindstrom . . . a brief synopsis for Ali, if you will . . ."

The elevator whooshed closed and they sailed up to the Red Building's main entrance.

"As I said," Lindstrom began, "we picked up these small changes. Nothing important. I really thought that it was just fallout from the changes that occurred in 1941."

"But they weren't?"

"No, and this time the Iron Men were being damned clever. A lot of very clever groundwork was being done, slowly changing our history but not in any dramatic way. Then, two things happened. . . ."

The elevator stopped. The doors slid open, and McManus hurried out. "Come on," he snapped, "we've already kept them waiting far too long."

The old scientist whipped down the hall to the main lobby of the lab building.

Ali caught a glimpse of blue sky outside. Bare trees. It was late fall. How many days have I been gone? she wondered.

She saw some figures, shadowy hulks standing just inside the lab entrance.

"Where are *your* guards?" she asked, "Don't you still have your guards?"

"Yes, but—oh, do get on with it, Lindstrom."

"Our computer finally picked up a new focal point for the changes . . . a new date," the historian said, whispering to her. "It took a while, but then there it was, clear as day. And when we saw these guys," he nodded in the direction of the dark figures waiting for them, "then we knew that something very bad was up."

She heard McManus clear his throat in preparation for speaking to whomever was waiting for them.

'But wait," Lindstrom whispered, bending his face close to hers, "you'll see what I mean. . . ."

They entered the lobby, an open area with an ornate vaulted ceiling two stories tall. She saw Toland standing just inside the door, flanked by two men out of a comic book. They wore bright blue suits that looked metallic—a type of body armor, she guessed. And tight skull pieces with a thin stalk of an antenna sticking out. Their mouths were exposed, but that was about it. A blackish band covered their eyes. Built-in infrared detectors? Ali wondered.

They carried short, snub-nosed automatic rifles, high-tech uzis, sleek and ominous.

And the last thing she noticed, as she came to stand right in front of them, were the small glistening badges implanted right into the dark blue body armor.

NYPD.

New York Police Department.

"Doctor McManus," one of them said, "we expected to hear from you yesterday. . . ."

She felt the other cop staring at her, looking her over with an interest that made her wish she had stayed down below.

"Who is this?" the second cop asked.

Lindstrom jumped in. "A grad student . . . she's helping input our data."

The cop nodded, while his partner returned to questioning McManus.

"We told you that the building must be put under

our complete protection by 0500 hours. That is only a few hours away, and I don't see—''

Ali saw McManus smile. Who are these people? Ali wondered. What happened to nice blue uniforms and friendly cops with bushy moustaches?

These guys looked like storm troopers from the planet Mongo. She saw them handle their guns as if they were so itchy to get off just one quick burst.

''Why, we're certainly going to comply with the Northeast Security Directive. It's just that—''

Ali slid closer to Lindstrom. ''The Northeast what?''

She saw one of the high-tech cops still looking at her.

McManus was talking. . . . ''Just let us get all straightened up in here, and—''

The double doors to the lab flew open and someone came in wearing a junior version of the cops' bizarre costume. Only now the color was a pale blue, and instead of a cop's badge there was the crown symbol of Columbia University.

And whoever it was wore the same kind of helmet-cum-mask. Must be all the fashion rage this season. . . .

''Campus security has taken a position at the entrance,'' the newcomer said.

Ali recognized the voice.

She looked at the weak chin.

The weak chin looked back. A small smile, more of a sneer, crossed his lips. He nodded to her.

It was Martin.

Martin, the pining romeo who hoped to win her love in spite of the fact that he played football and his IQ was a good twenty points lower than hers.

What was *he* doing dressed up like Judge Dredd?

''Martin . . .'' she said.

''I haven't seen you around, Ali.''

She walked up to him. She guessed that he didn't recall anything about sneaking her and Jim into the Time Lab, getting them started playing with time in the first place. He'd been outside. Who knew what he now *remembered* as his history.

"Don't you . . . er, work here?" she asked him.

The two cops were talking with McManus, who was still quietly trying to reassure them that everything was okay.

"Yes, but today's one of my duty days."

She nodded, figuring that it was best to play along as if she understood what he was talking about.

Duty days. Sounds like a concept she could do without.

"The Physics Department has begun File Removal Procedures against you," Martin said. "If I had known you were here, I could have . . ."

She saw that Martin toted a miniature version of the gun fondled by the high-tech cops. There's a scary thought, Martin with a gun. . . .

"I—I'll work everything out," she said. "I'm just—"

The cops backed away. Their body armor made it a bit difficult for them to move. "Very well, Dr. McManus" one of them said. "Until 0500 then, at which time we will expect compliance with the new Security Directive whether you and your staff are ready . . . or not."

McManus smiled weakly.

Lindstrom reached out an arm to guide Ali back.

"Just keep nodding . . . and smiling. . . ." Lindstrom whispered. "Everything's okay. Everything's hunky-dory. Just wait a second and—"

The cops turned to leave. But Martin stood there a moment, watching Ali, his exposed lips revealing his confusion. Then Martin turned and followed the police out.

"Let's go . . . keep walking," McManus hissed as soon as the cops were out the door. And he rushed back to the elevator.

The bus stopped at a junction of three narrow roads with a jigsaw of cracked asphalt. They were paved roads, though, and a steady stream of peasants in black pajamas moved past the bus.

"What are we waiting for," Jim asked Burnett, who had finally stopped jabbering in his ear and succumbed to looking out the window. Jim looked at Burnett once, looking at his face suddenly gone lifeless. And Jim guessed that Burnett was thinking about what was ahead.

Thinking about it.

Thinking about bad stuff.

Stuff that I don't have a clue about. . . .

"Waiting for trucks," Burnett answered laconically. "Unless there's some rock 'n' roll ahead. Don't hear anything, though. . . ."

Jim nodded.

Rock and roll? What the hell was that supposed to mean?

Then he heard the sound of deep, growling engines, and a pair of trucks came from the east.

"There we go," Burnett said quietly.

The door to the bus whooshed open, and all the big kids carrying duffle bags instead of Snoopy lunch boxes stumbled out of the somber bus.

Half the group headed towards one bus, and half towards the other. Jim waited, watching Burnett to see which he selected.

"Ain't you comin', Jacko?" Burnett asked.

Jim smiled.

The peasants, some wielding thin branches to herd scrawny goats, paid no attention to the soldiers. And the soldiers paid no attention to the peasants.

He climbed on back of the truck, sliding into an empty space on the bench-style seat. Most of the space was taken by shiny-faced privates, judging from the single stripe on their uniform.

The bus backed up, turned around, and roared back down the highway to Saigon.

Another link to civilization cut, he thought.

He started to get an uncomfortable feeling in his bowels.

Hunger, he wondered? Or something even more primal?

The truck engine came to life, startling him. The other truck started. They separated, one heading towards the east, while Jim's moved to the north, towards the dark jungle in the distance, toward the sculpted, rolling hills.

A smoky haze hung over the trees.

Probably just a fog, an early morning mist that would burn off.

But then again, he thought, maybe it won't. . . .

"Now, will you tell me what's going on?"

Ali sat down near Lindstrom's pile of yellow pads.

She saw the monitor flashing. Noncorrelated Data, each line said, followed by a string of numbers. Every few seconds, another line crept up from the bottom . . . more noncorrelated data.

Noncorrelated. The difference between outside the Time Lab, and inside the Time Lab. She saw Lindstrom watch the string of messages. He licked his lips.

"I *really* should check these," Lindstrom said.

"They'll wait, Dr. Lindstrom. "Please," she said. "Bring me up-to-date. Please." She touched his hand.

Lindstrom smiled. "Interesting expression, that. 'Up-to-date' . . . What does that mean when dates and events themselves have no constancy?" His smiled faded. "I'm afraid we're losing, Alessandra. They're too well organized, too fast. I don't think we can beat the Iron Men this time. And god, they haven't even started to play their big card!"

McManus had come over to them and stood behind Lindstrom. "Don't listen to his moaning, Ali. We have plenty of time to turn things around. And Dr. Jacob says the generator is all set, so—"

"That's the problem with your not being a historian, McManus," Lindstrom barked. He dug through the pile of yellow pads, pulled one out, and slid it to Ali. "Here, you take a look, These are the major changes, and, as I said, only small ripples have been introduced into the temporal continuity."

Ali looked at the list.

"The Inner City Consortium, founded 1975," she read.

"A post-Vietnam coalition of activists and politicians," Lindstrom explained. "It organized the homeless, the hungry, and the disenfranchised to elect a presidential candidate unconnected with either of the two major parties."

"What's so bad about that?" Ali asked.

"Read on," Lindstrom said, licking his lips. She looked at him for a second, wondering whether he was still suffering under McManus's alcohol ban. The old boy looked like he was hurting. . . .

"The Blair Amendment?" Ali asked, reading the next line.

"Oh, just a little fine-tune to the constitution," Lindstrom said. "Just a little paragraph that ripped the first amendment to pieces. That's where the thought police upstairs came from. Apparently, crime got a little out of control after we lost the war. . . ."

"Lost the war? I don't see *that* here."

"No. Not yet," Lindstrom agreed, shaking his head. "The Vietnam debacle is still down there, in the outside records, as a withdrawal, but it's become more of a rout. But all the supporting data for that withdrawal is slipping away, literally disappearing. The past is in flux, and the outside record is becoming confused and unclear."

McManus put a hand—meant to calm her—on Ali's shoulder. "What Dr. Lindstrom means, Alessandra, is that—by working backwards—we are seeing indications that the war will be lost. Not abandoned, not merely escaped, but *lost.*"

Lindstrom nodded angrily. "Yes, lost, like a real goddam war!"

"But how? How could we ever lose the war?"

Lindstrom sighed. "If I knew that, I'd know what your friend Jim should be doing. As it is, I can only guess."

"But," McManus said, "we do know the time frame for the projected changes and it's only a few days."

"When?" Ali asked.

McManus smiled, then squinted his eyes.

"The Tet Offensive, Ali."

"Tet Mau Than. The Year of the Monkey," Lindstrom snorted. "But god knows what the hell we're supposed to do there."

"But you'll figure it out, won't you?" Ali asked.

Lindstrom laughed. "Such faith. A charming attribute, Alessandra. I certainly hope so . . . for your Jim's sake . . . for McManus's sake."

She turned and looked back at the gaunt doctor. "Dr. McManus? Why?"

McManus smiled sheepishly. "Because I'm going back there, Ali," he said quietly.

The truck roared into the camp and stopped. The driver ran to the back of the truck and pulled the rear panel down. Suddenly the soldiers streamed off the truck, their heavy boots clopping noisily on the ridged metal floor. A helicopter, no little commuter chopper making a run out to Kennedy Airport, roared overhead. Jim watched it land with what looked like incredible, reckless speed, gently setting down near an empty spot to the left.

He felt Burnett urging him forward.

And Jim jumped down to the ground, pulling his duffle bag behind him.

Burnett walked away.

And Jim stood there alone. "Hey," he called to Burnett, his lifeline. "Wh-where are you going?"

Burnett—his duffle bag slung over his shoulder—shot Jim another what-the-hell's-the-matter-with-you look.

"Where do you think I'm going? I'm checking with my top and then I'll try to catch a few winks before party time."

Burnett kept walking away.

The soldiers scurried left and right.

And Jim stood there alone.

Great, he thought. I don't have the foggiest idea what to do.

I'm likely to get shot as a spy as soon as they figure out I don't know what to do. I'm just a VC clone of Jack McShane.

C'mon, he thought. There has to be something just near the surface, something shred from McShane's memory, that could help him get through the next few hours.

He closed his eyes.

Feeling like The Cowardly Lion. "I do believe in ghosts. I do, I do, I do . . ."

Nothing came.

He smelled the air. There were tall palm trees ahead just beyond the stand of tents with splotches of camouflage. To the right, he saw sandbag piles and a heavy machine gun. He saw the two soldiers watching him, studying him. He smiled back at them.

I'm okay, fellows. Just trying to figure out what the hell I'm supposed to do.

He looked left. He saw a large tent, perhaps some place troops slept, he reasoned. He heard a guitar.

And he recognized the song. An anthem from the sixties.

"Where Have All the Flowers Gone."

A breeze blew and he missed a few chords. Then he heard the tinkling of the guitar's metal strings. And voices, faint, whispering the song. A few voices. He picked up his duffle bag, entranced by the music.

I can't believe that they could sing that song here, he thought. Won't the officers freak out?

Because the flowers go to young girls, and the young girls go to soldiers, and the soldiers go to graveyards.

Every one.

When will they ever learn?

The song didn't have an answer to that one.

Jim moved towards the big tent, and he caught a whiff of food cooking, the smell growing stronger with every step he took. Good, he told his rumbling stomach, at least I know where the mess tent is.

The voices were clear now, reaching the last verse of the song. The helicopter took off again, its rotors slapping around in a loud ominous rhythm. A bird from hell, swooping over him, blotting out the end of the song.

He felt someone tap his shoulder.

He turned around.

A big black guy, a giant hulk wearing a green baseball cap with a permanent crease in the center. He had his sleeves rolled up, showing the thigh-sized arms of a weight lifter or a fullback.

He was one mean-looking motherfucker.

But he smiled.

And Jim looked at his shoulder, and saw the three stripes of a sergeant.

He's a sergeant and I'm a lieutenant. Got to remember that I outrank him.

"Welcome back, Lieutenant," the sergeant grinned. "I hope you had a good time."

Jim nodded.

(C'mon, he begged McShane's dormant consciousness. Who the hell is this? Give me a break, McShane, if you're in there. *Who the hell is this?*)

"I'll walk you back to the captain . . . things have been quiet over the weekend. So we should have it nice and easy tonight."

Jim nodded.

Then—bingo—

It was there.

Sergeant Clarence Howell. From a not-yet-terrible section of Brooklyn.

And Jim knew, as he picked up his bag and walked

alongside his top sergeant . . . his Top, sure, he *knew* that this man was the number one reason that McShane had survived his first six months in the 'Nam.

And that—Jim thought—was a good thing to know. A very good thing . . .

5

The helicopter carried no markings to indicate that it was anything other than a standard army chopper out on patrol.

That gave General Westmoreland a bit of comfort. But the few officers at MAC-V he had told of his plans thought that he was crazy in the first place.

He signalled the pilot to take off, and with a great whirring sound the helicopter rose above Ton Son Nhut airport.

Too much depended upon this intelligence, Westmoreland thought. He couldn't go into the next week without making himself convinced about what he was being told.

What Scorpion was telling the Americans . . .

It all sounded too incredible.

His G-2 was convinced.

The evidence that Scorpion provided was very detailed, his intelligence officer argued. There had been small skirmishes and raids that completely confirmed the intelligence.

The pilot cut a great arc to the north and the afternoon sun suddenly filled the small cabin. It was a good time to fly. As soon as the copter cut to the east, the sun would be behind them. The chopper would be lost in the glow. . . .

Westmoreland took off his hat and rubbed his short hair. Corporal Kline, his solid if unimaginative operations officer, was watching him. It would be Kline's job to take notes on the meeting.

Below, he saw the Saigon River, and then the open fields that stretched to the east, to Cambodia, the VC's playground. Behind him was the death trap of the Mekong Delta.

He thought of the boys who had died in this country. And the enemy they had taken with them. . . .

Attrition.

I've made that word famous, he thought. Attrition. This isn't a war in any ordinary sense. No, they whittle at us while we whittle at them. But there's no doubt that we'll win. We have the guns, the supplies, the tremendous economic might of the greatest power in the world.

And we have the men.

But that was the problem.

These damned protests at home were downright subversive. Courage and doing your duty were now out of fashion. How could his boys go off to the jungles, to the rice paddies, while punk traitors—that's what they were—burned their draft cards at home? Damn, some even wore North Vietnamese flags!

It was hurting the war effort.

He saw that in LBJ's face. The president's words spoke of his complete support, of his determination to see this through.

But his face, that hangdog expression, and his eyes, narrow and weary said that the stress was beginning to tell. On the presidency . . . and the country.

We can win the war, Westmoreland thought. If we have the will.

If our will is greater than theirs.

He straightened up in his seat.

And he had no doubt about that. None at all.

"Oh, yes," McManus smiled. "I've decided that I will go there—and do whatever is necessary."

Lindstrom snorted. "Whatever the hell *that* is."

"Well," McManus said, turning to Lindstrom, "I assume that you'll be able to give me *some* idea of how the great arch of history is being twisted . . . and how to put it right."

Lindstrom looked at his monitor. Ali, looking over his shoulder, saw the steady flow of messages, more noncorrelated data. She looked back to McManus.

He had a smile on his face, a gallowslike grin that was struggling mightily to look cavalier about his journey.

But Ali guessed that he was absolutely terrified.

"But Dr. McManus, what about the stress . . . I mean won't you—?"

McManus turned away as he answered, as if embarrassed by her question. "Oh, I'm not too terribly worried about that. Why, with what I've been through for the past few days, I doubt that using the Time Transference process could do very much more—"

"The old fool," Lindstrom muttered. "I told him that he'll kill himself." Lindstrom came to her. "I told him that I'd go, that even I'm in better shape than he is."

"And that is out of the question. You must stay here, Lindstrom, to follow the changes. Other trouble spots might pop up. You know that. We can't afford to lose our historian." McManus looked at Ali, his jaunty smile now melted into something resigned and pathetic.

There's no way he'll come back, she thought.

"I'm the only one that's expendable. . . ." McManus said. "The only one—" McManus's face suddenly seemed lost in contemplation of something strange and tantalizing. "And, it's going to be doubly strange."

"Why?" Ali asked.

Lindstrom laughed.

She heard Dr. Beck chuckle.

"Why?" she repeated.

"You see," McManus said, "I'll be going into the mind of a young woman."

And despite McManus's exaggeratedly grave expression, Ali laughed out loud. . . .

The captain looked up from his field desk, a pile of papers in front of him. While walking there, Sergeant Howell called him 'Captain Cool.' Jim thought it was some kind of base joke.

Now, standing in front of the captain, he saw the man's name. T. Cool.

Captain Cool looked up.

"I'm sorry, Lieutenant, there's been no word on your request. Maybe tomorrow . . ."

What request? Jim wondered.

To get the hell out of here?

"And, er, we've been getting these conflicting reports that—hell, I just can't make head or tail of them. Sergeant Howell?"

"Sir," the sergeant said from behind Jim.

"Have you gone over these with Lieutenant McShane?"

"No, sir, he just—"

"Here," Captain Cool said, handing Jim some papers. "Our intelligence people in Saigon say there shouldn't be anything to them. Why would supplies be moving past us, heading south? There's just no reason. But a few of our more loyal farmer spies say that it's been going on for three nights now."

Cool looked up at Jim.

"You okay McShane? You're awfully quiet."

"I'm fine, sir."

"Good. Well, as I said, it's probably nothing. But I'd like you to take a look out there tonight. Tell your men it's just a routine S&D. But it will more than likely turn out to be nothing more than a peaceful stroll in the woods, an easy Clear-and-Secure op. You should have just a sliver of the moon near dawn. Head out sometime around 1700 hours. It should be nice and quiet. . . ." Cool smiled. "And I'll probably know about your request by the time you get back in the morning."

Jim started to hand the papers back.

Cool grinned. "Don't you think you'd better keep these, Lieutenant? Unless you've got a photographic memory. . . ."

"Yes, sir," Jim said.

He turned to leave the tent. Cool cleared his throat.

"Lieutenant . . ." Cool said, his face all scrunched up as if he didn't understand what the hell was wrong with Jim.

"Yes . . ." Jim said.

Cool made a little saluting gesture.

"Oh," Jim said. He saluted in what he hoped was a properly military fashion. And then he walked out of the tent.

"I've already briefed the men, sir, if you want to get some shut-eye," Howell said walking beside him.

"Er, yeah," Jim said. He scrambled to think of a way to find out just where his bunk was without asking Howell.

This was getting embarrassing.

"Would you mind, er, walking over with me. I'd like to take another look at these. . . ." Jim looked down at the papers. One page had a few lines of words, all capital letters. SUSPECTED NVA SUPPLY ROUTE. He flipped to the second. It had a map. There was a dark black line, and two others in red.

"Sure, sir."

Jim stood there. He took a step.

"You're going to your tent, Lieutenant?"

"Oh, yeah," Jim smiled at the sergeant's big but now thoroughly confused face. "Right . . . Lost my bearings. . . ."

Jim took a step the other way, and the sergeant fell in beside him. Jim let Howell take the lead, letting Howell's movement set their course.

"Sergeant," Jim said looking at the map. He pointed at the circled area. "How do we get here?"

Howell laughed. Then, seeing Jim's face, he stopped. "Sir, the choppers will drop us and pick us up near dawn."

Jim saw a tent ahead closed in the sides, off by itself.

That had to be it, he thought. That had to be where the officers, the young cannon fodder of this war, said their evening prayers to save their asses before trying to replace their living nightmare with more pleasant dreams.

"Sergeant," Jim said, "I'd like you to take the lead tonight. I'm a bit—"

Jim thought of what the captain had said. *My request*. I've asked to do something. And that could be on my mind.

"I'm a bit preoccupied today, Sergeant. I don't know—"

"Yes, sir. It won't be anything I can't handle, sir. As the captain said, it's just a security operation."

"Good," Jim smiled.

Howell stopped just before the tent.

"I'll have the men in formation by 1630 hours, sir."

Jim nodded.

Looking past Howell, he saw some soldiers playing volleyball, whooping it up, spiking the ball. Actually enjoying themselves.

Now how the hell could they be enjoying themselves? Jim wondered. How in the world was that possible here?

He shook his head, and turned to go inside the tent.

"You can't go," Ali said.

"Oh, yes I can, my dear. Lindstrom must stay, as well as Doctors Beck and Jacob. I'm afraid—"

Ali laughed again. "But a *woman?*"

"Yes," McManus said with discomfort. "A woman. She's apparently a vital link to the Iron Men's plans and—as far as we can tell—they haven't tampered with her."

Ali looked at McManus's eyes. His fear was right there, close to the surface. She wondered whether it was fear of putting his body through the stress of the process, or fear of changing his sexual orientation so late in life.

She knew what she had to do.

"I'll go," she said.

"No," McManus said, dismissing her suggestion with a wave of his hand. "That is out of the question. You've just returned. You're still not one hundred percent, isn't that so, Dr. Beck? No, I'm afraid—"

Ali walked over to the pencil-thin scientist. It's funny, she thought. She didn't know a thing about him, not really. Nothing about his personal life. Is he married? Does he have children—god—maybe even grandchildren? Who is he, this sad-eyed man trying to save the world?

A job that was turning into a full-time occupation.

"Dr. McManus," she began . . .

"Oops," Lindstrom said standing in front of his monitor. She saw the historian lean close, then look down at his crazy jumble of yellow pads. "Oh, god, there it is," he said. "Here we go. . . ." Lindstrom turned to them. "I've got our first major clue. It just—" Lindstrom was excited, his cheeks flush, his eyes wide with excitement—"popped up, just like that. Something really extraordinary must be happening right now—" Lindstrom caught himself. "I mean, back then in 1968."

McManus took a breath. "What is it?"

"The outside data log on late-twentieth-century terrorism. It just damn well disappeared."

McManus looked confused. "That's all—just disappeared?"

Lindstrom nodded, still grinning nervously. "Yes," he said. "And it's been replaced by another entry."

"So . . ." McManus said cautiously.

"Another entry!" Lindstrom said. "Dated ten years

earlier. The whole history of terrorist activity in the goddam postmodern world has just been rewritten. Do you have any idea what that might mean?''

''But who's involved?'' McManus asked.

Ali walked over to Lindstrom's monitor. He had punched up the data on the screen.

And—unlike Lindstrom—what she read made her feel very scared.

And overwhelmed.

(It's hopeless, she thought. We're outmatched. We can't do a damn thing about this. Not a thing . . .)

''It's General Westmoreland,'' Lindstrom said. ''The man in charge of the whole misbegotten adventure. It starts with him!''

The copter was flying low. It looked, Westmoreland thought, as if the trees could reach up and snare the runners of the copter.

They caught no fire. They were moving much too fast, for one thing—and the area they flew over was supposedly secure.

But the man he was about to meet was going to tell him otherwise.

He had thought about the possibility that this was a trap.

After all, what protection would I have? Two platoons on the ground, waiting, the chopper, radio contact with Saigon, and a heavy artillery unit miles to the west.

It was a risk. Possibly a crazy risk. . . .

But the pressure was on. Support for the war was eroding. His request for two hundred thousand more men still sat on the president's desk.

And, Westmoreland thought, if I'm going to be convinced, I'll have to see the informant myself. Ask him questions myself.

Because, if it's true, Tet will be an incredible victory for us. It will end the war. An opportunity for a major engagement, a completely crushing blow delivered to NVA regulars.

And, once they're gone—the so-called guerillas—the peasant guerilla army will melt back to their farms and rice paddies. The battle for the hearts and minds of the Vietnamese will be over.

"Do you want me to do a sweep before landing, General?" the pilot asked.

"No, let's just set her down."

"Sir," Corporal Kline said. "I think we'd better just do one loop around the block, sir, just—"

The general shook his head. "I want to just get in," he said, "let's meet this man, and then get the hell out."

It had been Scorpion's request, this prerequisite that I meet with him. If the early intelligence hadn't been so good, I would have refused.

But it had been better than good.

It had been perfect.

This source—if bonafide—was unparalleled.

It would mean the end of the war.

The copter swooped down to an open field.

Westmoreland leaned closer to the small window of the Sikorsky chopper. He saw the platoons, the men looking up at the chopper, and then left and right, uncomfortable at standing in the open. And then he saw the other soldiers.

The North Vietnamese Regulars. They were dressed in their black *ao baba*, the pajamalike uniform the GIs came to hate. And he saw someone in a blue uniform.

Everyone watched the chopper land.

"All set, sir. . . ." the pilot said.

Westmoreland found his eyes searching the horizon for a sudden burst of fire that could blow the helicopter out of the sky.

He smiled. That would deliver a tremendous blow to the American presence in Vietnam.

I wouldn't be easily replaced, he thought.

The copter landed and, according to procedure, the main rotors stayed on in case of an ambush.

"Alright," Westmoreland said to the corporal. "Let's get to it," He stood up and went to the hatch, just as the pilot opened it. "Radio MAC-V and tell them that Eagle-One has found its nest. . . ."

"Yes, sir," the pilot answered.

Westmoreland hopped down to the ground. It was hard and dry from the past few weeks of uncommonly cool, clear weather. A pair of lieutenants came up and saluted. Westmoreland gave them a perfunctory salute back.

"Keep your men checking the trees. I don't want any surprises."

He looked over at the North Vietnamese contingent. The NVA Regulars looked grim, holding their AK-47s tightly, almost protectively. Their eyes, dark pinpoints in their tight, tan faces, looked grim and deadly.

And not for the first time Westmoreland thought—

Our soldiers don't look that way.

And as for the South Vietnamese Regulars, the ARVN—forget about them. Ever since 1962, when the first American "advisors" died on Vietnamese soil, it was well known that the ARVN soldiers and their generals didn't like to fight. Out on patrol they'd cough, or rattle their guns. Anything to alert the VC to just get the hell away.

They didn't want any engagements.

There had been some improvement. The younger generals, trained in the states, were giving their men real leadership, the right inspiration to meet the enemy on his ground, day or night.

But if Uncle Sam wasn't here, Westmoreland thought, it would be all over for South Vietnam.

He walked over to the NVA soldiers, towards their leader who stood back, waiting for the great American general to walk over to *him*.

This is too damned risky for all of us, Westmoreland thought. Damned dangerous.

But more so for Scorpion than me.

And so he kept walking, smiling now, extending his hand—

To the man who he knew only by his code name.

An apt name for someone who was ready to betray his cause.

And he watched Scorpion smile.

6

Jim stuck a last forkful of the hashlike mixture into his mouth. The food made his dull tin plate look as if it had been sloppily emblazoned by a particularly mushy cow pie.

But, despite his initial revulsion at the meal's odor, texture, and taste, Jim quickly devoured the plateful and the crumbly biscuit that was served with it.

He was hungrier than he ever remembered being.

Things moved fast now. Howell, his top sergeant, had let him doze to the last minute—on the wrong bunk, Howell pointed out to him. But what the hell. And then they caught the bottom scrapings in the mess tent, probably catching, with the hash, a few spoonfuls of whatever glop was last night's dinner.

And Howell briefed him as he ate.

Acting as if Jim knew what he was talking about.

A wild goose chase, that's how Howell described the evening's scheduled activity. A new supply route just south of Bien Hoa, moving material south. To here? Howell laughed.

Towards Saigon?

Very dubious.

Jim nodded, filling his face with the foul hash.

Once Howell fixed him with his intelligent eyes—eyes that didn't look like they missed a trick—and he asked Jim whether there was something wrong.

It must be in my face, Jim thought. That bewildered

look that didn't befit a lieutenant who had been in the bush for six months.

And again he had to wonder . . . why this guy? Why did the Time Lab pick Jack McShane? What's his role in the upcoming festivities that makes him so goddam crucial? And he looked around the tent, thinking . . . there has to be a contact here, someone else from the future who can clue me into what's happening.

I sure the hell hope so. . . .

But everyone looked liked they belonged here.

There was no going up and saying, excuse me . . . but are you from the future?

His plate was empty. Howell looked at his watch.

"If you're all set, sir, I have the men at Launch One. We can check out equipment and head out."

Jim nodded.

"Er, sir, could I see the map?"

Jim dug the folded wad of paper out of his back pocket. He had tried to forget about it, like the time he got a two-hundred-dollar parking ticket parking outside Carnegie Hall.

Just for five stupid minutes, just to buy tickets to the Mahler Second.

A present for Ali.

He had tried to ignore the parking ticket, crumbling it up, stuffing it in his pocket.

But he didn't have the balls to just toss it away.

(They always get you, he knew. Sooner or later the electronic watchdogs track you down and send a crackerjack squad of traffic police to raid your apartment. He could picture himself, like James Cagney, holed up in some farmhouse, screaming out to hundreds of cops with their tommy guns trained on the house. I'm not comin' out, coppers. I don't care if it was a fucking "No Standing Zone"! Come in and get me!)

He handed Howell the map.

It was worse than a parking ticket.

Howell unfolded it, pushing aside his half-finished

dinner plate. "You see, sir, this is where they supposedly have the traffic. See, three reports just this week. Sounds pretty dumb to me. But what I recommend we do—" Howell looked up at Jim. Checking to see if I'm awake, Jim wondered. Maybe it's time for me to go into a new body, a new time. Ding-dong, welcome to the Watergate Hotel. Hoo-hah, and yessir, this way to the American Embassy in Teheran.

There are other fun places to play Time Bandit.

"Yes," Jim said. "Go ahead."

"Well, what I think we should do is set down right about here—" Howell pointed to an area on the map with no elevation squiggles, "—and then move up the hill this way. Then, we can wait until after midnight, and follow the trail down." Howell smiled. "And, if it's being used for a supply route, we'll be able to nail the VC with the goodies."

Now, Jim thought, this could be the most cockamamie plan ever devised. Or, on the other hand, it might be perfectly logical. How the hell am I to judge? he thought. So he simply said, "Okay. Sounds good. . . ."

Howell folded the map and gave it back to Jim. "Then I'd better start getting the men ready. . . ."

Howell picked up his tray and Jim, looking around and seeing that the mess tent was empty, stood up and followed him.

And already the hash was sitting mighty uneasily in his stomach.

"Of course I should go," Ali said. "I'm younger, stronger. I'm in better shape than anyone else here."

"True," Lindstrom said.

"Not true," McManus said sharply. "You may have been, but you're very weak from your reentry. Dr. Beck hasn't had time to study the effects on your body. For all we know, you might be on the verge of a stroke. Isn't that right, Dr. Beck?"

"It's possible." Beck said, looking like the odd

woman out in the discussion. Ali sensed that the doctor wasn't really overly concerned about the state of her health. And that was some comfort. If she doesn't think I'm going to die, then maybe I have a chance to go there and back again.

Because there was one reason—more than any other—that she wanted to go back.

What could Jim think happened to her? He must have spoken to her German host, Fraulein Elizabeth Stolling . . . he must have discovered that she was gone.

So now what is he thinking?

Either that I've returned to the future crazy, or that I made it. In which case, he'll expect me to help him.

Which is exactly what I damn well plan on doing.

"No," McManus said, turning away, missing real support from his peers, "it's out of the question. I will *go* and you will *stay.* There, its decided."

Then Ali suspected something.

"This isn't about my health, is it, doctor?"

"What?" McManus said turning, his owllike eyes narrowing in alarm. "What do you mean?"

Ali took a step towards him, sensing victory. "Just this. I went, I came back, and I'm fine. A bit woozy perhaps, but none the worse for wear."

"And . . . ?"

"And now you want to do it? Isn't that it, Dr. McManus? You want to do it bad enough that you'll even risk the lab, risk the chance to set history right . . . even risk being a woman—"

Lindstrom snickered.

"Just so you can use your wonderful machine."

McManus flushed. He stammered. But—for a second no words came out. And Ali went close to him, so close, that he couldn't turn away and ignore her. "And that makes sense. Who wouldn't want to try this wonderful machine? But you can see that now is not the right time. It would be an experiment with your body. We don't know what the stress might do to an older person.''

Lindstrom muttered into his stack of printouts. ''Especially a wizened old crow like—''

Ali shot the historian a warning look.

And then she grabbed McManus's hand. ''There will be time for you after this all over. Jim is there and I want to be the one to help him.''

''She's right,'' Lindstrom muttered.

McManus pulled his hand away.

''Oh, I don't see—''

The scientist stopped and stared off into the distance.

Everyone in the lab was quiet for a few moments.

Then McManus turned, and smiled at Ali. ''Alright then, we'll send you.'' She beamed. ''But I hope you're still as happy when you find out who you will be . . . and what you'll have to do. . . .''

More silence, and Ali imagined all sorts of terrible possibilities. And then Lindstrom cleared his throat.

''If you have a few moments, kiddies. I have the latest news from the everchanging outside world. And the news, as the hangman told the horse thief, ain't good. . . .''

The soldiers stood on the open tarmac, their rifles standing next to them, their backpacks bulging.

Howell was talking to them. ''Now, listen up,'' he barked. ''I don't want any noise tonight. You make damn sure—'' Howell repeated the last two words with venomous power—''*damn sure* that I don't hear a sound.'' Howell walked up and down the line. ''And I want every buckle, every damn latch secure.''

Howell paused dramatically, letting it sink in.

''And keep your guns tight against your body. There will be no damn rattles. And RT—''

A thin soldier with glasses jogged forward. He had a blaze of freckles on his face and what looked like a hot dog wagon on his back.

Then Jim saw the antenna.

RT. Radiotelephone.

He was an important person, Jim figured.

"You," Howell said waving a very serious finger at the radioman, "have to keep that damn radio equipment quiet. I don't care what the hell you have to do, even if you have to walk on your tippytoes—"

The men laughed, and in that moment Jim saw that they had a lot of affection for the sergeant. Made sense, Jim thought. He was the type of person who saved lives by being a bastard.

And then Jim wondered. What kind of lieutenant am I supposed to be? Does McShane know what the hell he's doing? Or is he a fuckup? What's his scorecard?

Couldn't be too bad, he figured. Not if he's been through six months of this shit and—hey, mom, I'm still alive.

Howell stopped. He hadn't noticed Jim standing behind him.

"Oh, sir, didn't see you. Anything you'd like to add, sir?"

Yes, thought Jim. Just want to say that I'm not the real lieutenant, guys. So you can't depend on me for diddley—

"No," Jim said. "I think—"

Then, from the southeast, he heard the death whirr of helicopters. He turned and saw two choppers flying together, low to the ground, gliding right towards them.

"Alright," Howell yelled, "split into your C&S squads."

The men separated into two groups. Howell turned to Jim.

"Sir, did you forget your gun . . . your pack . . . ?"

"Oh, right," Jim smiled. "I'll go—"

"Henderson, go get the lieutenant's gear," Howell yelled at one of the privates. He turned back to Jim, his face filled with a concern.

"Sir, do you think—"

Jim smiled. This was looking bad. They're going to send me to the army's version of Wingdale if I don't get my act together. Ward Eight. That's what it's called. The happy place for the grunts who go over the edge.

Crackersland. The place for when you've heard one shell too many explode in your ear . . . when you've seen too many bodies ripped to pieces by shrapnel . . . when you've watched one head too many pop a hole from a .35 mm bullet.

"Let's just get the men lined up, Sergeant," Jim said, trying to make it sound something like an order.

And Howell nodded.

The choppers landed and kept their main rotors spinning. The side doors slid open and one of the army airman—standing next to machine gun—waved them in.

"Alright!" Howell yelled. "Load up!"

Henderson, a tall black soldier, appeared with a pack and a rifle.

Jim took the gun.

He looked at it.

This, he thought, had to be the famous Armalite, the M-16. The weapon of choice for the well-heeled Vietnam grunt.

Now how the hell do you use it? he wondered. It had buttons and latches that made it a more complicated machine than the WWII rifle he last fired.

Pull the trigger, right. But is that all, is there anything else?

He held it in his hands.

And his thumb flicked down a switch—without his thinking—then hit a button. His right hand closed around the trigger.

God, he thought. My hand just knew what to do. Took the—what. Yeah, the safety off. And then, I hit this button.

Sure, the M-16 was a semiautomatic. You could shoot one bullet at a time, or blast away.

("I ain't comin' out, coppers!")

He looked up. The soldiers were crowded into the two helicopters.

"All set, sir," Howell said, yelling over the roar of the rotors.

"Okay," Jim said.

And he jogged behind Howell to the nearest chopper and climbed in. It was crowded with the soldiers and there was barely room for him. He smelled their camouflage khaki, and the gun oil, and an ancient jungle smell that must have been tracked into the cabin by hundreds of other missions.

Jim spotted a small space on the bench near the front and he sat down. The rotors picked up speed. The pilot, his helmet scratched, with only a few letters of his name still visible, turned around.

"Ready, sir?"

"Ready," Jim said. Much too quietly, he knew. And he repeated it louder. "Ready!"

And—as if by magic—the chopper rose into the air, wobbling a bit before streaming away from the camp.

He looked around, and then out the plastic window near his head. He saw the tarmac landing point.

Someone had painted a red death's head in the center.

A macabre bull's-eye.

Cute, he thought. Real cute.

He felt his insides twist, turn, and tighten like snakes chilling.

He looked up at the other soldiers.

They sat there, looking straight ahead, their eyes glassy, as if staring into a pit that ran to the bottom of the universe.

Which, he thought, maybe it did . . . maybe it did. . . .

The North Vietnamese general used an interpreter, though Westmoreland guessed that he must know some English. General Tuan Ngoc Chau, was, if nothing else, worldly. He had been part of the negotiating team that parleyed with the French after their disaster of Dien Bien Phu. Chau had spent time in Paris, then later England, before the treaty and the elections in the south fell apart.

Chau had fought for nearly two decades for one ideal.

Why would he change now?

"The general says that he is honored that you agreed to meet with him."

Westmoreland glanced around, uneasy standing out here in the open. He saw the squads—all rangers—looking left and right, checking the sky, the trees. His helicopter was only about a hundred feet away.

"I am honored to meet the great North Vietnamese general."

Westmoreland knew that there would be these pleasantries, this ridiculous protocol to go through. Though he'd love to take the commie bastard and add his name to the day's body count.

The NVA general spoke quietly to his interpreter, saying a few words and then waiting for them to be translated. He barely made eye contact with Westmoreland. He seemed quite willing to let the interpreter radiate the good will for both of them.

"It is important that the leader of the American invaders understand that this information comes from the very highest source. And that it must be used wisely."

"Ask General Chau why he's doing this," Westmoreland said interrupting the interpreter. "Why is he telling us this?" And Westmoreland caught the smallest smile on the Vietnamese general's face . . . even before his question was translated.

Then Chau nodded. Then he spoke, quickly, angrily.

"The war is being—ah—mismanaged by Premier Ho Chi Minh and his cabal of—renegades. They lose sight of other ways to attain our goal. They have—turned our friends in the Kremlin, in Peking, against us. They want results at any cost."

"So why betray his country?"

Chau's face turned even angrier. A small spray of spittle flew from his mouth as he talked.

"No . . . no . . . he doesn't seek to betray his country. But Ho Chi Minh *must* be removed from power. The expensive war must change. We can negotiate—if we have—"

Now Chau smiled, and Westmoreland saw the wily general's game plan.

"New leadership. If this battle fails, that will be possible. It will become—necessary."

And then Chau signalled to the interpreter and the small man fiddled with a satchel at his side. Chau was still talking, but what he was saying wasn't being translated. The general seemed to be scolding the interpreter.

Then the interpreter pulled out a thick stack of papers.

"It is all here. The rest of the great offensive. Everything. After this fails, you will give us a twenty-day truce and—ah—"

The general said a last few words and then stood with his arms folded.

"Then we will negotiate with you for the future of Vietnam . . . as equals."

"I guarantee it," Westmoreland said.

The interpreter translated, and then Chau nodded to his interpreter. He pointed at the papers, indicating that they should be passed to Westmoreland.

"Corporal," Westmoreland said, turning to his operations officer. Corporal Kline stepped forward to take the proffered information.

Then Westmoreland made what he hoped was an appropriate gesture. He saluted.

But Chau just nodded, and turned his back, walking with his men back into the jungle.

"Well," Westmoreland said to his corporal. "I guess that's it."

And the American general knew that if the pages that Kline held were anywhere near as reliable as the samples that Chau had sent earlier, then the United States was about to win it's greatest victory since the whole Indo-Chinese adventure began . . . back when Kennedy was telling the world that America was ready to play worldwide policeman. . . .

He took the papers from Kline.

Chau and his handful of soldiers were almost at the edge of the forest.

It's an incredible risk Chau just took, he thought.

But then, Chau's an ambitious man. . . .

Westmoreland walked back to his helicopter. And, once inside, he said, "Let's get the hell out of here."

Ngo Tran Trinh was one of six pallbearers. He had asked his boss for the day off from the Continental Hotel where he bussed tables during lunch and dinner, and then cleaned up after the last meal had been served.

The boss was a plump mamasan who—when angry—sounded like a screeching bird yelling at him. She said he was more trouble than he was worth. He didn't appreciate the job he had, didn't appreciate the piasters that let him live here in Saigon so much better than the stupid peasants, those who drifted into the city hoping to feed off American crumbs.

She should let him go, she said.

Then she sighed, rolled her eyes, and said, just go. Go to your funeral. . . .

But he was to come to work as soon as the miserable body was laid in the earth.

The mamasan didn't ask who had died. People always died. Soldiers. Babies. VC. Americans. People die in Vietnam. It didn't matter, none of it did.

He tried to wriggle his shoulder. The plain wooden coffin, merely a box in the shape of a body, was painfully heavy. The coffin's corner dug into the indentation between Trinh's shoulder blade and his neck. It ached. Soon it would throb from the pain, from the rocking, digging motion, as they walked the coffin through the streets of Saigon.

How much farther? he wondered.

He couldn't see ahead at all.

There were other mourners walking next to him, an old woman, a boy, crying, clutching each other. Making wonderful wailing sounds of sadness. People in the shops, some buying jellied ducks, others holding a long loaf of bread, stopped and watched the bleak procession pass by.

He saw a sign.

Ton That Dam Street. The procession turned right, away from the Saigon river, away from the docks.

Towards the heart of the city.

The pain in his shoulder became unbearable.

He wished they could stop, just take a break for a minute. But still they ambled on, following a rhythm that sent the coffin rocking left, and right, and left and—

Until they came to a corner, and—across the way—a building with two double doors.

People would look at the procession filing into the small warehouse and think that it would be a waking place. A resting place before the body was brought to a church, or a graveyard, or maybe burned in one of the cheap incinerators that were in the city.

A short man with powerful arms threw open the double doors and the procession ambled in. It was dark and cool, in here.

The mourners stopped outside. They had to wait.

Someone at the door made sure that only the pallbearers came in.

Then the short man shut the doors. And bolted them.

He started yelling at them in a rough dialect that spoke of years in the north, near Cambodia.

"La! Lay nhay," he said pointing to three sawhorses in the center of the room.

A few more feet, Ngo thought. Just a few more feet and I can put this down. . . .

Then he yelled for them to stop, to lower the coffin onto the sawhorse. Ngo left his corner slip forward, off his body, as he reached up and took its great weight with his hands.

Now the pallbearers struggled to hold the tremendous weight with just their hands, sliding it down, groaning, while the man yelled at them to be careful, not to be stupid.

Ngo thought his hands would slip. He felt the wood digging into his hands, pulling them down with irresistible force.

Then lower, until just his arms and his fingers held his load.

How much lower were the sawhorses? It could only be a few inches. But it took forever.

"Ni!" the man said poking him. "You! Keep bringing it down."

Then Ngo heard the other end of the coffin hit the wood strut of one of the front sawhorses, and then everyone let the weight go. It fell only a few centimeters, but the sawhorses creaked and groaned under the tremendous weight.

The small man came up and pushed Trinh away. He had a tool in his hand, something for opening the sealed coffin. He pried at the edges, talking excitedly to himself, laughing. The other pallbearers rubbed their necks, and groaned at the pain, all of them feeling the terrible bruise the weight had made. But then Trinh, like the others, came close to the man working at the lid.

He was nearly done. He pried open just the last sealed bit, and then the man grabbed the lid and threw it open.

A white piece of silky material lay on top, reflecting the one light bulb above them.

Trinh stood there, transfixed, amazed—this was a wonderful moment. The man snatched the white cloth and threw it to the side, into the darkness around the coffin.

And Trinh marvelled at the weapons, packed tightly together.

Russian rifles, sitting on boxes of ammunition. And grenades, whole cases full of them. And at one end, rocket launchers. Two, maybe three, Trinh couldn't be sure.

He could imagine what it would be like to fire one of them. What a wonderful sound it would make. The great explosion. The screaming.

He imagined firing one at the mamasan while she sat behind her desk, counting her hotel's money and its towels.

He imagined her looking up while he shot a great rocket right at her.

And he smiled.

But it was just a fantasy.

Because he knew this man taking the barrels out, holding them up to the light, studying them, happy, laughing now, had other plans.

And soon he'd tell Trinh—who was, after all, just a guerilla soldier—what those plans were. . . .

7

Ali walked over to Lindstrom, who was cursing at the screen.

"What is it?" she said to him.

"Damn! More trouble with the police. This—this—" he sputtered, turning to McManus—"is intolerable. I can't believe they're getting away with it!"

"Believe it. . . ." McManus said quietly.

Ali tried to see the screen, but Lindstrom's body, twisting and turning, made that impossible.

"More funny uniforms?" Ali joked.

Lindstrom gave her a look that showed he was clearly not amused. "No, Alessandra. *Not* more funny uniforms. They've set camps up." Lindstrom spun around in his seat and hit the keyboard. A map appeared showing Manhattan, The Bronx, Brooklyn, Staten Island, Queens, and a bit of the surrounding suburbs. Lindstrom hit another key. And three dots began flashing.

"They've set up three internment camps, right in the center of the worst poverty hellholes of the city." He looked over her, speaking to McManus. "Do you want to know how large they are, McManus?"

McManus answered, his voice distant and defeated, "How large?"

"Each one is the equivalent of over twenty square blocks, more than four square miles each."

"That's very large," McManus said, his voice lost, quiet.

Ali looked at him.

God, she thought. He's losing it. And if he loses it, we're done for. And not just here, the whole of civilization will become the plaything of the Iron Men. We're in over our heads, she thought. Way over our—

And that's when the idea occurred to her. She'd keep it to herself for awhile. Thinking about it, just trying to see if there was something wrong with it. Thinking about it *over and over.* Until she knew, in the end, it was the only way. This is a war, she thought. The beginning of a war. These are just the first skirmishes, feeling each other out, before the battle was really joined. And those battles lay ahead, in days to come. And for those battles, Ali knew they'd need something more than just Jim Tiber, more than herself jumping back and forth in time, more than McManus—who already looked in trouble.

They'd need an army.

She turned to Lindstrom.

"Who are they putting in the camps?"

Lindstrom shook his head and turned back to the screen. "It's hard to tell. The damned media is controlled, so the data going into the outside computer is completely tainted. If it wasn't for the shielding on the Red Building, we wouldn't have a clue about the way things are supposed to be. But the labels being slapped on those being incarcerated sound . . . familiar."

"What do you mean . . . familiar?"

Lindstrom tapped the screen with his finger. "Undesirables. Political Agitators. Social deviates. I haven't found any religious groups being picked up. At least, not yet."

She turned back to McManus.

"We have to get moving," she said. "Things are happening much faster this time, Dr. McManus."

"Yes," he said, looking up at her tiredly. "You're

very right. Peter . . . would you be so kind as to brief Alessandra, I really must—''

And then Ali watched McManus fall to the ground, crumpling like a balloon with its air slowly wheezing out. She called out to him just as his head rolled back and hit the floor hard.

''God!'' Lindstrom said, pushing his chair away from his terminal. ''The old fool—''

Dr. Beck hurried over, calmly kneeling beside McManus. ''I told him that he couldn't go on like this without any rest. It's crazy,'' the woman said. The doctor looked up at Ali. ''He hasn't been eating a thing.'' She turned back to McManus. ''He'll die, and then where will we be?''

''In very bad straits. . . .'' Lindstrom said.

''Here,'' Beck said, cradling McManus's head. ''Help me get him up.''

Ali came to one side of McManus and helped Beck move the scientist's gaunt body off the ground. His eyes were shut, but the lids fluttered. He felt light, almost like a child. ''Did he have a heart attack?'' Ali asked.

''His pulse is good,'' Beck said, shaking her head. ''This is exhaustion. Here, move him onto his chair. . . .''

Beck guided McManus onto the contoured chair vacated by Ali. The doctor took his pulse again, and then examined his eyes with her light. When she shined the pinpoint of light into each eye, McManus groaned. ''I could use a medical lab,'' Beck muttered. ''His breathing is ragged.''

''Can I help?'' Ali asked.

Beck shook her head. ''I'll put him on an IV and give him some oxygen. Maybe a sedative—''

Lindstrom cleared his throat. ''Er, I don't think that we can afford a—''

Dr. Beck shot him a nasty glance. ''Dr. McManus won't do you much good if he completely collapses from exhaustion, Dr. Lindstrom.''

"Quite right," Lindstrom said.

Ali walked over to Lindstrom. "I think we'd better make the transference," Ali said. "Can you tell me what you know, what you think I have to do?"

"Yes. Come over to my 'office'," Lindstrom said, smiling, indicating his cluttered table. "I'll tell you our plan. . . ." He paused and gave her an embarrassed smile. "But I don't think that you're going to like it. . . ."

It became quiet inside the helicopter, until Jim thought he'd go crazy just listening to the steady whirr of the rotor.

Whopp. whopp, whopp, as though the sound was nicking at his mind, shaving pieces of sanity off and flinging them out the door to the jungle below.

But sitting there quietly was better than the horror show of the landing.

His copter tilted to the left as if it wanted to shake all the soldiers out, then quickly snapped back, righting itself. Then it landed with a bumpy thud and Howell shot up, screaming at the men.

"Alright, move out. Get your butts going. Come on, come on, *come on!*"

And Jim shook himself out of his ice-cold stupor and hurried to obey, belatedly flashing on the still untenable concept that he was in charge.

We're in big trouble, kimosabe.

He hopped down to the ground, which had a springy sponginess that gobbled up a good two inches of his boots.

"Clear the chopper," Howell yelled, and Jim saw the sergeant glance over at him, surprised that Jim was just standing there as if he had just gotten off the Miami shuttle, expecting Uncle Arnold and Aunt Martha to be there—tanned lizards—grinning and greeting him.

"Sir," Howell shouted to him, "Do you want to

head up by that clearing?'' Howell pointed to a open spot that seemed to lead into black jungle.

Damn, it was dark. Jim nodded. From his protective crouch, he looked up. Through the swish of the blades that seemed hungry to lop off his head, he saw an inky dark sky streaked with purplish clouds trailing to the south like angel hair.

''Sir!'' Howell called again.

And Jim nodded and ran over to the clearing, with Howell and his men following.

The ground sucked at his feet. He was sure it was squishing, but he couldn't hear anything except the choppers. Then he heard their engines rev up some more and the sound whined madly away into the sky.

They're leaving, Jim thought.

And he never felt so abandoned.

As he joined his men, he saw that all of them were looking up at the twin birds soaring away from them, and he knew that his horrible feeling was shared by everyone there.

''Right,'' Howell said, breaking the silence. ''The lieutenant wants to talk to you.''

I do? thought Jim.

He cleared his throat. And he looked at the men.

They were, he guessed, a standard-looking squad of GI grunts, circa 1968. There were four black men, one with wire-framed glasses that caught the light in a way that looked dangerous. A couple of the men wore what looked like black warpaint. Their faces were lean and spooky. The smudgy black lines made them look like they were up for an evening's party.

''Yeah,'' Jim said. He thought his voice sounded thin and unsure. ''Yes,'' he said, throwing as much forceful huskiness into the sound as McShane's voice box could manage. ''This is not just another—''

Jim paused. What was it called?

''This is not just another Search & Destroy. The captain's been getting reports of movement along the trail just to our—''

Jim looked left and right, wondering what the hell direction he was facing.

He heard one of the men, one wearing the warpaint, mutter, "Jesus. . . ."

Howell pointed to his left, and said, "West, sir."

"Right. West." Someone coughed. Or was it a laugh? "So what we're going to do–is, er Sergeant Howell will lead you a bit to the west. We'll loop around, and stay out of sight until after midnight. Then we'll follow that trail and see just what we can find."

Someone else muttered. Something about wild geese.

"Lissen up!" Howell barked.

Jim looked over at Howell. "Henderson and Oran will take point, Clarke, you bring up the rear," Howell said. "Lieutenant?"

"Yeah?" Jim said.

"Do you want to check in with camp?"

Jim nodded. "If that's what we're supposed to do."

He heard someone mutter, "Oh, God . . ."

"It's a good idea, sir."

A bunch of the men tittered.

"Shut the hell up!" Howell barked. "RT, front and center."

The radio man ran up beside Jim, unstrapped his bulky radiotelephone, and unhooked the phone.

Jim knew that the guy was about to hand the phone to him. Jim looked up at Howell. "You tell the base where we are and where we're going, sergeant."

"Yes, sir," Howell said.

Jim backed away.

What do they think? he thought. If McShane was a competent lieutenant before–which, it seemed, he was–what in the world do they think now? Maybe I'm stoned. . . .

No. Jim didn't think that would wash.

Though some of the men in the squad looked like they could have sampled a few tokes of dat old debbil mary jane before takeoff. Glassy eyes, laughing at things a bit too easily.

Things weren't that funny here.

If this was a movie, it would have a nifty sixties soundtrack. Some kick-ass Stones, maybe. Or Jimi Hendrix wreaking havoc with his guitar. Grace Slick advising everyone to feed your head.

Grace Slick, Jim thought. Now, there was a lady he wouldn't mind meeting. Great voice, great face, the ultimate sixties hippie star.

One pill makes you larger—

The other makes you forget you're in the fucking jungle.

But there were no sounds, except for the soldiers whispering, and Howell talking into the radio. Then the sergeant gave the handset back to RT.

A bird called from a nearby tree.

Jim looked up.

At least, he thought it was a bird. It was so dark, he couldn't see anything. And once they moved into the jungle, it would be even blacker.

(And then there was something. A piece of McShane's memory. A lecture. Back in the states, at Fort Hamilton. Before shipping out. McShane's memory. But it was there, as near as the sweetest childhood memory Jim could remember. A lecture on the flora and fauna of Vietnam. The teak and mahogany trees make a canopy in the jungle, the lecturer explained.

Yes, he said, pointing to a slide, even during the day, the broad, flat leaves make it dark and shadowy. And at night, the blackness can be total. It can help the VC. But it can help you, too.

If you move, if you make a sound, they can spot you and kill you. But it works the other way too. If *they* move, if *they* make a sound, you can get them before they get you. . . .)

Jim looked at the trees, and at the near-total blackness ahead. There was one problem with that theory—and he realized that the problem must have been in Lieutenant McShane's mind all the time.

We'll be the ones moving, *we'll* be the ones making noise.

Sergeant Howell came up to him. Jim felt the sergeant's eyes on him. The man's worried, Jim thought. His lieutenant appears to have a screw loose.

I should tell him, Jim thought, tell him what the fuck is going on here.

Right. As if anyone would believe that.

Anybody have a spare straight jacket? We've got a crazy officer here. Check it out. Thinks he's from the future.

The bird called again.

Human or animal? What a fun game. . . .

"Sir, if you're ready we'll move out. . . ."

"All set, sergeant."

Howell held up his arm in an L-shape, and pumped it up and down. The men fell into a line. Jim joined them.

And they entered the blackness of the jungle.

Ngo Tran Trinh eased his bicycle out the door, pausing to make sure that there was no one outside on the street that could see him. There'd be questions . . . what are you doing in there? If it was someone from the hotel, they'd want to know . . . *what are you doing, Trinh?* We thought you were at a funeral. What are you doing here?

But it was night now, and Trinh pushed his bicycle out the door, and then hopped on, pedaling hard, getting away from the stash of weapons.

It excited him, to think about the Russian rifles and the rocket launchers sitting there, waiting for him and the others who would help the NVA regulars end this war, end the interference of the American imperialists.

The streets were crowded, filled with the poor fools who abandoned their farms and the meager livestock, hoping to feed off the crumbs left by the Americans.

Trinh bicycled to the hotel. The mamasan said he had to work that night, since she let him go to the funeral. He passed them, the fools from the countryside. Their faces were hollow, depraved. They were like poor animals, with Americans stumbling around—the drunk soldiers—and the MPs patroling the streets as if it was their city. And everywhere the black market! American cigarettes, American jeans, American music . . .

American garbage.

It would all end soon.

He turned the corner.

And there was the most hated thing, the clearest symbol of the American invaders.

They called it the Monument to the Unknown Soldier.

It was a giant statue of a soldier, bigger than even the American soldiers who towered over the Vietnamese. Immense, it stood guard over the boulevard, its giant head grim and determined, holding a rifle ready to fire. Most people didn't look at it.

But to Trinh it was the perfect symbol of the Americans in his country.

The perfect symbol.

And on the day the city was taken, the statue would be torn down, smashed to hundreds, *thousands* of pieces until it was just an unrecognizable pile of rubble.

Trinh stopped pedaling. A crowd was in front of him, a few cyclos hustling piasters. To his left was the pathetic lure of the bars, the lights and music calling the soldiers to come defile the young women of his country, women that should be raising children—

An opening appeared and Trinh kicked off, pedaling hard to get away from the crush of people wandering the streets.

Yes, he thought, seeing the hotel ahead, its broad porch filled with only Americans and Vietnamese servants in starched white coats, yes, in just days the statue will crash down to the ground.

And then America itself will be brought to its knees!

8

General Westmoreland shut the door to his office.

Corporal Kline stood there, with the maps and papers from Chau.

"You didn't, I hope, give them any idea where they came from?" Westmoreland said.

Kline smiled. "No, though they sure asked me enough times, General. I simply said it was a restricted source, well placed with the NVA Regulars. They were *very* skeptical of the bonafides of the material." Kline pronounced the word "boner fee-days" as if it were a new puppy chow. Westmoreland found Kline efficient, but his officiousness was damned annoying. "That makes sense. But we have to keep this very tight. So what did the intelligence people come up with?"

"Well, I think they'll want to speak directly with you, sir, and the support staff at MAC-V, but everything fits the pattern that their intelligence operatives have been coming up with. One of the events has already happened. . . ."

"Oh, what's that?"

"Some strafing up at Khe Sanh. The commander reports some local action, a buildup in the DMZ just north of the valley. He's having the marines hunker down while requesting some air and army support up country."

"See that gets done."

Kline stepped forward and handed Westmoreland the stack of papers. "Yes, sir. I told them that you wanted to keep these . . . to look them over."

Westmoreland nodded.

"So they all think that it's convincing stuff?"

"Yes. Though," he paused . . . "they're confused about Hue. I mean, it's been an open city for so long—"

"Up until now. Taking the ancient capital would deliver a striking blow to the South. It's a very powerful move. Just the kind of thing we have to stop." Westmoreland nodded. "We have to stop that one dead in its tracks. . . ."

"Yes, sir . . ." Kline said.

And Westmoreland looked up, thinking that his corporal was holding something back.

"Alright Wally, what the hell is it? Out with it. . . ."

"Well, sir, it's just that Com OP 3 near Bien Hoa has been getting scattered reports of traffic moving south and—well, there's nothing in Chau's reports about any movement heading this way."

"No, there isn't. Have they checked it out?"

"They are now, sir. They've airlifted a few squads to check all the known supply routes . . . just to be safe."

Westmoreland took a breath. "There you go. The farmers are always seeing strange things in the dark. Especially when there's no moon and the jungle gets so damned dark. At any rate, we'll know more in the morning."

"Yes, sir."

Westmoreland stood up and stretched. What time was it anyway? he wondered.

"I'm going to turn in, Wally, but I want to head up to Hue in the morning. Look things over before we head into the Tet cease-fire. We'll go at first light."

"Yes, sir," Kline said.

And then Westmoreland left his office, telling himself that he wasn't really troubled by the odd reports from the supply routes.

Probably won't check out.

Nothing to get worried about.

But thinking, as he walked briskly down the hall and out to his driver who was sitting in the nearly deserted parking lot, what if it is?

Damn . . . what would that mean about the other information? What would it mean about Scorpion?

And just what was he going to do about it?

Big mosquitos, more like hummingbirds than mere insects, hovered near Jim's face, waiting for him to falter a moment before swatting them away.

He looked behind him.

Funny, no one else seems too bothered by the monster bloodsuckers. Do you just get used to them, or did I forget to use my army brand of industrial-strength insect repellent?

Then he felt one of the little buggers breaking through his skin and he slapped his cheek.

The slap stung and the sharp sound reverberated under the cavernous canopy of the jungle.

"Hey, quiet down back there," he heard Howell hiss. The sergeant couldn't see that it was his own lieutenant who was making the noise.

I guess I just have to let the buggers feast, Jim thought glumly.

The walking was difficult. They climbed up a long slope, and the pack made each step hard. They crossed a stream that cut mushy rivulets into the slope. And there were vines—ropes ready to snare his feet—all but invisible in the blackness. He stumbled three times before finally getting hooked cleanly, and he tumbled to the ground.

The line of men behind him stopped and waited while he struggled to his feet.

Jim hurried to catch up with the rest of the column.

The smells here were incredible. One second he'd

get a whiff of something that reminded him of a florist's shop on mother's day—the dizzying mixture of scents, all jumbled together too sweetly.

Then he'd get a snort of something foul and decaying. Old wet leaves turning into a loamy compost. Or something dead, the stench of a couple hundred roadkills piled together, little bubbles of methane popping out of the decaying bodies.

There was no breeze in here.

It almost felt like there was no air.

Jim took a breath, still climbing. He wiped his brow with his sleeve. His tongue felt dry and crusty in his mouth. He reached behind him for the canteen buckled to the side of his pack.

He unscrewed the cap and took a slug.

Then Howell was there, a small flashlight in his hand.

"Sir, we're about five klicks from the supply route." Howell looked around. "I don't think we're going to run into anybody, at least not until we get closer. We could rest here, or we could get to the crest." Howell held a map in front of the small pool of light made by his flashlight. Jim heard that bird sound again. And he imagined some tiny VC guy sitting in a tree, calling to another tiny VC guy farther away, who calls to another VC guy, who finally tells a whole army of pissed-off VC guerillas where they are.

Jim took a look at the map.

He saw the ridge, the squiggly oval that indicated it was the highest point.

"And where are we?" he asked.

"Right about here, sir."

Jim looked where Howell was pointing.

"So we could stop here, or move up there, and then—"

"Then wait until midnight." Howell smiled. "The witching hours for Charlie's supply convoys . . . if they're real."

Jim felt the pack harness digging into his back.

McShane might be used to this shit, but the pack didn't feel too good to Jim.

Once he had it off, it would be nice to think that the rest of the trip was downhill.

"We'll go to the ridge, Sergeant," he said.

"Yes, sir," Howell answered, nodding and folding up the map. Jim watched him jog up to the front of the line.

Then, like overgrown scouts who have lost their way, the line of men moved up the slope.

"How's he doing?" Ali heard Lindstrom ask Dr. Beck with what sounded almost like genuine concern.

"Dr. McManus is doing fine. With some rest, he should be alright. But how are you?"

Ali saw that Beck had the historian fixed with her eagle eyes. "Me? Oh, I'm fine. Wonderful. Not that I wouldn't appreciate a spot of Jack Daniel's—just to take the edge off."

Lindstrom smiled, but Beck shook her head and went back to the room with Jim's sleeping body.

And Ali watched her.

I can't go in there, she thought.

It was too strange to look at Jim's body, the plastic tubes dangling from the IV bottle, the steady readout of his pulse and respiration glowing in the dark room. It was as if he was dead.

And she always told herself . . . He's not in there. That's just his body. He's somewhere else.

If he were to wake up, it wouldn't be Jim.

It might be nobody. . . .

McManus had said that he was worried about what could happen should the host's personality become conscious. He didn't think it could happen . . . it hadn't happened yet. But it was something that frightened him, he said offhandedly.

"Nasty old woman," Lindstrom muttered under his breath to the departing Beck. "I never did like doctors, so full of all their healthful advice. . . ."

"She knows we need you," Ali said.

"And I *need* a drink!" Lindstrom said. "What is this," he said louder, for Beck's benefit, "a prison?"

Dr. Jacob came into the lab, oblivious, as usual, to everything that wasn't connected to his machines. Strands of his thin gray-white hair were sticking up. Ali guessed that he had been sleeping in one of the empty rooms, and he looked half-asleep in the brilliant glare of the Time Lab.

"Are you ready?" he asked Lindstrom.

"No, I'm not ready," Lindstrom said. "I haven't even begun."

Jacob made a big "O" shape with his mouth, and shuffled over to his beloved generator.

Then Lindstrom took Ali's hand.

"We don't know as much this time as we did last time," Lindstrom said to her. His hands were warm, comforting. He's trying to reassure me, she thought. "The Iron Men are playing it much more cleverly this time. Much more . . . the small changes are keeping the big pattern hidden. All we have are indications of when and where . . . but the 'what' remains elusive."

Lindstrom's eyes narrowed, as if checking to see how Ali was accepting all this. "I understand," she said quietly.

"Good. That said, let me tell you what I *do* know. It involves the Great Tet Offensive. What do you know about that?"

"Not much, I'm afraid."

"Well," Lindstrom said, pulling his hands back, rubbing them together, an old lecturer once again in harness. "Tet was a military victory for America and the ARVN. North Vietnam sent its regular troops—a massive attack—against key points in the south, from the marine base at Khe Sanh to the old imperial city of Hue. Saigon itself was even attacked, and the walls of the new American Embassy were breached."

"And what happened?"

"Tremendous losses for the north. Tremendous. The

Saigon intrusion was terrible, scaring everyone, but there were enough soldiers from the 199th Division to end that threat in hours. Khe Sanh was held, at a terrible cost to the NVA regulars. And Hue was held. The entire guerilla framework of the south was irreparably disrupted, never to be rebuilt. From that point on, the war would be against the regular army of the north. The guerillas, the dreaded VC, were out of the picture."

"So we won?" Ali said.

Lindstrom smiled, and shook his head. "No, we won *militarily*. But in every other way, Tet was the greatest blow of the war."

"How could that be?"

Lindstrom laughed. "Wars are more than battles won and lost, Alessandra. The north showed that they could attack the south with impunity. They demonstrated that after six years of American intervention, after an influx of over half a million men, they could attack—at will—almost anywhere in the country . . . even to the point of besieging the American Embassy. Westmoreland had been feeding LBJ—" Lindstrom looked over at Ali to make sure she knew that he was referring to the thirty-fourth president. She nodded. "Told him that Vietnam was now a war of 'attrition,' one that America would undoubtedly win with its tremendous resources. The Great Tet Offensive showed that it was all an illusion. . . ."

"So what happened, I mean, if the North lost the attack. . . ?"

Lindstrom took a breath. "In Washington, they turned a corner. Under the increasing pressure of the agitating students—you know, back then students used to get involved in social issues—why, I myself once—"

"Dr. Lindstrom," Dr. Jacob called from across the room. "The generator is at full power. We should carry out the transference as soon as possible—"

"Yes, yes," Lindstrom yelled back. "Well, with

Robert Kennedy breathing down the president's neck—he wasn't a candidate yet—and the dove McCarthy doing very well, and all those marches in Washington." Lindstrom paused. "After Tet, the war was over." Lindstrom dug through his stack of papers and pulled out a sheet. "Though it would still take us five years to get the hell out of there."

"It seems like such a waste. . . ."

Lindstrom turned and looked right at her. "Ali, it's one of the saddest stories I know in all of history. Idealism and hubris came together to produce a great tragedy."

He handed her the sheet of paper.

"Wh—what's this?" she said.

"I don't know what the big plan is—I told you that, not yet at least—but the Iron Men are playing with Tet. What they're doing isn't clear. But we can be sure it's going to hurt the US and bring about the kind of staunch hardliners they want in the Kremlin, perhaps in all of Europe. Here," he said, pointing to the sheet, "I've jotted down the changes we've picked up."

Ali looked at the list. There were some South Vietnamese names, places where Lindstrom noted that battles happened. And terrible emigration of refugees. And then, the people traveling from one place to another.

"We have one constant in all the changes, a man who is to be linked to everything that's happening."

She saw a name, near the bottom.

She tried to read it. . . .

"General Tuan Ngoc Chau . . ."

Lindstrom corrected her too-hard pronunciation. "Chau was a very important man in the NVA. He also—for a brief time—supplied information to American intelligence in what our intelligence took to be a postwar bid for power."

"And it wasn't?"

"Not at all. It was bogus intelligence, and later it was easily disproved. Chau was strung along, as if the

Americans believed him. But we knew he was a phony."

"So what's changed?"

"There," Lindstrom said, leaning forward and showing her some names on the bottom of the sheet. "That's information from Chau. Only now, it all *pans* out. Great caches of weapons were captured. Guerilla networks shut down. Chau has become the ace star in MAC-V's network of spies."

She nodded. "So the Iron Men have really turned him into a spy?" Ali didn't understand.

Lindstrom laughed. "No. Not at all. It's just that he's acting much more cleverly, he's after bigger game. And whatever the hell he's doing, he will use the Tet Offensive to change the world. I only wish I knew what that was. . . ."

Ali looked at the last two names on the sheet.

"Scorpion . . ." she read. "Who's Scorpion?"

"Chau's code name. It's always been Scorpion." Lindstrom shook his head. "Except now Scorpion isn't what he used to be." Ali looked up. "No. Chau is still Scorpion. But Scorpion is one of the Iron Men."

Ali looked down at the sheet, at the last name.

"Khan Ha," she read.

"Yes, Khan Ha. Reportedly very beautiful. Long black hair, deep, almond eyes. I've seen photographs. She was stunning, as a matter of fact."

Ali chewed her lip, watching Lindstrom's face, hearing him clear his throat. The historian turned back to his desk.

"She was Scorpion's mistress and—my dear Alessandra—I'm afraid she's the person you're about to swap places with. . . ."

They reached the ridge and, for the first time in hours, Jim saw open sky.

"Lieutenant, should we stop here?"

Jim rippled his back, sliding the heavy pack around to the front. Already he felt how wonderful it would be when he finally let the monster pack slide off his aching shoulders. "Fine, Sergeant." Jim looked around. The top of the ridge was exposed as if the trees had been burned off. Perhaps, he thought, it had been napalmed. He remembered seeing old news footage of napalm runs, of the deep green jungle exploding into a brilliant strip of orange. We just went in there and tried to burn anyone alive.

It was a strange, sick image—the high-tech jet vs. the incredibly dense jungle.

It was a hopeless image. . . .

He looked around, enjoying the air now free of the jungle smell. And he thought, if we stay here, there's a damn good chance we'll be spotted.

"Let's move down the slope a bit," he said to Howell. "Then everyone can scrunch down and—" he looked at his watch—11:15—"wait a bit."

"Yes, sir."

Howell led the squad down the slope while Jim stayed behind.

"Sir, do you want to call base?"

It was the radioman, a soldier named Tuttle. His face glistened with sweat. The radiophone had to be a bitch to carry. I don't know how to use that thing, Jim thought. "No . . ." he said. "Let Sergeant Howell check in."

The radio operator nodded.

And Jim stood there, a hint of a breeze drying his sweat. The crazy stew of smells was below him, and he felt as if he could breathe through his nose again without gagging.

He saw a flash to the north. A fire? Someone shooting something? It just popped up in the blackness and then disappeared, leaving only a bluish afterimage dancing on his eyes.

Howell came back up to him. "The men are all set, sir. I told them they could rest and have a bite to eat."

Jim thought of the glow to the north. "But no smoking . . ."

Howell smiled. "No, sir. Of course not. I—"

Jim saw Howell rub his cheek as if he was about to say something.

My confusion is bothering him, Jim guessed. And he's getting damn close to saying something about it.

"Good work, Sergeant. I'll be right down there. . . ."

"Yes, sir." Howell turned and walked away. And Jim took one last clear breath, and then he slogged down the hill. The squad lay in a shallow gully cut into the side of the hill. Most of the men were eating out of small tins that caught whatever light there was, and he heard the tiny sounds of their small forks rattling against the cans. A few others looked like they were sleeping.

How the hell could you sleep here? Jim wondered.

He saw an empty spot near one end of the gully and he wriggled out of his pack. He let it fall to the ground with a loud jangle that made his men look up. But Jim ignored their stares. It's okay, gang . . . he thought . . . the old lieutenant ain't quite himself tonight.

He took his helmet off. The inside had its own tangy odor and the cross straps were damp from his sweat. He put the helmet next to his pack. And he finally lay down on the rocky dirt.

Which felt like the most comfortable spot on the earth.

The mamasan breezed through the dining room. She threw Trinh a sneer.

Trinh smiled, and worked harder to finish setting the tables up from the morning's breakfast.

(Oh, just one rocket, he thought. Aimed right at her big mouth. Oh, that would be *very* nice.)

He didn't mind doing this work, folding the stiff napkins into tent shapes, and making sure the knives and forks were perfectly straight. No, it wasn't so bad—not when he could think of the guns and weapons waiting.

What's a few more days of this when soon, very soon, it would be all different. And the ones who collaborated, the Vietnamese who helped the American invaders—the ones like the hotel's mamasan—would be in prison.

Or maybe just shot.

And Trinh would help run the new city that would rise from Saigon's ashes.

There was one thing that bothered him, though. . . .

(He heard the mamasan yelling at another busboy, scolding him for not setting the table properly for breakfast. Her shrieks echoed in the empty dining room.)

One thing bothered him . . . the plans had changed. Trinh had seen the other "funerals," the caskets filled with weapons, making their way into the city right under the eyes of the stupid Americans. Everything seemed set for a great attack, to capture the city.

He folded the napkin tight and placed it on the white china plate. He felt the mamasan's eyes on him.

But now the plans have changed.

Not that he was told that directly. I'm just a soldier, a member of the guerilla army. It isn't my position to question decisions, and plans, and strategies.

My job is just to fight.

But the short, stubby man, his leader whom he knew only as Giang, had come back from a meeting acting very confused. He told Trinh and the others that the battle would now be even more important than they imagined. The losses would be even greater.

He said—and here Giang looked away, as if struggling to picture it—that they would do something that had never been done before.

But that's all he said. The rest would have to wait until the night of the battle itself, until the night of Tet.

And Trinh could hardly wait, he was so excited. It was only days now.

He finished his last napkin. He stood up.

He looked at the great clock set in a frame of gilted gold.

He watched it travel the last few seconds. To midnight.

Then it was January 27th. . . .

And, as if by magic, it was all one day closer.

9

Jim was dreaming.

He knew that. Even if he didn't know *whose* dreams he was having. His first feeling, inside this dream, was the pleasant rush of familiarity. He saw a street on a hill, lots of red stone houses, a small apartment building, a small grocery store.

That's *my* block, he thought, as he watched friendly, open faces float past him, smiling under a crisp blue sky. I *know* these kids, and the adults. They're my friends and neighbors. They mean safety and memories of Christmas and birthdays, chipped teeth at Little League games, a twisted ankle during the last soccer game in fifth grade.

Except—except—and he was real late on flashing on this—they're not my memories.

He saw his dad's beat-up Trump Wagon parked outside the small apartment building . . . looking as if it had been through the trenches with the family. And he saw shops, the pizza place run by a short, stubby Greek man and his thin brother, two guys who looked like Mutt & Jeff. They never smiled, as if making pizza was their own personal purgatory.

But Jim knew that he was dreaming about things not from his subconscious.

They're not my memories, he thought. Even inside the dream.

He floated towards the apartment house, to the top

of the hill. He looked down the other side of the hill under the beautiful blue sky, looking down to a gleaming bay that glistened under that brilliant sky.

He turned away from the water, the golden sea.

He looked at the small apartment building, and then Jim floated past the faces, the shops, up the stairs. He heard a voice as he flew up the stairs, his mother talking loudly, standing at the door, asking him where he had been.

Only it wasn't *his* mother.

No, this big-chested woman built like a linebacker was McShane's mother. He knew that. Even in the dream. And Jim watched, fascinated, as he went into the apartment and she went on haranguing him, yelling at him for dawdling on his way home from school, for buying candy, for wasting his money on comic books.

But never looked at him. She just kept bustling about the tiny kitchen, stirring a pot that—yes, now he could smell it! It was a great chicken stew, bubbling, filling the tiny room with its wonderful smells.

Jim turned.

There was someone else down a dark hall, standing in the shadows. The dark figure who came out into the sickly fluorescent light of the kitchen.

It was a kid. Four, maybe five years old. Jim looked at the boy. His big eyes glowed in the darkness like a boy in one of those tacky paintings you'd buy at Woolworth's.

I'm dreaming about McShane's childhood, he thought. This is *his* dream.

And Jim relaxed now, enjoying it. Dreams are okay, he thought, once you have your bearings. Nothing can go wrong in a dream.

Then he heard himself asking something in the dream.

"Where's dad?"

His mother went on stirring the pot, faster, working at it, as if something was giving her trouble.

The other boy—his brother—turned and ran away. Back into the darkness.

In the dream, Jim took a step closer to his mother.

"Where's dad?" he repeated.

And he noticed that the window over the stove was open. And breeze snaked its way in, cold and icy, clearing the wonderful smell out of the room. His mother—McShane's mother, he reminded himself—kept stirring the pot.

As if something was giving her trouble, harder, and harder, as if it was tar or macadam thickening, growing sluggish. The woman used two hands now, pulling at it, tugging, grunting, talking to her stew, her concoction.

But there were no stew smells now. Nothing except the cold, and his mother working so hard, talking.

He heard her.

"I—can't—" she said.

Jim saw her face all red, pulled tight. Tears glistened in her eye sockets, and then, gaining weight, they rolled down her cheek.

I can't.

He felt itchy.

Standing there, in the ice-cold kitchen.

Something at his neck.

His wool sweater against bare skin, he thought.

So goddam itchy.

In the dream, he reached behind his back and played with the sweater, trying to tug his tee-shirt up, to protect his skin.

The woman finally looked at Jim.

Her wooden spoon was stuck in the middle of the stew, standing straight up, like a shovel buried in dirt, like a makeshift cross on the battlefield.

"I can't," she sobbed.

And now he itched all over, as if his whole body was covered with the coarsest, scratchiest wool, until he itched in a thousand places all at once and—

He stared at the spoon.

Standing in the center of the pot. It shook. It vibrated.

Then Jim saw something reaching out of the pot. Black and red, holding onto the wood with a pincer, easing itself out of the pot.

His mother kept repeating over and over, "I can't help him, I can't help him, I can't—"

And while Jim heard her, he just kept watching the stick, this thing coming out with pincers, clawing its way out of the stew.

And then he woke up.

To the real nightmare.

"Ready," Ali said, sitting in the contoured chair she had only recently left.

And she thought about McManus. Funny, but for the second time he was going to miss her departure.

"How does that feel, dear?" Dr. Beck asked her, patting her wrists which she had just been strapped to the table.

"Fine," Ali smiled. And she wondered if she hadn't been too brave to volunteer to put her body through this again. It was all so new, and there was no telling what effect time-jumping back and forth might have.

And, more than anything, she was scared about where she was going.

To North Vietnam. To go be involved with an NVA general, who was actually one of the Iron Men.

Maybe there's some way he'll be able to tell about me, she thought . . . some way he'll figure out that I'm not who I say I am.

And she imagined all the nice tortures he could dream up.

So she could take a message back to the Time Lab.

To say that they're playing for big stakes.

After all, now Communism existed only as a word, even in the heart of USSR. The Iron Men were out to change all that.

Lindstrom hovered nearby, out of his element with

all the tubes and wires leading from Ali. She gave him a smile.

"You're sure you want to go through with this?" he said, smiling back.

Ali nodded.

"Well, we'll let you stay until just the night of Tet. The same for Jim. Of course, if Dr. Beck starts picking up any indications here that you're in distress, we'll—"

"Don't worry," Ali said. "I'll be fine."

"Okay," Lindstrom said. "Well," he sighed, turning to Dr. Jacob. "Are you all set, Jacob?"

"Yes—we should start the transference. We've been making tremendous demands on the power. If the outside is monitoring us, I'm sure they'll find it very strange—"

Lindstrom waved his concern away. "Don't worry about that." He turned back to Ali. "Well, Alessandra, goodbye for now." Lindstrom stood there awkwardly, she thought, as if he wants to kiss me. She made her fingers reach up and he came closer. He cupped an imprisoned hand and gave it a reassuring squeeze.

"Yes," Dr. Beck said. "Good luck."

"Now?" Jacob asked.

Lindstrom nodded, his eyes locked on Ali, and she realized that he was worried about her. "Now . . ." he whispered, keeping his eyes locked on hers. His hand was still entwined in hers. Then Dr. Beck leaned over and tapped the back of his hand, and Lindstrom slowly let go.

Ali kept smiling.

She heard the tachyon generator whine as the flow of subatomic particles was finally allowed to accelerate, faster and faster in the labyrinthine coils of the generator, faster and faster until they reached a point where time and events no longer had their iron lock of causality on things.

She listened to the sound.

In a moment, her own brain waves would be attached to the stream.

Her consciousness would depend on information from the movement of the particles.

And her mind would travel until it finally came to rest at another point in time, inside someone else's consciousness, like a bookmark in history.

She heard the whine rise up another few notes.

She still saw Lindstrom's face. His burly beard. His large cocker-spaniel eyes. She felt Dr. Beck's hand brush her forehead as she kept close watch on all the biofeedback data.

The tachyon generator screamed, a subatomic roller coaster careening from atom to atom.

Then—as she knew would happen—she saw and heard nothing.

Jim was half awake. His eyes were shut. He felt the hard ground of the gully he had been resting in, dreaming in. . . . He felt dozens of little stones digging into his back, unnoticed when he first lay down, but now feeling like a bed of nails.

And, as he blinked away in the cool Vietnamese night, he reached behind his neck.

Because—damn—it felt itchy back there.

He reached behind, touching his collar, and—

His eyes blinked open, crusty with sleep. He heard other sounds, snoring, grunting, moaning.

Then someone yelled out, "Oh, God." Then again, the same voice or maybe someone else's. Jim wasn't sure. "Fucking hell!" someone screamed.

Jim saw the two guards Howell had put on duty standing up from the gully, hurrying over now. Looking down at them.

Jim's fingers crawled under his collar and he felt something move.

It was the type of feeling that you'd get sitting on a dark porch watching the lighting bugs dart about and the bats swoop overhead, visible only as birdlike dots flitting across a gray cloud or milk-white moon.

You feel something moving. Your fingers close around it, and then you realize it's a bold mosquito about to chow down on your blood.

This was like that.

Only a thousand times worse.

He felt something move. Something big. And he thought it was a leaf or something that had worked its way under his collar. But as he tried to pull it out, it moved—goddam, it *moved!* Scuttling away, farther, down into his shirt.

And he heard more yells form the men, heard them moving around, trying to stand up. Screaming, cursing, yelling.

And Jim didn't have a clue as to what was going on.

Whatever had moved past his neck was now down. He brought his other hand around and started to rip under his green khaki shirt, feeling the thing crawling along his back, trapped, working its way to the front.

Now he was yelling, standing up, and yelling.

"Hell! What the hell is—"

The soldiers on guard were hissing, telling the squad to pipe down. But Jim saw that everyone was up, dancing around, grabbing at their backs, their clothes, doing a shadowy voodoo dance under the moonless sky.

"Damn!" Jim said, ripping the shirttails out, and then he felt his skin, felt the thing moving sideways.

And then—a moment of mixed blessings—his fingers closed around the animal.

It was big. About twice the thickness of a cicada with the same chitinous texture.

It felt like a goddam land lobster, writhing in his fingers.

He didn't waste any time playing guess-the-object.

But as he whipped it around and chucked it behind him, grunting and making a weird "Eeeeyaah!" scream, he saw just what the hell it was. The twin pincers in front, the little side legs, and the tail that curled into a backward 'C' ready to jab whatever was spoiling the scorpion's fun.

A fucking scorpion, Jim thought, standing, sweating, shaking, breathing hard. Aren't they poisonous? he thought. Can't they kill you or something? And all the men who had lain down in the depression were doing the same dance, wriggling around, trying to get rid of the suckers. Those who had escaped the scorpions were helping guys get out of their shirts and their pants to get the scorpions away.

Wouldn't want one in my pants, Jim thought.

No way.

He saw Howell, bare from the waist up, the whites of his eyes wide and bright like beacons. He stood on the ridge just atop the gully.

"Better get out of there, sir. We bedded down in a damned scorpion's nest."

"Great," Jim said. He snatched up his pack, noticing a pair of scorpions exploring it.

"Yuck!" he said, kicking them away.

He heard one of the men moaning. The rest of the squad was crawling out of the gully.

"How the hell did that happen?" Jim said.

"Damned if I know," Howell answered. "It looked clean in there, no animal holes. "Shit, nothing at all."

"Is everybody alright?"

"Clarke got stung—right on his butt. He didn't get to the sucker in time, and then he kinda squeezed in, jiggling around and everything."

"What will happen to him?"

"Boyle's working on him, Lieutenant. But I think he got to it in time, cut the venom out and shit. But sir," and here Howell grinned. "He's going to have a helluva sore behind for awhile."

Jim rubbed his eyes. I'm cold, he thought. And freaked out from scorpions! I want some hot coffee. And a crumb bun from the Columbia Student Union. They were hard as bricks, but they went down just fine if you soaked them in the tarlike coffee.

He pushed against his hair—what there was of it. The bristle cut probably looked even stranger than it felt. He scratched at his neck, remembering the feel of the scorpion.

(Remembering the dream.)

I'm in charge, he thought. I'm in charge.

Jim looked at his watch.

11:50.

"It's close enough," he said to Howell. "Get the men away from the gully. And move them down the slope a bit. Get their uniforms back on." Jim took a breath. I'm giving orders he thought, and damn if it doesn't sound as if I know what the hell I'm doing.

"And then we'll pick up that supply route and see what's going on . . ."

She was lost in the ozone again.

Well, Ali thought, "lost" isn't exactly the right word. She knew where she came from, and she knew where she was going. . . .

But for the first time she wondered—what is this place? What is this cloudy, filmy nowhere that you travel through? Where is it?

What is it?

She realized that it probably wasn't a place at all. It was simply the response of her optic nerves to the stimuli picked up from the endless stream of high-speed tachyons.

But—and this is something that would bear more thought—there did appear to be a *someplace* here. She could "see", or perceive, a distance, and flashes . . . as if there were other places to go rather than just the stream she followed. Just what was out *there?* she wondered. What were those brilliant flashes of color that she saw.

And then—a scary thought—what would it be like to suddenly change direction and go down one of the thousands of pathways that always seemed to radiate from whatever point she happened to occupy. . . ?

What if there was a way to do that? she thought.

And—while she was enjoying speculating about that—she rather abruptly arrived at her destination.

Her first sensation was the overpowering smell of garlic and oil. . . .

10

Howell pushed close to the point, holding the map tight in one hand while Henderson struggled to make his way through the heavy brush. We're moving off the slope, Howell knew, moving damn close to the trail.

But this was all new growth they were humping through. Something must have burned this part of the jungle, burning off the teak and mahogany, and leaving it wide open for the thick vines and bushes that were a real bitch to cut through.

"How you doing, Henderson?" he whispered to the scrawny soldier. Henderson's arms looked like bean poles, but he was doing a damn good job of whacking through the brush.

"Fine, Sarge. I'll be glad—" Henderson fought his way through some more vines . . . "when we're through—this shit."

"Yeah, I hear you. It's one thing to go to the woods, but this is like another planet. Just keep it up . . ." Howell looked back to see the rest of the line. He saw four soldiers just behind him and then, looking lost, Lieutenant McShane . . . stumbling along, left and right.

Like a scared rabbit.

Something's wrong, he thought. Something's *real* wrong with the lieutenant. At first Howell thought McShane was just hungover, or maybe stoned. It's an occupational hazard in Nam. And in a few hours, he'll snap out of it and take charge again. McShane was one real smart lieutenant—not gung ho. He was too smart for that, too smart to waste his men doing stupid jungle prowls. But if they caught some smoke, he was the best, real cool, getting everybody calmed down and in the best position.

And he didn't call up heavy fire from home unless things were real bad. They always drop their loads short, he laughed. Better off without the shit . . .

So, Howell thought, what the hell is wrong with him?

He seems like a damned different person.

It made Howell real nervous.

Henderson whispered back to him. "Better hold them up, Sarge. I got a fuckin' briar patch to cut through here."

Howell turned back to the line and pumped his arm.

He saw the men halt—all except for McShane, who stumbled ahead a few more feet before noticing that his men had stopped moving.

Damn! What the hell is it with him?

He heard Henderson's blade snapping through the vines, the gentle whistle of the blade in the air, the heavy *thwack* as it cut into the tangle of vines.

"Almost there, Sarge. Just—a few—"

Then Howell thought he heard something, above the noise of Henderson cutting.

"Wait a minute, man!" he whispered. Henderson didn't hear him, and he made another stroke. "I said, wait a damn minute!" Howell repeated louder.

Henderson froze, breathing hard.

And Howell turned left and right. There were noises. Shit, there were always noises in the jungle. Small animals skittering around on the ground. A rat snake snatching a jungle rat and squeezing it until it split in two. Always damn noises . . .

But this—

Hell, they sounded like *voices*.

I thought this was supposed to be a wild goose chase, Howell thought. A quiet night with no action.

Nothing. Just checking out a dumb story.

Howell slid his gun off his shoulder.

Damn, he thought. We're closer to the supply trail than I thought.

Much closer, and Charlie might have some action waiting down there for us.

Howell flicked the safety off his M-16.

He turned and saw McShane, back in the gloom, watching him.

Come on, man, I need you tonight. Don't freak on me. We can't afford not to have you on board.

One of the men down at the end of the line coughed.

Howell raised his arm up and pumped. Three times. Charlie ahead. The silent message was passed on down the line.

And then—he turned to Henderson and nodded.

He whispered to him.

"Nice and gentle now, Henderson. Just as sweet and quiet as you can do it."

Henderson's sweaty face was scrunched up, not understanding Howell's concern.

But now he attacked the viney barrier more delicately, chipping a smaller pathway leading down to the jungle trail that lay ahead of him.

And Howell set the button of his rifle for automatic firing.

Because, he thought, it looks like we're going to rock n' roll tonight after all. . . .

Lindstrom stood there, looking at Ali. Just staring at her face. So very pretty, he thought.

She's like sleeping beauty. So peaceful, her eyes gently closed as if she was dreaming about young princes and wonderful castles.

But there are no princes anymore, and all the castles have been turned into condos.

"Shall I take her?" Dr. Beck asked.

Lindstrom nodded. "Yes. And check on how Dr. McManus is doing." Lindstrom rubbed his eyes and let out an uncontrollable bellow of a yawn.

"You should get some rest, too," Dr. Beck said. "It will do us no good if you're flat on your back, too!"

"There's nothing wrong with me that a few sips of Scotland's finest wouldn't cure."

Dr. Beck shook her head disapprovingly and started wheeling Ali's chair back to the dark waiting area, the shadowy room that Lindstrom thought had the smell and feel of a morgue about it. Except the bodies were all alive.

But not really.

"Scotland's finest . . ." Beck muttered, walking away. "I'd like to see what your liver has to say about that."

Lindstrom laughed and then said, to himself, "My liver hasn't issued any complaints . . . so far."

He turned and looked at his table, now overflowing with notes taken from the computer printout. Unlike the last adventure of the Iron Men, the changes—so far—were small, almost uneventful.

But he knew the danger of what they were playing with.

Every century has its fulcrum points, Lindstrom knew. Points that determine the course of history for decades, maybe even centuries to come. Most people thought that Hitler's rise, and the Armageddon of World War II, was one of those points. And it was, but not in the way most people think. That war and Hitler's mad racist schemes only disrupted the natural course of events. The United Europe that emerged in the Twenty-First century was merely postponed by that war—not stopped. Of course, if the Iron Men had been successful with their attempt to fortify the Soviet hard-liners with stolen German loot from World War II, well, then, anything could have happened.

But we stopped them there, he smiled.

No. A real turning point, a real fulcrum of history, was the Tet Offensive. Its effects lasted well beyond the Vietnam War. American society, its entire global outlook, was forever changed. America wasn't simply chastened by the experience. Nearly two-hundred years of bumptious, jingoistic naivete was dispelled. And then began the difficult job of building an understanding of the US's real place in the world.

But—and here's the thought that chilled Lindstrom—what if that naivete hadn't been dispelled?

What impact would *that* have on history?

Lindstrom could well guess. The Iron Men were clever this time, selecting Tet. And, as far as Lindstrom knew, they had made only one mistake.

Me.

They didn't plan on me.

Sure, Ali's back there, and—if all went well, Jim too. But Lindstrom knew that before this was over he'd have to go back, to guide them through the necessary machinations to save the whole damn business.

Yes, they didn't plan on *me*, he thought. And is there anyone in this country who knows more about that whole misbegotten adventure . . . the Vietnam War?

Doubtful. Very doubtful.

No. And he remembered why.

He remembered the day as a small boy in Iola, Wisconsin. It was fall. Halloween was just the next week. His mother called him in from outside, away from the great golden piles of leaves he was jumping into with his friends, burrowing under, smelling the fall, savoring it while winter was years away.

He ran into the small house that always seemed too warm when he ran inside. His mother stood in the hall. She knelt down close to him. She held a piece of paper in her hand. Her eyes glistened in the half light of the hall. Her cheeks looked—he took a step closer—wet.

It took forever for her to tell him. He stood there, still smelling the leaves, the cold wind outside. Stood there listening to words that came out in small, controlled gasps. Until, slowly, oh so slowly and painfully, a glint of meaning emerged.

And he knew what mom was saying. He knew that his dad—this giant, shining figure who was only around for a few weeks, and then gone again—wasn't ever going to come home ever, not ever again.

He heard his mom say that he died fighting for his country.

And when he heard that word . . . died . . . he thought of other dead things. A raccoon he saw on a road. A baby robin that fell out of its nest. A pile of fish in the bottom of his grandfather's small boat.

He knew what "dead" was.

Lindstrom took a breath, the scene playing through his mind for the thousandth time.

And that moment, back in Iola, is when Lindstrom knew that this war would be the one thing he'd learn everything about. Absolutely everything. . . .

The leaders, the battles, the politics, the mistakes, the madness, the weapons.

Everything.

It would be his way of not letting go of his father.

Lindstrom rubbed at his eyes again.

They didn't plan on me, he thought.

Now isn't that too damn bad?

"Give me a fuckin' break," someone hissed from behind Jim.

Jim saw Howell look back, his black face nearly lost in the foliage. And Jim knew the sergeant wanted him to come to the front.

"Excuse me," Jim said awkwardly, squeezing past the soldier in front of him who said, "Yes, sir," the soldier said, acting confused by Jim's politeness.

Jim weaved his way to the front of the line.

It was even darker than before, with no hint of the moon in the east. He knew that there'd be a tiny sliver of a crescent somewhere near dawn. But there'd be no light before then.

He came and crouched beside Howell and the soldier who had been walking point.

"What is it?" Jim said.

"We've got some voices down there," Howell pointed. "I think Charlie's doing something, Lieutenant."

Right. Jim nodded. Now what the hell do we do?

He looked at Howell. "Any ideas?"

Howell took a breath.

"Well, it sounds like they're coming this way, movin' south, just like the reports said. Now, if we can just wait here, stay low, and then move behind them . . ."

Jim listened. And he knew that he should probably just agree to Howell's plan, but something about it bothered him.

Something about it wasn't right.

But how could I know what to do? he wondered.

Then he saw the problem through. And he knew it was coming from McShane's training.

"No," Jim said, shaking his head. "If we fall in behind them, they could turn—and if there's another line of troops behind them, we'll be caught right in the middle."

Henderson had his face down close, listening. Howell shot him a look. "Do you mind, Private?"

"Oh, sorry, Sarge."

Okay, Jim thought. If Howell's plan is no good, then what do we do?

And—amazingly enough—he saw another possibility.

"Why can't we run alongside the trail, get parallel to them and wait—" Jim looked to the south—"yeah, wait along the trail along the hill that we just climbed. We'll wait until they're just there, just right beside us, then we'll lay down some heavy fire, B-40s and—"

B-40s? What the hell am I talking about? Jim wondered. But the words, the plan, just came rumbling out.

"That's good, sir. But damn, I wish we could set some claymores. But there's probably no time."

"That's right."

Jim looked at Howell. Was it Jim's imagination, or did he see great relief etched into his sergeant's face? God knows what he's been thinking is wrong with me.

Jim stood up. Can't get cocky. I got a little pressure, a bit of adrenaline, and some much-needed information surfaced from old McShane's dormant consciousness. Great, terrific, but when this is all over I'll probably go back to being incompetent.

"Okay, let's get the men moving. I want them in position before the enemy has a chance to hear us."

"Yes, sir. And Lieutenant—?"

Jim turned back to Howell. "Yes?"

"There's one thing that I'm worried about. I mean, I just want to mention it. It's just—"

"Yes, what is it?"

"I mean the Charlies, the VC, whoever the hell is coming this way. I don't get it? Why the hell are they talking, making noise? You'd think they'd be moving their shit nice and quiet. If we can hear them from here, what the hell are they up to?"

Good point, Jim thought.

"I don't know, Sergeant. Beats the hell out of me. . . ."

Which, Jim thought, was certainly no lie.

The vapor lifted and this overpowering smell filled her nostrils.

I don't like garlic, she thought. Never had, not since her father had hired this cook for the summer who put it in absolutely everything—much to her father's delight.

Dad had made his first few millions shuttling between Paris and Marseilles, and he used garlic the way most people used salt.

"Khan Ha! An xong lai viet?"

Ali blinked. She stared down at the bowl of rice and vegetables on the smooth parquet table with beautiful dark and blond wood set in an intricate pattern. It was beautiful, and now even this garlicy dish smelled wonderful. She reached out and touched the wood.

It's real, she thought. I'm here, and someone's talking to me—shouting—

"Khan Ha!"

She looked up, and there was this man, old, though she couldn't say how old. He had a black silk robe on, marked with brilliant gold-and-red swirls. His eyes narrowed, studying her.

"Sao anh lai lam the?"

He's asking me a question, and she looked down, realizing that her hand was still caressing the wood, feeling its shiny smoothness. The man shook his head.

And she looked up to him.

And the next time he spoke she understood exactly what he was saying.

"What is wrong with your food?" The man gestured to the air. "I will send it back and get a new dish, if there's something wrong. It is your favorite and—"

"No," Ali said. And she realized that she was speaking Vietnamese. It came out easily and she took a breath.

I'm here, she thought. I made it. I'm Khan Ha and this man looking at me is General Tuan Ngoc Chau.

Except it isn't General Tuan Ngoc Chau at all.

He's Scorpion. One of the Iron Men.

And now she knew she was in danger.

If I make enough wrong moves, he will begin to suspect me. In fact, I may have already aroused his suspicion.

She moved uneasily on the low chair that hovered on short wicker legs only inches off the floor.

There was only one thing she had going for her. If she was new to being Khan Ha, well then this creep was new to being General Chau. And if I don't screw up too terribly, he won't suspect anything.

"No," she said, smiling. "I just felt dizzy just then."

She looked down and saw a small crystal glass with a light, purplish liquid.

"It must be the wine," she smiled.

Chau nodded. And then he picked up his chopsticks and took a forkful of food. She watched him eat, still smiling, and she saw that he wasn't handling his sticks too well.

I can do better than that, she thought.

Thank heaven for dad's expeditions to Shun Lee West in New York. That's one skill she had down by the time she was six.

She picked up her sticks and deftly began eating her bowl. And despite her loathing for garlic, she found the pungent food wonderful, detecting hints of ginger and mustard mixed in with sprouts and snow peas. Tiny bits of meat were hidden in the rice, pork, and beef, she guessed.

Chau ate hungrily, but he sent a constant spray of rice flying down to the table.

"It is late," he said. "Finish up."

Then his face wore a catlike grin.

She became aware of her garment. She wore a long silk gown that fell against her body—Khan Ha's body—molding itself to the young woman's curves.

And then—odd thought—she felt that she had no underwear on.

Hope I don't get hit by a truck.

She reached down and took her glass and sipped the wine, a delicate plum wine.

I may need another glass, she thought, if Chau has in mind what I *think* he has in mind.

(And isn't it interesting that every time I appear as a woman in history I find my sexual organs under assault? Well, at least that's one good thing about the future. That kind of pushy male crap is relegated to cheap holo-soaps.)

She put down the glass, feeling the silk go tight against her breasts, and then slip away. She felt Chau watching the show.

"I'd like more wine," Ali sang sweetly in what she hoped was a properly submissive voice.

And I'd like to squirt sesame seed oil in your lecherous eyeballs. Chau grinned—and again Ali felt secure that he wouldn't know whether that was appropriate or not. Am I supposed to ask for another glass of wine, or anything?

Who knew?

A server appeared from behind a small partition, a little man who brought over a porcelain decanter decorated with a giant maroon dragon. The server nodded to Chau, and then to Ali, and then knelt down to refill her glass.

"Enough," Chau barked when the server had finished filling her glass. "You may leave."

The server bowed again and walked over to a door. As he opened it, Ali saw a bed, low to the ground. A pale, yellow light filled the room.

I wished I had picked morning, she thought. After the evening's main event.

"Finish," he said, gesturing at her with his empty wine glass.

She nodded, trying to hide the gulp she made.

And she took only a few more bites. Suddenly, she had lost her appetite. She chugged her wine, though, wanting as much fortification as possible.

Chau got up.

How bad could it be? she wondered. It's not like I'm a virgin.

I'll just have to—er—move things along.

Quickly.

And I've done my share of acting, she thought.

Chau walked over to her. He reached down for her hand.

Ali put down the now unfortunately empty wine glass.

She looked up at Chau, guessing that he, too, was naked under his splendid robe.

And it looks like he's ready to unsheathe his ceremonial sword.

Her smile felt rubbery, like a prosthetic device sitting on her face. She wondered if she could complain of a headache.

Not tonight, dear. You see, I just came from the future and—

But instead, like a good time warrior, she reached up and took his strong, demanding hand.

Three lines wound their way alongside the trail. The men were on their own, cutting a path through the thick bushes and the vines that stretched like a net between the trees.

And Jim felt excited.

I'm not scared, he thought. Now what the hell is wrong with me that I'm not scared? This has got to be some bad news we're facing, and I feel goddam exhilarated.

He saw that Howell had one group down low, almost off the hill, right near the trail.

Howell stopped his group and hustled up to Jim.

"This looks good, sir," he said, and Jim saw that he was excited, too. Damned strange. . . . "We've got a clear line of sight on a solid chunk of the supply route. If you set the other men up there," he grinned, "we should be able to have a fine party."

And once again Jim found himself overriding Howell's suggestion. "No. You keep your men down there, but I want the B-40s up higher. That will give us some cover if we have to fall back."

Howell nodded. "Yes, sir."

"Okay, carry on," Jim said, and Howell crawled back to his position.

Jim turned to his squad.

"Spread out along this hillside," he said. "Make sure you've got a clear view of the trail . . . and don't squat your butts behind some bush or tree. We can surprise them, but it's no damn good if you don't get any decent shots off. And wait for my signal."

Amazingly, the men scattered away, melting into the overgrown ground, laying still so that Jim felt like he was almost alone.

Rockets.

Who has the rockets? he wondered.

He waited a second, hoping for some miraculous answer.

But when none came, he leaned down close to a nearby soldier, his M-16 frozen against his cheek. One eye squinted through the gun sight, while the other scrutinized the trail.

It was Boyle, the man who carried the medical supplies. "Boyle, who's got the rockets in the company?"

"Sir?" Boyle said, squinting at him.

Jim repeated his question.

"Private Oran, sir. He's our—"

"Thanks," Jim said. "Oran!" he called to the night.

Oran, looking too pudgy to be a soldier, stood up and looked back at Jim. "Sir?"

Jim ran over to him and knelt down beside him.

He looked like a boy, his round white face dotted with mole-sized freckles. Jim saw that he had the pieces of the B-40 and shells laid out beside him.

"Oran, I don't want you to stay here."

"Sir?"

Jim nodded reassuringly. "I want you to go back up there, back up near the top of the hill."

"But sir, it will be a lot harder to make a good hit. It's real dark. If I stay right here, I can—"

Jim put up a hand. I've got to remember I'm in charge here, he thought. This isn't a democracy. There's no voting. *I make the decisions.*

And I hope to hell that McShane keeps feeding me good advice.

"If you go up on the hill, you may miss a few shots. Let me worry about that. But just how fast do you think you can hustle with that cannon if Charley starts streaming up the hill?"

"I don't know, sir, I just—"

"This way we'll have a secure position, a place to fall back to while you can keep on firing."

Then Jim heard a hiss. In the darkness below, he saw Howell pumping his arm.

They're coming.

Jim pointed at the hill, and nodded. Oran started gathering his rockets together. Then he climbed up the hill with surprising agility.

Now I need the radio guy. . . .

He saw him to the right, his rifle propped up against a rock beside him and the radio open.

Good to know where he is, Jim thought. Just in case.

Just in case . . .

He listened.

Then he heard them. The voices, the faint sounds of men moving along the trail.

And—so strange—not being too damn quiet about it.

And Jim knelt down, and he listened to those sounds, and his own breathing. . . .

11

Toland pushed open the door of the Time Lab.

And—Lindstrom was chagrined to see—he wasn't alone.

This, he thought, is what we were afraid of. . . . They hadn't even considered the problem at first. But it was obvious.

As soon as the Iron Men knew about them, knew that there was another Time Lab trying to undo each knot they tied in history, well, they'd surely take steps against the lab itself.

Not directly. That would be risky for them, at least before they had their changes in place. But they could create the proper repressive climate so that the Time Lab would fall under official scrutiny.

Lindstrom was flanked by two security police, two beefy, grim-faced goons in bright blue kelvar. They hefted what looked like very powerful pulse weapons.

The *new* New York City was a police state . . . and they wanted to know what the infamous Red Building was up to. . . .

No way we could explain to them that we're about to change history back so that you never existed.

"I—I tried to stop them, but they threatened force, Dr. Lindstrom."

Lindstrom smiled. "That's alright, Toland. Thank you."

One of the security police stepped forward. "You

are not in compliance with the Metropolitan Security Directive 02030567. . . .''

''Oh, that one,'' Lindstrom smiled.

Though the cop's face was covered, his lower jaw sneered at the wisecrack.

''And we have been authorized to occupy the lab until such time that its procedures have received approval from the Experimental Research Division.''

Lindstrom gestured at them. ''Does that mean you have to stand right here.''

''Yes, and furthermore, you may not continue working here until—''

''Poppycock!''

A familiar voice barked from behind Lindstrom. The history professor turned around and watched McManus walk over, his eyes still slitted from his sedated sleep. ''Utter poppycock and rubbish!''

There we go, thought Lindstrom. Nothing like McManus's crusty voice to cut through the—er—bullshit—and set matters on a proper course.

''We cannot *leave* here, no more than doctors working in a hospital can leave. There are people in there,'' McManus said, gesturing back at the dark room he just emerged from. ''*People* who are under our care. Interfere with our experiment—make us *leave!*—and they might die.''

''Our commander has ordered us—''

''Yes, yes, I know. Secure the building. Occupy it until we are in compliance. All of that nonsense. Very well, then. Stay if you must. But let us work or you'll have those people's lives on your head!''

McManus turned away, as if the matter was concluded.

Bravo, thought Lindstrom. That's the way to deal with those fascistic dolts.

But the head cop's jaw seemed to chew up and down, mulling over the stalemate.

''Our commander will be informed of your continued noncompliance.''

"Yes," McManus said turning back. "And be sure to tell him that, if we have to leave the Lab, he will be killing innocent volunteers."

The cop stood still a moment and then turned to his equally grim-faced companion. "Take a position inside this lab. I will check with the Central Security Office at Dinkins Center." He turned back to McManus. "Until then—"

And he spun on his heels, his heavy duty pulse rifle swinging from his shoulder.

The other cop adopted a stern pose with his arms folded behind his back.

"Great," McManus muttered, "now we have this monkey to deal with."

Lindstrom put a schoolboyish finger up to his lips, telling McManus that it might not be a good idea to irritate the cop.

But McManus shook his head. Lindstrom saw both Beck and Jacob looking at the old physicist. And for the first time, they both looked scared. "No matter," McManus said, rubbing his eyes. "We'll use the language of innuendo." He looked over at the guard. "You don't speak innuendo, do you?" he said to the guard. The guard said nothing. He just stood there.

"Ah, didn't think so." McManus shook his head. He took a breath and looked away. "I feel so woozy . . ."

"Perhaps you should rest some more," Lindstrom suggested.

"No, I'm afraid the clock is running, my dear Lindstrom. I see we have our new entry in the historical sweepstakes in place. . . ."

He means Ali, Lindstrom thought. "Yes. And she has as much background as I could give her."

"Good. Well then," McManus said, looking over at the guard, "All we can do is watch how her, er, research develops . . . what effect it has." McManus looked away. "But I'm afraid we may need yet another candidate. . . ."

Lindstrom nodded.

Another candidate.

Another time traveler. Lindstrom had the same thought. When more data emerges, they might need to send someone else back there.

Lindstrom rubbed his beard.

And he knew who that must be. . . .

The sound of the enemy grew closer. From all the noise they were making, they obviously thought that they were safe.

Sure, thought Jim. They're moving through an isolated part of the jungle, well away from any roads or major villages.

They probably think that the trail is completely safe.

He picked up his binoculars, checking the trail—which still showed no activity—and then Howell crouched low and close.

He saw Howell look back in his direction. The sergeant nodded, and smiled.

Damn, Jim thought. I should be petrified, frozen with fear, but instead my heart is thumping like a drum, my palms are sweaty, and I can almost taste the tension.

Whatever this is, it isn't fear. . . .

He looked at the other men on the hill slope. Oran, squatting next with his rocket. Then other men, their guns held tight, their cheeks pressed close to their barrels, waiting for something to move, something human to wander into their sights.

Maybe I'm not afraid because I know this isn't *my* body. If I die, hell, it might not do anything to me.

(On the other hand, he wasn't really too sure about that. It could be that death is death. And if McShane buys the farm, my body might end up helping with the planting.)

He licked his lips.

"Sir," he heard a soldier hiss.

Jim snapped out of his reverie and pulled up the binoculars.

And there, at the northern edge of the trail, he saw the first enemy soldier.

In uniform.

He didn't expect that.

He expected someone in pajamas, wearing a funny peaked hat. This soldier, disappearing and then reappearing through the brush, wore a real helmet and black khakis.

The soldier said something.

"What?" Jim said, still watching the enemy through his binoculars.

"NVA regulars, sir. They're not VC, not guerillas. What are North Vietnam Regulars doing so far south?"

Good question, Jim thought.

Now more of them entered the exposed part of the trail. And more, until Jim began to get the idea that this wasn't no little squad.

It was bigger than that. A division perhaps, loaded down with supplies, weapons, cannons, and heavy machine guns.

All of sudden things didn't seem exciting anymore.

He felt a disturbingly loose feeling in his midsection. His body had picked up on his growing terror.

He moved his field glasses to look at Howell.

He saw the sergeant looking up at him.

Waiting for my order, Jim thought.

Goddam, waiting for my order.

No doubt about it, he thought. I'm over my head.

Way over.

He licked his lips . . . and brought up his arm. . . .

General Chau's technique wasn't exactly inadequate.

Though Ali realized that this guy wasn't really Chau, but one of the Iron Men. Still—once she accepted the fact that he expected to bed down with her—she took a breath and tried to act as though the bedtime fun and games were a normal course of events.

If he figures out that I'm not Khan Ha, she thought, I doubt he'll let me live.

Chau gave her body some careful attention that—despite her disinterest—fed her laissez-faire feelings. . . .

The lights were off, and in the moonless night Chau was a wiry, thin body rubbing against her. Khan Ha's apparatus, she noted, seemed quick to respond.

And then she was surprised to hear herself moan.

This, she thought, is pretty bizarre.

But her unexpected cry urged Chau to hurry, and he quickly mounted her, grunting. Now she could look up and see his eyes glisten, his teeth exposed as he pulled back his lips.

Whoever this guy really was, it must have been a long time between drinks of water. . . .

Then it was over quickly, and Ali was left lying there, listening to Chau breathing. He caressed her bare legs, squeezed them as if assaying the value of her flesh. He patted her flat midsection.

Just the way you'd pet a dog that fetched the newspaper.

In seconds she heard Chau snoring, an erratic buzz saw.

So much for romance, she thought.

And while she listened to the sound, she thought about how she'd get the information she needed. What does Scorpion really plan for Tet?

I have two days, she thought. Two days to get the information . . . and get it to Jim.

She reached down to the floor and pulled on her black dress. It was chilly in the room, and there was only a thin blanket on the bed.

And she thought of Jim, where he might be, and what he might be doing. . . .

Jim waited until all the exposed part of the trail was filled with the NVA soldiers.

And his hand was suspended in midair.

Maybe we should just back out of this, he thought. Maybe we should let them keep on shuffling past us. And then get the hell out of here.

But if I do that, I'll probably be arrested. We're here to kill the enemy, and there's a whole bunch of them down there. Besides—ha, ha—we have the advantage. We'll surprise them.

Who cares that they probably outnumber us three-to-one . . . four-to-one . . . maybe more?

His hand felt like a thin reedy stalk growing up from his shoulder. It almost felt as if he couldn't bring it down.

I'm crazy to bring it down, he thought. Totally crazy.

But he did, anyway.

He pulled it straight down . . .

The next few seconds were horrible and wonderful at the same time.

There was the noise . . . Howell's orders and the other men yelling, their words covered by the rattling sound of their guns firing, the screams of the North Vietnamese soldiers being cut down on the trail.

And then there was the first explosion of Oran's B-40, the shrill whine of the rocket streaming down to the center of the trail. And then more firing.

It was as if Jim had pulled the plunger on an outrageously large fireworks display.

Ka-boom!

But then the NVA soldiers fired back.

Their guns sounded different, the explosions had a different pitch, the guns made muffled sounds coming from the trail.

Belatedly, he realized that he should start firing his own gun.

He crouched low to the ground.

Oran let go with another rocket, whooping so loud that Jim heard his voice above the din.

Jim looked through the gun sight. A long ribbon of blue smoke now covered the trail. He saw movement there, but the enemy soldiers were under cover, firing back. Jim pulled his trigger. But only a singe blast fired, and he realized that he had the M-16 switch set wrong. In the blackness, he fingered the gun until he found the button that set it for semi-automatic fire.

He pulled the trigger again.

And the gun rattled like an explosive rattlesnake, jiggling in his hand.

If he hit anything other than trees, it was blind luck.

Then he heard Howell yelling.

He said, "Boyle!" . . . the medic. And Jim heard someone crying out. Calling on God, cursing, then God again.

Somebody was hurt.

Oran let another rocket go and the trail exploded into light.

But now Jim heard the enemy's guns taking bites out of the young mahogany trees and the vines. More yells and screams.

The blue smoke drifted up from the trail, blotting out Howell and the lower part of the hill.

That's no good, thought Jim, I can't see shit now. And Oran, with his chunky rocket launcher, can't possibly get a clear shot.

"Sir," Oran called down, "I can't see—"

"Yeah," Jim said. "Hold on a bit . . . maybe the wind—"

Maybe the wind will what? The wind sent the smoke creeping upwards. He heard Howell screaming, yelling above the gunfire, the screams of hurt men. "Fall back!" Howell yelled. "Get moving! Come on—come on—come on—"

A small window opened in the smoky swirl and Oran said. "I got a shot, sir!" And he fired a rocket right into the center of the hole. If there was still any NVA soldiers standing on the trail, the rocket just got them.

But then, through another clear pocket, Jim saw some of the enemy soldiers moving up the hill. Two three, maybe more.

He looked to the left, and he guessed there were some moving that way, too.

They'll surround us, he thought, encircle us, and then move in with their AK-47s blasting.

Jim stood up.

"Fall back!" he yelled, echoing Howell.

The soldiers near him, including Bloom with his radio and Clarke, his helmet askew, didn't need to hear it twice.

Jim stood there, waiting to see Howell and the others come up.

Then he saw Boyle—the medic, carrying a soldier.

It was Henderson. Jim ran down to give a hand. Howell was just behind him, firing, crouching, yelling at his men to move their goddam asses.

"They're moving' right up, Lieutenant. It's got to be a fucking division down there."

Jim nodded, then pointed to the left and right.

"They're moving up the sides, too, trying to trap us."

"Shit," Howell said.

Jim let Henderson drape his other arm around his shoulder. "Get everybody up to the ridge," Jim said.

Jim took some of Henderson's weight on his shoulder and the soldier screamed. The onetime grad student turned around and saw a bloody crater near Henderson's shoulder blade. It looked at least an inch deep. "You're okay, Henderson," Jim said right into the moaning soldier's ear. Then Jim supported him more from his chest, walking in tandem with Boyle.

Howell screamed at the last few men who were still down the hill.

Then Howell ran up to him.

"We've lost Scott, and Jackson. Maybe a few others."

Jim nodded, panting, struggling up the hill. The men above him were firing—hopefully over their heads. A rocket roared overhead, and he felt the blast behind him.

Howell helped move Henderson up the hill.

"What—the hell—do we do? Howell?"

He felt Howell look at him.

Not the right fucking question, Jim thought.

Too fucking bad. I don't have time to play lieutenant now. McShane might be in my head somewhere, but he was nowhere in sight now.

"I don't know, Lieutenant. Hold the hill. Call for some heat. I—"

Then Jim had a thought.

Only he knew it wasn't his.

And the thought seemed crazy and dangerous.

But he knew that if he was going to get anyone out of here alive, it was maybe the only way.

"Keep everyone moving, Howell. Past the crest of the hill. And get Bloom and his radio ready."

A chunk of wood, a pulpy piece of teak, chipped away from a tree, letting Jim know that someone was getting a bead on them.

Henderson was crying. Calling for his mother. Jim felt the scrawny soldier's blood dripping into him, making a sticky wet spot on his shirt.

"RT!" Howell yelled.

And Jim hoped that the radio and its operator were both in good working order.

Another bullet whizzed too close, and Jim thought . . .

We're having some fun now, Jimbo, now aren't we. . . ?

Some real fun. . . .

12

Sometime in the night, Chau turned to her, grunted, and said, "Leave."

Ali—stunned awake—slid out of the bed, pulling her black, silken dress close. She pulled it over her head while Chau turned away and his raucous snore once again filled the room.

Leave? Just where am I supposed to go? Ali wondered, standing there on the cold wooden floor. There must be some other place I live. . . .

She pushed Khan Ha's fine, jet black hair off her face and groped her way to the door leading out of the small room. A tiny sliver of light showed her the way to the dining area. As soon as she stepped out, an old woman, Chau's mamasan, appeared.

"I'm . . . leaving. . . ." Ali said.

The mamasan smiled, and backed away, clearing an imaginary path to the door outside.

It's got to be cold out there, Ali thought. She stopped and turned to the old servant. "Did I bring a coat or—?"

The woman shook her head and smiled. "No, you did not, Khan Ha."

Oh, Ali thought. Perhaps Khan Ha expected to stay the evening.

Ali took another step.

And then she decided to risk something.

She turned back to the mamasan.

"Er, where should I go now?"

The mamasan nodded and smiled. "To your mother's cottage. Yes, your great-uncle General Chau will expect you to go there."

Uncle?" Ali thought. God, bad enough the old commie is sticking it to someone half his age. But his niece?

What a creep.

"My mother's cottage?" Ali said.

"Yes," The mamasan answered. And then Ali saw her tilt her head—just a bit—to the right.

Okay, I go outside, out to the cold, and then go right. And if I'm lucky I'll find the cottage.

"Goodnight, mamasan," Ali said. The woman bowed.

"Good night, Khan Ha. . . ."

And Ali left General Chau's house.

It was raining bullets. They flew through the brambles and the vines like superfast insects ripping through the jungle. The soldiers crawled up the hill. crablike, while the bullets zipped through the air.

Jim stood on the ridge and fired down into the dark valley, well away from his men.

He was watching one soldier near the ridge when a bullet ripped through the back of his helmet and then exploded, leaving an ugly gaping hole at the front. The soldier fell forward like a toddler stumbling over an unobserved rock.

"Damn, hurry!" Jim said. Howell was bellowing at them, all the time sending a spray of bullets chugging down at the NVA soldiers.

Then Jim felt a tap on his shoulder.

"Sir! I've got base on the radiophone. They want to—"

An explosion interrupted Bloom's message. The radio operator adjusted his cock-eyed helmet and then started again. "They want to know what you need."

I need a fucking way out of here, Jim thought.

The last man reached the crest.

Then Howell had them lie down and fire at the enemy.

At least this part was working, Jim saw. We have a good position; now if they want us, they'll have to fight for every inch. Something exploded down below, and he saw a whole teak tree fly into the air. Then another explosion, and he saw Howell tossing grenades.

"Lieutenant!" Bloom yelled over the thundering explosions, "What should I tell them?"

Jim nodded. Why not, he thought, why not tell them . . .

He ran back to the phone, well back from the crest.

"McShane here."

The voice on the other end was almost inaudible, covered by static and the burping noises of all the guns.

"Yes, Lieutenant. Do you want artillery cover . . . aircraft support. . . ?"

Wrong, thought Jim. He might be new to this but he had heard enough about the limitations of artillery. . . . especially from miles away. And aircraft support couldn't do a damn thing if they were smothered by the jungle.

"No. I want the two choppers at our launch point. In fifteen minutes. I want us pulled right out of here."

"But sir—" more static, and Jim lost the next words.

"Could you repeat that?" Jim said.

The radio voice crackled on. . . . "But they'll be exposed. It's too—"

Another lost word, but Jim guessed it was "dangerous."

"We can hold them on this hill for ten minutes, and then get there just as the choppers land." Sure, why not, Jim thought. Isn't that what John Wayne would do, the old Duke?

On second thought, maybe not. He'd just dig in, hold his ground and wait for reinforcements. The cavalry always showed up in time to save his bacon. . . .

Fuck that, Jim thought. I *know* how this war turns out.

Or at least how it's supposed to turn out.

"Sir, we don't—"

"Fifteen minutes. Get moving on it now!" Jim yelled. "Do you hear me?"

Jim heard the radio operator at the other end talking to someone, another scratchy voice. And then the radio operator came back.

"The choppers will be at launch at zero-four-one-seven hours, sir. You copy?"

"Yes, I copy. And tell everyone thanks a heap. . . ."

He handed the phone back to Bloom.

"Forget the radio, Bloom. If you've got a gun, I suggest you start using it."

Bloom nodded. "Yes, sir. . . ."

Jim stood up and Howell was beside him.

"Henderson's dead, sir. There's two more wounded. We can't stay here much longer. . . ."

"We're out of here, Sergeant. Tell Oran to shoot his load. Just keep pumping the rockets down there. Leave two men to set up some covering fire and then—"

Something was there. An impulse, a goddamned impulse from McShane—

And Jim said it before he could step on the stupid thing, and squash it like a bug.

"Take the rest of the men to the launch area. I'll stay and help keep the rear covered . . . the choppers are getting us out of here in—" Jim looked at his watch. "Eleven minutes."

"No, sir. You'd best take the men—"

What the hell is this? Jim thought, as the absolutely stupidest most idiotic words he ever heard kept pouring out of his mouth. "No, you get moving Howell. Now."

Howell stood there, shook his massive head. And then the sergeant turned and started yelling at the men, leaving two hot dogs to lay down some smoke, while the rest of the men followed him back to the open grassy area beyond the hill.

"Good luck, sir." Howell said.

"See you in a bit," Jim smiled. And then Howell turned and led his men up the hill, into the jungle, suddenly swallowed by the old trees.

And Jim turned, hearing the sound of the NVA soldiers firing, calling out to them, bullets chipping at the trees.

And he wondered. . . .

What the hell is wrong with me?

McManus leaned over Lindstrom at his worktable. He quickly glanced at the nouveau cop, but it was impossible to tell if the stern figure was watching them or not.

"We can't go on like this," McManus whispered with a smile, making sure plenty of teeth showed. "We have to do *something*."

Lindstrom looked over at the guard and smiled. "Yes, and look at these, the latest news from outside. . . ."

McManus watched Lindstrom push a printout closer to him. He saw that Lindstrom had circled something.

"The ESAC? What on earth—"

Lindstrom pointed to some lines farther down the paper. And McManus read them.

"The European Socialist Advisory Committee. What on earth could that be? Not good?" McManus said.

Lindstrom made a hollow laugh. "Not to put too fine a point on it, McManus. Not good at all. But here—this is even worse—"

Another sheet appeared and a stupefied McManus read the words aloud. "The Antarctic Conflict. Oh, dear no. I—"

Lindstrom looked at the guard, who seemed to shift his weight a bit at McManus's exclamation. "Do try to keep your voice a bit on the quiet side, McManus."

"I can't believe that they'd go to war over the Antarctic!" McManus whispered.

"Too many potential goodies," Lindstrom said. "Apparently a unified Europe and USSR carved up the continent between them."

"And the US?"

"Well—" Lindstrom shuffled through some more papers as if disgusted by them. "It appears that the US was too busy enforcing its new, revised Constitution. When the riots broke out five years ago—"

"Riots?" McManus said. "What riots?"

Lindstrom shook his head. "Just take my word for it," he whispered. "There were riots, throughout the country. According to the revised history, the economy was on the ropes, the social fabric destroyed. After the formation of the united EurAsia, America became part of the third world. There have been attempts to tinker with the Constitution for decades . . . you remember the right-to-lifers . . . and the anti-immolators who were aghast at the burning of the flag? This time things got so bad that they've opened the book on the whole thing. Though—" Lindstrom squinted and looked at the pages in his hand— "for the life of me I can't imagine what the Supreme Court must have been doing. Talk about asleep at the wheel . . ."

The cop started to walk over.

"Does that mean that the Iron Men have made progress?"

"Very much so. We must be way behind them . . ." Lindstrom flicked the papers away . . . "Way behind them . . . But I've done something here, with the computer, in case—"

The cop stood behind McManus.

"Is there something wrong?" the helmeted officer said.

McManus stood up, pasting a smile on his face.

"Oh, no, we were just running some, er, tests on

the old computer network.'' McManus broadened his grin. ''It's very important to check those microcircuits and—''

The guard reached past him and picked up the sheets of paper.

''Oh, that's nothing,'' Lindstrom blustered. ''It's just—''

The cop looked at the papers. Studied them.

Then, looking from McManus and Lindstrom, he folded the paper neatly in half and secreted it in a pouch strapped to his side.

''A decision about the disposition of this facility will be forthcoming . . . I will hold this as evidence. . . .''

He walked away.

''Christ.'' McManus sputtered. ''This is very bad, Lindstrom . . . very—''

Then he heard steps from outside.

Many steps.

McManus looked over at Dr. Jacob standing at his tachyon generator, looking like a lost boy. Dr. Beck obviously heard the steps, too. She came out of the room that housed Jim and Ali's dormant bodies.

''Elliot . . .'' she said looking to McManus.

Think, he ordered himself. There has to be a way out of this. We can't lose now, we can't turn history over to those criminals, those madmen—

The lab doors flew open.

And four security police came in, each holding a massive rifle as if they expected the scientists to start blasting away.

One cop came forward.

''By the order of directive 020345901, this experimental facility is ordered closed until such time that it be granted a permit by the Metropolitan Research Committee.''

The cops moved quickly, one to each of the scientists, grabbing them by their arms and pulling them out of the lab.

"But you can't!" McManus sputtered. "You can't take us out of here!"

But they could . . . and they did. . . .

Oran kept firing the B-40. He looked like a kid running through a box of cherry bombs on the Fourth of July.

"Good work," Jim said between blasts of his own gun.

The NVA Regulars had stopped, holding their positions, hiding behind twisted trees, scrunching down into holes.

They're regrouping, Jim guessed. Figuring out just how they'll take the hill.

He looked at his watch.

Five minutes until the choppers come.

We've got to go, he knew.

But what if the North Vietnamese are too close, what if they get up too fast?

The could blow the helicopters right out of the air.

He looked at his watch again. 4:12.

Then 4:13.

He looked east, back to the jungle that hid the grassy, flat plain. He saw a slight glow in the sky.

Too early for the sun.

Right. It's not the sun at all. It's the moon. Coming to shed some light on our dismal situation.

Just what we don't need.

"We're splitting," Jim whispered. "Pass it along."

He looked at his watch. 4:14.

It was now or never. He thought he heard a sound. The welcome whirr of engines.

"One more blast," he said to Oran. "Let's leave firing. . . ."

Oran, baby-faced and miscast for the role of heroic rocketeer, turned and said—"I'm down to my last shell anyway, sir. . . ."

He fired, and Jim stood up. Yelling at the men. "Come on. Hustle, hustle, hustle!"

He waited while they ran back toward the jungle

behind them. And Jim sent a spray of bullets into the night air.

He heard the enemy moving and firing. Two big shells ripped up the ground near them. He followed Oran, who moved slowly, too damn slowly, picking his way through the maze of trees and vines.

Then a shell exploded right in front of Oran.

It appeared—as if by magic—right in front of him.

Oran fell backwards.

Back towards Jim.

Oran's arms were spread out, and he tumbled back like Wily Coyote running into a cartoon door just slammed in his face.

"Oran," Jim yelled.

(And he heard the choppers, just ahead now, minutes away, maybe already landing, picking up Howell and the others. . . .)

"Oran!" he yelled again.

But Oran's only answer was to keep pivoting backwards until Jim could see the damage.

He caught some smoke.

That was the expression.

Some real bad smoke. . . .

The whole front of his face was gone as if it had been pulled away.

Oran plopped back on the ground with a thud that mixed with the firing of the soldiers chasing them. Another shell chewed up the ground to the left.

Jim knelt down.

He thought he saw Oran's lips move.

Saying something.

Maybe something like . . . I guess I caught one, huh, Lieutenant? Caught one bad. I guess I did—

The lips looked like they were moving. But it was just the steady stream of blood gushing out.

Oran was dead the moment the shell hit.

Jim stood up and ran, hearing those engines.

Move, he thought, leaping over vines, dodging branches.

The crush of the trees became more dense, as if they were trying to stop him. He imagined the whine of the engines as the choppers left, leaving him behind, leaving him for dead.

Then the jungle opened up. He saw tall grass waving in the wind.

Waving in the wake of the chopper's giant rotors.

He saw Howell, waving at him, helping the last grunt get on board.

He saw the sliver of a moon, just peeking over the broad leaves of the trees.

He ran full out.

Bits of dirt danced around his feet.

They're firing at me, from behind me. They're trying to fucking kill me.

He pumped at the air.

Knowing that he wouldn't make it.

Howell was in the chopper now, yelling at him.

"Come on, Lieutenant! Come on!"

One chopper took off, and swooped away. The other seemed eager to join it.

Ten feet away.

Jim saw someone next to Howell. One of the helicopter crew was manning a big-barreled machine gun.

Jim reached for Howell's hand.

The crewman started firing at the NVA soldiers that Jim knew were just behind him. He heard an explosion.

Please, he begged, don't let them get the chopper. Not because of me. Don't let them—

Howell pulled him on—a good thing, because suddenly Jim's feet were off the ground, dangling in the air. There was nothing, just Howell's hand hauling him aboard, and the scream of the chopper's rotor as it lifted them up, and then—the chopper tilted away.

Jim looked at the machine gunner next to him, his teeth gritted, blasting away like a crazy man. He heard the ping of bullets smacking the side of the helicopter.

And he lay curled on the floor until, finally, the sound of firing faded into the distance like a bad dream.

Howell handed him a canteen.

"You okay, sir?"

Jim nodded. Then he pulled himself off the helicopter's ribbed floor so that he was sitting up. He saw the soldiers sitting against the wall. One lay near the back, moaning at the ceiling while Boyle bandaged his arm.

"How is he?" Jim asked, leaning against the metal bars of the chopper's wall. He saw strips of machine-gun bullets draped over the bars, and dark green gunny sacks. The floor was dotted with great red smears.

"He lost a lot of blood, sir. But if he can hang on 'till we get back to base, he should be fine. . . ."

Jim nodded.

Howell seemed to hesitate a moment. "And Oran?"

Jim shook his head. "I saw him die. It was over in a second. . . ."

"That's bad, sir," Howell said. "He was a good man . . . real good . . ."

The helicopter turned a bit and now seemed to be flying straight at the crescent moon.

"It happened so fast," Jim said. "A shell just blew up in his face. . . ."

And now Howell squatted close. He talked low, whispering. "You know, sir . . . I once got a few days down at Can Tau Beach for some short-time R&R. And—shit—I hadn't really seen much action yet. I was still doing evening patrols and catching chicken farmers poaching on each other."

Jim nodded, not knowing where Howell was leading. He heard the wounded soldier moan. And he heard Boyle comfort him, gentle as a mother.

This is a sick place, he thought. Sick . . .

And I've got to get the hell out of here soon, before—before—

"And I see these guys playing soccer on some field

they made behind the mess tent. I wandered over to watch it. And I see them playing this game, laughing, having a great time.'' Howell took a breath. ''The only thing is—the thing that bothered me—was that the ball didn't seem to move, too. It moved like something was wrong with it. More water, sir?''

Jim shook his head. His eyes were locked on Howell, absorbed by his story, letting it blot out the last hour's madness.

''So I go closer, and then somebody does a bad kick and this ball rolls right towards me, round and round stopping at my feet. I guess—'' he laughed—''It was in the out-of-bounds area. I don't know. I went to kick it back. . . .''

The copter dipped down, hugging the tree line.

''I went to kick it. And, shit, I saw it was someone's head. It was a head, sir, some VC they killed, some creep who set a bobby trap just outside of the camp that blew up half a squad. They caught him. And that's what they did to make themselves feel better . . . I backed away.''

Jim looked at Howell. ''And what happened?''

''They ran over and kicked it back into play. You know I felt sick. But they felt fine. You see, he was the *enemy.* He killed their buddies. And damn, if that didn't make them feel a lot better.''

Now Howell looked away. ''There's always time for a payback, sir. It always comes. . . .'' Howell nodded. ''For us, for Charlie, for everyone . . . all of us stuck in this damn war . . .''

And Jim wanted to tell the sergeant then. Tell him. Hey, I'm not who the hell you think I am. I mean, you're right . . . I sure am *not* myself.

But instead he just leaned back against the cabin wall, shut his eyes, and listened to the roar of the engines. . . .

13

Ngo Van Trinh got up early, well before he was supposed to go to his job at the hotel. He got up when it was still dark and the city of Saigon slept. He was so tired that all he wanted to do was pull his thin blanket over his head. But he forced himself to look at his small electric alarm clock—an American clock—and then, with torturous steps, he slipped out of bed.

There were no voices in this normally noisy building. The bar girls and their rotation of lovers were gone. The angry families fighting over too little of everything were now at peace, asleep.

Trinh stood there and rubbed his eyes. He heard a car a few blocks away. He heard the steady whirr of his clock.

He shook himself and slipped into the same clothes he wore the night before, pulling on the thin, dark pants and top, and the worn slippers that never lasted more than a few months.

I'm cold now, he thought, but in a while I'll be pedaling through the empty streets. I'll wake up, my blood will flow, and I'll feel warm.

He felt the emptiness in his stomach, an emptiness he'd have to ignore until he got to the hotel and could snatch some hot sticky rolls fresh from the bakery.

But that was still hours away.

It was January 29th. . . .

And Tet was one day closer.

* * *

Ali found the cottage. It was easy, since it was the only building back away from the flimsy-looking barracks. A guard stood duty, and he smiled as she nodded to him, opening the door.

A small light glowed from a table just inside the entranceway.

Then an old woman swooped out of the darkness. She grabbed Ali's arm and squeezed it, holding her hard.

"Did you tell him?" she croaked. Her eyes were wet and filmy. They looked as if they barely saw through her thick coating of mucous.

The woman squeezed her arm again.

"Did you tell him?"

Her arm hurt and Ali tried to pull it away. Who is this? she wondered. But the woman held her fast and wouldn't let go.

"Tell him what?" Ali said.

The woman licked her dry, cracked lips. The tongue looked shriveled, lizardlike, snaking out futilely to lubricate the words. "About our leaving, for Tet Mau Than . . . to visit our cousins to the south. Did you tell Chau?"

And Ali gave the only answer that she could be sure of. . . .

"No . . . at least I don't think so. . . ."

The woman slapped her, a great stinging smack that belied the old woman's small size.

"Stupid girl! Stupid, stupid girl!" she shrieked, louder now. Ali felt her stinging cheek, the warm glow of the slap.

Then she heard footsteps in the hall. Two boys, tall, but not yet men, came out into the small pool of light in the hallway.

"What will happen to your brothers if we stay?" the woman shrieked. "How long do you think they'll live fighting for Ho Chi Minh, dying for the 'One Who Knows.' Your mother is dead, your father is dead, and they are next." The old woman took a step closer and grabbed at Ali, snaring her hair.

What the hell is she talking about? Ali thought.

"You give yourself to that pig night after night. Now," she said, tugging at her hair, "*now* is the time to get his help." The woman pulled again and Ali yelped. "You will wait until he wakes up and ask his permission." She let go of Ali and grabbed the two strapping boys, their dark eyes looking fearful in the pale light. "I will not let these two die."

And Ali tried to make sense of what was going on here. These are my brothers. And this old woman—she must be my grandmother and she wants them out of the country, away from the armies of the north. And I'm supposed to get permission to visit relatives during Tet.

(During the cease-fire—*yes!*—the thought was there as if it was her fondest childhood memory. Tet is a time for visiting friends and relatives not seen for a long time. What better time than the cease-fire to do that?)

"You will ask Chau's permission and we will leave by nightfall. Do you understand?"

"Yes. . . ." Ali said.

And then what? Was this supposed to happen, she wondered? Will this help her get to Jim? Will this help her learn what the Iron Men plan on doing?

It must, she thought, or Lindstrom wouldn't have sent me here.

Unless . . . unless . . . she thought history had been twisted so out of whack that this Khan Ha was no longer the key person she used to be.

The old woman turned and walked back to the dark rooms in the back of the small cottage. And as she walked, she muttered. . . .

"Stupid girl . . . stupid. . . ."

And Ali stood there. Tired. Cold. But—more than anything—confused.

* * *

Jim felt the helicopter's bumpy landing. He looked out and saw the soldiers waiting to help the wounded. Jim stood up, and helped Howell ease out the wounded soldiers to the waiting medics on the launch pad.

One soldier groaned as his body was gently lowered onto a stretcher and then slid down to the ground.

"How is he?" Jim asked Howell.

"It's a bad wound, sir . . . lots of blood loss. But he's real strong and he'll get great care. The base doc is a real magic worker." Howell turned to Jim. "I'll get the men settled down, sir . . . you get some rest, too. . . ."

Jim nodded.

It all seemed like a dream now. The explosions, the North Vietnamese soldiers crawling up the hill after them, Oran getting his face blown away.

No, not a dream. A nightmare. . . .

He looked out of the cabin of the helicopter, and saw the ring of tents, lights on, and the first purplish and crimson tinges in the east as the new day began.

The day seemed ready to wash away what happened during the night. He looked at the soldiers helping his men unload, a concerned welcoming committee who knew that they'd had a bad time of it.

Jim crouched down to jump out of the chopper.

And he saw Burnett.

The other lieutenant was dressed in camouflage fatigues, but he looked neat and unruffled. If he had been on patrol, then he obviously had a quiet night.

"Heard you caught some real bad smoke, Jack."

Jim nodded. There was no grin on Burnett's face, none of that good old boy bumptiousness. And that was good, because Jim knew he couldn't handle it. Not now . . .

"You lost some good men."

Jim nodded. He stepped down to the tarmac and said, "There was a platoon. Maybe a couple of platoons. They nearly nailed all of us."

Burnett allowed a small smile onto his face. "Good thinking calling in the choppers. From the looks of things, another ten minutes and no one would be coming home."

Right, Jim nodded. None of us.

And where the hell is home for me now? Here? Back in New York, at Columbia?

Or nowhere?

And who the hell am I? I can't even tell what are my thoughts or Jack McShane's anymore.

I've become totally schizoid. Maybe this is dangerous. Maybe I'll just snap, and start blowing people away.

Or maybe I'll just blow myself away.

He felt his eyes sting. Damn, maybe a bit of grit blew into them. Or something.

He felt them grow wet and blurry.

I'm crying, he thought. Jesus, I'm crying. I'm weeping like a baby.

Jim took a step away from the chopper, hoping Burnett wouldn't see. We've all got to be men out here, don't we? That's our role. You see, you're a man. And men fight and die and they damn well don't cry. Men just don't do that.

Fuck it, Jim felt like saying. Fuck the Time Lab, fuck the Iron Men. There was only one thing that gave him any comfort, one thing that made him think that he could take a breath and maybe get back on track, become a good little time warrior fighting the good fight for the historical record.

Ali.

If I knew Ali was alive, he thought, then maybe I could go on. I wouldn't feel so damn alone.

Burnett put an arm—a big, powerful arm with a chunky hand that looked like it used to arm wrestle grizzlies—right on Jim's shoulder. He sees me crying, Jim thought. Great, now I have this cotton farmer trying to console me.

"Jim . . . before you report to the captain . . . I thought I'd better tell you something. . . ."

Jim stopped, turned and looked at Burnett. Burnett's face, catching the first orange glow of the dawn, was somber, serious.

"The order came in a half hour ago. They approved your request, man. It's been approved, Jim. . . ." Burnett smiled.

And Jim nodded.

Let him think I'm shell-shocked. Let him think I've had my eggs scrambled by too many exploding rocket shells. What the hell does it matter?

Jim nodded, and then asked, "What fucking request?"

McManus turned to Lindstrom, who was beside him, both of them being propelled out of the Red Building with equal speed. He heard Dr. Beck behind them, arguing with her bullheaded escort, complaining that he was hurting her.

"Peter," McManus said, jogging to keep step with the thrusts of the cop at his back.

"Yes . . ."

"I'm very worried about something, Peter. . . ." and McManus looked back at the cop who held him. I hope Lindstrom can read between the lines, he thought. Because I can't very well talk freely with these goons so close. They apparently don't have a clue about the true nature of the Time Lab. And the longer we can keep that from them, the better.

"I was wondering," he said, as they were pushed into the elevator, "just what the effect will be when we, er, go outside."

"Effect?"

"I mean, you know . . . as Proust might put it . . . Récherche du temps perdu. . . ?"

The cops pressed a button and the elevator zipped up the three flights to the main level. The doors whooshed open with jarring suddenness, and Mc-

Manus could see the doors leading out of the Red Building.

And he saw Toland.

Good, he thought. They're letting Toland stay on. That's good. That might be helpful . . . later. If we can ever figure out what in the world to do about this.

"I'm not sure I follow you, Elliot. Récherche du what? I'm afraid my French—"

Damn, McManus thought. How could the professor not know Proust's classic work, *Remembrance of Times Past*. The point McManus was trying to make had to be clear.

Namely, what will happen to their memories once they're outside.

They'll be subject to the revisions set in place by the Iron Men. Even their memory of the Time Lab and all their work would disappear.

It would be, McManus suspected, the final victory for the other side. The Time Lab would be out of commission. And he, and Lindstrom, and the rest, wouldn't have a damn clue that anything was wrong.

Their escorts, whose blue kelvar outfits squeaked as they walked, seemed to hurry them up as they neared the entrance.

Lindstrom kept repeating the words over, and over again. . . .

"Récherche . . . du temps . . . perdu . . ."

Until, finally, his great bushy eyebrows went up, and he grinned—

Rather an inappropriate gesture, McManus thought. Lindstrom turned to McManus, still smiling. "Oh, I understand. Proust. Certainly. I never dallied much with French literature. . . ."

Alright, you historical dolt, well, what about it? McManus wanted to scream.

They were only steps away from the building's entrance.

McManus saw Toland standing sheeplishly inside the entrance, flanked by yet more of New York's finest.

Lindstrom looked over, his smile melting, giving way now to furrowed brows and down-turned lips that made his oversized red beard look positively droopy.

"Yes," Lindstrom said. "I would say that *is* a problem . . . a very large problem."

And having heard Lindstrom's bleak analysis, McManus found himself ushered out of the chronological safety of the Red Building into the crazy revisionist world as created by those ideological lunatics, the Iron Men. . . .

With the first light, the Saigon streets began to fill up. Soon the small Renaults and cyclos were darting around, while peasants hurried on foot to the open-air markets, hoping to get delicacies for the upcoming holiday.

Trinh looked at his watch.

It said Timex, but he thought it was something cheap from Hong Kong. But it worked. He had to be at the hotel in one hour.

Plenty of time, he thought, as he saw the warehouse entrance at the next corner. He pulled up to the door and knocked. Three times. And then twice. And then once.

"Who's there?" Giang called out.

"Ngo Van Trinh."

The door unlocked, and Trinh eased his bicycle into the large room. Giang slammed the door shut behind him.

"You're late," he said.

Trinh nodded. There were other people there, and they had the weapons spread out, rows of rocket launchers, and AK-47s from China, and Russian hand grenades. "There was traffic . . . very early. Because of Tet."

Giang, a gnomelike man who looked very strong, grunted.

"Come," he said, "there's been an important change."

Giang walked over to a desk near the corner. Trinh leaned his bike up against the wall and followed him.

When he reached the desk, he saw Giang had spread a map of Saigon out on the table.

Giang pointed to a black dot near the bottom of the map. "You're not going here anymore," Giang said.

It was the radio station, Trinh saw—the target for Trinh and four others who were to go with him. And he thought he had done something to anger Giang, that now he'd be left behind, perhaps to guard the warehouse, or just to give out the weapons, while everyone else got a taste of the glory.

Giang went on. . . .

"There is something else we need you to do. I want you to go here." He pointed to another dot on Thong Nhat Street. Trinh tried to remember what was there.

Giang looked up at him.

"Do you know what that is?"

Trinh looked, tried to remember. "I—er, it's—"

Giang nodded. "It's the American Embassy, Comrade Trinh. The new embassy . . ."

The embassy. Trinh fought to keep the smile off his face. Why, this was even better than the radio station. The American Embassy. It was almost too incredible to believe. . . .

Giang threw a glassine envelope onto the table.

"Go ahead," Giang said. "look inside."

Trinh was excited, but he felt confused, scared. Why the change in plans? What was he to do, exactly, with the American Embassy? It was a new building, with a big concrete wall. And it was heavily guarded.

He picked up the envelope.

And shook out three photos onto the table.

They were Americans. Dressed in suits. Smiling.

"Do you know who they are?" Giang asked.

Trinh shook his head.

"They are the ambassador—Mr. Ellsworth Bunker, Mr. George Peterson—the attaché for intelligence, and General Cao Ky."

"Ky?"

"Yes. He will be at a party that night . . . to watch the fireworks. The embassy will be heavily guarded, but you and the other squads will be well armed."

Trinh fingered the photos. He looked up at Giang.

"We—we are to assassinate them?"

Giang shook his head.

"Not at all, Trinh. Not at all. In fact, you must keep them alive. . . ."

"My request?" Jim said. "What did I request?"

"Jack, maybe you'd better stop in at the medical tent. You're looking a tad out of focus."

"No. I'm fine. But my request . . . approved . . . what—I don't know what you're talking about."

Burnett shook his head disapprovingly. "I still think you'd better see the doc. . . ."

"What request?" Jim said grabbing Burnett's arm.

"You got your twenty-four hours, Jack. They gave it to you because it was Tet, because of your father. You'll get to see him before he dies."

Jim looked away, waiting for some help, some crumb of information from McShane.

Then he remembered the dream.

The street, the apartment building. The block on the rolling hills of San Francisco. Where McShane was born. And the woman crying, the woman stirring the pot.

His mother.

His father was dying. He knew that now.

So I'm out of here, Jim thought.

For twenty-four hours. Then back again.

Is that what's supposed to happen? Or are things getting all screwed up? Did they plop me in the wrong guy, somebody who can't do diddley to stop the Iron Men from playing with Tet?

"Come on, Jack . . . you've got to check in with the captain. . . ."

Jim nodded, and followed Burnett to the Military Command tent. ''When do I leave?''

''That's the bad news. You leave from Ton Son Nhut at 10:00 hours. Just enough time for you to wash up and get your butt back to Saigon. You've got a military transport direct to Pearl, and then a commercial flight to San Francisco International. . . .''

I'm out of here, Jim thought.

And maybe I'll get real lucky.

And I won't have to come back. . . .

14

Westmoreland sat at a desk inside the Military Assistance Command center at Hue. It was past midnight when he left Saigon, sleeping on a cot in a closet-sized room. He woke up as the sun cut across the narrow streets and the stone buildings of the old capital city.

He opened the report while Kline got him another cup of coffee.

It was, of course, more news from Khe Sanh.

His eyes went immediately to the estimated size of the NVA buildup.

Thirty thousand.

Thirty-thousand NVA Regulars surrounded the northern marine outpost. *Thirty thousand* and even that was considered a conservative estimate. The shelling increased every day, and the soldiers were hunkering down, fortifying their underground bunkers. The airlifts now included not only food and ammunition, but sandbags and two-by-fours. The base commander reported that the "heavy incoming" was incessant.

And Westmoreland was worried.

Not that he wasn't prepared for this. Scorpion had given him the information days earlier. It was turning out *just* as he had said, a major assault on the marine's outpost, the guardian of the south.

But he had to make sure that the marines held on, that Khe Sanh had absolutely everything it needed to hang in there.

Elsewhere, the cease-fire was being observed. It was as if Khe Sanh was the only hot spot exempt from the yearly lull in NVA and VC activity.

And that—according to Scorpion—just wasn't true.

He felt the morning sun, warm on his cheek, making the polished desktop glisten. No, according to Scorpion, by the evening of the thirty-first, *dozens* of cities would be hit. And the small towns—the provincial centers of power—would be attacked by guerillas reinforced by NVA Regulars. Even Hue would be attacked, in a desperate battle to capture this ancient prize, this symbol of ancient Vietnam.

Westmoreland didn't doubt the information.

Everything Scorpion had passed along had come true. And, in a little more than two days, the US forces, with their slowly more-competent allies, the ARVN, would deliver a massive, perhaps decisive, blow to the enemy.

Kline knocked on the door.

"Come in," Westmoreland said, and his corporal brought in a large cup of coffee that sent up a wispy steam in the cool room.

"I also brought a brioche, General . . . thought you might be hungry. . . ."

Westmoreland smiled. In a while, he'd make the rounds in the city, let the men see him. Give his commanders some last minute advice. Make sure that nothing could go wrong.

"General?"

He looked up at Kline as he put down the cup and the delicate roll.

"Yes, Wally?"

"We just got a report in—from the south, sir. It's underneath the status sheet you requested. . . ."

Westmoreland moved the status sheet aside—the up-to-the minute record of how prepared his troops were to stop the upcoming offensive.

And he saw a report, just a few pages.

It came from south of Phu Cuong, in the low-lying

hill area that sprawls down to the Mekong and Great Delta. He looked at the report, recognizing the captain's name. Cool. Not someone he'd want to depend on, Westmoreland thought. More of Saigon warrior than anything else. Liked his time *out* of the bush and back in the city.

He read the report.

A skirmish on a supply trail. A big group of enemy, a good-sized platoon . . . maybe larger.

Now, what the hell are they doing so far south? Westmoreland wondered.

And then he saw something else.

They were NVA Regulars.

Now that was interesting. NVA Regulars . . . moving south.

What on earth for?

He turned and looked up at the wall map of South Vietnam. He saw Bien Hoa. And then, to the right, Phu Cuong.

And below, past the hills and the jungle, sitting on the river, Saigon.

"That's mighty peculiar," Westmoreland said, standing up and walking to the map. "How many enemy?" he asked Kline.

"It was only an estimate, sir. The report, you can see, mentions a platoon. I would guess that the C&S squads must have run into better than a hundred NVA Regulars."

Westmoreland rubbed his cheek. One hundred. He touched the map . . . and then let his finger trail down, towards Saigon.

"I don't like it . . ." he said to himself.

And more than that, he didn't like the fact that Scorpion had told him nothing about it. Was it an insignificant patrol, some NVA troops moving to help the VC squads in the surrounding villages?

Or was it something else?

Something that had to do with Saigon.

And Westmoreland got an uncomfortable feeling in his gut.

He'd finish his tour of Hue. He'd check on the airlifts to Khe Sanh.

But by tomorrow, he was going to be back in Saigon.

"Let me know if anything else strange shows up, eh Wally?"

"Yes, sir. . . ."

And Westmoreland was still looking at the map when the corporal left.

"You can go on board, sir," the crisp-looking sergeant said to Jim.

And Jim smiled and walked past the open gate to the big green military transport. The plane sat on the runway, its belly open and with stairs leading up to a passenger section.

Jim felt strange. He had on a crisp shirt and pressed pants. His face was shaved, and scrubbed clean of the grit and dirt from only hours ago. The battle, and their rescue, seemed like a lifetime ago. He carried a small duffle bag, with just a change of shirt and pants, some underwear, his razor . . . a toothbrush. He found where McShane kept his money, buried at the bottom of his footlocker under an issue of *Playboy.*

When he had come out of the shower, his body superheated, steaming, from the near scalding water, he dug out the money. And he leafed through the issue of *Playboy,* stopping at a pictorial.

The Girls of James Bond.

He looked at them, their flat stomachs, their breasts that defied gravity. Their vapid, all-American smiles.

There was nothing erotic about them, he thought.

At least not this morning.

He flipped to the jokes.

He read one about a dentist using laughing gas and filling the wrong hole.

Ha, ha.

Nothing very funny about the joke.

He took the money, threw it on his cot. He put McShane's copy of *Playboy* back.

He might need it later, Jim thought. If he has to come back here.

(Hoping, praying, he thought, that it won't be *me* that comes back. How do men survive, how can they last?)

But he knew the answer to that one.

It was just something that he had missed.

You get here, and you give it up. You say—that's it, it's *all fucking over, baby.* Life—as I knew it—is gone, finito. Now, I can just cruise along and see just how far I can go before someone nails my ass.

And with that kind of attitude, hell, every day comes on its own terms. Play it as it lays. In a way, you don't have to be crazy to work here—but it sure helps.

Because only crazy people could do this.

Five hundred thousand crazy people. All wishing they could go home, to the world of *Playboy*s. And jokes. And vapid smiles.

Not knowing that some of them would never really leave Vietnam.

Even if they did get back to the states.

It was the war that the country wanted to forget.

Unfortunately, they forgot its warriors, too.

Another soldier stood at the stairway leading up to the passenger compartment of the transport. "Good morning, sir."

Jim nodded and walked up the stairs.

He looked around. His last look at Vietnam? he wondered.

It was a clear morning, a crisp, blue sky, a bit of a chill in the air, and only a few wispy clouds dancing just below the sun.

Jim walked up the stairs, feeling with each step—

I'm losing it. . . .

If you guys at the Time Lab pick up anything from me, get this. . . .

I need out.

I can't do this.

I'm just a fucking grad student, for Christ's sake.

He reached the top of the stairs and walked in.

The transport was filled. There were soldiers laughing, happy, talking loudly. One guy had a radio on.

The Saigon station was playing The Beatles.

Can you believe it? Jim thought, working his way down the aisle to his seat. Can you believe it?

You say hello . . . and I say goodbye. Hello . . . goodbye.

Pretty profound lyrics. Nothing like LSD to improve one's poetic gifts. And Jim remembered that *Magical Mystery Tour* had just come out . . . accompanied by the self-indulgent home movie of the same name.

He remembered how this all started. My thesis on The Beatles. I was going to do some first-hand research, thanks to the good old boys in the Red Building with their handy-dandy time machine.

Jim found an empty seat next to a marine who sat on an aisle seat, his legs sprawled out. The leatherneck kept his eyes fixed on the aisle, the front of the plane, anywhere but out the window. Probably saw enough of this beautiful country. "Excuse me," Jim said, taking the window seat.

He put his small bag under his seat. The seats were narrow, but not too uncomfortable.

There would be no stewardesses this flight, he knew. Another song came on the radio. An organ playing a dirge. A raspy voice wailed out the obscure words. . . .

"We skip a life and dangle . . . turn cartwheels on the floor . . . the band refused to play while the crowd cried out for more. . . ."

Heavy, Jim thought sardonically. Too fucking profound for me. He looked out the window. And he saw a forklift move to the plane, to the open cargo section. The forklift was filled with coffins, stacked on a wide pallet.

Coffins, three high.

Each one was covered with an American flag, covered perfectly, covering the coffins as if they were a product with uniform packaging, being shipped back to the folks at home.

Be the first one on your block to have your boy come home in a box.

He twisted in his seat and watched the forklift pull right up to the green transport's open belly. He heard the whirr of its motor as it raised up the pallet and then pushed the colorful coffins into the belly of the plane.

No one else was looking.

"A Whiter Shade of Pale"—Jim remembered the song—was still playing. He felt the thud as the pallet was lowered, and then he watched the forklift back away from he plane, its dirty work done. The belly shut with a grinding of gears and the scream of unoiled hinges. Then the engines started, the propjet mixing the old-fashioned sputtering of propellers with the whine of the jet engines.

He sat back in his seat as the plane moved towards crisp, brilliant flags covering them. And he thought of the line from the song. . . .

The crowd called out for more. . . .

How many more? Jim wondered. How. Many. More. And what the hell am I supposed to do to stop it?

Ali paused by General Chau's quarters. She looked at the stern-faced guards who stood at his door.

"Is General Chau up yet? I would like—"

The guard nodded. "He was up before dawn. He is leaving for the North."

Leaving, Ali thought. How could she get permission to go with her family if he's gone?

(And that *is* what I'm supposed to do, isn't it? If I don't go south I'll never see Jim, never get a chance to help him—)

This is crazy, she thought. I'm like a blind person groping around in someone else's house.

"He's left already?" she said.

The guard shook his head.

"No. He is leaving by river launch. But he will be gone soon. . . ."

"Thank you,' Ali said. The soldiers knew who she was, knew that she was a special person favored by Chau.

His concubine.

And she turned. Where was the river? But then, through tiny racks in the leafy green wall, she saw tiny golden shimmers, the sun reflecting off the water. And she ran.

She found a winding trail that led past the thatch-covered barracks. Soldiers stood outside and watched her run down the hill. She heard the motor of the launch, rumbling, idling.

It's going to leave, she thought. It will leave and I'll be stuck here, trapped here.

She yelled, hoping that they'd hear her down there.

The boat's motor was louder. Perhaps it already left.

She wasn't paying attention and she tripped over the exposed root of leafy acacia tree. She felt a thorn dig into her ankle.

"Ow, damn!" she said. Then she gasped. She had said it in English.

She turned to see whether anyone had heard her.

And there was a soldier standing against a tree, watching, his face impassive.

But she just struggled to her feet and started running again.

The jungle opened up and she saw the dock, a sturdy wooden dock that stretched nearly to the middle of the river. Chau's launch was a substantial vessel, with a large prow and two machine guns, fore and aft. It looked fast, and the guns looked powerful.

Chau was nodding to someone, and then he turned, about to step onto the gangplank leading to the ship.

"General Chau!" she yelled.

And everyone at the dock turned. Now Ali came to some wooden steps carved into the hill, steps that cantilevered in and out, more treacherous than just a long, steady slope down the hill to the water.

She ran full out.

Even though she could see that Chau looked angry.

The other North Vietnamese officers looked at each other, embarrassed.

This is probably a real bad thing to be doing, she thought.

Chau puckered his lips, and his eyes narrowed as she reached the wood of the dock and she ran up to him.

"General," she said breathlessly . . .

She was aware of everyone watching her.

The general's mistress. Merely his plaything.

Making a scene. Embarrassing him.

"I needed to ask you—" Ali hurried on.

"I am leaving," Chau said. "We can talk—when I return—"

Ali reached out a hand, but she dared not touch him. "I needed to ask you . . . My grandmother, my family . . . we wanted to visit our cousin near Kontum . . . for Tet Mau Than. We need—"

Chau shook his head. Ali knew he was about to say "no."

Unless she could do something to turn that decision around.

"Please," she wailed, "please, my general. My grandmother is an old woman, and without your help, she'll never see—"

Now the other soldiers shifted on their feet. They stepped back from the embarrassing scene. She saw that Chau was even angrier. His knuckles were white and bony. Then he spat out an answer. . . .

"You should have told me this before." He raised a hand. "This Tet will be a dangerous time to be traveling. You shouldn't—"

Ali took a chance and reached out and touched Chau's arm. "Please . . ." she groveled. "She is an old woman. . . ."

And Chau nodded. The launch sounded eager to be away.

"Very well," Chau spat out the words. "Talk to Captain Hien. He will tell you how to go . . . where to travel." Chau turned and walked onto the boat. "Just do not travel on the night of Tet, eh?"

Chau was on board and the soldiers pulled the gangplank away. "And go today. As soon as you can." Now a bit of a smile played on Chau's face. "In a week, everything will be different. . . ."

He said this loudly, as if it was for the benefit of the other officers on board the launch. She saw him nod to the captain. The lines were undone, and the launch roared away. Ali stood there, waving at Chau.

Waving at the man from the future.

And she had a thought.

Maybe I should have killed him last night.

When I was with him.

But no . . . then she wouldn't have a chance of getting away.

That was the important thing . . . no matter what Chau was up to.

And she turned back to the log stairs leading up the hill and back to the camp.

15

Amazingly, the high-tech cops escorted Lindstrom to his office in the History Department and then turned to leave. Lindstrom stood there, watching as they led McManus and the rest away. Perhaps they think a lowly historian isn't worth the trouble, Lindstrom thought.

"Er, excuse me," he said to the broad blue backs of the police.

They stopped and looked back at him.

"Perhaps my friends might wish to stay here—and help me write our application to the Metropolitan—the Metropolitan—"

Damn, he thought what the hell is the name of that stupid bureaucracy that has the city by the *short hairs?*

"The Metropolitan Security Commission." One of the cops offered.

"Yes, I mean as long as they're here and everything . . ."

One of Lindstrom's peers, a squat little gnome of a man whose field was the Mediaeval Europe, bustled by Lindstrom without so much as a nod of the head.

Hmm, Lindstrom thought, now that's odd. Old Fennel never was the most outgoing of fellows, but he was not, per se, rude. But then there's likely to be a lot of odd things out here.

The two cops looked at each other—at least, it seemed as though they were looking at each other.

Their metallic visors gave no clue as to what their eyes were really doing.

Finally, one turned. "That would be acceptable. As long as your entire team, Dr. Lindstrom—"

Lindstrom saw McManus wince at that usurpation. . . .

"—understands that the Red Building is off-grounds until further notice."

Lindstrom smiled, as broad and warmly as he could manage.

"Gotcha, gentlemen," he said walking up to McManus, Beck, and Jacob, who looked like renegades from some highly experimental, and dangerous, lab.

Lindstrom escorted McManus and the rest to his office door. For the first time, he noticed the black stencilled letters on his door. They read: Dr. Peter Lindstrom, Assistant Chairman, History.

He dug out his key ring and tried the lock, hoping that his pre-change key still worked. The police stood there, studying him. "Yes," he said, sotto voice, "We'll draft an immediate proposal to the Metropolitan whatever, and—" The lock clicked open.

Lindstrom turned the knob, and ushered the scientists in. He smiled and turned to the police.

"Good day, gentlemen," he said and he entered his office.

Hoping that he wouldn't be disappointed by what he'd find there.

After all, he thought, the future of the world hangs on the next few minutes. . . .

Trinh reached up to pull down a stack of gleaming white plates. The breakfast service was nearly done and it was time to prepare the tables for lunch.

And he felt the mamasan, Madame Thuy Au, watching him, her beady-black eyes like the eyes of vipers, bulletlike, burning into his back.

Trinh fought to keep from cursing the horrible woman.

He wished that he had been allowed to quit. Why did he need to show up at this stupid job? he thought. In days, it would be all over, All over, and there would be no more serving meals to the pig fascists who sit at the tables covered with white linen.

But Giang said the instructions were quite clear. Nothing is to be different, nothing is to change, until the moment it all begins.

There should be no clues, no alert.

That was part of the plan.

"Careful, you stupid man. Careful with those dishes."

The mamasan's voice shrieked in his ears.

I'd love to just throw the dishes down on top of here, let them smash into her head.

Instead, Trinh tightened his grip around the plates, and stretched a bit more, making sure of his grip.

When he felt something move, something slip from his pants.

From the back pocket.

He felt it move, and then he heard it flutter to the ground and land with an obvious smack, right at the feet of Madame Thuy An.

He turned, still struggling to hold the plates.

He saw the envelope with the photos. He watched her pick it up.

He hurried to step down the ladder. He felt warm, almost feverish in this back storage room. He smelled the overpowering scent of Madame An's perfume, a foul, sickly sweet smell.

"Ey?" she said. "And what are these? What do you have here?"

Step, step, step, he went as fast as he could, the dishes feeling like they were ready to slide out of his suddenly very-sweaty hand.

"They are nothing," he said, loudly, trying to keep

the panic out of his voice. "They are nothing but some photographs."

She stared at the park of photos. He watched her dig a long, perfectly manicured thumbnail into the envelope, edging the photos out of the envelope.

And Trinh yelled at her, *yelled* at the mamasan, something that was unheard of. He heard his voice, suddenly full and strong, filling the cramped storeroom, echoing off the walls, bouncing off the puckered and splintery ceiling.

"No!" he yelled again.

Her nails were making it difficult to get the photos out. But she had edged the tightly fit stack out a centimeter or so. Trinh looked frantically left and right, looking for some place to put down his stack of dishes.

He saw a small table and the tray filled with cutlery. He put the stack down on top of the tray and then, just as Madame Thuy had one photo nearly halfway out, he snatched the pack from her.

She was giggling, then laughing. He didn't think he'd ever seen her smile, let alone laugh. "Pictures of your girlfriend?" she laughed. She looked at the packet in his hand while he forced the photos back into the packet. "Or perhaps—your boyfriend." Her smile evaporated. "I wouldn't be surprised. Now hurry, and get those tables ready."

He stood there, watching her, still breathing hard, remembering how scared he was, how his voice sounded when he yelled at her.

He watched her, and she shook her head and walked out.

And Trinh looked down at the photos. She didn't see anything, he thought. She didn't see the picture of the white-haired ambassador and General Ky.

I'm safe, he thought.

He took breath, and then he stuck the photos into his front pocket, a deeper pocket.

She didn't see anything, he thought.

Because if she did, he thought—if she did, I'd have to kill her. . . .

Jim fell asleep, a dreamless sleep this time. And when he woke up, the plane was emptying.

He turned and looked out the window.

It was an airport and the soldiers were streaming off the plane. He rubbed his eyes and grabbed his small duffle bag. He followed the soldiers off the plane, he saw that most of them streamed back to a building off to the left.

R&R in Hawaii, Jim thought. Not a bad deal.

But damn, it had to be damned hard to go back, to get back on a plane and go back to Vietnam.

He stepped down the ramp.

A sergeant waited there and spoke to him.

"The plane to San Francisco is boarding in Gate #3, Lieutenant. In the main terminal . . ." Jim nodded, and followed the other soldiers into the building.

Into the real world.

Or as real as 1968 could ever seem to him.

He walked into the building and he was assaulted by the colors. Everyone wore brilliant shirts with swirling floral patterns, as if they had to yell, scream, *I've been to Hawaii!* A few even wore plastic leis. They wobbled around, men and woman, their faces beet red from too much sun, the proud badge of a dream vacation.

He saw souvenir shops with Hawaii ashtrays in the shapes of volcanos, and endless native girls in mid bump and grind doing the hula.

Jim licked his lips. I'm thirsty, he thought. And hungry. He smelled some food, hot pretzels and hot dogs sold from a red-striped push cart.

Better find my gate, he thought. He looked up at the sign and discovered that Gate 3 was to the left.

Jim walked towards that end of the terminal. He felt people looking at him. It's the uniform, he knew. They're looking at me because I'm a soldier.

Not a good thing to be circa 1968.

Fighting the war that nobody wanted.

Certainly not the grunts in the field.

He saw a crowd ahead, checking into the TWA desk.

He read the plastic letters that said "San Francisco." And Jim joined the line of happy vacationers. He saw some turn away, embarrassed at their goofy garb now that someone from a grimmer resort just showed up.

And while Jim stood there, inching forward, he wondered . . . What am I going to do in San Francisco? Go to my parent's house—McShane's parents? See them, see my dying father?

And then come back?

Is that all? Is that what's supposed to happen?

While the Great Tet Offensive is starting, is this where I'm supposed to be? Or is something very wrong?

He moved up to the desk. An attractive woman with a beehive hairdo smiled at him with dark-red lips. "Good morning, sir," she said. "Flying home?" she asked cheerily.

Jim nodded, then, thinking it impolite, he said, "Yes."

"Good, well," she said, passing him back his ticket. "Have a wonderful flight."

He took his ticket and headed to the plane that would take him to a world that just might be even stranger than the jungles of Vietnam.

"Now, what are we going to do?" McManus said, bursting into Lindstrom's cramped office.

McManus looked around—holding his breath. The office looked even more cramped than normal, filled with papers, and books, and—he finally breathed—a computer.

"Thank heavens!" McManus said, hurrying over to the computer.

"Dr. McManus," Dr. Beck said. "Please, you'll get yourself too excited and—"

"Too excited?" he said, a crazed look in his eyes. "Dr. Beck, do you realize that we have been booted out of the Time Lab? That now we have *no* way of knowing what in the world is going on back in 1968? And—" he said turning away, looking disturbed by the thought—"that now we have no idea of what is real history?"

"Not quite, Elliot," Lindstrom said. The historian had walked over and turned the computer on and was looming at the screen. "Not quite—"

"What do you mean, Lindstrom?. There is no way we can tell what's real or not anymore. Let's face it, the Iron Men have won. They can do whatever they'd like with the story."

"Not . . . quite. . . ." Lindstrom said.

Dr. Beck came close to the screen now, and even Dr. Jacob who seemed lost without the massive wall of controls to his tachyon generator.

The screen flashed on. "Great," Lindstrom said. "It's working. Now, let me see if—"

"What good is this?" McManus said. "We're *outside,*" Lindstrom. Everything here is bogus. Lord knows what we've already started accepting as fact. It's all hopeless."

Lindstrom hit another key and the screen flashed.

"Current historical data—on line. Good," he murmured to his machine. "Now, cross your fingers, and we'll see whether this worked or not."

He hit another key.

Another message came on.

"Time Lab Historical Data Retrieval—On Line."

"What?" McManus sputtered.

"And now," Lindstrom said gleefully, "just one second. . . ."

Lindstrom hit the enter key with all the grace of a concert pianist finishing a Mozart concerto.

And the screen gave out a reassuring message, which

Lindstrom read aloud for the benefit of Dr. Jacob and Dr. Beck, who couldn't squeeze in close enough for a good look at the screen.

"Dichotomies and Variations from true history—ready to print. Ready to print!" Lindstrom shouted standing up and patting the frail McManus on the back. "We're back in business, gentlemen, er, and Dr. Beck."

McManus watched the list of items being scrolled through on the screen. Lindstrom turned on his office scan printer and in a moment he had a copy of the list.

McManus kept on reading, shaking his head. "What? There's no EurAsia?" He turned to Lindstrom. "That's not—er—real? And the USSLA—that's not a real thing, either."

Lindstrom smiled. "I guess not, my friend. Think about it. . . . You know about the Time Lab, right, and what we were trying to do?"

Mcmanus's eyes took a fuzzy, unfocussed look. "Yes. I mean, we were trying to stop the Iron Men, who were . . ."

"Yes?" Lindstrom prompted.

"Who were—well, for the life of me, I can't recall what they were doing. Something about changing history. But in what way, or why—well, I just don't—"

"Precisely," Lindstrom laughed. "You see, once we're out of the Time Lab we—our memories, our own personal history—everything is absorbed into the new time continuum. There is no past as it really was."

McManus nodded.

And then he looked down at the computer screen. "Then, what about this—this computer. How can it tell us what should be, and what shouldn't?"

Lindstrom raised a finger in the air. "I thought ahead. I could see that the police, or whoever they are, weren't about to let us stay much longer. So, I arranged for a line to be run from the Time Lab's computer out to my office. I'm using the Communication Syndicate's fiber lines, so we're not free from being discovered. But there wasn't any time to do anything else. And hopefully, by the time they discover what we've done, we'll be ready for the next step. . . ."

"I don't understand. . . . You mean, Lindstrom, this computer is in contact with the Time Lab's computer?"

"Precisely, and as such it's shielded, protected from the ongoing revisions of the Iron Men, and of course Scorpion."

"Scorpion? What's Scorpion?"

"Their operative, Elliot. Not that I could personally recollect that information. My memories are as completely addled as yours. But the computer here has been keeping tabs on Scorpion and what he's up to."

Dr. Beck came close.

"And what of Jim Tiber, and Alessandra . . . do you know how they are doing?" Dr. Beck asked.

Lindstrom shook his head. "Only physically. . . . I made sure that your monitors were connected to the main program in the computer. So if I just—"

Lindstrom hit a button.

"There. You see that everything looks—" Lindstrom leaned closer to the screen—"okay. Jim and Ali are both fine. For now."

"For now?" McManus said.

Lindstrom scratched his beard. "Yes . . . I'm afraid that the hard part of their assignment is coming up. Not that I remember it. But I just skimmed through the stuff here. It's going to be dangerous. And I just 'learned' something else."

McManus still looked dubious. "And just what is that?"

"I mean, I must have known it—we must have known it—back in the Time Lab. It's just a bit of a shock to, say, rediscover it."

"Yes." McManus said.

"It appears," Lindstrom said, "that one of us will have to go back there to help them. The last part of the plan we concocted, apparently."

"Back there . . . back to 1968?"

Lindstrom nodded.

"And to do that," he said, "we're going to have to get back inside the Time Lab within the next twenty-four hours. . . ."

McManus nudged Lindstrom's elbow. "And just how are we going to do that?"

Lindstrom laughed and shook his head.

"I haven't a clue, McManus . . . how about you?"

16

Ali stood outside General Chau's small command hut, awaiting an audience with Captain Hien. Khan Ha's grandmother, a bone-thin crone, was always at her elbow, jabbing at her, hissing like a snake.

"You should have arranged all this . . . before your general left. Now, we may never get to leave!"

Ali, who wanted nothing more than to pick up the old lady in black pajamas and rubber tire sandals and toss her into the nearby river, just smiled.

As she imagined the dutiful granddaughter should do.

They had been waiting for a long time when the door to Chau's hut flew open, violently, and a guard said that she could go in. Ali heard laughter inside, the sound of men laughing deep and ominous. As she stepped past the guard, she smelled smoke. Normal Vietnamese Grade-D cigarettes? She wondered. Or were they indulging in a bit of the local strain of wacky weed?

When she entered—bowing her head—Captain Hien waved the other soldiers away.

Ali had felt that—as Chau's concubine—she would be safe, even surrounded by a whole battalion of horny soldiers. But with Chau gone, now that she was alone, she was beginning to have her doubts.

Hien sat on a wooden chair, his boots up on a desk.

And though it was early afternoon, he had a tumbler out and a bottle of Russian vodka.

A bit of Stoli to celebrate the upcoming Year of the Monkey.

"Yes, Khan Ha?" he said, making no attempt to hide his scrutiny of her. Ali bowed again, a natural impulse, she reasoned, that must be imprinted in Khan Ha. You breathe, you bow. Simple as that.

"General Chau said you would help arrange our passage. My grandmother wants to go south for the Tet, and—"

Hien laughed. He took his boots off the table and poured himself another tumbler full of vodka, not seeming to care as some dribbled over the side onto the table.

"Oh, he did, did he? You know the south isn't a very safe place to be going? He told you that, didn't he?"

Ali nodded. "Yes, but my grandmother is very old, This may be her last chance to see her relatives in the south."

Hien shook his head. "It is too dangerous. You should stay here. With us. Until it's all over . . ." He pulled another glass out from the desk drawer, a filmy tumbler. "Some vodka, Khan Ha?"

Ali shook her head. Too quickly? she feared. What if I offended him? Then I'll be stuck here . . . and whatever purpose I'm supposed to serve would be nullified.

She also had another worry.

Hien didn't like Chau. That was clear.

But that might even be useful.

"The general said that you are to help us," Ali said, raising her voice a bit. "He has given his permission for us to go. . . ."

Hien nodded.

"You should stay here," he repeated. The captain rubbed his cheek and finished his drink.

"Perhaps. But I am leaving with my grandmother."

Hien kept watching her and Ali knew that he'd love to jump her bones, a prospect that made her feel bilious.

"Then go. . . ." he said, sniffing at the air, sensing the force of her words.

"We need help. General Chau said you could help. There are areas we should avoid. We need help getting to the border."

"He should have told me himself. . . ." Hien muttered. But then he stood up and went to a giant teak cabinet. He made a small belching noise.

I hope that he doesn't pass gas the other way, Ali thought. This is a small room, and she already smelled the captain's sweaty body. She watched him open a drawer and pull out a stack of oversized charts.

He threw them down on the table.

"Now then," he said. "Just where are you going?"

"Kontum," Ali said, repeating the name told her by the old woman. Kontum, and then onto Cambodia for her family . . . while she went on to Saigon.

To find Jim . . . if he's where Lindstrom said he would be. . . .

Hien arched his eyebrows. "That far south. You will be—" he laughed here, a sound that scared Ali. "You will have a long, tiresome journey." Hien shuffled through the stack of maps until he came to one labelled Kontum province.

"You should stay to the west," he said. "Travelling along here. . . ." He pointed to a road leading through mountains and heavy jungle. "Kontum will not be attacked." Again, Hien laughs. "At least, I have not been told it will be attacked. There are many loyal comrades there." More laughing, punctuated by a belch.

Hien sat down again.

Fine, thought Ali. But Lindstrom said that Saigon was the key. Everything he was getting indicated that the problem had to be in Saigon.

She had to find out what was planned there. She fingered the stack of maps.

"Can we—" she stared to say . . .

"What are you doing?" Hien barked. Then, with his eyes glassy and distant from the alcohol, he smiled dopily. "Those are secret. Very secret. Special plans created by your . . . general."

"Yes," Ali smiled.

Now came the hard part. She had to be nice to this creep. Nice, so that he'd let her nose through the maps, and see what Uncle Ho had planned for the holiday season.

"I appreciate your help, Captain," Ali smiled, trying to radiate some warmth to penetrate Hien's alcoholic haze. He looked up, responding to the sweetness in her voice. "I will tell General Chau how you helped us. He has told me much about all these plans . . . about your great help. . . ."

More interest ignited behind Hien's eyes.

"He said that the plans for the capital were inspired by you. . . ."

She was close to him, close enough so that she could reach out and touch his shoulder. A dangerous gesture, she guessed, but—unfortunately—necessary to manipulate Hien the way she wanted.

She touched his shoulder. He looked up at her, smiling, and then licking his lips.

"Oh, he did . . . I don't recall my saying much at all."

Ali pulled her hand back as if she had touched a stove.

"Oh, but the general said you did. . . ."

Now Hien stood up again and came over to the maps, pawing through the pile. "There have been so many crazy schemes," Hien said. "Changes from the plan. Khe Sanh abandoned, Hue only encircled. And then—" He pulled out a map.

Saigon, Ali thought.

She studied the map as Hien babbled on.

"I could see attacking the city, attempting to take it. But this—" Hien jabbed a finger down on the map. "I—I don't understand."

Ali looked at where Hien was pointing.

She read the street names. Hong Tap Tu Street. Thong Nhat Avenue.

She saw a building. It was circled. A red line led away from it, to the distant corners of the city.

"What is that place?" she asked, hoping the question sounded casual, almost disinterested.

Hien turned, as if suddenly aware of the impropriety of this whole thing. "He didn't tell you about this?" Hien laughed. "I thought you knew . . . I thought he told you about his plans . . . I thought—"

Ali stepped back, bowing again. "Yes, Captain. He said that there would be a great battle in Saigon. And that you inspired him—that's what he said—inspired him for the great part of his plan."

Hien shook his head.

"Inspired him?" Hien looked back at the map. "To do what? This crazy plan of his?" The captain jabbed a meaty finger on the map, right on the building. "I don't understand this . . ." Hien said.

Come on, Ali thought. You've had enough booze. Let it spill out. You'll feel better.

(And she had a thought then. An idea. It wasn't something she and Lindstrom talked about. But it made sense. She flashed on a way to make life a bit difficult for Chau . . . a.k.a. Scorpion. . . .)

"Why take the embassy?" Hien asked. "If you can't take the city, why take the embassy?"

So that's it, Ali thought. It's just the attack on the American Embassy—the attack that failed. But that's not a change, that's the way things really happened. The walls of the brand new American Embassy were breached and, according to Lindstrom, they were secured with just the normal MP guards on duty. It scared everyone, but nothing happened . . . not really.

Hien licked at his lips as if he tasted something bitter.

Then he turned and looked at Ali. "He is taking hostages . . . *hostages!* Is that how wars of liberation are to be fought? With hostages?"

Hien walked back to his chair, while Ali studied the map, the red lines streaming through the streets of Saigon, converging on the embassy.

So that's what it is.

The Iron Men were using that well-honed technique of the late-twentieth century.

Hostages.

Then she had a strange thought.

Why? Why take the hostages?

Sooner or later, they'll have to be let go. Let go . . . or killed.

There's no way that the VC, even reinforced with NVA regulars, could take and hold the city, let alone the embassy.

What the hell good would hostages do?

She shook her head. She could try to figure that out later. For now, she knew what she'd have to do.

She had an appointment in Saigon.

With Jim Tiber.

Though he doesn't even know it.

And god—she thought—I hope he's there.

Ali backed up to the door. And she spoke again, removing the sweetness from her voice.

"You can help us get to Kontum?"

"Eh," Hien said. Then, "Yes. But you should get going soon. I will arrange for a truck to take you into Quang Tri. From there, you can travel south."

Ali nodded. She reached for the doorknob.

"General Chau said that even the Americans admired the plans. . . ."

Hien nodded. "He feeds them lies and tricks that they swallow greedily. . . ."

Standing at the door, Ali let her face fall. "But that's what confuses me. . . ."

Hien looked up.

Ali continued. . . ." He told me that the American general laughed when he heard about the attack on the embassy."

"What?" Hien said.

"He told me that when the battles are over he will have great power in Hanoi, that he will remember *your* part in the—he used this word—fiasco."

Hien walked up to her.

"You say he told the Americans about Saigon . . . about the embassy. . . ?"

Now Ali turned away. "I thought you knew. I thought you were part of his plans. To end this war, to give our country a new ruler. . . ."

"Of course . . ." Hien spat. "Yes."

She watched Hien's face cloud over as he considered the various possibilities . . . considered whether she was merely mixed-up . . . that Chau had merely fed the Americans more false information . . .

But then—like an eagle zeroing in on a panic-stricken field mouse scurrying through the grass—Hien's face became set.

He bought it.

Now, she thought, he suspects Chau of selling out the north for his own personal political gain.

And—if all goes well—Scorpion will find that he's not the only one who can do tricks with history.

I'm pretty experienced myself, Ali thought.

And she let herself out the door, leaving the captain to his wild and bemused thoughts. . . .

Somewhere along the way it occurred to Jim that he had entered the world of the Sixties and—so far—it wasn't what he expected.

In fact, outside of the hairdos and the proliferation of polyester and leisure suits, it would be hard to tell what year he was in.

He had expected to see hippies, but the TWA flight to San Francisco seemed to be carrying nothing but refugees from the sunny world of sitcoms. These were people out of *Leave it to Beaver* and *The Dick Van Dyke Show* on vacation. And the cultural revolution—like the war—was happening someplace else.

Only when he entered the San Francisco International Airport did he begin to see signs of the Age of Aquarius.

First, there were bell-bottoms—long-haired boys and girls with razor-straight hair, wearing floppy sailor-style jeans emblazoned with patches. Some wore backpacks as if they were catching the next flight to Yellowstone. He guessed most were heading back to college for the spring semester.

And boy, was this a great year for college!

He also watched some followers of Krishna handing out pamphlets and selling incense. Beefy airport security cops prowled the large airport, hustling the unwanted proselytizers out of the terminal.

For a few seconds, Jim just stood there in the fluorescent glare of the lights, as weary travelers made their way to the parking lot, the Hertz and Avis mannikins, or the cabs and busses outside.

I'm going home, Jim thought, feeling weird and awkward holding his too-light bag.

It was late. Near twelve.

He'd have to wake his parents up.

McShane's parents.

And then talk to them.

How am I going to do that? he wondered. I can't pretend to be their son, to immediately fall into those crazy patterns that families have, the memories, the guilt, the jokes, the pain, the hundreds of disappointments.

I couldn't hack that with my own family.

And now I have someone else's to deal with. . . .

He saw the large clock overhead creep past twelve.

I have less than twenty-four hours before I go back, he thought. And I still don't know what I'm supposed to do. Perhaps I should hit Chinatown and buy some fortune cookies. Maybe visit a palm reader.

He saw a kid walk past him. Long hair, straggly, unkempt. Ripped jeans. A leather vest. He wore a broad-brimmed hat with a feather and a peace button.

Right, thought Jim. Check back in a few years when you exchange your peace button for the Mercedes Benz symbol.

Jim stared and the kid turned and stared back. Then he gave Jim the finger, laughed, and turned away.

I'm the bad guy . . . Jim thought. The government sends my ass to Vietnam, and *I'm* the fucking bad guy.

He felt like taking the kid and beating the—

Whoa! What the hell is wrong with me? I'm thinking like I'm the vet, that this is my war.

I'm losing it, he thought. I knew it would happen. Total schizophrenia. Complete absorption of my personality into McShane's.

Jim shook his head. He saw the door leading out to the outside. He saw cabs lined up, the drivers standing outside, bored, waiting for a big fare.

That's me, Jim thought. A big fare. . . .

He walked out the door, pushing the archaic spinning doors open, and he approached the first cab he saw. . . .

"Thanks," Jim said, getting out and handing the driver twenty dollars for what Jim suspected was a rip-off.

He got out and, as the cab squealed away like some night creature with a fresh kill, Jim looked at the apartment building.

It was the same building, he knew. The same one from the dream.

He looked around at the dark block, lit by ordinary street lamps before the arrival of the ultra-high wattage tungsten lamps that turned night into day. He saw other buildings, the small grocery store, a few cars, sleek, finless monsters that guzzled gas with wild abandon.

He shifted his small bag from one hand to the other.

He heard a cat meow down the block. The house was on a hill. He saw the bay in the distance, the blinking lights on the water. And there, down the other way, he saw the park.

(Golden Gate Park, he thought. Dad took me there, to the Morrison Planetarium. We played horseshoes on the courts there. And sometimes he took me to Fisherman's Wharf for oysters. Or Ghiradelli's for fresh chocolate, the smell overwhelming, intoxicating, wonderful. And he'd take me to the Presidio on Veteran's Day, because that's what we did, and that's why—)

No . . . not my dad. Not *my* dad. . . .

Jim started up the steps. He reached the door. He heard sounds in the hallway, though it was near one a.m. TV. Some voices. The lingering smell of a thousand meals, absorbed into the very plaster and wood of the apartment.

I grew up here, Jim thought, his hand shaking as he grabbed the smooth handrail.

I grew up here. Between the boredom and the chowder. I've dashed up these stairs hundreds of times. No, more times than that. My feet knew every step, every curved depression.

Jim found that he was walking up. One flight. Turning. Then up the next.

Until he stood at the door to the apartment. Three-A.

There was a buzzer, but it didn't work. He knew that. Never worked. Not as long as he knew.

He knocked. Gently at first, almost a tap. Then harder. Once. Twice. He heard steps from inside. And someone muttering. And—the safety chain in place—the door creaked open. . . .

17

Lindstrom watched McManus scroll through the computer screen, shaking his head one moment and shrugging the next.

"I'm afraid that most of this doesn't mean very much to me, except, of course, the most egregious changes." McManus looked back at the screen. "I'm afraid I haven't really kept up with current events. It all seems correct—"

Lindstrom went over and clapped him on the back. "That's exactly my point, McManus. *Exactly.* If we just relied on our memories, why, this would look just fine. I mean, I remember voting for the maniac that proposed the Metropolitan Security Council. But the thing is—" and here Lindstrom leaned close to the physicist's ear—"it never happened. None of it."

"Well," McManus said sadly, "I can see that this computer is our only link to sanity. And—"

Dr. Beck—standing near the door to Lindstrom's tiny office—went "shoosh!"

She held up a finger in a schoolmarmish kind of way.

Lindstrom turned away from the befuddled McManus and cocked an ear. He didn't imagine they'd leave them alone for too long. Just as soon as the bureaucracy creaked itself to further action, he was sure they'd be banished from the campus until "further investigations". . . .

Which meant that they didn't have very much time.

No, he thought . . . I don't have much time.

"So, what do we—" McManus went on, lost to the monitor.

Lindstrom tapped his shoulder and gestured at Beck, who stood at the door, rigid with fright.

Now they could all hear the footsteps. Walking down the hallway. Boots, Lindstrom guessed, the preferred footwear of fascists the world over. And that's what these goons were, this whole Metropolitan Security nonsense. Emergency laws—born of fear—signed away rights in exchange for some elusive hope of safety and, yes, security.

Instead, as in *A Clockwork Orange*, the thugs get to wear the uniforms.

The footsteps came closer.

Dr. Jacob sat on a small settee overloaded with Lindstrom's dozens of reviewers' copies. He had the blank, wide-eyed stare of a rabbit feeling the cool flap of a predator's wings just over his shoulder. . . .

Lindstrom was sure that the steps were slowing.

Damn, he thought, they're coming here! If that happens, then it's all over. There will be no hope, nothing to be done. And Jim and Ali were probably better off stranded in the past.

The steps were just there, just outside the door.

Dr. Jacob made a small mumbling sound. Lindstrom looked over at him. The poor bastard is petrified.

Beck stood at the door, Charlotte Corday at the ramparts, ready to cut the throat of any royalist who dared to interrupt their plotting.

Lindstrom listened.

But then the footsteps kept moving.

And everyone waited until they heard nothing.

"Whew," Lindstrom said. "That was mighty close."

"Now," McManus said, not missing a beat, picking up the thread of their discussion, "the way I see it,

Jim Tiber and Alessandra won't be able to change things on their own, even if they succeed with their various difficult and unlikely escapades."

"Yes," Lindstrom agreed. "I figured that out back in the Time Lab."

"So, then—we must send someone back to help them . . . especially on the night of . . ." McManus peered at the screen . . . "the thirty-first. This embassy business. That seems to be the key."

"Exactly."

McManus turned and faced Lindstrom. "And it's also clear that we have to get back inside the Time Lab."

"Right again."

McManus rubbed his chin in thought, feeling its gaunt, knobby shape. "And it's obvious that one of us must go back."

"Uh-huh. . . ."

McManus stood up, a Galahad to the stadium, Lindstrom thought. . . .

"And that person shall be me!"

To which Lindstrom responded, "Wrong."

"Jack . . . Jack?" The woman's voice was cracked, layered with the unsettled quality of age and interrupted sleep. "God in heaven . . . Jack! Sweet Jesus!"

And all Jim saw were the woman's eyes peering through the crack. She was a large woman—again the dream was accurate. He heard her fumble with the door chain. "Oh, Jack. Why didn't you call, what ever made you—"

The door flung open.

And anything else his mother might have said was lost as she threw her arms around him and hugged him tight. The squeeze was incredibly strong, pumping the air out of his body, while she cried and mumbled into his chest.

And Jim could look over her shoulder at the apartment, so eerily familiar. There were photos on the wall. And diplomas. He saw a football trophy on the table. Beyond the small table lamp in the hallway, it was dark.

I know this place, Jim thought.

It's home.

The woman—his mother—Mom—finally pulled away and took his face in her powerful hands, and held his face.

He saw her puffy face wet from her tears. Her eyes were red, "Let me see you. You look starved. What have you been eating?"

Jim watched her quickly look down at his hand to see the small bag he carried.

"What's this?" she said.

"It's just my bag, Mom," he said with surprising naturalness.

The woman stood back and looked at him. "Your bag? That small thing? How could—"

"I just got one day, Mom. Maybe a bit less now. They let me home to see Dad."

He watched the woman bring her hand up to her lips, as if Jim had just reminded her of something nasty, something she had forgotten.

She took his arm, and walked him inside the apartment, shutting the door behind.

She took him left, to the kitchen with the ancient formica table, and chairs that had been repaired with tape.

The woman nodded, as if talking to herself. "You have to go back . . . I understand now. They just let you come—to—to—"

"To see Dad."

Jim looked up. There was one window. It overlooked a courtyard. And in the summer you could hear all the other neighbors. Laughing, fighting, crying.

Making love.

And when you saw the neighbors outside, you acted as though their secrets were safe.

McShane's mother took a chair, slid it back, and then sat down tiredly.

Jim took another chair, facing her.

Now that she knew he was leaving so soon, that he was going away again, it was as if she couldn't look at him. Her eyes wandered over the kitchen, to the tabletop, to some distant never-never land where mothers cry and worry about their sons.

"Mom, I—"

God, Jim thought. What do I say? I had a hard enough time communicating with my real mother.

This is too much.

She looked up at him. "Food . . . you must be hungry." She started to stand up. "I'll fix you some eggs, scrambled. Some potatoes. I know you love—"

But Jim reached up and grabbed her arm. He had the dinner from the airplane rumbling around somewhere in his gut, that and too many bags of nuts. All he wanted was to do what he had to do here. To carry off this charade, get some sleep—

"I'm not hungry, Mom." He held her until she sat back down.

"Oh," she said.

"How's Dad?"

She looked up at him again, with eyes dulled by some very sad truth.

"He's dying, Jack. I try to make him comfortable. There's medicine for the pain. He sleeps a lot. At night I hear him wheeze, he catches his breath. I run in. He's going, Jack. That's what I told the army when they called." She nodded her head. "That's why they let you come here."

Jim nodded.

It wasn't fair, he thought. If this is McShane's time to say goodbye to his father, I shouldn't be here.

I shouldn't be here playacting.

"I'll see him in the morning."

But his mother shook her head.

"You'll see him now, Jack. *Now.* Not in the morning."

She stood up, pushing her chair on the bumpy, cracked, linoleum floor.

Right, he thought. I'll see him now. Though I've been flying all day, though I'm a good eight hours past Saigon time, I'll see this man.

And then, as Jim stood up he felt something funny.

A tightness in his gut.

A strange quiver of tension.

And he sniffed at the air . . . as though he had a cold.

But he knew he didn't. . . .

"What do you mean 'wrong'?" McManus stammered.

"I really don't think that your body could withstand the strain of the Time Transference process. In fact—and correct me if I'm wrong, Dr. Beck—but the process induces both a temporary arhythmia and strokelike symptoms from the brain—"

McManus waved away such concerns. "That's nothing. Why, I've had a stroke. And look at me! Fit as can be."

"Doctor McManus!" Beck said with imperial authority. "You never told me that you had a stroke."

"It was during my vacation. You see, as long as I am working, I'm fine." He turned back to Lindstrom. "And that's why I'll be fine using our device . . . no matter what physical strains there are."

"I doubt that very much, Elliot. We have no idea what the effect might be on a body as old as yours."

"Yes, that's true. No idea. And there might be *no* effect. What will my body be doing, after all, but simply sleeping in a chair."

"There are the strains of the transfer, dangers—"

"—That we know nothing about. Yes, my dear Dr. Beck. But they may also be dangers that don't exist."

Lindstrom shook his head. "You know, I joined this

project as a junior partner, McManus. In fact, if I knew that you'd be keeping the lab 'dry', I probably would have made a quick retreat. But it's clear that *I* should be the one to go."

McManus shook his head. "And why do you say that?"

"For two reasons: I'm dispensable. And I'm younger, a tad healthier than you. Dr. Beck has to stay. That's obvious. And Dr. Jacob is—" he looked over at Jacob, who didn't appear to be listening at all—"if anything, older than you. Besides, he has to run the tachyon generator. So that leaves you and me, and in that case there's no contest."

McManus made a small laugh.

"That's where you're wrong. Lindstrom. Granted, you might be a bit healthier than me—even though I'd hate to see the condition of your liver. But you've made a major miscalculation. . . ."

"Which is?"

"You are *not* indispensable. In fact, you are the only rudder on this chaotic ship. Without you, I dare say history will be bolloxed-up completely. No—you must stay to keep history organized."

Lindstrom looked at him. The old physicist had a point there.

"As for me, well, Jacob runs the machine, and once I'm launched, the return can be carried out by any one of you. I am not needed. You must stay here. That leaves me, I'm afraid. . . ."

Lindstrom saw that McManus was enjoying his logical dance. He's looking forward to time travelling, Lindstrom suspected. That's what this is really all about. The old coot wants to try his machine.

And damn him, he's right. Things were so complicated now that if the Iron Men got away with this it would take a *team* of historians to figure out what to do to set things right.

He's right. I am indispensable. Which means that

McManus has to go. But God! What if he dies? Then what will we do.

McManus's smile was broad and triumphant.

"There. You see, I must be the one to join our intrepid adventurers."

Lindstrom nodded.

Dr. Beck stepped away from her post at the door. "Aren't you two forgetting something?" she sputtered.

"And what's that?" McManus said.

"We aren't in the Time Lab. We can't do a thing here. And I don't see a way we can get back in."

And they all heard this tiny sound.

Very quietly, Dr. Jacob cleared his throat.

"Er," he said. And when everyone finally turned and looked at the short man sitting down, he continued.

"I do," he said quietly. "I know a way we can get back in there."

And—for the first time since Lindstrom ever met the master of the tachyon flow—Dr. Jacob smiled.

18

The truck rumbled up one bumpy dirt road, climbed one more hill, then down again, winding its way to the No Man's Land of the border between North and South Vietnam.

Ali looked at Khan Ha's two brothers, two young boys, only a year or two away from the time they would have to join the great war of liberation. They were good-looking boys, their tan skin matched by the deep brown of their eyes.

They're worth saving, Ali thought.

As are a lot of other children in this war. How many innocents have to pay for this stupid war?

They're worth saving.

But Ali knew she wouldn't be able to help them.

The old woman—Khan Ha's grandmother—talked to her before they got on the beat-up truck. She talked to her about a plan that had been set for a long time.

They would get down to Kontum. And then they'd escape across the border to Cambodia.

It's safer there, the old woman said, clicking her tongue and nodding her head. Safer . . .

Ali wished she could tell her what history had in store for the poor people of Cambodia. But maybe history's agenda has been changed. Maybe Cambodia wouldn't become the killing fields, the final, bloody coda to this sad year.

But Ali knew this . . . although the old woman and

the two boys might go on, across the border, she'd have to keep on moving south, moving to Saigon.

The truck hit a rut and it sent her flying up in the air. The old woman looked up, shaken awake. She pulled the two boys close to her, one on each side, bookends, holding the old woman up on the wooden seat. Then she closed her eyes again. It was nearly dark.

The hills to the south were shifting from a lush green to dark, brownish color as twilight gave way to night. And that was the idea. Get to the border at dark. The truck would take them as far as possible, perhaps even across the border. The dirt roads were seldom watched, seldom patrolled.

At least that's what Hien said.

Then they'd make their way on foot, sticking to the road. There might be other travelers, other people trying to get to relatives in the south during the cease-fire.

In the morning, they'd find a ride. Some small farmer taking goods south. Maybe one of the infrequent busses that rumbled its way through the maze of small villages.

We'll get there, Ali thought. She was sure of that.

The only thing is . . . will I get to Saigon in time?

The truck hit another rut.

"Ey!" the old woman shouted. She leaned over the rail of the truck, shouting at the driver. "Watch the holes. You nearly bounced me out of the truck!"

The woman turned back and looked at Ali, her rumpled and wrinkled face even more prunelike. Ali smiled. The woman was ninety-going-on-forever. She was as brittle as the bamboo that stood in the swampy fields. But just as hearty . . . just as persistent. It would take a lot to kill her.

They reached another hill.

Not far now, Ali thought. Then we'll be in the south. The truck started its roller-coaster plunge down a hill, into an ever-darkening valley.

The air felt chill and damp.

And she thought of Jim. . . .

This woman, his mother, led him into the dark room.

Jim couldn't help sniffing, the smell of old bed clothes and spilled medicine, and bedside meals eaten sloppily, all mixing together in the cloistered, almost sepulchral room.

Mrs. McShane gave his wrist a squeeze.

"He's sleeping . . . Mom . . . maybe we'd better—"

Another squeeze. And she pulled him farther into the gloom.

Jim's eyes adjusted and he saw the bed, a white bedspread, the shape of a body, the dark form of a head.

"Tom," the woman whispered, still edging Jim closer, pulling him forward as if he was a reluctant schoolboy.

This is crazy, he thought. I don't even know this person and I'm being brought to his death bed.

"Tom," his mother said again. "Tom, look who's here . . . look who's back with us."

She pushed Jim forward, propelling him toward the bed.

"Go ahead," she whispered. "He'll wake up now. Go on. Say something. . . ."

"Dad," Jim said hoarsely, too quietly, he realized to awaken anyone. He cleared his throat. "Dad."

Then he saw the man on the bed, the still body, stir. And two glistening pools appeared.

His eyes were open.

The man mumbled something.

"It's our Jack," the woman said, again at his elbow. "It's our boy. He's back from Vietnam, Tom. He's back."

The man's eyes blinked. Once, and then again. He mumbled something again, and Jim wondered whether the man was already lost to the blessed incoherence of the painkillers.

"Sit close to him," his mother whispered. "Go ahead. Sit down next to him. . . ."

Jim did as he was told. He sat down on the too-soft mattress, threatening to tip the man over. He had to move farther onto the mattress. He sat touching the man's body. And now, his eyes adjusted to the darkness, he could see the face. The hollow cheeks, the wispy strands of hair standing up at odd directions, the lips, cracked to the texture of alligator hide.

The man muttered something.

"Give him some water, Jack," his mother said, touching his shoulder.

Jim looked at the end table and saw a plastic water bottle with an L-shaped tube. It was surrounded by a small army of white-capped medicine bottles. Jim took the water bottle and held the tube up to the man's lips. He opened them slowly, birdlike, and sucked.

And Jim could feel the blessed wonder of the water covering his mouth, wetting his dry tongue.

The man kept sucking. And then he stopped, and shook his head.

"That's enough," the woman said to him gently.

Jim nodded, and put the water bottle down. The old man looked at him, his eyes a bit brighter, a bit more aware. The man smiled.

"You're . . . okay?" the old man croaked.

Jim smiled. "I'm fine, Dad. Just great. It's the New Year over there, so they let me come home and visit. . . ."

The man nodded, the smile still there, just barely, fading, as Jim watched his face darken.

The pain. It's probably always there. The man probably only gets a few minutes of consciousness before the pain makes it necessary to take the pills and push it away, Jim thought.

He felt the man's hand, big, lined with fat veins, cover his. Jim smiled.

This isn't right, he thought. I'm not the one who should be here. This is too important for me to be pretending. It's as if I'm stealing something from McShane, stealing a too-important moment from his life.

The man squeezed gently.

"It's good to see you," he said.

"It's good to be here," Jim said.

The man licked his lips.

"More water?" Jim asked.

The man shook his head. But his face looked troubled now.

"I—I want you to find Will."

"Excuse me. . . ?" Jim said. He turned back to McShane's mother. But she stood a few steps back.

The old man talked past him, trying as best he could to raise his voice. "You didn't—" he coughed, looking up at his wife. "You didn't tell him?"

"No, Tom. He just got here. I didn't think."

The man squeezed his hand hard. "We've lost him, Jack. Will's run away. To join those crazy people, those—"

"Hippies . . ." His mother added with what Jim found almost humorous venom.

Except there was nothing funny about being here with these people, with their pain and fear.

1968. It was a good year to lose your kid.

Especially in San Francisco.

"Find him for us, Jack. . . ." the old man said. "Get our Will back. . . ."

Jim nodded. "I—I'll do what I can."

The old man smiled.

His eyes fluttered closed.

"Come on," the man's wife whispered. "We'll let him rest now."

Jack stood up.

He followed the woman out of the dark room.

Well, Jim thought, at least I know what I'm going to do tomorrow.

"I've fixed your bed," the woman said.

"Great," Jim said. And he thought: I'm going to look for my brother.

Now all I need is a photograph so I know what the hell he looks like. . . .

The truck stopped. Abruptly, in the middle of nowhere.

Ali heard the driver get out and come running to the back.

"Out, out," he yelled unhinging the metal flap to the back of the truck.

Ali looked around. "Here?" she said.

The driver nodded, agitated, nervous.

"That village there," he said, pointing at some distant lights just visible through the trees, "is South Vietnam. I can't go any closer."

The old woman was up now, pulling along the two sleepy boys. "Close . . . close? Are you a scared rabbit? A baby . . . ?"

Ali grabbed her bedroll and jumped off the back of the cab. She turned around to help Khan Ha's grandmother down.

"Hurry!" the driver barked.

Well, thought Ali, if he's so scared about being discovered here, what does that mean for us? What happens if we're found by some wandering South Vietnamese patrol.

She thought of My Lai. She thought of the famous picture of the Saigon police colonel sticking a gun up to some VC's head and blasting away.

Bad things happen here.

"Come on," she said, taking the old woman's hand. "We can get to the village before dawn. We'll be fine. . . ."

The old woman shook her head.

"I'm hungry," one of the boys said. Ali dug a piece of bread out of her bedroll. She also had a small canister of mint tea. And just a little bit of money.

The driver ran back to his cab and started the noisy

truck engine. They were engulfed in smoky exhaust. He turned right, and began backing up to turn the truck around. Ali ushered the old woman and the boys to the side of the road.

"Coward," the grandmother yelled. "You could take us closer!"

But the driver didn't even look at them as he finally straightened the truck and gunned past them, sending a dusty spray drifting back towards them.

"Come on," Ali said. "It's not too far. Soon you'll—we'll be able to get across the border."

The old woman grumbled something low and unintelligible.

And Ali followed the road into the flat jungle ahead . . . unaware that someone was watching them.

Ngo Van Trinh didn't follow his normal route home from the Hotel Continental.

No, even though he knew where the embassy was, he wanted to see it up close, to study its walls, its gates.

So he went down busy Ha Ba Trung street, dodging the crazy cyclos who cursed and shouted at him, looking at him as an amateur taking up their precious biking space. The drivers paid pedestrians and bicyclists no heed.

You stayed out of their way . . . or else.

Already the city had a festive air. There was the sound of fireworks, not the big displays that would come in two nights, but the little snaps and pops of people lighting their small firecrackers. The workers had already started their vacation for the great holiday.

They were on the streets, laughing, going to bars, mingling with the Americans, who looked bothered by so many Vietnamese filling the streets.

Ngo thought these things and nearly pedaled into a car that suddenly stopped in front of him.

He backed up, and his rear tire screeched at the pavement. The car started up again.

Trinh looked left. He saw the great cathedral, all lit up now.

It made him think of when his mother took him to church.

It made him think of how responsible the church was for the terrible problem of Vietnam. They told the people to wait . . . and pray . . . and hope.

When what they really needed to do was *act*.

Quickly and decisively.

He passed the cathedral and came to another busy road, Thong Nhat Street. He turned the corner. He saw the row of buildings, the embassies and the official residences, looking so wonderful and proud while most of his people lived in crowded rooms, living off American crumbs.

He noticed a policeman watching him.

He's wondering what I'm doing, Trinh thought. He felt like giving him the GI salute.

The magic middle finger raised up.

Then he biked harder, and faster, until he came to the embassy . . . and then he slowed. He saw the main gate, guarded outside by only two marines. But he was sure there were more inside.

The walls weren't terribly tall, but they were topped by spikes and barbed wire. And he saw a tower to the left. On his map, it was marked as a fire station. But there were probably more guards there with powerful guns.

And—as he passed the gate—he knew that there were marines inside. A special detachment to protect the embassy.

They would have to be fought and defeated quickly.

There would be other VC, Giang said. Many groups, all entering from different points, some near the back where the embassy parking lot was, and others near the terrace filled with plants and a tree that overlooked the compound pool.

Like snakes slithering after fat rats through a hay rick.

One of us will get through.

The others will kill the marines.

We'll take the captors.

Trinh took a breath, speeding up as he felt one of the guards studying him.

And then—with our hostages—we'll give the Americans an ultimatum.

He pumped hard now, biking past the embassy's walls.

Nguyen Binh Khiem Street was ahead. He'd turn there, and come back by the river, enjoying the cool breeze that blew off the Saigon River.

And Trinh wondered. . . .

What happens after the ultimatum?

What will the Americans do then?

Giang hadn't said anything about that.

Nothing at all.

And—Trinh supposed—it really wasn't any of his concern. . . .

19

They all waited, Lindstrom noted. Beck, McManus . . . as well as Lindstrom himself.

They waited for Dr. Jacob, as he took a step into the center of the room, his normally vacant, distracted-looking face appearing—by God—almost excited.

"There is a way back inside. . . ."

Finally Lindstrom couldn't handle any more waiting. "Do you mind sharing it with us?"

"No. Not at all. It's just—" Jacob turned and smiled at them. "It's just that I'm trying to remember how it goes. What exactly the path is. . . ."

"Path?" McManus said. "What kind of path?"

"You see," Jacob continued, "when the tachyon generator was built, we knew it would make enormous demands on the university's electric supply. *Unprecedented* demands, actually. And that's why we decided to do something about it."

Lindstrom looked at McManus, whose face was screwed up, trying to remember what Jacob might be talking about. "Special arrangements? I remember the installation of the shielding—we knew we had to do that. And of course, there are special water lines, and—"

"And electric lines. We didn't tap into the university's system, Elliot. Did we?"

McManus smiled. "You're right."

"There was a special line installed, running from

the Red Building directly off the campus, with a special feed hooking to the Big Alice generator's special industrial lines."

"That's very interesting." Lindstrom interrupted. "But I don't see how that helps us."

"Oh," Jacob turned, nonplussed by Lindstrom's query, "but it *does*. You see, we had no idea what effect the accelerating tachyons would have. We all felt there was the distinct possibility of electrical feedback—"

"What he means," McManus interjected, "is that the particles could magnify the electrical power and actually feed back into the lines."

"Yes," Jacob said. "And if that happened, they'd melt. They'd short out."

"Precisely," McManus said, his face now wearing the same idiotic, beatific grin sported by Jacob. I hope they decide to let me in on the fun, Lindstrom thought. "So we had to make the lines accessible . . . for repairs . . . for monitoring."

"They run through the campus," Dr. Jacob added. "There's a half-dozen places you can get at them. And they all lead right into the Red Building."

Lindstrom walked over to Jacob. "You're sure?"

"Absolutely."

"That's perfect," Lindstrom said, turning now to McManus and Beck. "We can get back inside."

But he saw that a new cloud had passed over McManus's face.

"Yes, but there's still the problem of what to do once we're *back* in the lab."

"What do you mean?"

"They'll have the Time Lab guarded. We can't just show up and take over again. They'll just escort us out and make sure we don't break in again. . . ."

Lindstrom scratched his beard. The vision of easy success had once again been replaced with a grim picture of hopelessness.

"Perhaps . . ." a voice said.

They turned, and this time the unlikely plotter was Dr. Beck. "Perhaps there is way . . ." She looked at Lindstrom and McManus.

She shook her head. "If only . . ."

"Well don't beat around the bush, Dr. Beck. If you have a plan, then out with it. I have to be sent back as soon as possible."

"No, Elliot," Lindstrom said, "I do—"

Dr. Beck nodded. "I wish you were both twenty years younger . . ." she said sighing . . . "but here it is. . . ."

And they all gathered close to her.

Chau's launch stopped at a small dock and he got off the fast patrol boat while a woman cleaned clothes by the river.

A car waited for him there, a large black Russian car that he knew would jiggle terribly on the dirt road.

This gets wearying, he thought. Pretending to be this general . . . but I have to stay here until the attack has been set in motion, irrevocably. Then, near midnight, I'll be pulled back to the Georgian stronghold of the Iron Men.

He sat in back of the oversized luxury car used only by important politicos. Its plush, gray seating was amazingly uncomfortable. There was a small cabinet in front of his seat—perhaps for a bottle of vodka and a bucket of chipped ice. But he flipped it open as the car pulled away, and it was empty.

Too ascetic, these Orientals. But they had an envious dedication to the task at hand.

Oh, it was a dedication he and the other Iron Men could match. Hadn't they started planning years before the end, years before the dawning of the loathsome Russian Republic?

They talked about democracy, about all the curses it would deliver on the strong peoples of the USSR. They talked until there were no longer any Soviet Socialist Republics, only a weak, liberalized Russia.

They talked . . . until only one man gave them the key to turn things back.

He was a scientist, not even a military officer. And scientists usually make for weak, muddle-headed people. Leave them in their labs, but don't let them talk about politics.

But this one was a dedicated Communist and he was welcomed to the inner sanctum of the Iron Men.

He brought news of this machine, this incredible machine of his. Experimental, mind you . . . he cautioned. Perhaps dangerous. But it was an invention unlike any other.

And the Iron Men saw the potential. . . .

The scientist was given a code name, as they all were. Outside the Iron Men's compound, they used their normal names, their normal titles. Inside, only code words were used.

He had taken the name of Scorpion. . . .

The scientist was called Sabre.

Such a powerful name for a small, owl-eyed man. . . .

But he brought with him the power, the real strength to change the world.

Of course, the first attempt ended in disaster. No one knew that there was another Time Lab—invented by the Americans. Hard to believe. The Japanese, yes, that would make sense, but the Americans?

But their power seemed limited, and Sabre explained that the Americans didn't seem able to go back and forth.

Mistakes were made. A few of the Iron Men suggested that World War II was too large, too unwieldy to play with.

Perhaps they were right.

It was my idea, Scorpion thought, to use the Tet Offensive to achieve our goals. It was so clear, it stood on the history page declaring its importance. And I had a plan, an amazingly simple plan that would achieve the Iron Men's goals.

Others argued for more ancient times, that history can only be really 'rectified' at its roots. One of the Iron Men insisted that the answer lay in Ancient Rome.

But I argued well for my plan.

It was so clear, so *simple*.

And it was approved.

Unfortunately, he thought, I was selected to carry out the plan . . . a major annoyance.

He looked out the window. The driver was going slowly, taking care not to rattle him around too much.

It won't be long, he thought. We'll get to this temporary headquarters and they will approve the final arrangements.

He looked at his watch.

Midnight. January 31st.

I can wait, he thought, shifting on the plush seats. . . .

I can wait.

General Westmoreland walked down the broad avenue that separated the ancient imperial city of Hue from the newer section, most of it built during the years of the French occupation.

He looked at the quiet streets, the sandbags piled near the corners, a tank lurking at one end of the road . . . a sleeping dragon ready to awake and breathe fire.

He turned back to his jeep.

The whole day had been spent inspecting Hue, checking its defenses, briefing his commanders.

Some of his commanders seemed to doubt the general's assurance that this would be the site of a major attack . . . perhaps *the* major attack of the offensive.

They doubted, and he smiled and said—"trust me. . . ."

Now, having seen the city and its defenses, the battalion of ARVN and the assorted American companies scattered around the city, he felt he could relax.

Hue could resist even a massive assault.

He got back into the jeep.

Kline was talking on the radio.

"General, there's nothing more about that NVA supply column. It's no place for aerial surveillance."

Westmoreland nodded.

That story—if it was reliable—bothered him. It was one thing for a squad to catch a few VC hustling weapons from one rat hole to another. But this was a lot of men—well-armed, regular soldiers.

What were they doing so close to Saigon?

Scorpion had said nothing about Saigon.

"Okay," Westmoreland said. "And what's the news from Khe Sanh. . . ?"

Kline hung up the radiophone and started the jeep. He backed up, and started driving back to the American Military Headquarters.

"The same, sir. The shelling is constant. But there's been no frontal assault on any of the positions. . . ."

"The airlift is still going on."

"Yes, sir. More weapons, and, anything else they need, it's all being dropped by the hour. If it stays clear, it will go on all night."

Westmoreland nodded. Khe Sanh had to stand. Scorpion warned that Hue and Khe Sanh would be the major goals of the offensive. To lose either would deliver a humiliating blow.

And he remembered President Johnson asking, almost pleading, that the US not suffer the humiliation of a Dien Bien Phu.

That wouldn't happen.

But still—something nagged at him. . . .

Despite all the confirmation that Scorpion's information—his intelligence—was correct, something bothered Westmoreland. . . .

Scorpion had been right so far.

But what if now he was wrong?

What if the whole scenario fell apart when this offensive began?

And he tried to think . . . where are we most vulnerable?

He might have thought of any one of a dozen provincial town and cities, all important outposts, all holding the key to an important part of the south.

But instead he thought of the mysterious supply column moving through the jungle.

They were only detected by chance. . . .

Only engaged because the platoon was clever—

He thought about that supply column. . . .

And he worried.

"Should I take you to your quarters?" Kline asked.

The general shook his head. "No. Take me back to our command post . . . and when we get there, ring up MAC-V in Saigon."

"They'll probably be gone for the day, sir. Just some operations officers on duty."

"No," Westmoreland said. "Get me General Greene . . . and whoever the hell is the overnight intelligence officer. And I don't care if you have to wake them up!"

"Yes, sir," Kline said. Westmoreland watched Kline press down on the gas pedal, instinctively—and correctly—reading the general's impatience.

20

It was the kind of feeling you'd get in a car, Ali thought. You'd be driving along, daydreaming, not really paying too much attention to anything, when you felt it.

Someone was watching you.

It was as if you could feel their eyes, some preternatural heat boring into you, radiating from a person's eyes.

And nine times out of ten you'd turn, and there he was—it was always some guy. Looking at you as if he hadn't seen a girl in a year.

That's what this felt like.

There was no other signs. Nó noises, nothing. The dirt road, almost a path, just meandered its way through the jungle. The two boys helped their grandmother, who grunted and groaned at every step.

Still, as Ali took the lead, she had the definite feeling that they were being watched.

Once she stopped and held up a hand, signalling the rest of her new family to be quiet.

And she stood there, and listened.

She heard her own breathing, and then, if she wasn't crazy, the rhythmic tattoo of her heartbeat.

It's all in my head, she told herself. There's nothing. we're just in the jungle and I'm getting spooked. Just have to get a grip on myself . . . calm down. Soon we'll be at the village. And by morning we'll be going south.

And by tomorrow night I'll be in Saigon.

She was telling herself these things, pushing aside her fear, her irrational fear, when she heard a sound.

It was the snap of a branch being walked on. She hoped that there would only be that one sound. Just that, and nothing else. But then there was another sound, another snap.

She licked her lips and looked around, trying to sense where they were coming from. Were the sounds ahead of her, or behind her? Were they close or far away?

We have nothing, she thought. No weapons, not even a knife.

She laughed, a cynical, frightened sound. That's the thing about borrowing other people's bodies, taking over other people's lives . . . she thought. Makes you kind of cavalier about danger.

After all, it isn't *your* life.

More sounds. More snapping branches. Closer too, right there, she thought, just in front. . . .

Maybe we should back up, she thought. Get back to the north, back to the no-man's-land . . . at least until morning.

Yes, you borrowed other people's lives. But while visiting, you get to feel whatever they feel.

"Khan Ha!" the old woman said too loudly. "Why have you stopped? What's wrong?"

"Grandmother," Ali whispered. "I hear—I think I hear—"

Then she felt it again, only more intense.

Someone watching her.

From behind.

Looking at her back.

She saw the old woman's face fall open, angry and surprised. Her two brothers clutched close to the old woman.

And Ali slowly turned around. . . .

* * *

The soldier was dressed in a different kind of uniform, dabbed with garish splotches of camouflage that stood out even in the dark, moonless night. The other men arranged themselves in a circle, surrounding Ali, her grandmother, and the two boys.

Two of the soldiers held flashlights and kept their glaring lights tightly focussed on Ali.

"Where are you going?" the man snapped, walking back and forth. "What are you doing here?"

"I—I—" Ali started to answer, but she heard a few soldiers laugh and say things to each other. Low, dark things.

More laughter, and Ali could tell that the men had been drinking. They're standing here with their guns, she thought, in the middle of nowhere, and they've been drinking.

And what's worse . . . they're South Vietnamese soldiers . . . and they know we came from the north.

They could kill us.

But then she *knew* that they didn't want to kill her.

The leader came closer. He was a dark shadow, and she smelled sweat and the sweet smell of wine. He stood so close to her Ali could smell his breath.

"We are travelling to see relatives . . . in Kontum. For Tet." she said. "For the cease-fire."

The leader laughed. "Cease-fire?" He said. "There is no cease-fire. Not here. Not for us."

His men laughed.

"We're just visiting—"

The leader's hand came out of the darkness and entered the pool of light that bathed Ali's face.

She stood there as his fingers, rough, blackened things, touched her cheek, caressed it.

"You are very beautiful," he said.

His comment brought laughter from the other men.

There was silence. The man's hand stayed on her cheek. The men sounded closer, tightening their circle. The big flashlights were right in her eyes, blinding.

"Very . . . beautiful. . . ." the leader said, his hand trailing down off Ali's cheek, and then into the sleek line of her neck.

One of the boys ran up to her and clutched her tight. It was the one named Tuan. He held her protectively. She smiled down at him, his beautiful eyes now blinking in the light.

There has to be something I can do, Ali thought.

Because it was quite clear what these soldiers had in mind.

A little New Year's party.

With me as the favor.

And then what? What would they do afterwards? Just let us go?

She doubted it.

"Please," Ali said. "My grandmother is very old, very weak—we must—"

Ali gestured back at the woman. A few soldiers stood close to her and the old woman was curled up, shaking, twisted by her terrible fear.

The leader's hand trailed down farther until Ali felt it very gently surround one of her breasts. Then, less gently, he closed his hand around it and squeezed.

Screw this, Ali thought. These drunken bastards are going to kill us, anyway.

Screw this standing here and letting him maul me.

"No!" she screamed. And she backed away, out of the light, pulling Tuan with her. "Get away from me. You're drunken pigs. What kind of soldiers are you that you'd bother women and children? Go, crawl back to your holes."

The leader laughed, and so did his men. But there was too much tension for them to let go that easily. The flashlights found Ali again. She stepped back from the light and a twisted root caught her foot. Damn, she thought. Don't let me fall. Don't let me fall to the fucking ground, not with these animals here. Please, god—''

She sprawled backwards, flailing out, trying to grab Tuan for balance.

But she fell down. And when she looked up, the men were there. Laughing, talking.

''Get away!'' she screamed.

The leader had unstrapped his gun.

Then he pulled off his jacket and handed it to another soldier. They were all muttering now, the excitement incredible. Ali tried to squirm backwards, crawling back like a crab away from the men.

And all the time they kept their great lanterns aimed at her. She heard Tuan pounding at one of the soldiers, beating his fists against the soldier's chest while the soldier laughed and held the boy effortlessly.

The leader was just visible in the pool of light.

Ali saw him undo his belt. The men's chatter grew, until it was the most horrible thing Ali ever heard. Like hungry pigs, she thought.

There was nothing human about them.

''Come here,'' the leader said to her. And he laughed, finally undoing his belt. Ali skittered back another foot but ran into a wall of a soldier's legs and boots. They nudged her forward, towards the leader.

''Come here!'' he snarled.

Ali clawed at the ground, scraping a pitiful handful of dirt in each fist. I'll throw it in his eyes, she thought. And I'll kick the bastard in his balls. I'll get his gun and blow his head off—

She held the dirt tight.

Knowing that it was all a sad fantasy.

He was going to rape her. And then all the men would rape her.

And then—most likely—they'd kill her.

So that no one would ever know what they did, what living in the jungle and killing people could do.

''No!'' she screamed.

The leader let his pants fall. And it was a sick, comical gesture.

Ali was crying. She heard the old woman keening. Moaning to the air.

And then—

She thought it was her imagination. I've lost it, she thought. I've lost it!

She heard another voice.

It had been Dr. Beck's suggestion that they all get some rest before putting into effect her rather remarkable plan.

Lindstrom sat in his chair, watching the computer screen flick back and forth between the land of what is and what should be. He had listened to Beck's plan, thinking that this was all the more remarkable coming from such a respectable presence. That's one very tough woman hiding behind her quiet facade. . . .

And now she simply lay on the floor, covered by the tattered blanket that Lindstrom kept on a top shelf of his book case for those moments the university shut down the heat. Lindstrom had a tendency to leave off grading reports until the day before grades were due. Often, he was the only one in the building.

McManus and Jacob shared the small couch, their bodies twirled together like disgruntled lobsters snared in a net.

Lindstrom said he'd sleep in his desk chair.

Which was true.

Even if that wasn't what he was doing now.

No. There was something else he wanted to do now.

Something he had to do.

He supposed he wouldn't have noticed it. The phenomenon of acquiring new memories as soon as history was changed appeared rather natural. One second you remembered this . . . and the next, you remembered that.

But planted in the back of all their minds was the

one thought that—thanks to the computer link-up—couldn't be eradicated. It's all wrong. Bogus.

That thought remained, despite all the nonsense that they "knew" to be correct.

Lindstrom looked at the screen. All the nonsense . . . Like the memories that he had now. Memories of his father . . . Home from Vietnam. Coaching his Little League team. They had won their division that year. And he had taken the team out for pizza. And then the summer at Long Beach Island, flying kites, crabbing, body surfing while dodging the jellyfish that always clogged the surf whenever the water hit the perfect temperature for swimming.

And more . . . teaching the boy to drive . . . helping him apply for the scholarship to Princeton . . . growing old, not understanding what physics was all about, but giving love and support and everything a boy needed to grow up.

Except . . . *Except—*

Lindstrom looked at the monitor. It was right there.

My father died in Vietnam. He was killed in Vietnam. When I was only three years old. That's the real truth, that's the real truth I'm trying to preserve. Lindstrom rubbed at his eyes. He looked at these memories with a funny perspective.

If I succeed, they'll all be blown away. A whole life with my father *blown away.*

He touched the screen—a link to the man and their life together.

And it's in my hands. . . .

He heard McManus turn over, snorting, gulping at the air with surprising noise for such a gaunt, skeletal man. Lindstrom saw one of the physicist's feet flop onto the face of Dr. Jacob, who brushed it away with much loud twitching and smiling.

Dr. Beck slept stone quiet on the hardwood floor. They all slept, gaining energy for the next day's adventure. But Lindstrom knew that he wouldn't sleep.

I have this night, he thought. To keep those memories. To remember all those wonderful times, as I grew up and my father grew old. There's just tonight.

And he knew he wouldn't waste a moment of it sleeping. . . .

The soldiers stepped back and Ali felt cool air touch her cheek. A breeze tried to push her hair off her face. But it was stuck to her cheeks by the salty glue of her tears.

The leader turned, a baggy-pants comedian.

"What is going on here?"

Ali couldn't see the man. But his voice had authority. And, if nothing else, it got the soldiers to back up.

And their leader, who had been ready to unsheathe his rapier, stood there, stunned.

The man came closer. The flashlights, which had fallen away from her to point down at the ground, sent a spray of reflected light up onto the man.

Ali stood up. The two boys ran over to her, followed by their grandmother. She was crying, sobbing terribly. And she, too, fell against Ali.

"Is this how we fight our war?" the man said. "Is this how you win the people of our country?"

The man—an officer, Ali guessed—stepped close to the baggy-pants leader. He slapped him hard with the stock of his gun, and her would-be rapist grunted and tottered backwards, falling to the ground.

"Get back to your camp . . . now. You will all be dealt with in the morning."

For a moment Ali thought that they'd disobey the officer. Maybe they'd kill him, too.

It was that kind of war, wasn't it? Ali thought.

But they stumbled away. And the leader stood up, pulling up his pants, hurrying to join them. Ali watched as they disappeared into the jungle.

"You are alright?" the officer asked.

Ali nodded. "Yes. And thank you. . . ."

The officer tilted his head back in the direction of

the men. "This war has done terrible things to our country." He looked at her. "It has gone on too long for men to stay decent, for women and children to be safe. . . ." He paused. "It has gone on too long. . . ."

The old woman was still crying, leaning against Ali. Ali had her arm around the woman holding her tight, comforting her.

"Where are you going?" the officer said.

"To the village," Ali answered. "And then, on to Kontum to see relatives for the holiday."

The officer nodded. "It still is not safe here," he said. "Even though there is a cease-fire. It is not safe."

"I know," Ali answered. "But my grandmother—she is old—"

Ali couldn't see much in the darkness, but she saw the officer's intelligent eyes looked at the woman pressed tight against her. "Yes," he said. "I understand."

Then he looked around, as if listening to the wind, to the jungle.

He turned back to Ali. "I will take you to the village. It is only an hour away. There are people who will let you rest with them until morning." He reached out and ran a hand through Tuan's fine, black hair. "There's a bus at midday. There are many like you travelling through the countryside. It will take you south, to Kontum."

"Thank you. . . ." Ali said. She felt her tears drying on her cheeks, the thin strands of her hair sticking together. "This bus—" Ali said, pausing to think about how to phrase this question.

"Yes."

"This bus, it stops in Kontum? It goes no farther?"

The officer started to guide her along the road.

"No," he said. "It keeps going south." He laughed, a warm, reassuring sound after the piglike howls of the drunken soldiers. "It takes forever, but it eventually ends up in the capital, in Saigon. Why do you ask . . . ?''

''No reason,'' Ali said. ''Just . . . curious. . . .''

And she walked beside him, thinking about her good fortune. And wondering:

What are *you* up to tonight, Jim Tiber?

And if I do get to see you again . . .

(she smiled at the thought) . . .

Who will you look like this time?

21

It was breakfast, and Jim savored the experience of a lost era.

He sat at the McShane kitchen table, a genuine objet d'Americana. It was a red and white swirl of formica, filled with *modern* kidney-shaped clusters. And as student of American cultural landmarks, Jim knew that it was at just this type of table that Lucy and Ricky would sit down.

Mrs. McShane refilled his coffee cup while he shoveled in another lighter-than-air spoonful of puffed rice.

Jim read the box.

It stated that there was dinosaur inside.

He was nearly done with his puffed-up chow when he noticed that McShane's mother was acting mighty quiet, as if she was hiding something.

Perhaps, he thought, it's because I have to go back tonight. That has to be eating her alive. Or maybe she's scared because she's going to be left alone with her husband, alone to watch until the cancer finally takes him away.

And he thought of how that man, this father, looked last night . . . sitting in near total darkness. Sunken cheeks, eyes bulging out of the tight sockets. Thin, wispy strands of hair, like a wheat field gone fallow.

He took another spoonful.

The man looked like those skeletal men and women liberated from the concentration camps at the end of

World War II . . . so dessicated that they were no longer human, but pathetic, shambling caricatures of people, so horribly different from the hearty GIs.

"More coffee?" his mother said.

She was trying to act casual.

Jim shook his head. Maybe she's upset about her runaway son. Well, it wouldn't be the first time old middle-America would lose a son to the counterculture.

There would be worse eaters of children in the decades to come, he thought.

Much worse.

He looked at this woman, as broad as her husband was lean. Bustling about the tiny kitchen as if she had dozens of important tasks to be about. A fancy-dress dinner, perhaps, a grand party in the foyer. She wiped, and moved and rearranged. Anything, but stand still and look at him.

Why? he wondered.

For the last time.

As there came a knock on the apartment door, and Mom hurried to answer it. . . .

This girl walked into the kitchen, while McShane's mother trailed behind. Jim still had his spoon in his mouth. And his first thought—seeing this girl wearing so much makeup and a turquoise sheathe dress—was: I look like a slob.

Jim wore a tee-shirt, with bare feet and a good day's growth on his chin. Thanks to McShane's brush cut, he didn't have to worry about the top of his head.

Who is she? Jim thought. This Avon lady.

(An odd suspicion began to grow, undefined, but slowly coming into focus.)

He sat there with what he thought must be a dumbfounded expression. The girl stood at the entrance to the kitchen, grinning from ear to ear, waiting expectantly.

For what? he wondered.

Fortunately, Mama McShane jumped into the breach.

"Well, Jack . . . aren't you going to give Susan a kiss?"

Jim stood up. The girl's quivering excitement seemed to be ready to explode as Jim gave full rein to his confusion.

"Er, right . . ." he said.

He saw the girl's face fall a bit when he didn't leap to embrace her.

"Susan!" he said, too loudly, hoping to dispel his initial impression. (Who the hell is she? he thought. But then that became obvious.)

It was Susan.

The girl I left behind. No, scratch that. The girl *Jack McShane* left behind.

And then he looked at the girl's face as he walked over to her, extending his arms, her smile returning. The whole thing in slow motion. And, like a photo album tumbling to the floor, sending a random assortment of snapshots flying out, he got peeks of Susan and Jack.

In the back seat of a Ford Maverick. Grabbing under her dress. Her protests. Her squeals. Then her laughter, until all the teenage fun and games turned deadly serious as McShane hit, as he told his friends, home plate. Susan closed her eyes as he grabbed her shoulders and pulled her close.

And he could see her then, her girlish giggles melting into something more heated, more serious.

It was her first time, in that Maverick. And—and—

It was just before McShane shipped out for wonderful Vietnam.

Now Jim pulled her close. And he kissed her and she kissed back. Just a touch of her tongue coquettishly touching his lips before he broke up the embrace.

"Jack!" she gushed. "Jack, I couldn't believe it when your mom called and said you were home. I had to come here before I went to work." She grabbed his hands and squeezed. "I don't care if I'll be late."

"Great . . ." Jim said.

"Well, I'll let you talk," his mother said. "I want to check on your father."

And his mother moved discreetely out of the scene . . . leaving Jim with Susan to catch up on old times.

Whatever they were . . .

Dr. Lindstrom stood outside the door to his office with the burly Dr. Beck beside him.

He looked at her. A woman like that gives a man confidence, he thought. She looked like she could pick up one of those security guards and toss them over her shoulder.

But where were the security guards?

It was nerve-racking standing here, waiting, and all the time thinking that Beck's plan might not be such a hot idea after all. Maybe there was another way, he had said.

Not that he had any alternative.

"Do you think," he said quietly, "that maybe we should check on the others? They might be getting—"

Beck shook her head. "No. Let them stay where they were. It would be just our luck to go back in there and then have the guards come in."

"Right," Lindstrom agreed.

But he had to wonder . . . where did this woman get the moxie . . . the sheer cojones to think they'd be able to pull off what they had to pull off.

He had asked her: where did you get *this* idea from?

"From the movies," she said deadpan. "It works all the time."

And as no one else thought that that was a particularly stupid answer, Lindstrom shrugged. There were no good alternatives.

But this waiting outside his office was driving him crazy. Last night it seemed as if the guards came past the office every fifteen minutes. Now, the hall was a ghost town. A few assistant professors darted into their closet-sized offices to snatch up some lecture notes or a handful of ibuprophen. Full professors, Lindstrom well knew, avoided any class before 10 A.M.

Great intellects require much sleep. And Lindstrom himself was not beyond cancelling a class if he had too many bells ringing in his head.

He looked left and then right down the deserted hall.

"Where in the world are they?" he said.

As if in answer, he heard steps on the broad staircase near the center of the building. Dr. Beck stiffened.

The steps moved in unison, Lindstrom noted. This was precision walking. It's wonderful how security cops and other fatheads make such a big deal about the dumbest things. Click-clack. Click-clack. Then, as they reached the hall, Lindstrom heard the jingle of their guns.

He thought of their guns. That's the part that scared him.

He looked over at Beck to see whether she was scared by that, too. But she wore a big grin. Hooray! her face proclaimed. We're having a wonderful adventure.

"What about the kelvar?" Lindstrom asked. Beck waved away his concern.

Then he saw them.

Beck gave him a "straighten-up" nudge to his ribs. The guards saw them standing outside the office and—again with that wonderful precision—they turned and started walking towards them.

"Here we go . . ." Lindstrom said through clenched teeth.

Beck said nothing.

She asked him about the war. Jim shrugged and said he didn't want to talk about it.

Which was certainly true.

She gave him updates on all their mutual friends.

And their activities. Tom was off to Guam with the Air Force. He was doing some top-secret stuff. Janie and Bill broke up . . . she found out he was playing around. Meanwhile, Janie was dating this guy she met at the City West Bank, a teller . . . but this time she was going slow.

And then—as she looked right in his eyes—she said:

"Sarah Kessler and Mark announced their engagement. . . ."

And her eyes locked on his.

Jim looked away, at his cereal bowl, at the kidney swirls on the table, anything but Susan's heavily made-up eyes.

Her hand crawled over to his, covering it. "Isn't that neat?"

Jim nodded.

"Great," he repeated.

She squeezed his hand.

"I've got to go. . . ." she said.

Jim nodded, smiling.

"Do you remember what you wrote?"

Her eyes still had their laser lock on him.

What I wrote? What I wrote!

"Er . . . what do you mean—"

Her face made a small pout. She was hurt. It was obviously something important.

"You don't remember?"

He patted her hand covering his. "I write a lot of things, Susan. Just tell me, honey—"

He wasn't sure 'honey' was the appropriate pet name . . . but he hoped it passed.

"About us, of course. About what you said. That when you came back, well—" she laughed, then sort of turned away, embarrassed.

Let me guess, thought Jim, feeling that there was nothing he could do to stop this train.

"You mean about our, er, getting married . . ."

Now she brightened, back from the land of teenage heartbreak to the world of future domestic bliss.

"Right, silly. You said we could just do it when you came back. Right away. And—"

Jim tried to pull his hand away from hers . . . but she didn't let go. There's a fair amount of tenacity in this gentle flower, he thought.

He wondered . . . did McShane really write that? Did he really mean it? I don't exactly feel authorized to make any major decisions in what is clearly *not* my life.

"But I'm not really back, Susan. I'm just here . . . to see my dad . . . before—"

She nodded. "I know," she said sternly. "I've been here nearly every day . . . since your brother left. To see if they need anything . . . to help."

Deeper and deeper, Jim thought, sensing the true warp and woof of this tightly webbed plot.

"It would make them happy, Jack. Your dad told me that. 'Give him something to live for,' he said to me." Her hand squeezed his again. "I want to give you that, Jack."

Jim nodded.

Things were quickly spiraling out his control.

He laughed, a nervous explosion that he hoped would nudge away the irresistible force of Susan's plans. "But what can we do? I'm leaving at 11 P.M. Fifteen hours later I'm back in Saigon, Susan. How in the world—?"

Her smile broadened further as the cat swallowed the canary whole.

"Reverend Dimme said he could do a simple service . . . anytime tonight." Another squeeze. "Anytime."

And then, before Jim could perform his impersonation of Jackie Gleason going "ha-me-na, ha-me-na, ha-me-na!" Susan got up and walked over to Jim, where she slid, quite comfortably, right onto his lap.

And as she wriggled her still-demure bottom on his

lap, he felt a primitive stirring that added a whole new element to the discussion.

Maybe, he thought philosophically, this is what McShane really wants to do. Maybe he really wants to marry this—

Another wriggle, and she leaned close to him whispering into his ear.

—not unattractive girl.

"We could have a quick service," she laughed, "and then a quickie."

Screw the service, Jim thought. Let's just go for the quickie now.

But then, on cue, his mother entered the kitchen and Susan sprang up from his lap, straightening her sheathe dress that wore the telltale ribbing of their too-brief tryst.

"I've been talking to him, Mrs. McShane, about Reverend Dimme—"

She nodded, and Jim saw that the woman didn't seem overwhelmed with joy at the prospect of the instant marriage. That was something to keep in mind, Jim thought.

He stood up, forgetting that he still bore the telltale traces of the physical interest aroused by McShane's girlfriend.

"Susan, let me try and find Will . . . let me find my brother. Then we'll meet back here."

Her eyes narrowed, sensing a tactical loss. He walked over and gave her a reassuring hug. "I'll see you here, we'll have dinner. Around five-thirty or so. You'll be off by then?"

She nodded. "My shift in Junior Wear ends at five."

"Great," Jim said, smiling. "Super! We can talk about it then and—"

"Should I call Reverend Dimme?"

Jim shook his head. "No. Just wait, honey. I mean, there's my dad. . . . and Will . . ."

She nodded, a sad puppy now. She turned to leave, stopping opposite McShane's mother.

"Thank you for the call, Mrs. McShane."

The woman smiled and hugged Susan.

"You come for dinner?" she said. "I'll fix Jack's favorite dish."

Not kielbasa, Jim hoped. Enough surprises for one time trip.

Susan stepped to the door, pausing to give him one last, doe-eyed look that only a cad could refuse.

"I'll see you then, Susan," he said.

"Yes," she said quietly, theatrically, and then she left. The door slam carried the proper expressive weight.

He turned to McShane's mother, puttering about the kitchen again. "What do you think?" he asked her.

She turned to him.

Her eyes were rheumy, wet pools. There's a lot of sadness here, he thought. Too much sadness.

"I think I want you to find Will."

22

There was a bus.

At least, the villagers called it a 'bus.' The grayish-green vehicle had seen better days. But Ali and her new family were lucky to get places. By the time the bus left the village—no more than a scattering of huts, some farmland, and a tiny Catholic church—it was filled. People stood in the aisles, laden with fruit and cuts of meat to share with family and friends.

But everyone seemed happy.

Everyone . . . except Khan Ha's grandmother, who sat grim-faced, her wrinkled lips locked together. She cradled the youngest boy close while an excited man sat next to her, loudly talking to a friend three rows away.

Ali sat with Tuan. She felt close to the boy even though it wasn't really her brother. He was quiet. And she sensed his sitting with her comforted him.

He thinks I'm taking him out of this country, she thought. Soon he'll learn that isn't true. . . .

Would they manage, Ali wondered. . . . The old woman, the two boys. Would they be all right?

God, she thought. I'm feeling guilty. Why the hell should *I* feel guilty? They're nobody to me, just more characters who don't realize that they're traveling with an imposter.

She looked at Tuan. And he—so alert to her every move—looked up.

He trusts me, she thought.

Damn. Why the hell does he have to trust me?

The bus—coughing up smoke and brushing against the leafy fronds of the trees near the edge of the road, bounced along, moving south. . . .

Very slowly. . . .

She fell asleep. And then she woke up. The bus was stopped. She had been lying against Tuan and he had born the weight of her head on his thin shoulders without complaint.

"Where are we?" Ali said.

"They stopped us . . ." the boy answered.

Ali tried to see through the forest of bodies that clogged the bus. The window—grimy, mud-splattered—offered only blurry shapes near the front.

"Who stopped us?" she asked.

"Soldiers."

"Soldiers?" Ali groaned. After the last night's encounter, that wasn't a good thing to hear.

She could see the grandmother sitting across the way, gumming at the air, muttering to herself . . . probably complaining about the stop.

And then she saw the greenish uniform of an ARVN regular. He was working his way through the bus . . . looking at people . . . asking them questions.

Ali leaned forward, trying to catch a few words.

He pushed through some more people, moving near her now. He turned and looked at her.

"Where are you going?" he asked roughly.

"To Kontum," she said. To see relatives. . . ."

Ali caught the old woman looming over her, her face doing nothing to cover the alarm she felt.

The soldier nodded. "And who is traveling with you?" he asked.

"My brothers, and my grandmother . . ." Ali pointed across the aisle.

The soldier turned and nodded.

"And where are you from?"

And Ali drew a blank. A name suggested itself . . . Tien Thuy. But she knew it would be the wrong thing to say.

She opened her mouth, but there was nothing she could think of—

The soldier stood there.

Until finally Tuan spoke up. "Con Thien . . ." he said.

The soldier nodded. "You may have trouble getting back. It may not be easy. . . ."

"That's alright," Ali said, trying to recover. "We can stay . . . at Kontum . . . as long as we need to. . . ."

The soldier nodded again and then, taking a breath, he pushed past some more people, towards the back of the bus.

"Well done," Ali said, leaning down close to Tuan. The boy turned and smiled at her.

Ali smoothed his shiny black hair.

Why does he have to trust me? she thought. She turned and looked out the grimy window . . . and waited until the bus again burped its way to Kontum.

The security police stood of front of them.

The two were indistinguishable, Lindstrom noted, except the one on the right has a rather weak chin.

Kind of spoils the whole effect, he thought.

"What is wrong?" the other cop said.

"Dr. McManus has collapsed." Dr. Beck said breathlessly. "He had a convulsion, a fit, rolling around on the ground."

The weak-chinned cop spoke. "We can call the emergency services of the university. They can come and help—"

Dr. Beck shook her head.

"No. That will take too long. He needs help immediately. If you would just help me carry him to the infirmary—"

The cops looked at each other. One pushed at his

pulse rifle, a nasty-looking weapon if Lindstrom ever saw one. He examined it carefully, to see how it was strapped on. It looked as if it would just slide off his shoulder.

How does one fire it? Lindstrom thought. Just pull the trigger? He hoped so.

The weak-chinned one spoke again. "We'd better call the emergency series. This is not a responsibility that we—"

Dr. Beck shifted into her most stern, authoritarian mode.

"Dr. McManus may have another stroke—he may die—if he's not removed immediately. I am his personal physician." She took a step closer to the boys-in-blue-kelvar. "You know how valuable he is considered by the Metropolitan—"

Beck faltered, having forgotten the name of the super agency responsible for the city's current state of decline.

"The Metropolitan Security Council!" Lindstrom added, covering the breech.

Lindstrom watched the two cops hesitate. They obviously didn't know how important McManus was. So they carefully considered what Beck said.

"It will just take us five minutes to get him over there. . . ." Beck said, interjecting a more rational tone into her voice. "Five minutes, and then you can continue your rounds."

Like nightmarish Tweedle-Dee and Tweedle-Dum, the cops looked at each other and nodded.

"Very well, then . . . show us where the man is—"

"This way," Dr. Beck said. "But be careful. He has been having sporadic fits, violent thrashing and all that. Don't be alarmed."

Lindstrom watched the cops follow Beck into his tiny office. And Lindstrom wondered . . . why are my palms so sweaty?

* * *

Jim parked the car, McShane's infamous Maverick, on Waller Street, just blocks from the center of the Haight-Ashbury hippie mecca.

He had searched for the car keys until he was forced to ask good old mom where *she* thought they might be hiding. She found it odd that he didn't know but she told him to look inside his tool chest, with its impressively complete collection of mechanics tools.

I admire that, thought Jim. McShane takes care of his car himself. Not something I would try.

Unfortunately, McShane's mother couldn't tell him much about where his runaway brother might be. Will McShane had worked in a place called Roger Calkins Music Store. But when she called, they said he didn't come around anymore.

The truth, or were they covering up for Will? Jim didn't know.

But if Will was about to be part of the Woodstock Nation, there was no better training ground than San Francisco.

Jim locked the car. And then he dug the photo out of his pocket.

He had snatched it when his mother had her back turned. The picture was stuck into the corner of a formal photograph, a high-school graduation photo. In the big photo, Will's now-long hair was still pretty much in check. In the snapshot—the more recent photo—the hair was long, dangling down in ringlets to his shoulders. He wore an orange vest and a purple shirt.

Loud was *in*.

He studied the picture. He might only get a glimpse of him, on a street corner, in a store, somewhere. He had to make sure that he would recognize him.

Then he put the photo away and started walking over to Haight.

He checked the address and then looked up at the sign.

The large puffy letters—not quite Peter Maxish but

definitely of that school—read ROGER CALKINS MUSIC COMPANY.

And below it, in small letters, a call to political action. . . .

SOCK IT TO ME.

He pushed open the door.

The music pounding out of the loudspeakers was loud. And the incense was strawberry.

He stood there, looking at the genuine hippies—yessir, right here, hippius Americanus, in their native state—pawing through the record bins. Individualists all wearing bell-bottoms, fringed vests, and beads.

Jim listened to the song. It was one he had heard a few times when researching the Beatles. By a group called Starship . . . or—

No, now he remembered, The Airplane. The *Jefferson Airplane.*

They had that a great lead singer. The powerful lady with the clear, metallic voice. Grace Slick.

Boy, he thought, does research pay off or what?

"And if you go chasing rabbits . . ."

That's me, Jim thought.

He started to go up to the front desk. The clusters of hippies stopped and looked at him.

He heard a few mumbling to each other, and Jim was confused. What did I do? Why the hell are they looking at me, laughing, giggling, and—

He heard a word.

Straight.

Straight, he thought, searching for its meaning in his memory of jargon circa-1968. Straight . . .

Straight. Oh, yeah. The hair. My shoes, he thought, looking down at his black army shoes. Straight.

No drugs, nor rock n' roll, no free sex, no commune.

No way.

If they knew I was a soldier, what would they do?

And Jim felt angry, then. Who the hell are they to put me down because I got my butt stuck—

(Thinking: Gotta be careful. Don't want to lose it. McShane is McShane and I'm—I'm—)

In fucking Vietnam. Who the hell are they to—

"Can I help you, man?"

A clerk—another hippie, but taller, with few more years on his fringed belt, spoke.

"Yeah," Jim said, "you can."

He came closer to the counter, looking around at the hippies as they finally stopped looking at him and went back to their records.

"I'm looking for someone."

"Hey, man, we're not the police or anything here. You see, it's like a music store. You dig?"

Jim nodded. "Yeah, I dig. But—" he pulled out the photo and passed it to the clerk.

"This is my brother. He worked here and—"

The clerk looked at it and then passed it back. "Right. Will. He's a cool freak, man. He started to get into guitar here. I dug him."

"Yeah, well, he worked here, right? And I'd like to find him."

The clerk looked away, as if he was checking to see if someone needed any help. Then he looked back at Jim.

"Right, he *used* to work here, you understand? But he didn't go for the hassle of getting here on time and shit like that. So he quit."

"I know," Jim said patiently. He heard some more tittering behind him. More words.

Fucking straight arrow.

Jim clenched his fist.

I'd like to take these creeps, these draft-dodging punks and—

Whoa! What the hell is wrong with me?

"Hey, man!" the clerk said. "You're like bringing bad vibes into the store, you know? This is a music store. Nice people buying nice music. And your playing detective is a real bummer."

Jim sniffed. The incense was pinched into an electrical clip that sat in a metal ashtray.

And there, just beneath the strawberry scent that was everywhere, Jim detected another smell, something a bit more acrid.

Old Mary Jane.

It's amazing, he thought. Smoking marijuana was once a big crime. Everyone had to cover it up, burn some incense. And thirty years later, drugs would own the country.

Own it . . .

"So, maybe you can go somewhere else, 'cause—"

Jim felt like he was about to lose the only contact he had. He leaned closer.

"Can I tell you something?" The clerk stood there. "I don't care what Will is doing, what he's wearing, what he's smoking or—" Jim looked around. A few nearby freaks were straining to listen—"who he's balling."

That is the correct term, Jim thought. Balling. It was in all the R. Crumb comics he found in the archives . . . the best source for sixties street lingo.

"I just care about this . . . his father is dying. He may be dead by tomorrow."

"Heavy . . ."

"He's got cancer all over, man. And he'd like to see his youngest son one more time. Can you fucking dig it? Nothing else. Just a last goodbye . . . across the goddam generation gap."

"Heavy . . ." the clerk repeated. "I understand. I mean, I got parents, too. Though I'm pretty fuckin' glad they're dead." The clerk took a breath. "Okay, you promise that's all that's going down here?"

"I swear to god, man," Jim said, with what he hoped was authentic fervor.

The clerk leaned close, leaning down to Jim's ear, speaking in a whisper.

"Cool . . . alright . . . I'll tell you where you can find him. But Jesus, don't tell him I told you, alright?"

"You got it."

And as the clerk spoke, a new song started blasting from the speakers.

John Lennon's ghostly voice singing about "Strawberry Fields Forever."

Jim turned to walk out of the store, the eyes of all the hippies, the freaks, watching him.

I met him, Jim wanted to say. I *met* Lennon in fucking Hamburg!

But he knew . . . they'd never believe it . . .

23

The bus stopped just outside of Kontum, not far from a small farm with a few dull-eyed cows looking on as half of the passengers got off.

He said the stop was for ten minutes . . . just ten minutes.

Ali stood beside the bus and she watched Khan Ha's grandmother, revived with a tremendous urgency, take the two boys and hustle them up the hill to the provincial capital.

Ali looked around. It was nearly dark and she had spent the whole day on the bus.

And she knew that she'd have to spend the night, rumbling slowly through the dark single lane roads, moving closer to the flatland in the south.

The grandmother only took a few more steps before she stopped, and turned.

"Come on, Khan Ha!" she screeched, her voice clear and sharp.

Ali saw the two boys watching her. And she saw especially Thuy, the older boy, studying, understanding already.

"Come! We may not be able to find some place to sleep if you don't hurry!"

The driver vanished into a nearby cluster of bushes. Probably answering nature's call.

Ali took a step. And then another. And then, while the three of them watched her, she shook her head.

"I'm not going . . ." she said.

"Not going?" the old woman shrieked. "What do you mean . . . 'you're not going?' This is *your* idea. You were going to save your brothers. . . ."

Ali took another step. Thuy came close to her, looking up at her.

"I—I can't go," she said. "There is something I have to do in Saigon. Something I must do. . . ."

She felt the old woman fixing her with hawklike eyes. "What? What is this? What are you up to? Is this some adventure for your General Chau? Have you lied to us all along?"

She felt Thuy take her hand and squeeze it. And he said, "Please . . . Khan Ha."

She turned to him and smiled. She slid her hands over his smooth hair.

"Don't do this," he said.

Ali gave Thuy's shoulder a strong squeeze.

"You can still go to Cambodia," she said, looking right at the boy's beautiful dark eyes. "But wait until the Tet is over . . . don't travel during Tet. This whole countryside will be under siege."

"Bah," Khan Ha's grandmother said. "It is a cease-fire. It will be the quietest—"

Ali squeezed Thuy's hands. She shook her head. "No. It will be the worst battle of the war. Stay here, in Kontum, until the siege is over. And then leave."

"But what about you?" Thuy said.

"I will come later. I will find you. It won't be hard finding two such handsome, young men and a powerful woman."

Now the grandmother came close, her hand outstretched, pointing at Ali. "But what are you up to? What are you doing?"

The bus driver came back from the bushes, smoking a cigarette. The smoke drifted toward Ali, the sharp smell mixing with the fresh hay and offal of the nearby cows still idly chewing their cud, watching everything.

"I have to go," she whispered. She turned back to

Thuy. "You're the man, Thuy. You have to be in charge."

She felt the boy fighting back his tears, fighting away the fear.

But she sensed a reserve, a power in the boy. In a year, he would have been taken into the NVA army. He can be strong if he has to be.

"You go to Cambodia," she whispered to him. "And I will try to find you later. But if I don't, if *anything* should happen, remember this—"

Ali saw the driver throw his cigarette down and step onto the bus.

I have to go, she thought. I have to—

"Remember this, Thuy . . . don't stay in Cambodia, do you understand? No matter how easy or how good things look, don't stay. Do you understand me? Do you promise?"

The boy nodded. His eyes were watery, barely holding back the dam.

The bus engine started. Ali pulled him tight and kissed Thuy's forehead. She ran and gave a quick squeeze to the grandmother, who still muttered to the night air. Thuy's brother gave her a big hug.

And then Ali ran into the ramshackle bus just as the driver was pulling the door shut. And he pulled away even before she had a chance to turn and look at them standing there, before the town of Kontum, watching her disappear.

They stood there, wondering, where she was going . . . and whether they'd ever see her again. . . .

The next part of the plan was tricky.

They had to follow the two burly cops into the office and hope that everything happened just the way Dr. Beck hoped it would.

When Lindstrom pushed in behind Beck, he saw that McManus was playing his part admirably. The scientist was sprawled out on the floor, his legs and arms akimbo. He kept shaking his head as if possessed with tremors.

Lindstrom looked at Dr. Beck.

She had moved to the side, near the overloaded metal bookcases. He saw her fiddling with the books, digging out—

One of the cops turned. "Are you sure he can be moved? We might hurt him."

"Oh, yes," Dr. Beck said, resting her arm on the book shelves in a pose that looked—to Lindstrom—very suspicious.

But the cop nodded and stepped closer to McManus. Dr. Jacob squatted on the corner of the desk, near the window.

Lindstrom didn't dare look over at Beck for fear that it would—in some psychic way—signal the cops to spin around and catch her.

I just have to believe she'll do it, he thought.

That's all. Faith.

Never one of my strong suits but—unfortunately—it's about all I have right now.

He watched the cops step over McManus's quivering body. They both tried to push their heavy rifles to the back so the weapons didn't swing in front of them.

"Don't we need a stretcher or—" one of them said to Beck.

Please, thought Lindstrom, let Beck be finished with all her preparations. . . .

"No," Beck said. "He has not hurt his bones or anything like that. Go ahead, You can pick him up—just be careful of his convulsing."

They leaned down. One of the cop's guns slid to the front.

"Damn!" he said, and he pushed it off his shoulder.

Lindstrom watched them work their hands under McManus's shoulder.

Beck slid close to him.

Lindstrom licked his lips.

I never was very good at secrets, he thought. Never any damn good at all.

As he was directed, he held his hands behind his back.

And he felt Beck's hand touch his. And then, something plastic. He let his fingers gently surround it, explored it, until he felt the plunger of the hypodermic . . . and then the needle.

And he took it from Beck's hand.

The cops lifted McManus into the air. Not a very difficult feat, as the scientist couldn't have weighed more than ninety-five pounds.

But then—just as they had him at waist level, high enough so that he'd be hurt if they dropped him—he started twisting and spasming in their hands.

Lindstrom shifted on his feet. He watched McManus's rather remarkable display. The scientist lolled his head from left to right, letting his tongue dangle out grotesquely. He sent his pelvis flying upwards, bending his body in a U-shape, threatening to go flying out of the burly cops' hands.

"What the hell is he doing?" the chinless cop said. "What the hell is happening?"

"Be careful," Beck said stepping closer to them. And as if he needed reminding, she gave Lindstrom a nudge that sent him tottering a few steps closer.

Beck kept moving, sliding back to the cop near Dr. Jacob and the window. "You must be very careful!" she warned. "This will pass in a few moments. But hold him as tight as you can. Do not let him—"

Lindstrom went from watching McManus's display of his contortion abilities to Beck, who was instructing the cops while she made sure that she had Lindstrom's eye.

She smiled.

Showtime, Lindstrom thought, slowly bringing the hypodermic around to the front.

"Don't let him . . . *go!*" Beck yelled the last word—

the prearranged signal—and Lindstrom raised his needle like an assassin's dagger and leaped at the cop.

He immediately saw that he had made a mistake.

As much as McManus was writhing, the cop was moving back and forth, trying to hold him up, struggling to keep his balance.

Just as Lindstrom made what he thought was a daring leap at the cop's back—eyeing the exposed back of the neck, the one-inch band of skin not covered by the helmet—the cop backed up.

And, reflected Lindstrom as the air was kicked out of him, this was what it must feel like to have one of those linebackers plow into you. One second you can breathe . . . and the next you can't.

It threw Lindstrom flying against the door.

He held the hypodermic aloft, protecting it above all things.

He smashed into the door.

And when he finally could take his eyes off the protected needle, he saw that Dr. Beck had better success.

Her cop was reaching behind, to the back of his neck, trying to pull out the needle that she had planted. But it was probably all over. There was enough sedative to put the cop out for the next few days.

That left—Lindstrom was chagrined to note—the other cop.

The cop had let go of McManus's feet. And the physicist landed with a sound thump on the ground. The cop turned to face him while Lindstrom still held the needle aloft.

Lindstrom watched the guard slide his gun off his shoulder, moving it to the front.

I wonder how big a hole that would make in me, he wondered. He was only seconds away from finding out the answer to that intriguing question when help came from the unlikeliest of sources.

Dr. Jacob, after his surprising revelation of another way back into the Time Lab, had returned to his normally withdrawn and preoccupied self . . . even as they planned the unlikely pharmaceutical cold-cocking of the two cops.

Now, just as the barrel of the pulse rifle was being leveled at Lindstrom, the portly master of the tachyon generator climbed on to the desk and, with a whoop that sounded more apache than physicist, he leaped on the cop.

Jacob's aim was off.

He missed the cop's broad back.

But he was able to latch an arm around the cop's thick neck and pull him to the side.

And—even better—the cop's helmet slid up an additional few inches. Now there was more skin for Lindstrom to target.

C'mon, he told himself. Don't screw up this time! And he ran at the cop—keeping one eye on the now-wavering gun barrel. A warning shot could just as easily end their plans.

"The neck!" he heard Beck scream.

Lindstrom paused—just a second while Jacob dangled from the cop. Then—like a dart player taking careful aim—he squinted and ran the hypo home, just below the weak chin.

The man gagged. That must smart, Lindstrom thought. His finger fumbled with the plunger, nearly sliding off.

He regained his perch and pushed down.

Jacob flew off. And the guard brought his gun flying to the front. Lindstrom watched horrorstruck as the cop's gloved hand tightened around the trigger.

And then—like a party balloon suddenly being popped—the cop collapsed to his knees, and then fell to the side.

Lindstrom looked down, sweating and grinning, and back up at the others. He didn't see Jacob. It took a moment for them to hear Jacob's muffled cries . . . from under the collapsed cop.

* * *

It could have been any poor, inner city neighborhood.

Except—Jim thought—most ghettos aren't this colorful. The streets here were filled with kids, garish and clownlike in their fringed vests, broad-brimmed hats, and jeans dotted with a quiltlike covering of patches.

And the shops—which were once a cleaners, or a neighborhood deli—had also undergone transformation.

Jim walked past an establishment called the "Light Fantastic." It apparently did a brisk business in posters and ultraviolet lights.

There was a poster in the front window bathed in Ultraviolet light from a long bulb on each side. It showed a ship, some Rembrandt or Durer rendering, sailing into a swirling red and blue spiral. The UV light made the Day-Glo colors alive, the picture shimmering, almost 3-D.

Just the thing to study while turning on. . . .

Another shop offered pipes and papers, essential weapons in the countercultural revolution.

A loudspeaker above the door was transmitting marching orders to the freak army.

Jimi Hendrix thumped out the abrasive, kick-ass licks of "Purple Haze."

Man, thought Jim, would Hendrix be freaked-out to realize that the late-nineties brought a host of Jimi impersonators gigging everywhere from the money pits of Vegas to the Rainbow Room.

Even the hippies became middle-aged.

He crossed another block, and then turned off to Ashbury . . . following it down to a street named Clayton.

Someone hissed at him from a stoop.

"Hash, joints, bennies . . . Got what you're looking for, man."

Jim looked at the guy sitting on the steps. He was

balding. And though he had bell-bottoms and a goatee, he was about five years too late for this trip.

More of a businessman, probably dealing bad acid to the kids from Marin County who came into town to "blow their minds."

Jim shook his head.

And again he felt that anger, that nasty feeling inside. A feeling as if he'd like to smash the guy.

He'd a predator, a fucking predator.

The first of the legion that would come to own the cities.

"Peace, man," the guy, the vulture man called to him from the steps.

"Screw you," Jim said back to him.

Wishing—

That the guy would say something back.

(And knowing . . . this is McShane is charge. This isn't my thing. I'm about as nonconfrontational as they come.)

He kept walking down Clayton, and he saw other residents of the Haight area. Old ladies pushing their small wagons filled with two bags of groceries.

A bunch of black men stood around, talking, probably wondering where all the grinning, goofy-faced white kids came from.

And then he came to the building. The sign read: THE NEW HAIGHT HEALTH COLLECTIVE. In smaller letters . . . 'ALL WELCOME.'

He pulled open the door and walked in.

He was in a waiting room.

Of course, a waiting room. Some freaks sat on a couch. One kid, with hair tumbling below his shoulder, tapped his foot nervously. He banged at his knee. To the right, there was a big black woman with two little kids running around, hiding under the chairs. A girl in a big paisley dress—hiding what Jim guessed was a pregnancy—sat morosely by herself.

"Can I help you?"

A young girl with a headband sat at a desk, a yellow pad in front of her.

Jim nodded.

"I'm looking for someone," Jim said.

The girl's face clouded over. She loomed uncertain.

"Er, this is a health collective. We try to get people hooked up with free medical service. I don't think—"

"I'm looking for my brother," Jim said.

The girl nodded.

"Will McShane."

The girl looked to the back, to the rooms.

"He's busy now. Helping one of the counselors."

She chewed her lip.

"Okay," Jim smiled. Everyone—except the two little kids—were watching him.

The flower-child/receptionist squinted. "He's talking someone through a bad trip. I don't want to—"

Jim nodded. He smiled and said, "That's cool. I'll wait outside. Just tell him I'd like to talk with him. Tell him it's his brother."

The girl nodded.

And Jim went outside.

24

Jim stood outside, leaning against a "no parking" sign, the balmy winter sun on his neck. A cool breeze seemed to whip up the street. It sent a scattering of lost newspaper pages scurrying around as if looking for a trash barrel.

A red car went by, a classic Mustang with brilliant whitewalled tires.

And when Jim turned back to the Medical Collective door, he saw his brother.

No, McShane's brother. . . .

He had to tell himself that.

Because looking at this lanky kid, pushing his long hair off his face, brought this incredible tidal wave of feelings.

He saw Will as a kid, with a crew cut, running after him, wanting to go with him to the movies.

And McShane calling back to him to go home.

You're too little, he yelled. You'll get scared by the monster, Will. Real scared.

And his kid brother had stopped and McShane had taken a quick glance back before picking up his pace. Nobody wanted a little brother tagging along.

This was almost a man standing here. What was he? Sixteen . . . Seventeen? Still my little brother.

And Jim felt other feelings, undefined jealousies, anger—

"Hi, Will," he said.

Will nodded and looked up at the glistening sun.

"How'd you find me?" Will asked, acting casual and disinterested.

"I walked around, showed your picture around . . ."

"Fucking-a!" Will said, turning towards him, sneering. "I knew you were a killer, but a detective?" His brother nodded, up and down . . . "I'm real impressed, Jack. . . ."

"No. I'm not here to track you down, Will. It's just that—"

"Hey look," Will said, taking a step towards him. "I'm not going back home, can you dig that? I've got a place to crash, and I've got some good friends. I don't need my old man jumping on my case about my hair, or my music, and I sure as hell don't need you playing big brother."

What's going on here? Jim thought. What's the history, the years of buried garbage that I'm trying to deal with here?

That I can't deal with . . .

Jim nodded. He tried to read the words on the shirt Will wore. The letters were puffy, twisting, distorted balloon letters. Quicksilver Messenger Service. What is that? he wondered. A competitor to Western Union?

Then below a pair of art deco winged feet he read two more words . . . Fillmore Auditorium.

That's here, Jim thought.

I could go see it.

Incredible!

If I wasn't leaving tonight.

"So you can just, like, go? Alright?"

Jim shook his head. He reached out to touch his brother's shoulder, but Will pulled away.

There's a lot of pain here, Jim thought.

"Dad's dying. He's got cancer running from his neck down to his belly, Will. He's not going to be conscious much longer."

As if on cue, Will picked out a nearly squashed box of Marlboro cigarettes. He dug a wrinkled cigarette out, tapped the filtered end against the back of his hand, and then stuck it his mouth. He lit it with a metallic lighter, just like the Zippos the Vietnam grunts carried.

"So he's going to die. That's what happens. You get old—" he took a drag—"and you die."

Jim felt his body go rigid again.

He saw other pictures. He and Will fighting, rolling around in the snow. Laughing at first, but then turning serious as he climbed on top of him and pinned his brother to the ground.

I'm pinning you, twerp. Now say uncle.

Jim heard the words playing back in his mind.

Say uncle, twerp.

And Will wouldn't. Though he brushed snowy clumps at his little brother's face. Though he held him there, crying, yelling, shaking his head back and forth. No, no, no!

The Medical Collective door opened.

A man in a white lab coat popped his head out of the door.

"Will," he said. "We could use some help." Will nodded and the man closed the door.

"I gotta split. Thanks for the news." He took another drag.

Will turned.

And Jim said, "Hey." His brother stopped.

This time he's leaving me behind, Jim thought.

"I go back tonight, Will. Back to Saigon."

"Enjoy," Will said.

"Just come see him. Sit down next to him. Tell him you're okay. Tell him that he's okay. Let him die in peace. Then you can come back here, back to your world, your life." Jim looked up at the building. "It looks like you're doing some good work."

"At least I'm not killing anyone."

"Right," Jim said after a pause. "Will you think about it?"

Will shrugged. ''I dunno,'' he said. ''Hey, I gotta go . . .

And Jim—who never had a brother—watched Will flick his cigarette away and walk back inside.

He didn't walk right back to his car. Instead, he walked around Haight-Ashbury. After all, this street carnival didn't last long, he thought. Might as well see it as long as I'm here. . . .

It was difficult getting the blue uniforms off the now peacefully sleeping guards.

But it was much harder putting them on.

It was decided that McManus and Dr. Beck would wear the uniforms.

McManus looked like a wizened kid playing dress-up until Lindstrom got the idea to stuff some pillows into the uniform, filling it out Santa-style.

''There,'' Lindstrom said, pushing a cushion down, broadening McManus's chest by a good three inches. Neither of the two cops was very tall, so height wasn't the problem.

Finally, when McManus was well stuffed, he turned to the others.

''Well,'' he said cheerily, ''how do I look?''

''Not bad,'' Lindstrom answered. ''Just remember to walk upright and try not to bend your arms. It makes the newspaper stuffing crinkle.''

Dr. Beck, on the other hand, had no need of stuffing. In fact, she threatened to make the uniform bulge at the midriff, something that embarrassed her.

Dr. Jacob invented a makeshift corset from Lindstrom's dusty curtains.

''If it wasn't for my beard . . . and my girth, I would gladly volunteer.''

McManus held up a hand—the newspaper crinkled. But otherwise he looked remarkably like one of the high-tech security cops.

''Don't worry.'' he said. ''Dr. Beck and I should

pass inspection. Just make sure you meet us in the lab. I don't know how much time we have—''

''What do you mean? We should still have plenty of time to to get you back there and—''

Dr. Jacob came forward and explained. ''No. You see, the longer the generator is left on, with subjects in *media res,* the more erratic the time correlations are.''

''I don't—''

''We don't have a one-to-one relationship between the elapsed time here, and elapsed time there. Well, we never did. But the longer the machines are left on, the more erratic the swings get. A half-hour here could become twelve hours back there . . . or vice versa.''

''And there's no way to tell?'' Lindstrom said.

Dr. Jacob shook his head. ''I'm afraid not.''

Lindstrom scratched his beard. ''Then what the hell are we waiting for? Dr. Beck . . . our two guests are all taken care of?''

Beck nodded. ''We have a minimum of thirty-six hours . . . maybe more.''

He turned to Jacob, who seemed flushed with excitement since his daring attack on the cop. ''And you know where to find the entrances to the electrical tunnel.''

''Many entrances,'' Jacob said.

He walked up to McManus.

''You should leave first, McManus,'' Lindstrom said.

McManus, a trace of a smile visible under his half-helmet, nodded. Then Lindstrom stuck out his hand.

McManus, and then Beck shook it.

''See you in the Time Lab. . . .'' McManus said.

''See you in the Time Lab!'' Lindstrom answered.

And then McManus turned, followed by Beck.

And damn! Lindstrom heard the crinkling noises as McManus walked away.

He shook his head and shut his office door. . . .

''We'll leave in five minutes,'' he said to Jacob.

And Jacob, with his new-found taste for adventure, beamed.

Ali had fallen asleep but then the bus stopped, and she woke up.

She looked around. It was dark inside the bus except for the faint glow of lights from the front. She heard the snores of the other passengers. The bus had pulled off the narrow road. She grabbed the seat in front of her, pulling herself forward. . . .

A man was watching her from across the aisle.

She turned to him.

"Where is the driver?" she said.

The man grinned a toothless smile, and gestured over his shoulder. Ali turned and she saw someone sprawled out, lying across a benchlike seat at the back.

"He's sleeping," the man smiled.

Ali nodded, and looked away.

Next thing, she thought, this rice farmer is going to ask me if I want to party.

The driver's sleeping.

We probably won't get started again until morning. Well, what was I expecting, Ali thought. Greyhound?

"Are you sleeping?" the man said.

Ali nodded, then added for emphasis, "Yes . . ."

She leaned against the window of the bus. She was awake now. Maybe she could sleep again. Maybe she couldn't.

No, she thought. The next time I sleep I want to be in my own body. In my own time. This was homesickness of a new and especially horrible sort. I miss my life. I miss more than just my apartment.

I miss me.

She caught herself slipping into self-pity.

No, can't have that, she thought. That would be definitely counterproductive.

"Everyone's sleeping," the man said happily, hoping to lure her into a few more words of conversation.

She stayed absolutely still, resting against the

smudgy window. Then, she saw a fiery glow somewhere over the trees. It was far away, a brilliant flash that outlined the jungle and illuminated the clouds.

She forced her head not to move.

Then she heard a rumble. A deep, almost soothing purr. Fireworks? she wondered. Or has the Tet Offensive started already. And if it has, maybe I'll never get to Saigon.

And this whole thing will have been a waste of time.

She wanted to go shake the driver, and tell him to get up, and get the damn bus moving.

But I can't do that . . . she thought. No way.

"Are you sleeping?" the man asked again.

Ali answered by making a slow, rumbling snore.

While her eyes, wide-open, kept looking at the sky for more flashes.

Westmoreland had doubled the night operations staff at MAC-V.

He knew that the personnel would be confused, wondering what the hell was going on.

And to kill any grumblings, Westmoreland was there looking at the updates coming in every fifteen minutes from the commander of Khe Sanh. He had action reports from Binh Thuan and On Lai, both right on the money as far as Scorpion went.

He's still got his credibility.

Scorpion's still a good source.

"Carry on," he said to the captain in charge of the map room, and Westmoreland hurried to go back to the radio room.

He met Kline at the doorway.

"Any more news on that supply group?" Westmoreland asked.

"Er, no sir. They moved off all the known trails and disappeared."

Westmoreland kept nodding. "And what do the reports say about the action in the provinces."

Kline had to hurry to keep up with the general.

"As expected, sir. In fact, both our forces and the ARVN are having an easy time of it." Kline paused, and Westmoreland sensed that the corporal was holding something back.

"Alright, out with it. What's your problem?"

"Everyone's real pleased, sir. I mean, if this is the Great Offensive, then it's all over before it even begins, General."

"What about Khe Sanh?"

Westmoreland stopped at the door to the radio room. He didn't want anyone else to hear this discussion.

"Right," Kline admitted. "It's pretty bad up there. But it's been bad up there for a while. These new attacks. They're almost like—"

The door to the radio room opened. A corporal came out, saluted Westmoreland, and then hurried away.

Kline took a step closer. "They're like feints, sir. Small actions. Just to distract us."

"Distract us from what?"

Kline shrugged. "That's what I don't have a clue about, sir."

Westmoreland nodded. Kline was good, a real good operations officer. But he had his limits. Westmoreland opened the door.

The men inside stood up at attention.

"At ease," Westmoreland said. "What's new from Khe Sanh?"

One of the radiomen handed the general a piece of paper. "The situation's the same, sir. No more shelling than last night. . . ."

"And the airlifts?"

"They're getting through, sir."

"And what about air support for the small towns under attack?"

"It's been offered on an 'as-needed' basis, sir. . . ."

"And?"

"And no one has called in any fighter cover. The engagements appear small, sir."

Westmoreland nodded. Damn right they appear small. Because they are. He turned to Kline.

"Can you skip sleep tonight, Wally?"

The colonel nodded and smiled. "Yes, sir. No problem."

Westmoreland smiled. "That's good. Because I think you hit the nail right on the head. All this stuff is a feint. The real party is going to be somewhere else. . . ."

And where is that? Westmoreland wondered. Where the hell is that?

Ngo Tran Trinh turned over in his bed. He was asleep, but outside his windows there was the noise of firecrackers, going off rat-tat-tat. Their bluish smoke drifted up from the street, into his window.

And Trinh dreamed.

Wonderful dreams.

Leading his men to the walls of the embassy, and then scaling the walls, flying over the barbed wire as if it wasn't there.

And the enemy fell like puppets.

While Trinh's men laughed. This was so easy, *so wonderful.*

And they ran to the main building of the embassy, joined by dozens of other squads, small, and well armed, all converging on the main embassy building.

But Trinh and his men would get there first, unscathed. They would take the building. And while the others took positions by the windows with their AK-47s and rocket launchers, Trinh would speak to Saigon . . . and the world.

Trinh would bring the United States to its knees!

There were more firecrackers, more smoke, and Trinh turned over, twisting his sheet around his body.

And he smiled.

At his wonderful dream.

25

Dr. Jacob walked alongside Lindstrom as if he was a superannuated applicant touring the prospective campus.

"Please," Lindstrom said. "Don't act as if we've just robbed the Bank of England!"

"Sorry," Dr. Jacob said, and he stepped a bit to the side, putting a carefully measured few inches between them.

The cafeteria was just ahead.

And it looked pretty much as he remembered it, thought Lindstrom. The sleek, modern building standing amidst so much classic red brick and history. It was ugly but serviceable.

And—if Jacob was right—it would be their ticket into the Time Lab.

Of course, there were guards outside. But then the guards were everywhere, watching the students walking from building to building. This must be what higher education in Naziland must have been like. Well-behaved students, very docile professors, and all these fierce-looking police.

It created such an inspiring atmosphere.

Jacob bumped into him.

"Would you please move—" Lindstrom began.

"I see they're stopping people," Jacob said. "See."

And he was right. The cafeteria guards would let ten students drift in and then stop one. The students had to produce some card. It was examined, and then the person was waved in.

"What in the world . . . ?"

"It must be a pass, some kind of identification. . . ."

"Right," Lindstrom said. "But press on. We can't do anything about it now. Just walk in and—"

They neared the steps. Unfortunately, no crowd of students appeared to mask their entrance. They fell under the solitary scrutiny of the guards. Lindstrom started talking. . . .

"No, my dear doctor. You see, epistemological concerns are strictly redundant. Everything is phenomenologically situational, even the—"

Lindstrom had his arm around Jacob as they went up the three broad steps. He spoke loudly, thinking: perhaps they won't interrupt a private conversation.

Jacob—unfortunately—didn't catch on. "What are you talking about?" he said, much too loudly. "Epistemology? You know I never took any philosophy and—"

Lindstrom felt the heat of both guards staring at them.

Out of the corner of his eye he felt one of the guards shifting on his feet.

Damn! Lindstrom thought. He's going to move. He's going to stop us and ask—

The guard took a step.

And at that moment the cafeteria doors flew open and a bunch of students hurried out joking about barf bags and mystery meat.

The food mustn't have improved, he thought.

They were laughing, pulling at each other, fueled by the clear fall air, the bright blue sky.

Lindstrom, with his arm around Jacob, navigated through them.

The guards were held back, swept aside by the wave of students.

And then Lindstrom and Jacob were inside the main

dining room, an endless expanse of plastic chairs and simulated wood-grain tables that stretched the length of the building. There were smaller dining rooms, for private department fetes, to the left and right.

"Which way?" he said to Jacob.

Someone at a table waved to Lindstrom . . . a student, and Lindstrom waved back.

"Quickly, Jacob. We're not exactly invisible here!"

Jacob looked left. "Down those stairs," he said, and the physicist hurried to stairs that led under the cafeteria.

Lindstrom followed, thinking. They're watching us now . . . wondering where we're going . . . what the hell we're doing.

The stairs curved around, under the dining hall, past a giant green metal door labeled 'boiler.'

"This way—I think," Dr. Jacob said. And he went down a long corridor, past a storage room, until they were nearly at the end.

They were at a door labeled, "Electrical."

"This is it. I mean, I think it is."

"Well, let's go. We can't waste any time—"

Dr. Jacob turned the door knob. It twisted about one-fourth the way around, and then stopped. The physicist looked at Lindstrom glumly.

"Go on, pull it!" Lindstrom said.

And much to no one's surprise, it didn't move.

"Damn! Now what will we do."

"There are other places we can enter the tunnel leading to the Time Lab . . ." Dr. Jacob offered.

"And they're all equally as likely to be *locked!* Do you have any idea how to get in here?"

Jacob shook his head. "No. I don't—"

Then he stopped.

"Wait. I do have *one* thought."

"How wonderful."

"But it might be a bit noisy . . ."

* * *

By the time Jim got back to his house, Susan was waiting for him.

She came running up to him and gave him a big kiss.

"Jack, I thought you'd be back sooner. I got off early from work and—"

Susan walked with him into the minute living room, dotted with a too-large chair and an uncomfortable-looking couch. The antimacassars were pinned firmly in place, yellowed flags of domesticity.

"I wanted to walk around," Jim said.

It had been wonderful, most of it. Seeing *Rolling Stone* on sale—the fourth issue! With Donovan and Jimi and Otis Redding on the cover. Otis—The Crown Prince of Soul—had just died in a plane crash.

And he thought, holding the issue, what is it with rock stars and airplanes?

He had walked past the Fillmore, walked up to the box office and got a schedule for the weekend. There were bands he didn't know—Blue Cheer, Mad River . . . and something called the Joshua Light Show.

Next week, the guy in the converted movie ticket booth said, Big Brother is coming. With Janis Joplin.

Now that would have been something to see.

His mother shambled out into the living room.

"Did you find him, Jack? Did you find your brother?"

"Yeah, Mom. He's fine." Susan clung possessively to his arm. He had to shake her loose to go up to this woman, McShane's mother, who was bearing her twin crosses with so much open pain. "He's fine. He's working with some doctors . . . helping people."

She looked up at him. Her eyes were dark and sallow, as if she had spent too many days in a dark room, the blinds drawn, waiting for death.

"Did you tell him about his father?"

"Yes. I did." Jim searched for something else to say.

The woman nodded. "Dinner's ready." She managed a smile. "Your favorite, spaghetti and meat balls. . . ." The woman shuffled back to the kitchen. Jim started to follow.

"Jack," Susan said, latching on to him, holding him in place.

Jim stopped and looked at her. "Jack," she sung more sweetly now, moving close. She was wearing perfume that was too sweet. And she had a lot of makeup on.

But she was pretty.

Especially when she pressed against him.

"Jack—when are you leaving?"

"Tonight," Jim said. "I have an eleven o'clock flight."

She kissed his lips, and he felt hers, rubbery and warm. She kissed his cheek whispered into his ear. "I called Reverend Dimme. He'll wait. We can do it, Jack, before you go back. Before you leave. We can get married. . . ."

Jim nodded. Now, he thought, that might not be such a bad idea. Why, it might even be what McShane wants.

Might be.

But I'm in no position to judge. None at all.

He wished he could tell her. Soften the blow a bit. I'm not who you think I am, sweetheart. It just wouldn't work, you see, a cute dame like you and someone renting a body like me.

He grabbed her hands and pulled her close.

"Susan, we can wait." He pulled her tight, once again feeling the quick responses of his body—which was saying, rather pointedly—go for it. "We can wait until I come back. . . ."

Susan was crying. Her tears were making her makeup go smudgy. Jim kissed her lips, tasting the salt. "We can wait. . . ." he said, "for a real wedding. Because I'm coming back, okay?"

Susan nodded, even as a fresh flow trickled down her cheek.

And Jim took her hand and led her into the kitchen. Not knowing whether there was a shred of truth in what he said.

"Explode it! You have to be crazy?"

Jacob put a finger up to his lips, shushing Lindstrom.

"No. You see, the stuff they use to wax the floors here has low flammability. But once ignited, it tends to expand. . . ."

"And how do you know that?"

"I've seen the night man work in our building. The chemical formula is printed right on the side of the container." Jacob reached out and touched his arm. "Oh, it's perfectly harmless. Unless you compress it in a small space, and, as I say, ignite it."

"Then what?"

"An explosion." Jacob smiled, and Lindstrom imagined the kind of demented teenager Dr. Jacob must have been.

Lindstrom looked at his watch.

"Alright then, but let's hurry. We don't have a lot of time."

Jacob ran back to the row of storage rooms, opening the doors, looking for the floor wax. When he found it, he hauled the large canister near to the door.

"Now, we need something to wrap it up in, like a ball, and—"

Lindstrom saw the physicist eyeing his tie, a Royal Blue with the Swedish Crown.

"Yes," Jacob said, fiddling with Lindstrom's neck. "This will do wonderfully. Perfect, as a matter of fact."

"Get your hands away. This was my father's tie and—"

Jacob shook a finger at him. "Do you want to get back to the Time Lab or not?"

Lindstrom sighed, shrugged, and undid his tie. He worked it back and forth until it was loose. He gave it to Jacob, who promptly dug a ball of the floor wax out of the canister.

"Horrible stuff," Jacob said. He fashioned a ball of the goop and then wrapped the tie around it until it was completely covered.

"Now . . ." Jacob said, as he used the tail end of the tie to fasten the ball tight to the doorknob. "That should be close enough to the lock. Now, all we need is a fuse." Jacob looked down, lost in thought. "Aha!" He bent over and started undoing one of Lindstrom's laces.

"What're you doing now?"

"A fuse, Dr. Lindstrom. I'm wearing loafers."

"If we run into any more problems, I'll be naked. . . ." Lindstrom muttered.

Jacob pulled the laces off one of Lindstrom's shoes and then coated it with a thin covering of the floor wax.

Then he stuck one end into the explosive.

"And I believe you have matches?"

Lindstrom—who hadn't had a pipe in hours—dug out his matches and handed them to Jacob.

"Now, we're all ready. If you'll just step back and—"

Jacob wasted no time lighting the lace. For a second, nothing happened. The laces seemed fireproof. But then they started sputtering and burning, slowly, leading up to Lindstrom's tie.

"I suggest we step back," Jacob said, wrinkling his nose.

And Lindstrom backed up watching the lace burn, wondering whether this crazy thing would work.

"What about the noise?" Lindstrom said.

"Hmmm?" Jacob answered, lost in rapt attention, watching the last two inches, then another inch burn—"

"What about the noise, won't the explosion—"

Jacob shook his head. "Oh, no. It's very low-level stuff. There will be some sound, true. A pop, really, but nothing—"

And at that point the explosion went off.

And inside the corridor the roar was deafening.

"Could you pass the meatballs?" Jim said to Susan.

She was still sitting sadly, a perfect match for his mother, who only played with her food.

As for Jim, he thought, that there's nothing quite like mom's home cooking . . . even if it isn't your own mom.

He speared a meatball and then covered it with more of the homemade sauce.

"Will you get to come back again . . . before your tour is up?" Susan asked.

Jim shook his head. "I don't think so. But I'm half-way done, you know?"

"You father won't live to see it," his mother said.

Jim answered by cutting his meatball in two.

Nobody said anything for what seemed an eternity. It got so quiet that Jim heard Mr. McShane sleeping in his room, that perfect, restless sleep that heavy medication can bring.

Jim took a bite of the crusty Italian bread—fresh from the bakery. Maybe I didn't do such a good job here, he thought. And he wondered whether it would have any impact on what happened back in Vietnam.

And for the hundredth time he prayed . . . help me. Someone. What am I supposed to do? If something is wrong here, show me how to fix it. . . .

But—as far as he knew—he was all alone.

It grew so quiet that Jim heard the clock ticking in the living room, marking off each second, part of the deathwatch.

And then he heard steps. Starting at the bottom of the stairs, and then winding their way up. Step after step.

He looked up.

McShane's mother had noticed them, too.

Neither of them said anything.

Jim looked at his watch.

I've got to go, he thought. I've got to get a cab and get out to the airport.

And he wondered what time it would be when he got back. Am I traveling with the sun—or away from it? Do I lose time . . . or gain it.

Funny idea, that. Losing time. Gaining time. That was something he was getting to be an expert about.

The steps kept coming. Until they stopped at the door.

The door opened.

His mother held her napkin twisted and weaned between her fingers, a tattered paper lifeline.

"Mom," someone said.

The woman looked up and then—quickly—at Jim. Her eyes spoke of thankfulness. Of joy.

And Will came into the kitchen. He looked from his mother, and then to Jim. And Jim saw that some hurt, one of those wounds that families inflict on each other, had begun to heal.

Or maybe Will had just been ready to come home. If only for a visit . . .

He nodded to Jim, and then said: "Where's dad? I—I've come to see dad."

Jim smiled. He turned and looked over at Susan.

Whose disposition, he noted, still hadn't improved.

26

The explosion echoed up and down the corridor, back and forth. Lindstrom covered his ears. He saw Jacob close his eyes.

And when the rumbling finally stopped, he said to the squat physicist:

"A small 'boom', huh? A pop! I wouldn't be surprised if everyone in the cafeteria comes running down to see if there's been a bloody earthquake!"

At that, they both turned and looked down the hall, ready to see the herd galloping down to see the spectacle up close.

But there was nobody.

They waited a few more seconds. . . .

"Do you think—?" Dr. Jacob began.

Lindstrom held up a hand, cutting him off.

Then . . .

"That's amazing."

"What is?" Jacob asked.

"That cafeteria must be so noisy with all the trays and talking, and the floor here so thick, that nobody even heard your pyrotechnical display."

"Or maybe it just seemed real loud to us, since we're right here . . . right next to it."

Lindstrom shook his head and then hurried to the door—

There was a hole in the door. But the door knob was still there. And the door frame looked intact. Lindstrom reached into the hole but—as he suspected—there was nothing to unlock the door with on the other side. Having postponed the inevitable as long as he could, he tried the doorknob.

It made a one-quarter turn . . . and then stopped.

"Damn!" he said. "It's still locked!"

Dr. Jacob walked over to him. "That's impossible. I placed it right by the lock and—"

Dr. Jacob bent down to examine the door, the lock. "I don't—" He reached out and gave the knob a hard twist. It caught again and then—as Lindstrom was about to storm away and curse at the walls—it clicked, and the knob turned all the way around.

Dr. Jacob popped open the door.

"After you," he said to Lindstrom.

Lindstrom walked in. The room was a mass of great metal tubes and circuit boxes . . . but not just for the cafeteria. It looked like a meeting place for all the electrical circuits on the campus.

There was a single light bulb on, powerful, but it barely lit the murky corners of the large room.

"Now, where do you think the tunnel is?" Lindstrom asked.

Dr. Jacob looked around. And Lindstrom could see he was confused by all the massive tubes, and bundles of electrical cable.

"I don't know—it should be near that wall, but there's nothing right there . . . except—"

Jacob ran forward. He moved a table.

And when he moved the table, Lindstrom saw what was in the wall behind it, close to the floor.

"There we are!" Jacob said. He gave a kick at the small door. "That's it! It goes straight to the Red Building!"

Lindstrom knelt down and looked at the door.

"It's kind of small . . ."

"Don't worry," Jacob smiled. "We'll fit. In fact, you go first and I'll push you through if there's any problem."

"Sometimes I wonder whether it's worth saving all this historical nonsense," he grumbled. He pushed his head into the hole. The tunnel was lit by light bulbs inside metal cages, and the cavern led left and right.

We're going to have to crawl! Lindstrom thought.

And at that moment he felt Jacob peremptorily pushing at his backside, not knowing whether it was his uncertainty or his girth that was impeding his progress.

Jim got to the plane with only ten minutes to spare. The cab hat hit traffic near Golden Gate Park, and then crawled along Third Street, along the bay.

He ran to the gate, and then onto the plane just as they shut the door.

He sat down next to a man wearing a cowboy hat. And he hoped the man would pick up on his 'I sure as hell don't want to talk' vibrations.

But as soon as Jim plopped down, the man turned to him.

"Where are you off to, soldier?"

"Hawaii," Jim said buckling his seat belt and kicking his small bag under his seat.

Isn't that where this plane goes? Hawaii.

The man showed himself oblivious to the subtleties of body language. "You staying there or shipping out to somewhere else?"

"I'm catching a transport to Saigon."

Then the cowboy stuck out his hand. "Well, son, I'm proud to hear that. I support what you boys are doing over there. It's the front line of democracy, you know. You ever read *None Dare Call it Treason,* son? It's all in there, Nam, Cam-bow-dia, all them places heading down the Communist road. Just like Eastern Europe . . . which that pinko Roosevelt sold to Stalin at bar-gun prices."

I'm trapped, thought Jim.

Even if I don't respond. Even if I don't say a word,

this fellow can drone on with less than minimal reinforcement.

I'll sleep. That might help.

"You know, I'm not too happy with Johnson as president . . . though he's a damn sight better than that Kennedy. We sure pulled one out of the fire in that one. Let me tell you. But Johnson at least has the balls, son. He's backing you. Now, when I was in Korea . . . well, the thing was just about over. But . . ."

Jim didn't even nod. The man had him prisoner.

The jet engines started.

He had figured out when he'd land in Saigon. With the travelling time to Hawaii, and then to Saigon . . . and the time difference.

He'd land sometime around midday.

January 31st.

The plane started moving. The stewardesses were displaying the life vests. A baby cried, a disconcerting sound that he thought probably had everyone on edge.

He thought of watching Will sitting in the dark, listening to him talk to his father.

His father had tried to scold him. You should live here, the man said. With your mother . . . and me. The voice was weak, it cracked and rattled like brittle branches on a dead tree.

But the man held Will's hand. And Will didn't respond. He didn't argue. He nodded. He told his father about working in the Medical Cooperative. That he might take some classes at night . . . see where it might go.

The father nodded. And there bloomed on his face a thin smile. He dozed off and then snapped awake.

He complained about Will's hair. But he held the boy's hand tight. Caressing it.

Finally Jim leaned over and said, "I've got to go, Dad. I've got to get a plane."

And Jim kissed the man on his forehead. He hugged his mother, who whispered "thank you," to him.

And Jim backed out of the room, the apartment, their lives. . . .

The plane's engine started to rev up, the whine growing louder, threatening to drown out the Patriotic Cowboy. But the man just raised his voice.

"We can lick their yellow asses, son. *You* can lick them."

And Jim thought:

I didn't screw up. Maybe Susan's a bit disappointed—but McShane will have to figure that one out for himself. But I was able to bring a bit of peace into those people's lives.

And here's my reward—

A ticket back to the 'Nam. . . . and this blowhard sitting next to me!

The bus started moving near first light, shaking Ali awake. Her bones ached, and her left foot was numb, and then it filled with pins as the circulation came back.

There were a few more people on board.

She sat up, wishing she had a piece of fruit, or some water to drink, wondering how long it would be until they reached the city.

They hadn't gone far when the bus stopped.

There were soldiers outside, and a jeep was parked in the middle of the road, blocking it. One of the soldiers came onto the bus and spoke to the driver. Ali watched, and she tried to listen. But they spoke too quietly. She had to wait until the soldier got off, and the driver got up and faced his passengers.

"The road ahead is closed," he said. Everyone started groaning and complaining to their neighbor.

One man called out, "Does that mean we can't get to the city?"

The driver took over his khaki pith helmet and scratched his head.

"There is fighting down that road. Lots of VC."

"Is there another way?" the man yelled out.

Please, Ali thought. Don't let me come this far just to get stuck in the middle of the jungle.

"There is a road through the mountains, but it is miles away from here . . . much farther—"

"Take us that way!" people started yelling, and Ali joined in, yelling at the man.

The driver smiled. "It will be more time . . . and more gas . . . I will have to drive all day and—"

Ali stood up. "We'll pay!" She looked around to see if everyone else shared her sentiments. But they were looking up at her as if she just gotten off a spaceship. "*I'll* pay," she said. Khan Ha had acquired a sizeable nest egg . . . and Ali didn't mind using it.

The driver grinned. "Yes, then I can take you." He turned back to his seat and started the bus.

The other passengers clapped.

Ali smiled graciously and sat down. And then a woman sitting behind her offered her an orange, big as a grapefruit.

It was the best thing Ali ever tasted. . . .

There would be no work today for Trinh. Or tomorrow, or the day after or the day after that.

He smiled, as he got off his bicycle and propped it up against the warehouse entrance. The mamasan would think that he just ran off to celebrate. A lot of the workers did that, only to return to beg their jobs back.

He knocked on the door and Giang let him in. There were other men inside.

This was his team! Trinh thought proudly. These were the people who were going to fight with him.

Giang brought him over to the table . . . he introduced him to the men. Trinh nodded, not remembering their names. It didn't matter. They had been kept separate so that no one could endanger anyone else. If one was captured, that's all they'd lose. The weapons were already scattered around the city.

Giang pointed at the map.

"There are many squads," Giang said quietly. "Many . . ." Giang outlined the embassy. "The building is to fall as soon as fighting breaks out in the city . . . at six-thirty. They will be having cocktails inside. It will be dark."

Trinh nodded. This was a great moment, to be standing here, talking about this.

"But three of the squads have a special job," Giang said with emphasis. He pointed a figure at Trinh's chest. "And your squad is one of them."

Yes, I know, thought Trinh. He had memorized where to go, and what to say. I am prepared. thought Trinh.

"Perhaps one of the others will get there first. If so, no matter. You should help defend them."

No, Trinh thought. It will be *my* group. He looked at the men. They were young, all of them with bright, eager faces. They looked strong and he knew that they had received the same training that he did, in the distant villages, at night, learning how to use the weapons, how to fight.

Some may have been in battles before.

"I understand . . ." he said to Giang.

Giang nodded. "Today, you will study the plan, the attack." He walked around the table, nodding. "You will anticipate everything that might go wrong . . . and what you can do about it. You will learn where the weapons are and where the other groups will enter. And then we will go over the whole thing again and again." Giang looked up and smiled at them.

"Until it is time. . . ."

And Trinh, and the others all smiled back.

General Chau sat with the other generals, studying the maps of South Vietnam.

Some had doubted his plan. A few even questioned his loyalty behind his back. But when word was received that Ho Chi Minh himself gave his blessing, it ended the controversy.

And that, thought Scorpion, was easy.

It was easy to alert Uncle Ho to a viper in Hanoi, someone who plotted behind him. There was plenty of evidence to get the would-be assassin shot. And, of course, it brought great credit to General Chau.

No one dared question his plan now.

"But what do you think, Chau?" one of the generals said to him, he was an old man who walked stiffly, a valiant survivor of the years of struggle with the French.

I haven't been listening, Scorpion thought. Still, he nodded, and said, "It has much merit. . . ."

The old general said, "See!" and worked to convince the others of his ideas.

Whatever they were.

Scorpion looked at his watch. Nearly time . . . I'll be gone, and Chau will be back and—much to his surprise—he'll be responsible for an incredibly dashing and innovative plan.

A plan that will bring about the end of Vietnam. Maybe all of Southeast Asia. By the time the conventional war between the US and China—supported by the USSR—is over, the borders of Vietnam, Thailand, Cambodia, Laos, will all be a distant memory.

The United States will have suffered a major defeat, eaten up by turmoil within and devastated by a costly, cumbersome war.

The USSR will land on the moon. It will establish hegemony over all of Asia. Latin America will—with nary a word from the US—become a client state of a powerful Soviet nation.

The Iron Men will cease to be outcasts with a powerful technology.

The USSR will become our country.

He laughed. Forget that. By the twenty-first century, it will be our *world*.

The way it was intended to be . . .

He moved in his seat, as the old NVA general still droned on.

There was one thing that bothered him.

His information was that the other Time Lab—still at some place unknown—could only send its travelers on a one-way trip. And that—for the purpose of rectifying time—rendered their device all but useless. But it appeared, after our troubles in 1942, that that had changed. . . .

And if that was true, things might take a dangerous turn.

Because, he thought, we have our Achilles' heel, too.

True, we can go back and forth—within certain physiological limits. It isn't a shuttle, after all!

But—so far—we have only been able to have one time traveler in place at a time. Our generator just cannot do anymore.

And that could be dangerous.

Very dangerous.

He reached down and took a sip of his mint tea.

27

The tunnel narrowed . . . to the point where Lindstrom thought that he'd be stuck like a cork in a wine bottle. He saw the heavy electrical cables, bound together like hemp.

"Blast it!" he hissed back to Jack. "Are you sure this will take us there?"

"Yes. Quite sure. Just keep going, Professor Lindstrom."

Lindstrom grunted and crawled a few more feet.

Every now and then he thought he heard a sound. Distant steps echoing from above, from whatever building they were below. A high-pitched squeak . . . maybe a door opening, or a rat searching for a way out, a way to the wonderfully overflowing garbage dumpsters filled with cheez-doodles, kernels of popcorn, and the crusty bones of pizza.

He thought of crawling forward, through a dark spot between the naked bulbs that dotted the tunnel.

Crawling right into one of the rats.

He scratched at his chin, as if his beard could serve as a nest for a rodent.

The tunnel narrowed a bit more. "What is this, Jacob? This is going nowhere!"

"Just push on . . ." he urged him.

Lindstrom nodded. And then, the tunnel widened. As he came closer to the next light he saw that this was new construction. The tunnel curved a bit to the right, and then up to the left.

Damn, he thought. Old Jacob is right! This is leading somewhere.

"Keep a look out for an opening," Jacob called to him. "A manhole, some way to climb up. We should be getting near there . . ."

Lindstrom craned his head around but he saw nothing. He crawled—babylike—a few more steps. Still, he just saw the smooth ceiling of the tunnel. He started to lose hope. Maybe, he thought, there are dozens of tunnels. *Dozens.* And this could be the wrong one.

"Do you see anything?"

Lindstrom shook his head. He crawled a few more baby steps. "No, nothing here. Nothing at—"

Then he saw it. A small, round metal plate, just overhead.

That's it, he thought.

And then—another observation . . .

There's no way in hell I'm going to fit through that small opening.

The bus rumbled through the jungle. Someone produced a bottle of wine and passed it around. Everyone in the bus started singing, even the driver. And then—funny thing—Ali found that she knew the words.

"In our village, is a man . . .

"Who laughs every chance he can . . ."

And the chorus consisted of these great sung laughs.

Ali laughed too, looking at everyone, so happy that it was a holiday, happy that they could forget about the war.

Then, the bus started trailing down a hill. The thick covering of trees and bushes gave way to open farmland. And then they rumbled through a small town, causing its residents to come out and see what was making all the noise.

Until—through the sea of heads—Ali saw the city from the front window of the bus.

The skyline of the big hotels, the smoky plumes from the factories, the sprawl of huts and shacks that surrounded the city.

Saigon.

A Paris of the East, it was said.

Everyone stopped singing. They all watched the city come closer and closer.

"Get your clothes off!"

"What the hell are you talking about?" Lindstrom shouted.

"You are right. You will not fit through here if you're dressed. But if you're naked, it might give us the necessary few inches we need."

"And it might give me one hell of a case of nasty abrasions."

Jacob's face turned serious and severe. It was a look Lindstrom hadn't seen before. "Look, Lindstrom. We don't have a lot of time. Synchronization is out of whack . . . the generator has been working much too long. A few minutes here, could be *hours* there. We don't have the time!"

Lindstrom shook his head. He was quiet for a second, thinking about it. He heard another squeak.

Wonderful, he thought. How nice to be nipped on the bottom by a giant sewer rat while trying to crawl through a rabbit-sized hole.

There was something of the fantastic in all this.

Except he didn't feel like Alice out for a romp all on a summer's day.

"Will you just do it?"

Lindstrom hesitated.

"Because if you don't do it, I will go myself. You can stay here. . . ."

"Very well . . ."

Lindstrom turned around and, with much difficulty, worked his clothes off. His shoes first, and then he wriggled out of his tweed slacks and striped boxer shorts—

He looked over his shoulder to make sure that Jacob wasn't looking. The physicist was considerately studying the opening.

Then he took off his shirt, and his t-shirt. He got a sudden ripe whiff. Yes, he thought, it's been a while since a bath and a change of clothes.

Finally, like an albino sea lion stuck in a laundry chute, he turned around and said, "Ready."

"Good. I'll go through first . . . make sure everything looks okay. Then you can send your clothes up . . . and then I'll pull you through."

"Easier said than done."

Lindstrom was forward of the hole. He heard Jacob push on the metal plate. Then he heard the scrape of metal as Jacob slid it to the side.

"There," he announced. "That was rather easy. Now, I'll just—"

He heard Jacob make an "oomph" sound and then some huffing and puffing.

"I'm through!" Jacob whispered. "Back up and hand me your things."

Lindstrom crawled backwards and, when he passed the hole, he handed the scientist the wad of his clothes.

Jacob took them and then returned, extending his hand down. "Alright, let's go."

Lindstrom reached up and took the hand. And he crawled forward, guiding his head through the hole. That fit easily, he saw as his head and the one arm, emerged.

Now came the tricky part, getting his shoulders through the opening.

Lindstrom twisted left and right, before bellowing, "It won't fit!"

"Quiet!" Jacob scolded him. "Now, tilt your left shoulder down, just a bit. Tilt it . . . that's it—"

Lindstrom awkwardly forced his one shoulder down.

"Now, push up. That's it. Come on, push all the way."

Lindstrom pressed against the ground. He felt his

shoulder scrape the edge of the hole. It scraped, rubbing his skin raw. But then it popped through.

"There!" Lindstrom said, grinning. "I did it."

He looked around. They were in some kind of storeroom. It was dark, but he could see boxes and file cabinets. A thin band of light cut across the room from a door leading out.

"Now the rest of you," Jacob said. "Come on. Push through."

Lindstrom nodded. In his excitement, he had forgotten about his ample girth. He licked his lips and placed his hands on either side of him.

Alright, he thought. Here goes. He started to hoist himself up. There was no problem for the first few inches. But then he felt the most horrible squeezing sensation.

"It's not going to work!" he yelled. "There's too much of me."

"Yes it will!" Jacob ordered back. "Keep pushing!" And Jacob grabbed Lindstrom's head, holding him securely around the chin and pulling.

"Not there, you idiot! Grab my shoulders!" Lindstrom said.

And now Jacob anchored himself right over Lindstrom and pulled. And the history professor felt his stomach sliding through the hole slowly, torturously, easily scraping off a layer of skin.

If I get through this, I'll never eat another eclair as long as I live. I swear . . . he promised. Then—just as he felt his stomach passing through the hole—a miracle if there ever was one—the door flew open.

They were both covered in light.

And though the two figures at the door stood in the shadows, there was no mistaking the shape.

They were two of the Metropolitan Security Force, dressed in the fierce blue uniforms.

"Oh, no. . . ." Lindstrom groaned.

And what he heard next surprised the hell out of him.

* * *

Jim's second plane droned on, a military transport. It was quiet, half-filled with a scattering of soldiers that were—lucky guys—on their way back to Vietnam.

He had left the happy vacationers back in Hawaii.

Jim slept fitfully, waking up as the plane lurched from one altitude to another, trying to dodge some nasty Pacific storm.

He dreamed. Of bombs exploding all around him. Of white phosphorous lighting up the night sky. Of the bars of Saigon honking out their thumping siren call to drink and play because tomorrow . . .

And he dreamt of Ali.

As she was back in New York. Calm, cool, level-headed. Always in control, he thought. The perfect counterbalance to his own impractical enthusiasms.

And he dreamt of her as she had looked the last time they met. . . .

As a well-padded German fraulein. Each of them were in new bodies, touching and exploring each other, excited by the novelty . . . knowing that they were still the same.

The dream went on, fueled by the steady rhythm of the plane . . . as he pictured rolling around on Ali's new body, enjoying its fleshy fullness.

And he was still having that dream when the plane landed in Saigon.

Lindstrom froze. He saw Jacob put up his hands. And as uncomfortable and awkward as his position was, Lindstrom guessed that he should follow suit.

Though he did feel foolish raising his hand in the air, like an oversized rabbit caught about to nibble at the cabbage patch. The two guards stood at the doorway and then, after looking over the situation, they walked towards them.

And Lindstrom heard the crinkling of newspaper.

"Goddam!" He yelled. "McManus and Beck! You're here!"

Lindstrom struggled to get out of the hole, while one of them found a light switch and the room was filled with light.

McManus pulled off his helmet. "Of course we are. The guards outside the building didn't question our entrance at all, especially when I told them we were under the direct orders of the Security Council."

"What's that?" Lindstrom asked. "Should I know about that?"

"Oh, I doubt that . . . since I made it up."

Dr. Beck came forward, also removing her helmet. "We told the guards in the lab that they had to patrol the outer gates of the campus. We said that there were rumors of an attempt to break into the lab."

"Brilliant!" Jacob said.

Only then did Lindstrom finally say, "Well, would you mind helping me the rest of the way out?"

McManus came over to give Dr. Jacob a hand.

"And—er—Dr. Beck. Would you mind, er, turning the other way. I'm not—"

She grinned, and turned to the door.

McManus and Jacob had no trouble pulling him out of the hole. Lindstrom quickly got back into his clothes.

"And the lab?" he said.

"Oh, it's fine. Everyone is sleeping peacefully. Isn't that right, Dr. Beck?"

Dr. Beck—her back still to them—nodded.

"Oh, you can turn back now," Lindstrom said.

"We must move fast through," McManus said. "We can't be sure how far off we are from synchronicity. If it's as bad as I fear, then every few minutes here are vital."

"Then let's get going," Lindstrom said.

McManus reached out and grabbed the professor's arm.

"But Lindstrom, I will be the one going back."

"McManus, you're much too frail, and—"

"You *have* to stay here. I've explained it to you!

Who else can keep history on track?'' McManus turned to Dr. Beck. ''Dr. Beck agrees. And—'' he looked back at Jacob.

Lindstrom also looked at his erstwhile partner.

''Yes . . . I believe Dr. McManus is right. Of course, I'd go if I didn't have the generator to worry about.''

''Nonsense. I'll be fine.'' McManus clapped Lindstrom on the back of his shoulder. ''So let's get to it. I've been looking forward to this for a long time. . . .''

And Lindstrom followed McManus out of the storeroom, back to the Time Lab.

Which was a welcome sight indeed.

''Welcome back, sir!''

Jim had stepped off the stairs from the plane not really expecting to see anyone, still waiting for some apparition to appear and tell him what the hell he's supposed to be doing.

Instead, Sergeant Howell was there, a big grin on his face.

''Howell!'' Jim said. ''What are you doing here? Why aren't you back at the base—''

''New orders, sir,'' Howell said, falling into step with Jim. ''MAC-V has sent companies from II and III corps into the city. Don't know what for . . . just a precaution. We're here for a couple of days . . . then it's back to the woods. . . .''

Jim looked at Howell. The man was obviously happy to be out of the jungle. Saigon was music to most grunt's ears.

''Tonight we're on duty in the city.''

''Where?''

''The Armed Forces radio station. A detachment is to assist the MPs in guarding the station.''

Jim nodded.

Howell seemed to be waiting for him to say something.

Something intelligent, Jim thought.

Which wasn't forthcoming.

"I—I've got a jeep, Lieutenant. I can run you by MAC-V. You can check in, wash up. We go on duty at 0300 hours."

"Right. . . ." Jim said.

A radio station. He tried to think how that could be important. After all, I'm supposed to be a *key* person in a *key* place. But what the hell is this? A radio station? He never heard any story about the Tet Offensive involving a radio station.

"Lieutenant, how are things at home?"

"Home?" Jim said, half listening. "Oh, alright. I spoke to my dad. He's in bad shape. But he's comfortable."

"Sorry to hear that. . . ." Howell said.

Howell led him to a jeep parked by the main gate of Ton Sun Nhut.

"And everyone else, your mom, your brother?"

Jim smiled. "Better than before. I think—yeah, I think I helped."

Howell got into the driver's seat.

"And your girlfriend?"

"Oh, she's not too happy," Jim said smiling.

A large plane, a mammoth transport roared overhead. Howell started the jeep.

"But I think she'll still be there waiting when I get back," Jim said.

"Sure she will, Lieutenant." Howell pulled away.

Sure she will, Jim agreed.

Howell drove quickly out of the airport compound . . . while Jim followed the progress of the giant transport vanishing into some clouds to the north.

The bus stopped and everyone got off.

The city, the buildings, the river catching the light were still miles away.

"What's wrong?" she said to the driver.

"Eh?" he said.

"Why aren't you going there?" Ali said, pointing to the main part of the city.

"No. We stop here. You can take the city bus, or cyclos. I stop here." The driver smiled.

Shit! Ali thought.

This is like getting to Oz.

But I'm close, she thought. Saigon is just ahead. Saigon.

And the Radio Station.

And—please God—Jim.

She got off the bus.

And the driver rudely slapped the door shut behind her.

28

After stopping at MAC-V headquarters so Jim could check in, Howell suggested taking him to his temporary barracks to rest.

Jim touched his arm.

"No. I want to go to the radio station."

The streets were filled with people, clogged with the blue Renault taxis and the cyclos whose drivers cursed at each other as they juggled for space.

The air was laced with the intermittent pops of the firecrackers.

What a perfect set up for an attack, Jim thought. No one would know there was any real action until they caught a live bullet.

"No," Jim repeated. "Take me directly to the radio station."

"But sir, I thought you'd like to get some rest. I'm fine, sir. I have the men posted . . . they're on four-hour rotations." Howell nodded. "Everything's cool, Lieutenant."

Right. Except that Jim knew that if McManus was supposed to do something, he'd better make himself available. And sleeping through the attack in a hotel wouldn't do.

No matter how damn tired he was.

"I'm alright, Sergeant. I'd rather be on duty. Just make sure I get some coffee. . . ."

"Alright, sir. There's no need but—"

A cyclo cut across Jim's path.

The driver looked back at the jeep, his face sneering, cursing, until he saw the military green and small American pennant. And then he turned away. He looked as if—as if—

Jim watched him pedal away.

He looked scared.

As if he was hiding something.

Jim watched him turn in the other direction, away from Hong Tap Thu Street.

He didn't have a passenger.

But in the back of his cyclo, where a passenger would sit, there was something.

A box. A crate.

Something.

Funny, thought Jim.

Giang stood at the door.

"Remember," he scolded. "There are many teams. Stay to your area. Kill as many of the marines as you can . . . but do not waste your time fighting them. And do not damage the embassy wall."

Trinh nodded. He looked at the other men in his squad. They looked nervous. And so do I, he guessed.

But we all know what to do. And like army ants hurrying to gather the crumbs of bread dropped in the tall grass, we'll come together, groups from all over the city.

"You will call me as soon as the embassy is secure, as soon as you have your hostages."

Trinh nodded.

"Kill no one who isn't a soldier. They must all stay alive."

Trinh nodded again. He had heard this before, but now he knew it was the last time, the last review. . . .

It was almost time for action.

Giang smiled . . . and looked at his watch.

"You go in five minutes. . . ."

Trinh nodded. The cyclos . . . that was the wonderful part.

Hiding the weapons in the back of the cyclo! They'd be scattered around the building. While the army, the ants, converged on the building.

And—Trinh thought—the city will be ours.

Except, Chau thought, walking around the map.

Nodding, thinking . . .

That wasn't the real plan after all.

He had sold it to the other generals that way. And—despite some concern—they approved it. Of course, without the benefit of the Iron Men's historical hindsight, they couldn't see what the outcome of the plan would be.

The expected American withdrawal.

Perhaps simply an American willingness to negotiate.

No, they don't understand the United States.

General Westmoreland was about to ask for two hundred thousand men. And he was about to be rejected. The country had had enough, Johnson had had enough. And Richard Nixon—the one they call "Tricky Dick"—was ready to take the stage . . . the great international statesman who would end the war.

That was what was supposed to happen.

Now, Chau thought, it will all be different.

"General Chau," a soldier came up to him, holding a piece of paper.

He looked at it. There were the code names of all the VC divisions ready to swarm around Saigon. Most of them would create disturbances. Some sectors, such as Phu-Tho, were to be held and reinforced as VC strongholds . . . until the NVA regulars arrived.

But all of that—as wonderful and dramatic as it was going to be—was secondary to the main arena.

This is the dawn of the age of terrorism.

I will make the sleeping American dragon awake . . . before it decides to slumber on forever, Chau thought. And the result will be a world dominated by the Soviet Union, ideologically loyal to the principles of Marx, and Lenin, and Stalin. It will be controlled by the military, with the entire economic resources of the world ready to fuel its beleaguered economy.

And the cost?

Chau smiled.

World War III.

He crumpled up the telegram.

Not such a high price to pay, he smiled.

And as he waited for the next note, the one that would tell him that the attack had begun, he looked at his watch.

I want to get out of here, he thought.

All the interesting parts are over. . . .

Westmoreland walked up the steps of the embassy. On his way into the building he had checked the placement of the marine guards . . . spaced every ten feet. There were MPs as well at the doors to every building.

The embassy looked secure.

For anything but a full-scale attack, the compound was fine.

And that kind of attack was impossible. No troops could move through the streets. The streets were patrolled by MPs and Saigon police under General Loan.

By the time any force got within blocks of the embassy, a small army could be mustered.

He came to the doors of the main embassy building. The lights were on, making the building look like a chateau in a *son et lumiere* spectacle. The ambassador was hosting the traditional formal cocktail party and dinner for the Vietnamese government officers in Saigon. With Thieu's absence, General Cao Ky was the honored guest.

Ky knew that the US was growing more impressed with his style, as opposed to that of the phlegmatic Thieu, who seemed less and less interested in pursuing war.

An MP opened the door and Westmoreland entered and turned to the left, to the large reception room. He stopped and stood there.

"Champagne?" a servant asked.

Westmoreland shook his head.

"General!"

It was the ambassador, Ellsworth Bunker. Bunker was a dynamic supporter of Westmoreland's policies. If more troops were approved, it would be in no small measure due to Bunker.

Bunker extended his hand.

"No champagne?" Bunker asked.

"No," Westmoreland smiled. "I'm on duty. . . ."

The ambassador nodded. "Still concerned about Khe Sanh?"

"Yes. A bit." General Ky spotted him from across the room and he waved. Ky was wearing a jacket and tie—a change from his normal iridescent flamboyant scarfs. He looked back to Bunker. "But there's no change there. And no news from Hue . . . yet."

"You'll stay for dinner?"

Westmoreland smiled. "No . . . I really should stay at my headquarters and watch what happens."

"Well, then, a rain check." Bunker held up his half-filled champagne glass. "I will salute the new year in your honor."

Westmoreland nodded and watched General Ky disengage from a conversation with an attractive secretary and glide towards him.

Westmoreland sighed. Now he'd be stuck here for another ten minutes at least.

Bunker turned and saw Ky swooping down on them. "Oh, my condolences . . ." and then the ambassador abandoned him.

"Now!" Giang said.

He threw open the door, and Trinh and his men walked out, calmly, as if they were off to see a soccer game.

It was twilight. The sky was limned with purple, with streaks of fiery red.

"It's not going to rain, Trinh thought.

Perfect.

As instructed, he and his men separated, putting yards between them, stopping now and then to examine a window, or to examine some fruit in a stall, while they moved towards Thong Nhat Avenue, and the embassy.

At one point Ali had to push through a crowd of people. The streets were filled. Everyone was excited, talking loudly. She smelled the heady aroma of beer and wine, and the smell of fresh fish being cooked and sold right on the sidewalk.

Some men stared at her, followed her.

Now, every step hurt. Her ankle felt weak and wobbily, as if it would collapse in on itself. She stopped to buy a greenish banana—a plantain, she guessed. It was bitter, but she ate the whole thing as she just kept walking.

It got dark, and there were no brilliant street lights to guide her, just the warm yellow glow of the lights from the tiny bars and restaurants along the way to the center of the city.

And there were more firecrackers, a constant clattering now. She kept thinking, there, that's it. That's the attack. And I'm too late to stop it. All because of that damn bus.

She hoped to get a ride. A bus going into the city, a taxi, something. . . .

But everyone was on holiday.

And when she came to a small rise in the road, she still saw the main part of the city, the river, the docks, the big hotels.

The radio tower.

Were still in the distance.

I just never seem any closer, she thought.

She took a step. Her foot caught in a crack in the

pavement. It grabbed her foot and wrenched it. She fell to the ground hard.

A man behind her nearly stepped on her.

He yelled at her to get up, to get out of the way.

Ali's ankle throbbed from the pain. God, she thought, what if I can't walk on it? She rubbed at her nose . . . feeling as if she was about to start crying.

This is too much, she thought. I can't go on anymore. Too much—

She rubbed her ankle. Then, taking a breath, she stood up, testing her foot.

One step after another, she told herself. One . . . after another.

And she repeated that inside her head, a chant to get herself to continue, and then keep going.

Trinh looked over his shoulder. They were there, his men, trying to avoid looking at him.

And Trinh turned onto Thong Nhat Avenue. It was night, and they blended in with the hundreds of other people celebrating the Year of the Monkey.

Westmoreland finally escaped to his jeep, promising to have breakfast with Ky just as soon as possible.

"Home, James," he said to Kline.

"Sir, I just got a call that there's been an attack in the north section of Hue."

"And?"

"Nothing else, except that the ARVN troops are holding their own. They have asked that air support be made ready."

"Okay, Wally. It looks like things are starting. Anything else?"

Kline started the jeep and pulled around the circle in front of the embassy building.

"Scattered firing near Chu-Chi and three other spots. No details on the size of the attack."

Westmoreland nodded.

"Call ahead to my office in MAC-V," he said as

they passed through the embassy gates. "Tell them to have my intelligence officers ready. And put the air command on alert."

"Yes, sir."

The marine guards saluted as they pulled away.

And the general didn't take any notice of all the cyclos gathered near the wall.

McManus sat down right in the chair.

"Alright, Lindstrom. Tell me. Who should I be?"

"Wait a second," Lindstrom said. "Let me see if we have any clearer picture of what's going on back there. . . ."

Lindstrom bent over his computer. He heard Dr. Beck fiddling with the IV rack. Then McManus yelped when Beck jabbed him with the needle.

"I'm trying to get an idea of what kind of synchronicity we're running against. I have to match up your insertion with what Jim and Ali are doing . . . if they're doing anything. . . ."

This last he muttered for his own benefit.

Beck turned on the pulse and respiration screens.

"How do things look?" McManus said cheerfully.

Lindstrom glanced over. Beck studied the screens and shook her head. "Not wonderful, Elliot. This is against my advice . . . it's much too dangerous and—"

Lindstrom looked back at his monitor.

The changes were speeding up, from small things like the renaming of cities in honor of revolutionary heroes, to giant chunks of the US being lopped off and handed to her unfriendly neighbors.

It's a good thing we got back here when we did, Lindstrom realized.

He stared at another disturbing change.

It looked like independent institutions of higher learning had just become things of the past. . . .

He picked up his pad.

He had three names, three possibilities for McManus to jump into.

Two were not very risky. But they didn't seem to be the person that was needed.

The right person . . . at the right time.

The other was perfect.

But the risk factor was tremendous.

He wrote the names down.

It has to be McManus's decision.

He walked over to McManus who was fussing in the chair like a schoolboy visiting his dentist, Dr. Demento.

"McManus, I have some names. And the situations you'll drop into."

"Well, pick one," McManus said, excitedly.

Lindstrom shook his head. "No, I think this should be your choice."

He handed the pad to McManus.

The radio station was a squat building that sat beside a tower that was the highest thing for blocks around.

It was surrounded by some familiar faces who smiled as Jim got out of the jeep.

He saw Tuttle, his radio man.

"Welcome back, Lieutenant."

Jim smiled. And a few feet away, an M-16 hanging uncomfortably from his shoulder, he saw Bloom, the medic.

"Everything okay, Bloom?"

Bloom nodded. "Nice and quiet, sir."

Howell came up to him. "Should I get you a cup of coffee, Lieutenant?"

"Let me check everyone, Sergeant. Then we'll go inside and plan a schedule for the night. . . ."

As Jim went into the station, he heard some popping noises in the distance. More firecrackers, he thought.

Happy New Year!

But this time he was wrong.

"Oh, no . . ." Dr. Jacob said.

"What's wrong?" McManus said, turning his head

slightly. Lindstrom stood beside him, thinking McManus looked very odd sitting in the chair with a metal skull cap on and the wires leading to the black box.

Dr. Beck monitored his heart beat and respiration, and the IV rack stood to the side.

Lindstrom looked over at Dr. Jacob, who walked from one end of the tachyon generator to the other. "I don't know. . . ." Jacob said. "There's something . . . wrong." He scratched his head, looked up as if he had nearly snatched an idea from the air, and then shook his head.

A human computer, observed Lindstrom, carrying out a whole series of evaluations in his head.

But one thing was obvious.

At the moment Dr. McManus wasn't going anywhere. . . .

29

"Dr. Jacob—what's the problem?" McManus hissed.

"I—er—I don't know. Everything seems to be working. It's just that—"

Lindstrom walked over to Jacob, not that he'd be able to help. What I know about science, Lindstrom thought, you could fit on a file card. The two scientific words I'm most comfortable with are on . . . and off.

Still, he went and stood next to Dr. Jacob, showing solidarity with him in the face of his problem.

"You see," Jacob said, "everything is set the way we left it. For *two* people in different locations. I've added an additional input for Dr. McManus. And—well the readings are all wrong."

"Wrong?" McManus called back.

"We've never had three people back there, Elliot. Perhaps I'm missing something." Lindstrom watched Jacob do some more mental calculations, rifling through a new set of permutations.

"Wait!" he said to the air. Then he walked over to some screens on the generator. He touched a dial, Lindstrom saw a wavy line leap to life, zigzagging across the green screen.

"Interesting . . ." Jacob said.

"What is it?" McManus yelled, sounding clearly exasperated. "Have you found the problem?"

Jacob shook his head and turned to Lindstrom.

"No. But I've discovered something rather . . . interesting. Peculiar, actually. Something I didn't know about the tachyon flow."

"Will that help you send McManus?" Lindstrom said.

"Oh, no. But it should make an interesting monograph on the behavior of electrons and positrons in a moving tachyon field . . . very interesting. . . ."

McManus—prisoner in his chair—groaned.

"I hope everyone's having a great New Year out there . . . and watch the monkeying around. Now another hit from the top hundred of '67 . . . here we go with the Music Explosion and a 'Little Bit of Soul'. . . ."

The DJ's voice disappeared and the song—piped through the station's hallway—accompanied Jim on his tour.

"Now when you're feeling low—
And the fish won't bite . . .
You need a little bit o' soul—
To put you right. . . ."

"Can we get that off?" Jim said.

"Yes, Lieutenant," Howell said. "I thought it would be okay . . . the men might like it."

Jim shook his head.

"Can it." He spotted a door at the back of the bunker building. "Where's that door go?"

"There's a back entrance, out to a parking lot."

"And you have it guarded?"

"Yes, Scott is back there."

"Just Scott?"

Howell nodded.

"Put two more men back there. Is anybody actually *in* the building?"

"Six men, sir."

Jim kept walking. He saw the army DJ sitting behind a glass booth. Capturing the station might have some PR value, a kind of Tokyo Rose maneuver. But Jim didn't see how it had any real strategic importance.

"Get everyone outside. I don't want anyone coming near the building or—"

A soldier came running up to them. "Military Assistance is on the phone, sir. They want the officer in charge."

That's me, Jim thought.

He followed the soldier into an office. He picked up the phone and pressed the blinking button.

"Lt. McShane here," he said.

And Jim listened, nodded. He saw Howell watching him.

As some captain told him that—all of a sudden—Saigon was under attack.

Jim hung up. Isn't this just great, thought Jim . . . isn't this wonderful? He turned to Howell.

"Sergeant . . . where's my rifle?"

"You see," Dr. Jacob was explaining . . . "positive particles and negatively charged particles should neutralize each other. But that doesn't seem to be happening in the flow. I've never seen that before—"

"What does it matter?" McManus said.

"Oh, it matters very much. If there are particles that still carry charges, it would affect the tachyon flow—the stream itself could achieve polarity. And I don't have a clue what that might do."

Everyone was quiet for a second, while Lindstrom hoped that one of the two men would come up with a solution.

"Wait a second," McManus said, twisting in his chair. Lindstrom saw Dr. Beck shoot out a quick restraining arm. "We reversed the flow when Alessandra was brought back, correct?"

"Yes," Jacob said. "But now it's back to normal and—"

"Perhaps not. Perhaps only part of the flow was

switched back. If the tachyons are accelerating in two *different* directions, that might explain why protons and electrons aren't neutralizing each other."

More silence, while Jacob's face scrunched up and mulled this hypothesis over.

"Why, if that's true, it's fascinating."

Lindstrom took a step to Jacob. "And can it help you get McManus toddling off?"

Jacob looked at Lindstrom as if he had just asked the most sublimely irrelevant question. Then he grinned. "Of course. I mean, that would explain the problem. I just have to isolate the stream of particles that are going in the wrong direction, sort of traffic direct at the subatomic level. Then we should be all set!"

Jacob walked over to the massive machine, which—in reality—was only the controls and a monitor screen for a mile-long particle accelerator buried beneath the Red Building.

Jacob muttered to himself as he fiddled. "There. Alright, that looks good. And here . . . no. That will never do. Let me see . . . ah, yes, here we are."

Like a prima donna spinning around to face the audience after a difficult pirouette, Jacob turned to Lindstrom and McManus.

"All set, Elliot!" he announced proudly.

"Thank God!" McManus barked.

He sat back down in his seat.

Lindstrom walked over to him.

"Er, McManus—Elliot—I just want to, er—" Lindstrom was finding the words he wanted to say a bit difficult to get out. "I mean, good luck and all that. And I'll see you when you come back."

"Oh, stop all the solemnities, Lindstrom." McManus turned and shook a bony finger at the history professor. "And stay off the sauce while I'm gone. There's no telling what you could get into without me watching you. . . ."

"Yes . . ."

Lindstrom patted his shoulder.

"Let's go," McManus said excitedly.

Lindstrom looked up at Dr. Beck—one final check to see if she gave her approval. Begrudgingly, she nodded.

Lindstrom turned to Jacob and pointed at him.

"Five . . ." Jacob said. "Four . . . three . . . two . . ."

"This is wonderful!" McManus said, gripping the arms of his seat as if he was strapped into a space ship.

"One. . . ." Jacob announced.

And then—almost peacefully—Lindstrom heard a click, the high-pitched whine of the generator.

And McManus shut his eyes.

Her foot, the ankle, had gone beyond pain. She simply knew that she was taking one step, and then sliding the foot in front of her.

She knew the people, laughing, enjoying the wonderful clear night, were watching her.

Wondering . . . who is she? Why is she walking like that.

And why is her face so drawn, so haggard?

Doesn't she know it's the Tet.

But all Ali knew was that every step she took brought her closer to the tower, closer to the radio station.

Once she took a step and she tried to say his name. Jim. In English.

At first, another name came out, a Vietnamese name. Huan . . . Tuan . . .

She concentrated, and tried again.

"Jim," she said.

Someone heard her, turned and watched her shuffle down the street.

It didn't matter. Hearing his name, the word helped.

She wouldn't allow herself to think that he wouldn't be there, that something might have happened and he just wasn't there.

He'd be there. She'd tell him.

And he'd stop it.

The tower was in front of her, never getting any larger.

And then, she turned a corner and—

She brought her ankle around, taking another step.

I'm going to make it. I'll make it! she thought.

And for the first time since this long day's nightmare began, she smiled.

Jim stood outside.

"I don't see anything," he said to Howell.

"It's the VC, Lieutenant. They can come from anywhere. One of my buddies was in a bar and this woman ran in and dropped something. Just like she was delivering a loaf of bread or something. She just dropped this bomb and it blew up. Killed half the GIs in the bar."

Jim nodded.

The last reports said that Phu-Tho, at the corner of the city, had been taken by the VC and NVA Regulars. It was incredible. NVA Regulars in the city! And there were reports of the nearby villages being pounced on in the middle of the celebrations.

He hoped someone was getting some heavy-duty troops into the city.

But here—except for the pops that probably weren't firecrackers anymore—it was quiet.

Howell touched Jim's arm.

"Hey!" he said. "Wait minute. I see someone out there. Someone small. In fuckin' black pjs. Walking right here. Do you see him?"

Jim squinted. Beyond the pool of light made by the radio tower, it was black. But then he saw a shape. Moving slowly, awkwardly. Heading right for them.

"Who the hell is that?"

"Should I fire a warning shot, Lieutenant?" One of the soldiers said.

"Yeah—" Jim said after hesitating. "Give 'em a blast over their heads."

"I don't like this. . . ." Howell said. "Crazy fuckers . . ."

The soldier fired a few rounds into the air.

Jim watched the figure.

Still taking steps, still coming.

There, she thought. It's just there. I'm almost at the tower. I'll be able to sit, to get off this foot, and—

She heard more firecrackers. Closer now. And lights in the sky.

She rubbed at her exhausted eyes. Her knuckles digging in the sockets, rubbing away the tears, trying to fight the pain. She chewed at her lip.

I'm. Going. To. Make. It.

Please, she thought.

More firecrackers. And now voices yelling at her.

At first she didn't understand. The voices, the words. So strange, Sounding—

Oh, god, she thought, her vision clearing a bit from the tears. Oh, god, there are people *there*, and voices. Speaking in English. Then, Vietnamese. She shook her head. No, she thought. Please, speak English. Please.

She felt so tired, so confused. . . .

She tried to hurry, putting so much weight on her injured ankle that it sent horrible jolts of pain traveling up her leg.

She tried to call out. But instead she just coughed, and mumbled. She wasn't scared that anything might happen to her.

She was too happy to even imagine that anything bad could happen now.

"Look!" Howell said. "Lieutenant, the guy's still coming. He looks like he might be carrying something and damn, he's not stopping."

Jim looked. What's going on here? he wondered. Who is that coming here?

He thought of Howell's bomb story.

"Should I shoot, sir? Should I order someone to shoot?"

Jim chewed his lip.

"I—"

"Sir?"

Jim nodded. Then he said, "Yes."

Howell gave the order. Someone fired.

The person, the VC fell.

With a scream, a howl.

That was not a man's cry.

Trinh looked at his watch, at the crowds milling about outside the embassy. The other attacks, the diversions, had already begun. The embassy guards would be alerted.

But no matter.

There would be too many against them.

Trinh looked at the gate. He watched it, and he saw that—if he took his men in that way—he'd just be with the others, rushing in, shooting . . . being shot at.

There'd be no chance for him to get to the embassy first.

He looked down to the corner of the street.

The wall was lined with barbed wire. And, at the far end of the block, the wall joined the garage. And on top of the garage there was garden, with bushes and grass on top of the roof.

A place for the Americans to sit, secure, inside the compound.

That's where we should go in, Trinh decided.

He looked at his watch.

One minute.

He looked at his men, all of them waiting, all of them expectant.

Trinh pointed down the block, at the wall.

He heard a siren in the street. Soon troops would fill the streets, trying to stop the attack. But we'll already be inside.

Trinh looked at his watch.

Ten seconds.

The cyclo driver stood on the corner eating a sandwich, looking as if he was waiting for a ride.

Five seconds.

Trinh and the others walked over to the cyclo. We have to move fast, he thought.

He counted off the seconds in his mind with every step. Four. Three. Two. One.

And then he and his men ran for the guns hidden in the passenger seat of the cyclo. . . .

30

Trinh and his men took the weapons. People on the street screamed and backed away. As Trinh handed the guns to his men, he saw the others streaming towards the two marine guards just outside the gate.

The guards were slow to react, thinking . . . it's just more people in the streets, celebrating the holiday.

Then Trinh saw the other cyclos begin to move, ready to discharge their loads. He raised a hand to his men. They stopped, their foreheads already shimmering with sweat.

Trinh pointed down the block.

"We'll go down there," he said.

One of the men, someone very young, his eyes alive with excitement, took a step forward.

"What? And run from the fighting?"

Trinh acted quickly. It was important to do things fast, with a strong hand. If he wanted these men to follow him, he must be a leader—

He slapped the young man.

"No. The wall at the corner goes to the roof of the garage. And straight to the embassy itself." Trinh smiled. "We'll get there before any of the others."

He heard the guns firing, automatically sending a spray of bullets into the compound. There were screams from the streets . . . women dressed in beautiful ceremonial dresses crying, hurrying away, pulling their children behind them.

The young man nodded.

Trinh turned, and he yelled to warn the people on the street. They scattered, seeing Trinh and his men run down the street, along the wall. At the corner, he looked at the wall, topped with barbed wire.

And he thought; It will be hard getting over, having the barbs claw at my skin.

Hard, but not impossible.

The firing from the entrance still sounded like firecrackers in the distance. He heard a siren from blocks away.

"Come!" he ordered the man who had questioned him. "Help me up."

The man quickly came forward and Trinh directed him to bend down and make a foothold with his hands. Trinh stepped into the man's hands and then said, "Now!"

The man started hoisting him up while some of the others supported his back.

Higher, until his eyes were level with the patch of barbed wire. It had many strands, woven together, a nest of sharp nettles. Trinh felt the man's hands wobbling under him. And ahead, he saw the bushes of the rooftop garden and a white table with three metal chairs. And beyond that, the new embassy building, its windows filled with a warm, yellow glow.

Trinh extended his gun across the wire and then pressed down as hard as he could, pushing the mesh down.

It will catch me and cut me. There is nothing I can do about that, he thought. He pressed harder with his gun, and then, with another scream, he clambered atop the wall.

He felt hooks catch his clothing, his skin, scraping away his flesh. There was a sharp pain, and then he felt tiny, wet spots on his shirt. I'm bleeding, he thought. But it didn't matter.

I'm doing what I dreamed about!

He kneeled—into yet more barbs—and then threw

himself off the wall. Then he stood up, exultant. He saw the other groups, fighting their way into the well-protected compound, the ground becoming littered with bodies.

He yelled for the others to follow him.

And he turned to face the embassy.

Jim stood over the girl. She was young, and beautiful.

"Shit," he said. "Why the hell did we shoot?" he said to Howell. "What the hell was wrong with us?"

"Lieutenant, she just kept coming. You saw that. We didn't know what she was doing. She could have been VC. Hell, she may still have a bomb hidden on her."

A few of the other soldiers came forward.

Jim shook his head.

"Get—get someone out here to look at her."

"Yes, sir," Howell said, and he ran back to the building.

The Vietnamese woman's eyes opened.

They fluttered into crescent shapes. Open, then closed. Open, then closed.

She said something in Vietnamese.

"What's that?" Jim said turning to one of the soldiers, hoping they could speak Vietnamese.

"I don't know, sir, I—"

Jim knelt down close to her.

She was wounded. A trickle of blood rolled off her shoulder, down her arm and onto the ground.

"Don't worry," Jim said, close to her. "You're going to be alright."

She opened her eyes again.

She looked right at him.

"I—"

Jim thought it was just a sound. Not a word, nothing intelligible.

Then, again . . .

"I need—I'm looking for—"

"You speak English," Jim said.

She licked her lips with a tongue that was as dry and cracked as her ragged lips. "Get her some water! Quickly!" Jim shouted.

Jim smoothed her hair, pushing the stray strands off her cheek, off her forehead.

"I'm looking for—"

Her eyes widened.

And did Jim know what words she was about to say?

Or was it just that—when the realization finally hit him, it broke over him like an immense wave. Leaving him stunned, alone, looking at her face.

Her face.

"Lieutenant McShane," she said.

He nodded. "I'm McShane," Jim whispered. "I—"

And he knew who she was.

He saw her eyes begin to tear.

"Lieutenant," someone said, handing him a canteen. Jim cradled her head, and pulled her up. He tilted the canteen and poured the water between her lips. A tiny trickle that she lapped at hungrily, groaning.

"Easy," Jim said. "There's plenty of water. Easy. . . ."

Then the medic was beside her, unsnapping a box of bandages.

She kept on sucking at the water, and then stopped, breathing hard. She looked at him . . . and then whispered, quietly.

"Jim . . . ?"

He smiled. And nodded. He said one word.

"Ali."

She nodded. And while the medic worked on the wound, he leaned close to her, while Howell and the other soldiers watched. Closer to her dry, cracked lips.

"I've been waiting for you. . . ." he whispered.

And then he kissed her.

Giant flood lights came on, covering the rooftop garden with brilliant white light.

"Come on!" Trinh yelled, fearing that the men would stop.

He looked ahead. We're so close, he thought. There were large double doors and great windows leading from the garden into the embassy building. There would be guards inside, but that wouldn't matter.

They won't expect us to come this way.

Trinh brought his Chinese version of the AK-47 around to firing position. He made sure it was set for automatic fire. But he'd have to be careful.

It was not the point to kill people. Not at all.

He was just seconds away from the doors.

When they flew open. Three marines came running out, their guns burping bullets. The dirt kicked up in front of Trinh. He heard someone moan, and then cry out behind him.

"Keep running, comrades!" Trinh yelled. And he fired.

His gun tore up the wood of the doors, shattered the glass, and then—whether it was his gun or someone else's he didn't know—two of the marines fell forward.

The other marine backed up into the building.

Trinh grinned.

He reached to his side and picked up a grenade. Giang explained that the white phosphorous would explode with a great bang and leave a giant cloud of smoke. . . .

But no one would get killed.

Trinh pulled the pin. He counted to five—the way he had been instructed—and then tossed the grenade at the doors.

The explosion seemed to shoot a cloud right at Trinh, blinding him.

"Keep running!" he yelled.

And then he banged into the door frame. He heard screams and yells from inside.

We're here, he thought. We're right here at the building, and the reception hall is just below this room!

He found the opening and he went in, protected by the cloud of smoke.

Through the hazy cloud he saw men standing against the wall.

He heard their firing.

Trinh fired back, and he heard his men firing from behind him. Then, more screams and yells. But there was nowhere to go, Trinh thought.

Nowhere at all. The compound was surrounded.

And I'm about to take the building.

He emerged from the cloud.

Two more marines were at the other end of the room firing at the cloud. But Trinh got a clearer picture of them than they did of him.

He ran a line of bullets right through them.

"Yes!" he screamed. "Come on, we are almost there, comrades."

He had only four men left. But that would be enough, he was sure.

He jogged down the steps.

He saw the people at the party looking up at him, terrified.

More soldiers were at the main door, just to the left, shooting out at the courtyard.

They might turn and look over their shoulder.

They might see us, Trinh thought, grinning.

And if that happens . . . I will kill them.

He saw the people back away, some still holding fluted glasses in their hands, like the glasses Trinh cleared from the tables at the hotel.

Delicate glasses.

They held them—

As if their champagne could keep this terror away.

One of the marines did turn, but the man behind Trinh saw him and shot him.

The guests backed away even farther, pressing close together.

All around the building, the sound of gunshots and the screams of men being hit swirled around.

The one marine at the door turned and fired. He caught one of Trinh's men in the head. The man fell forward onto the red-carpeted steps, his blood and bits of his skull covering part of a step.

Trinh shot the marine.

The people cried out.

And Trinh pointed to his men, telling them to go to either side of the group, to herd the prisoners like sheep, to keep them close together and scared.

Trinh stayed on the stairs, his gun waving over them.

"You are now prisoners of the National Liberation Front."

He was proud of his English. That's not all I've learned, thought Trinh.

The gunshots were just outside. The other VC groups were drawing close. But we got here first, Trinh thought. It is our prize!

"I want Ambassador Bunker and General Nguyen Cao Ky to step forward."

The crowd stiffened. They looked around. For a second, Trinh thought that no one would move. That they'd just stay there, like that, a scared, frightened herd.

But then a man stepped forward. He had whitish hair, with a small bald spot. Then Ky—Trinh recognized him—came to stand beside him.

Trinh went down one step, his gun still waving back and forth.

"You are now hostages. You will be held until the United States withdraws from the city of Saigon. If they don't withdraw within twenty-four hours—"

He paused, checking that his words were being taken with the proper seriousness.

"If that doesn't happen, you—and all the people here will be killed."

There were frightened screams, and talking. Terrible cries that sounded wonderful to Trinh.

The ambassador cleared his throat.

"What do you want me to do?"

Trinh smiled.

"Call your army, call your General Westmoreland. Tell him not to attack the embassy or you will be killed. And tell him that he has twenty-four hours to have all his troops leave the city."

Trinh saw the ambassador nod. "He'll never agree to—"

"Tell him!" Trinh snapped. "Tell him, or everyone here will die."

It was quiet for a moment. The ambassador cleared his throat. "I'd like to use the phone . . . inside my office."

Trinh nodded to one of his men, telling him to follow the ambassador.

"Remember!" Trinh called out to him. "Tell them twenty-four hours. . . ."

And he smiled. . . .

Thinking that this plan was working wonderfully. Not knowing that it was designed to fail.

"It's bad, sir. The bullet passed through the arm. There's been a lot of blood loss, sir, and some bone damage."

They were inside the radio station. Ali lay on a black leatherette couch.

Jim sat at one end.

He ignored the looks his actions drew from the other men. Even Howell stood there, scratching his head. There's no way I can explain this, he thought. How the hell can I tell them what's going on here?

Besides, he had only one concern—Ali. To make sure she was comfortable, that she had enough to drink.

The questions he had . . . the thousand questions . . . would have to wait.

Like what happened to her at Ludwig's castle when she tried to stop the Time Lab from yanking her back. And did she ever get back?

And one very important question.

What is supposed to happen here?

What's supposed to happen . . . that won't happen unless he did something.

And what is it, that thing he was supposed to do?

Her eyes opened. She winced and then forced a smile.

"God," Ali whispered. "I thought I'd never see you again."

Jim smiled. "You're not exactly seeing me now," he said.

She smiled, a small, painful thing. "No. But it's you. I can tell. Even under that haircut."

Then a grimace claimed her face.

"You okay?" he asked. "Can I get you something? Some food or—"

She shook her head. And she tried to sit up.

"Hey," he said. "No. Sit back. You've got to get some rest, Ali."

Howell appeared at his shoulder. His voice was cold, confused. He doesn't know what the hell I'm up to, Jim thought.

Can't blame the guy.

"Lieutenant, I've put the men back outside. Is there anything else you want me to—"

Jim shook his head. "No, Sergeant." Then Jim turned to him. "And I'll explain everything later."

For example—why this Vietnamese woman is calling me Jim. . . .

"Yes, sir," Howell said noncommittally. And he walked away.

Jim turned back to Ali. She grabbed his hand.

"Jim. I know what you've got to do. I don't have time to explain everything now, but—"

A soldier walked over and handed Jim a report.

Jim looked at it. "More fighting in Phu-Tho. Apparently it's a big VC enclave in the city. Part of the Iron Triangle . . . never too friendly to Uncle Sam."

She squeezed his hand tighter. "Jim, that's not important. It's the embassy—"

"What about the embassy?"

"It's going to be attacked. And held."

Jim shook his head. "But it was attacked during Tet. No big deal. Some soldiers killed, but it failed and—"

She shook her head.

"Not this time. They're taking *hostages*. The ambassador. Ky. Hostages."

"I don't understand—"

"They'll make demands—for the US to get out and—"

She coughed.

"They'll demand that the US get out and—"

"It won't work. . . ."

"That's just it," Ali said, her eyes flashing. "It won't work. The hostages will be killed. And the US will be horrified. They'll give Westmoreland the 200,000 more men he wants. They'll start bombing the north. And—according to Lindstrom—it ends with China joining the war—a conventional war."

Jim nodded. "World War III . . . while the Soviet Union sits back and watches the two countries tear each other apart. What about nuclear weapons, won't—"

"No," she coughed. "The country won't stand for that. It will be too risky. It will be a conventional war. And it will leave America a third-rate power." She coughed again, moaning as she pulled at her shoulder bandage.

Jim touched her cheek with his hand.

"So what do I do?"

"Get out of here," Ali said hoarsely. "Take your men. Get into the embassy. Don't let anything stop you. Surprise the VC inside. Free the hostages."

"Oh . . . is that all?" he laughed.

But Ali's face was grim. "It's the only way, Jim. You've got to do it, or they've won. And everything, in North Africa, in the Ardennes, it will all have been for nothing." She patted his hand. "I wish," she said quietly . . . "I wish I could say hello to you the way we did last time . . ."

"I'll take a rain check," he said.

"You have to go now," she said. "I don't know how far they've gotten. It has to be now."

He started to stand up, saying: "Okay. I'll do it. And you stay here and—"

But she held his hand tight.

"No. Bring me along, I can stay in the jeep. Tell your men you need me to make identifications."

"But Ali . . . you're wounded. You've lost a lot of blood."

"No. Khan Ha has lost a lot of blood. I don't want to be separated from you again. I'll be there . . . until it's over."

She held his hand tight.

He smiled. "Sometimes I think you can talk me into anything."

Now she smiled.

"What do I tell the men?"

"Tell them I'm a spy. Tell them I brought you information about the attack. That you have new orders. You can do it. You're the officer."

"Right," he smiled. "I keep forgetting that. . . ."

And Jim went to the door of the station and yelled for Howell to get the men together. . . .

The pudgy general came up to Chau, his face all smiling, beaming. "You have heard the news, General Chau? I admit that I am surprised. It is incredible. We have caught them unawares, completely surprised. Your plan has worked."

Chau nodded, smiling back at the round gnomelike man.

It was almost too easy, he thought. Just introducing a concept a few years ahead of its time . . . in this case, pushing the indecisive American forces over the brink into a crazy war of revenge and indignation.

Too easy . . . he thought.

"Some plum wine?" the general said, extending a friendly hand.

Chau shook his head.
There will be time for wine later, he thought.
When it's all over.
He smiled.
When I'm back in the USSR. . . .

31

The streets were clogged with people, scared people running from the real-life explosion.

Jim sat in the jeep while his men trailed behind him in a truck.

But nobody was going anywhere. The street was impassable.

"This is no good!" he said to the driver.

He looked over at Ali, at this beautiful Vietnamese woman whose face was twisted by pain.

"I've got to get you out of here. . . ." he said.

She shook her head. "No. I'll be okay. There has to be another way through here—"

Jim nodded and—with the jeep stopped—he jumped out and ran back to the truck.

And when he got there Howell—holding tight to the steering wheel—looked grim. He doesn't know what I'm up to, Jim thought. And I don't think I can explain it.

"Sergeant," Jim said. "Is there another way to the embassy . . . some back streets. . . ."

"Yes, sir," Howell said without warmth. "We can cut down to Bach Dan Street and follow the river. If we go to Thi Hghe Bridge, we'll get to the back of the embassy."

Jim pounded the truck's door. "Let's do it. . . ."

Jim ran back to the jeep and told his driver to follow the truck.

As soon as they left the main road, the crowds thinned. Jim heard sirens and—when he looked down a street—he saw a fire engine screaming through an intersection.

And all the time he thought: I'm not going to have enough time.

I'll be too late.

He pulled Ali close, even though he saw his driver look over at him oddly.

They were by the river now, and there were boats there, moving away, alarmed by the fighting breaking out in the city. This is the real end, Jim knew. After this, there could be no more illusions.

If Hanoi could hit Saigon like this, it can do whatever it wants to. This is the end.

Unless something happens that I'm supposed to stop.

As they cut north, the streets were clear until Jim saw Howell's truck turn away from the river and head back into the city.

"We're close now," his driver said.

"Great," Jim said.

But as soon as they went up one more street, Jim saw the wall of the embassy and—surrounding it—troops, ARVN and American.

And it looked as if they were already too late.

"Pass him!" Ali said squeezing Jim's hand. "The truck!" she said. "Pass it and make it stop."

Jim nodded to the driver, who floored the accelerator and cut in front of Howell and the soldiers.

"Now—" Ali coughed. "Now, make them stop."

Jim stood up and signalled Howell to pull off to the curb.

And Ali turned to him.

"It's already a standoff, Jim. They're inside . . . and our troops are outside. If you go right up to the front, they'll stop you. It will be too late."

Jim nodded and licked his lips. He looked down the

street. He saw the soldiers, crouching, their weapons aimed at the gate, but frozen.

The VC already had their hostages.

Jim turned back to her. "So what do we do?"

She squeezed his hand again. "Find another way in. Surprise them. They won't expect you . . . but you have to—"

His driver was giving him strange looks. Then he said, "Sir, I think we'd—"

Jim held up a hand.

He looked at the compound wall.

We'll have to go in some other way, fast, before they get guards all over the place.

We'll lose some men. I might be shot. But it has to happen fast.

Howell came up to him, his face looking angry.

"What are we doing, sir?"

Jim kept looking at the wall, at the corner just ahead.

"Sergeant, we're going over that wall. Do you have some rope?"

And Howell looked away as if he was listening to a crazy man.

"It's the phone," one of the women, one of the American secretaries said, holding the phone out to Trinh.

Trinh nodded. He and his men were inside, holding the hostages. The other guerillas were outside, a defensive wall to stop any attempt to free them.

Trinh walked over to the white phone. He noticed how scared these people were, how his every step made them tense.

He took the phone.

It was an American captain . . . some name Trinh didn't know. He was telling Trinh that they were surrounded, that they should give up . . . it was only a matter of time.

"No!" Trinh screamed.

(And he saw the hostages, his prisoners recoil more. Like frightened animals pressing together.)

"No. You listen to me. I will kill these people in just twenty-three hours. One after the other, starting with your ambassador. Unless all American troops are removed from the city."

The captain tried to explain that it was hopeless, that they should give up. . . .

Trinh felt that it was time for some example of his power. He pointed to the woman who had handed him the phone. He smiled at her, and signalled that she should walk to him. She shook her head and made a gesture.

As if to say, me? You want me?

The ambassador tried to say something.

"Now, don't go scaring—"

"Quiet!" Trinh hissed. The captain on the phone droned on, about how hopeless it was, how more troops were coming and—

The secretary walked to Trinh with the small steps of a child.

Then Trinh—with a suddenness that felt wonderful—pulled the trigger of his gun.

A hail of bullets cut into her midsection. Her blood splattered all over the floor. She may have made a sound. It was hard to tell.

Everyone was screaming.

"Did you hear that?" Trinh yelled. "That was just some worker. Next time it will be General Ky . . . or the ambassador. . . . Did you hear that?"

The captain and his threats had been silenced.

"Next time, you let me speak with Westmoreland. I will tell him what we want."

Trinh looked at his watch.

The one that keeps on ticking . . . he thought, smiling.

"You now have less than twenty-three hours. . . ."

And he hung the phone up.

* * *

Howell handed Jim the coil of rope. And—at the same time—touched his shoulder.

"Lieutenant . . . what the hell is going on here? Why are you listening to that woman?"

Jim looked at the sergeant and he had a fear.

Howell could shut this whole thing down. The men were used to taking his orders. I might be in charge . . . but Howell ran the outfit.

He looked at the sergeant, almost tempted to tell him the truth.

I'm from about fifty years from now, sergeant. I'm a grad student—if you can believe that. But some really bad dudes are messing with history, and I'm stuck with straightening it out. . . .

Right, thought Jim. He's likely to buy that.

Instead he nodded and took a breath.

"She's a special agent, Howell. Someone I was briefed about. I couldn't tell you—orders. And now, she knows something that can save this city. If we move . . ."

Jim studied Howell's face to see whether he was accepting any of this.

"But I need you on board, Sergeant. And believe me—every goddam second counts."

Howell stood there, thinking about it.

Then he smiled. "Then let's get to it, sir."

And Jim turned back to Ali to give her the thumbs up sign.

But her eyes were closed. . . .

They got three ropes over the wall.

"It will have to be fast," Jim said, realizing he was talking to men who had no experience in dealing with terrorists. That kind of routine training was still a decade away.

"Keep low, stay out of the light. Shoot to kill, but don't risk hitting the ambassador or any of his people."

Howell and his men nodded.

"The sergeant knows the building . . . so he'll get us to the reception hall."

Jim stood there. It was quiet. There was the sound of distant gunfire, but nothing close. Just the stalemate at the entrance to the embassy.

And—he thought—if the Americans see us here, they'll shoot us as well.

We gotta get going . . . Jim thought.

"Okay," he said to Howell.

And with muffled grunts, three men started climbing up the wall, and over the barbed wire.

"The news is good?" Scorpion said to the radio operator, standing in the cramped room.

The radio man handed him a sheet of paper.

Scorpion took it and read the three short lines. Embassy surrounded. Hostages being held. No action from the Americans.

Perfect, exactly as orchestrated.

Except—yes, he heard some noises outside. The other generals, reading the same report.

Concerned now that the plan was going a little awry.

A little? thought Scorpion.

Your plan, perhaps. . . .

But not mine. Not at all. . . .

Jim followed the first soldiers up, gingerly jumping over the barbed wire.

And as soon as he crested the wall, he saw a problem.

They were on a squat building with a garden covering the roof.

And it was bathed in light by giant photo floods on the side of the embassy building.

Jim rolled to the side and joined the other soldiers.

They were still in the shadows, but as soon as they started going close to the building they'd be seen.

"Damn!" he hissed.

More of his men came over, and then Howell, who—seeing the problem—rolled next to him.

"What the hell can we do?" Jim said to him.

"Get the hell down and join up with the guys at the gate. They've got these suckers surrounded."

Jim shook his head. "No, we can't do that."

He looked up at the lights. There was only one thing to do.

"Get your best man to take some shots at those lights. And tell him not to miss. As soon as they're out, we move."

"And then what?"

"No shooting inside the building—not until we've got the VC spotted."

Howell shook his head. "You know, sir, this isn't the Wicked Witch of the East's castle. These guys aren't going to melt away. . . ."

Jim gave Howell an order. "Just do it. . . ."

Howell rolled away and spoke to one of the soldiers.

Jim waited.

Howell rolled back. "Ready when you are, sir."

"Okay," Jim said. "We move when the lights go out."

Jim nodded to Howell. And he waited. He heard the click of someone's rifle, just to the side. He took a breath.

There were three lights. Two right beside each other, and a third on top of the building.

Jim let his breath out. Then the gun cracked, so damn loud Jim thought that the plan was crazy. But he kept his eyes on the building. One light shattered. Then another.

A pause.

As the soldier aimed at the third light, atop the building.

Come on, Jim thought. Come on! Don't fucking miss it.

He fired.

And the light sputtered and shattered.

Then everyone stood up and ran, under the near perfect darkness, to the embassy.

Howell and one of the soldiers beat him to the door, and they grabbed two VC, surprising them, jabbing their ten-inch blades into their midsections and giving the handle the procedurally correct full twist.

"We're in," Howell said.

Jim nodded and—in the darkness—he gestured to the sergeant to take them down.

And Jim prayed, don't let these maniacs start firing at the hostages the minute they see us.

They went down the stairs as quietly as they could, but their belts and straps rattled, like drunken Santas tiptoeing through the house.

Jim went to the front.

I can't let this get screwed-up, he thought. We've got one shot and one shot only.

They saw the light below. The legs, people standing and—

Jim saw one of the VC turn. He turned and yelled at them, pointing.

"Damn!" Jim said.

And, without thinking, he and his men fell into a shooting crouch, bringing their guns up, picking targets.

The VC fired quickly, his trail of bullets eating into the steps.

Jim fired at him, as did his men—all of them taking the same target.

When he turned to pick another target, he saw that two of his men had been hit. He watched Bloom roll down the steps, tumbling over and over, still clutching his M-16.

A bullet chopped at the wall near Jim.

Bad position, he thought. We're on the steps, and the VC are down there, close to the hostages and—

We can't shoot, Jim knew.

We could hit Bunker or Ky or anyone.

And—as if to drive the point home, one of the VC

screamed and grabbed this man—a man with white hair and bald spot—and jabbed his gun right against his head.

"Stop!" he screamed. "Stop or I'll blow the ambassador's brains out!"

Jim saw the VC had his hand tight on his gun, nearly pulling the trigger, ready to blow him away.

Jim stood up and yelled, "Stop firing!"

He screamed it louder. "Lower your weapons. . . ."

And Jim saw the guerilla smile.

They won, Jim thought.

This time I was too late.

"The phone," one of the other guerillas said.

Jim and his men were still on the steps, their weapons lay on the ground. Two VC had them covered.

"Bring the phone here," the guerilla with Bunker said.

"Yes . . . yes . . . we have captured more of your men here!" the guerilla exulted. "They will die, too. The next time everyone gets killed! Everyone!"

The hostages—the embassy workers, the secretaries—screamed.

"Do you hear me?"

The guerilla listened and then he smiled and said: "Good."

He hung up the phone. "They will call in one hour to tell us what they are doing. Get their guns. . . ." the leader said.

There's got to be something I can do, Jim thought. Something. . . .

He took a step, then another, away from his gun. Closer to the leader.

"Who are you?" Jim said. "Do you have any idea what the hell you're doing?"

"Stay!" the man yelled. Then he smiled. "I am Ngo Tran Trinh. And I am forcing the United States out of our city."

Jim shook his head. He looked at the ambassador. Trinh had the gun barrel pressed tight against the ambassador's temple. The ambassador was scared, but he stood straight, impassive.

A brave man, Jim thought.

I don't want to be responsible for his death.

"No, you're not. The troops won't leave. You'll kill everyone here . . . and the war will only get worse. Your country, your beautiful country, will only become one massive battlefield, a charnel house . . . for decades to come."

Trinh sneered and shook his head. "No, they won't allow that to happen. They will leave and—"

Jim listened.

Behind him, he heard the other guerillas gathering the guns, and then bringing Howell and the other soldiers down. Jim looked at his sergeant. He had a wound in his chest. He hobbled across the wood floor, and onto the red carpet, leaving a filmy smear as he stepped.

"You're being fooled. . . ." Jim said. "You're supposed to die, and so are all these people. And then Vietnam will lose forever."

He saw the ambassador twitch.

Trinh's sneer faded a bit. He had intelligent eyes. Maybe he can see the truth of what I'm saying, Jim thought. Maybe—

The ambassador twitched again, and shook. Trinh held him tighter.

There was something funny here, Jim thought. Something very—

The ambassador closed his eyes. Trinh was explaining how it was all going to work, how the call was about to come in. . . .

Ambassador Bunker opened his eyes.

He looked right at Jim.

And then—with a familiar, almost impish smile, he winked at Jim. . . .

32

What? Jim thought. Why is Bunker winking at me?

Then—for the first time—the ambassador spoke.

"He's quite right there, Mr. Trinh. You see you and your brave men here are pawns in something you don't understand."

Wait a second . . . Jim thought. What is this . . . I—

Trinh jabbed his gun butt against Bunker's head.

"Ow!" Bunker said. "That hurt. I'm merely trying to point out the fact that—"

Jim turned a bit to the side, just enough to see that the other guerillas were loaded down with weapons.

He looked back at Bunker. Listened to him.

And Jim smiled.

Knowing exactly what happened.

"As Shakespeare wrote, 'There are more things in our philosophy, Horatio, than—' "

Trinh was looking at the suddenly garrulous Bunker prattle on. Jim took a step closer. Another. Until he was just four feet away. Three.

Trinh turned.

"Get back!" he yelled.

And that's when Bunker moved. "Than you've ever dreamt of!" he yelled. And then the ambassador ducked and pushed Trinh to the side. The gun—a loose cannon, ready to blow the people away—pointed into the air.

And Jim leapt up and grabbed the barrel as Trinh screamed, and tried to pull it back down. Jim and the guerilla were struggling. Trinh pulled the trigger, littering the eggshell-colored ceiling with holes.

"Oh, dear," the ambassador said. "Well, here goes nothing!" And Jim watched him kick Trinh right in the family jewels.

Trinh released his trigger finger, grunting and doubling up. Jim quickly took the freed gun and brought it around to aim at the other VC. But Howell, though wounded, had moved quickly once the gun was away from Bunker's head. He and his men turned on the distracted VC. A few blasts went off but no one was hurt.

The hostages gathered around Jim, talking, excited, almost giddy with relief. But Jim saw the phone, sitting on a table right next to Trinh. Flashy General Cao Ky came running up to him.

"Well done, Lieutenant!" he said beaming.

Jim nodded. "Call the troops outside the embassy. Tell them they can go ahead and storm the compound . . . tell them that we're okay in here. . . ."

And then Jim turned to Ambassador Bunker.

Who was grinning from ear to ear.

"I'll tell you—that was a marvelous experience," he said.

"I bet it was. . . ." Jim answered. "Welcome to Vietnam, er, Doctor. . . ?"

The ambassador's eyes went wide with surprise. "Dr. McManus, Jim." He lowered his voice and pulled Jim to the side, away from the other people. There were shots outside, and the sound of rockets being launched. It would all be over in minutes.

"You knew it was me?"

Jim nodded. "I knew it was someone from the Time Lab. It was as if, suddenly, there was someone else in the room. Someone who didn't belong."

McManus smiled. "Well I'm sure you know what *that* feels like. . . ."

Jim turned and saw Howell hobbling around, instructing the men to move the VC out to the door.

"Sergeant . . . thanks for going along with me."

Howell nodded, his eyes narrow and suspicious. He looked at Bunker. "Yes, sir. Just . . ." and he took a step closer to Jim. "Just someday I hope you will tell me the story." He looked from Jim and back to Bunker. "The whole story."

"You got it . . ." Jim laughed. Howell grinned and started moving the VC out of the room.

"Well, I don't know how long we'll be staying here. The synchronization with the Time Lab is completely out of whack, I'm afraid. We might be yanked any minute."

"Can't be soon enough for me," Jim said.

Out of the corner of his eye, he saw a soldier running up to him.

Something was wrong. . . .

What could be wrong? he thought.

"Sir," the soldier said breathlessly. "Sir!"

"What is it?" Jim said.

"The girl—the Vietnamese girl—she's—she's—"

But Jim didn't wait for the soldier to finish. He ran past him, out the door.

"They've retaken the embassy, General Chau!"

Scorpion looked around. The other generals surrounded him. And behind them stood a dozen soldiers with nasty bayonets fixed and ready.

And Scorpion smiled. "They've what?"

The short pudgy general took a step closer. "Retaken the embassy! Your plan failed miserably. We still hold Phu-Tho, but troops for the US II and III corps are moving against them!"

Scorpion took a step backwards.

Oops, he thought.

The best laid plans.

Of course, he knew that something was wrong. It's that other Time Lab, their damn interference.

He looked at his watch. 11:57.

"Er, this was not unforeseen, generals. In fact, the premier himself said—"

Just have to buy time, he thought. Just a couple of minutes. Then the real General Chau can deal with the fallout.

Yes, the other Time Lab has turned into a worthy opponent.

And perhaps it was time to try a different tack. The problem here is that we're working with modern events. We need to do more research, and play with something like the Dark Ages, or even the Roman Empire. Something that will be more opaque, less easily seen through, Scorpion thought.

Give them a Gordian knot that will really befuddle any attempt to untie it.

And—he must remember—the other proposal under study in the mountainous cavern used by the Iron Men. It was something called Retroactive Chronological Dissynchronization.

Or to put it more simply . . . using the future to derail the past.

Yes, that *might* be the way to go.

Next time. . . .

He looked at his watch.

11:59.

"Arrest General Chau," the pudgy general barked.

Scorpion smiled. He kept his watch up.

Two mean-faced guards came up to him. He watched the second hand sweep across the twelve.

Nothing happened.

Oh, no. . . . he thought. What is this? What the hell is happening? Why aren't I being pulled back.

The guard grabbed him.

And then—and then—

The watch must be off by a few seconds, he smiled. Everything started to fade.

A few seconds off, he laughed.

What does that matter . . . when you have all the time in the world?

"I—I think she's dead, sir. . . ."

Jim pushed the soldier away from the jeep.

"Ali?" he said. Then louder, coming close to her face.

"Ali . . ." he whispered to her cheek. "Please, don't. Not now. Now that we won."

He felt a hand on his shoulder.

"Jim, is she. . . ?" It was McManus.

But Jim crawled in the jeep, close to her. "No, baby. Now that we got this close." He let his hand trail down her arm and felt her pulse. "No . . ." he sobbed. He felt his tears run off his cheeks and onto hers. "No!"

"Jim." McManus said.

Jim pulled her up, and rocked her close.

And he sobbed uncontrollably, sitting there.

While the soldiers marched their prisoners away, while the ambulance sirens screamed through the streets, bringing help to the wounded.

Jim turned to look at the ambassador, this Dr. McManus that Ali had told him about. He was blurry through his tears.

"Please," he begged the man, as if he could somehow bring her to life.

"Please," he said again.

But his voice sounded hollow, empty. As if it was too thin—

As if—

Bunker's face went even blurrier. Jim blinked, trying to clear his tear-soaked eyes. He held Ali tightly. But then he couldn't feel her, couldn't feel the pressure of her limp body tight against him.

"No!" he yelled.

But he made no sound.

And he knew he was leaving Vietnam.

EPILOGUE

Even as he was going through it, it reminded him of only one thing. When poor Dorothy is hit on the head and blacks out in the face of a Kansas twister.

And all around her dance the real and twisted images of her little girl's life . . . Dear Aunty Em, and Huck and the other corny farmhands. Then Miss Gulch transformed into a cackling witch, chasing after her yippy little dog, Toto.

Jim didn't see any pictures as he floated through a hazy fog. But he imagined them, all the faces he'd seen.

Rommel. Goering. Howell. And again and again—Ali as Fraulein Stolling. Ali as Khan Ha.

And Ali . . . lifeless in his arms.

If he had a body, he knew he'd be crying.

But there was nothing, just this haze, and these flashes in the distance, like the rumbling of other wars, in other times.

Which—he guessed as it all faded to black—they might very well be. . . .

"Jim? Jim?"

He opened his eyes.

A big, bearded fellow stood in front of him. Jim craned his neck and he moaned. It hurt horribly.

"Steady," a woman's voice said. "You'll be very stiff. You've been in this seat for a long time. . . ."

He saw the large woman speaking. Then the man spoke again.

"I'm Professor Lindstrom, Jim. Professor Flynn Lindstrom. You've taken some of my courses."

Jim nodded.

"And this is Dr. Beck, the medical doctor in charge of the Time Lab."

"I'm back?" Jim said.

Lindstrom smiled and laughed. "Certainly you're back, my boy. You have, as they say, saved the day."

"You're a hero, Jim Tiber." It was another voice, thinner, coming from behind him. Jim turned again, making his neck muscle clutch into a painful spasm.

"Ow," he said.

"You must take it easy," Dr. Beck whispered to him.

Another man came and stood in front of him. "I'm Dr. Elliot McManus. I was there with you—as the ambassador." McManus turned to Lindstrom. "I do wish you had let me stay a bit longer. I barely got the feel of the time at all."

Lindstrom gestured to another man in a white coat, standing next to the enormous tachyon generator. "Dr. Jacob was hard pressed to tell us how much time was elapsing back then."

"It's a problem I'm working on, Elliot—" Jacob said.

Jim listened, trying to understand exactly what they were talking about.

McManus looked around. "But the guards—they are—?"

Lindstrom laughed. "Yes, they just disappeared. The computer is still an hour behind printing the changes, but it appears that nearly everything is shifting back to normal."

McManus smiled, his birdlike face uncertain. "Then it worked?"

"Wonderfully!" Lindstrom said.

Jim looked at them. They were so happy, excited. What the hell is wrong with them, he wondered?

"Why don't you have a party?" Jim said angrily. "Put up decorations. Get a cake. Have a celebration. . . ." He tried to sit up. But he groaned, and his weakened body defeated him, sending him back against the seat. "You've got your history back. And Ali is—"

He paused.

He saw Lindstrom tap McManus's shoulder.

McManus said, "You didn't tell him . . . ?"

"He just arrived. It took longer for him to come around."

"What are you talking about?" Jim said. "What's going on?"

He heard steps. From behind him, coming from the side room off the lab.

Steps coming close to him.

He tried to turn his neck, but he was locked into position by the pain.

The person came behind him.

He saw a hand touch his arm.

Another step.

And—out of the corner of his eyes—he saw her.

It was Ali.

They kissed a long time, completely oblivious to the people watching them. Jim just held the kiss. His arm was too weak to drape around Ali's neck, but she just kept pressing against his lips—*my* lips this time, he thought. My damn lips! Not someone else's. Her tongue teased his tongue and, despite the awkward circumstances he found his thoughts dwelling on the real reunion to come.

Someone cleared their throat. Once. And then again.

And finally Ali broke her kiss.

It was her face this time, angular, cut from the finest marble. Her straight, brown hair glowing even in the milky fluorescent lights.

"Hi, Jim. Welcome home."

"But—how? I don't get it?"

Lindstrom scratched his bushy beard. "I can explain, Jim. Dr. Beck detected the signs of severe physical stress in Ali's host. We both worried that she was dying—"

"And no one knew," Dr. Beck continued, "what would happen if someone died in a host during the Transference process."

"It was too big a risk," Lindstrom said. "So even though it was dangerous pulling Ali out when she was hurt, I felt we had no choice."

"In fact," Beck said, "she was back here well before you were."

"Then I arrived," McManus added. "You see, the longer you're in the flow, the longer it takes you to return. And it took you quite a while to regain consciousness."

"How do I look?" Ali said, grinning.

Jim smiled back. "Better than the last two times I saw you. And Khan Ha?"

"She died, Jim," Ali said quietly.

"Her life helped save her country, and our country, from a war that would change the world forever . . ." McManus said gently. "We will never forget her . . . or any of the others. Lindstrom is starting to document all of this, to keep a record of what the Time Lab does, what our 'Time Warriors' have accomplished."

Jim felt Ali's hand close around his, squeezing it. He thought of how this started . . . his rejected thesis on the Beatles. I'm back, he thought, but I still have my academic problems. But all he wanted to do now was just get out of here with Ali, to sit together and talk. And hold each other.

To click my sneakers together and say that there's no place like home.

And there would be time for that now . . . plenty of time.

"Yes, Jim, as a matter of fact I've started keeping

a record of things over here, now that the outside and inside tie line agree. And I—''

Lindstrom walked over to his computer screen. He hit a button. Jim saw the reflected glow of the screen flash on Lindstrom's face.

''And I—'' he started to say.

Jim looked at Ali. She was still smiling, but she was also watching Lindstrom.

So was McManus, his face pinched with concern.

''What is it, Lindstrom?'' McManus said. ''What appears to be—''

They all watched the history professor. Their smiles faded.

It was very quiet.

Then Lindstrom spoke.

''Everything's fine,'' he said slowly, measuring his words. ''Nothing has gone wrong outside . . . if you know what I mean.''

Everyone took breath. McManus started to say something, ''Well, I'm glad of that. I'm sure—''

''But,'' Lindstrom continued, raising a finger in the air, ''there's just this one thing. One small thing. I don't know. It may be nothing. Just some anomaly created by our trips back and forth—''

McManus took a step towards Lindstrom.

Ali leaned close to Jim, her body wonderfully warm and alive. She squeezed his hand tight.

And Jim listened.

''It's just—this,'' Lindstrom said almost laughing, tapping his screen. ''A curious thing . . . but, what in the world did King Arthur's Court have to do with Watergate?''

And—for the moment—no one had an answer.

THE END

About the Author

Matthew J. Costello is a contributing editor at *Games* magazine, and writes for *Sports Illustrated* and *Writer's Digest*. His interviews have regularly appeared in *The Los Angeles Times* and *Amazing Stories Magazine*. *Time Warrior #1: Time of the Fox* was published by ROC in 1990. His novels *Home* and *Darkborn* will be published in 1992. Costello lives in Ossining, New York with his wife and three children.